The fire in my gut morphed from anger to desire. And the reasons for coming here, my quest for answers and explanations, disappeared in the face of what I really wanted—what I'd been hiding ever since she'd found me.

I traced a finger along her knuckles. She took a step away from me, her eyes guarded.

"What are you scared of?" I couldn't keep the huskiness from my voice.

"Nothing." She jutted her chin at me as if daring me to challenge her, but her voice shook just a hair, and I knew she was lying. But more than wanting the truth, I wanted to pull her to me and taste her lips again.

"You know you give me some bogus line about faith and trust, but you have just as many issues there."

She shook her head. "I do not."

"I beg to differ. If we're keeping score, since that's a big thing with you, faith and trust are the same things. They're homonyms."

She raised her eyebrow. "Did you come all the way here to give me a grammar lesson?"

"No." I ruffled my hair, trying to remember all the things I planned to say on the drive here. "I came to say I'm sorry. I jumped to conclusions about Wade. I was wrong."

Her eyes locked on mine, and for a long moment, everything stilled. It was probably time for more than just an apology. I needed to tell her how beautiful she was.

Praise for Dianne May

"An edgy, engaging tale, brimming with perils and a romance worth rooting for."

~Kirkus Reviews

"*The Perfect Distance* is a delicious romantic suspense. Read it. You won't regret it. It's an intriguing, well-written, story with twists and turns that will keep you turning the page and wanting more."

~Isabel Jolie,
author of *When the Stars Align*

"I couldn't put it down. It was dripping with emotions. A well-constructed murder mystery."

~Lt. Col. David Brown (Ret.),
author of Devil's Den

The Perfect Distance

by

Dianne May

The Perfect Distance

Contact Information: info@thewildrosepress.com

Cover Art by *Kim Mendoza*

The Wild Rose Press, Inc.
PO Box 708
Adams Basin, NY 14410-0708
Visit us at www.thewildrosepress.com

Publishing History
First Edition, 2022
Trade Paperback ISBN 978-1-5092-3890-3
Digital ISBN 978-1-5092-3891-0

Published in the United States of America

Dedication

Dedicated to the men and women of the armed forces for their service to this country and all the homeless animals that cycle through shelters and kill pens across this nation. May you all find a safe place to land.

Acknowledgments

Horses have fascinated me for as long as I can remember, and I have been incredibly lucky to have shared my life with many, some of whom grace the pages of this story in some form, be it personality, color, or name. Thank you for the memories and the wings you gave me to fly. Thank you to my publisher, The Wild Rose Press, and my editor, Val M. Mathews, who worked diligently on this story to help it shine. Kim Mendoza for the awesome cover art and Sally Tanner for my branding and website. My first readers, Rebecca Kryshtalowych, Laura Ashley Cherry, Susan Young, Amanda Cooper, Jen Johnson, and Sheri Winkler for all your encouragement. Rebecca Wickerham, who read the very first rough draft and told me to keep going. Linda Blanchard for all the Southern phrases. My freelance editors Naomi Hughes and Kate and Ross Angelella, whose knowledge and feedback put me on the right path. Emilie Lukash, who reminds me not to give up writing, or riding, and listens to me stress about both. My Conn College Camel group for always making me smile and feel twenty years younger. My sister and best friend, Theresa DePippo, who is there for me no matter what and who keeps the crazy hours I do. Lastly, to my husband Bill and my kids, Bobby, Will, and Charlotte, who patiently share me with my computer and who challenge and inspire me every day.

Chapter 1

Finley

The thud of hooves broke my early morning baking marathon. I pushed open the screen door of our new rental house just in time to catch a flash of red mane. My breath caught in my throat. The horse skirted the edge of our lawn—flying hooves digging out clods of dirt, tail waving like a flag in the wind. It stopped, restless and easily spooked, and ripped at our grass. A red halter dangled off its head, and a long lead line trailed behind. A horse girl the first half of my life, I knew twelve-hundred-pound animals that could run thirty-five miles per hour were not easy to catch.

Cody nearly barreled into me, munching on one of my newly baked butter tarts. "Holy crap. Where's that horse from?" His voice sent the horse on another spin around the yard.

With his hair brushed back and still wet from the shower, Cody resembled Jack to a *T*. It sent chills up my spine. I pressed my fingers to the bridge of my nose. Our recent relocation and my new job had shortened my normally long patience. "I don't know, and those tarts are for work."

My boss at Peak Coffee House had agreed to a tasting of my pastries today. True to Murphy's law, I'd burned the first batch, so I was already running late and had few pastries to spare. For the last twenty years, this calendar day only held bad memories for me, and so far today, it was keeping true to form.

Ignoring me, Cody popped the last bite of crust into his mouth. "What are you going to do with that horse? He looks nuts."

The horse alternated between ripping mouthfuls of grass and trotting around in small circles as if it couldn't decide where to graze. With each frenetic circle, it stepped on the lead line and jerked its head, which excited it even more.

I dipped sideways to get a better view. "One, I think he's a she. And two, I have no idea. Does Mr. Bennett have horses?" Hank Bennett, one of our new neighbors and my college roommate's uncle, owned about one hundred acres.

"I don't think so. I've never seen any. If he did, I bet he'd feed it more." Cody licked his fingers one by one.

Excellent point. This horse's ribs stuck out pitifully, and even from here, her mangy coat cried out for brushing. A little pang radiated in my heart. Poor thing.

"What about the neighbor on the east side?"

He screwed up his face as if he didn't know compass directions, which surprised me. What the hell was he learning in school?

He turned, his interest in the horse gone. "I don't know. I'm going to get Jazz. Don't want to miss the bus."

"Be careful. She's in a mood." Jazz, fifteen and pissed off about our recent move, had a vicious tongue and a quick right hook—both of which she liked to practice on her younger brother. She'd missed tryouts for the travel lacrosse team in the area and had lots of pent-up frustration. I didn't blame her for being angry. But I'd made a promise to her dad before he died, and I wasn't breaking it. Teenage moods and anger be damned.

"She's okay, Mom."

Cody's loyalties, like his dad's, ran deep. No matter what his sister did, Cody always had her back. I planted a kiss on his head before he could leave and got a whiff of baked butter and cinnamon. "No more tarts for you."

He grinned sheepishly. "Yeah, yeah." He turned and headed back inside for Jazz. "Good luck with that horse. She's screwing up our lacrosse area."

Indeed, she was. The mare took another loop around the yard, almost knocking over one of the goals. *Damn it.* I didn't have time for this, but the odds of her getting caught up in the long lead line increased by the minute. I grabbed some carrots from the fridge and returned to the yard. From the corner of my eye, I caught Jazz and Cody waiting for the bus. Side by side, they made quite the picture: Jazz, tall and dark, focused on her phone; Cody, stocky with mahogany hair, bounced around jabbering. My breath hitched in my throat, and I closed my fingers around my horseshoe necklace and looked up to the sky.

"Keep them safe, Jack," I whispered. It was an impotent plea. Jack had died months ago, but it always eased the tightness in my throat.

Turning away, I found the mare at the edge of the yard staring at me, nostrils flared. I twisted my head right and left, trying to relax, and approached her.

3

Closer now, I held a carrot out. She sniffed and reached out to nibble the end. She clearly didn't trust me if her shifting weight and wary gaze were indications, but her hunger was winning out.

The second carrot disappeared quicker and with more surety. I lifted a hand, hesitated a moment, and when she didn't move away, stroked her neck. The mix of dirt and horsehair smelled like my first pony ride, and my heart swelled. I gave her a few more pats and threaded my fingers through her chestnut hair. She pushed her neck into my hand, and I smiled. She was dirty, skinny, and jumpy as a flea, but she wasn't mean. With a little love and elbow grease, she'd shine up like a new penny.

The crunch of her teeth on the second carrot filled me with joy, something I hadn't allowed myself to feel in a long time. I grabbed the lead line. The end had been shorn off, leaving ragged edges. I knotted it so it wouldn't slide out of my grip if she bolted.

In the distance, a dog barked. The mare jerked her head up, ears cocked to attention. The artery along her neck pulsed rapidly. Another bark. I tightened my grip on the lead rope and prepared for her flight instinct to kick in. She snorted but remained in place.

The barking echoed through the trees near my east side neighbor's property, and judging by the pattern of the hoof prints, it was where the mare had come from. I had no interest in being chummy neighbors with anyone—friendly neighbors meant sharing details. In my book, staying safe meant staying alone—but I had to get this horse home and soon, before I was late for work.

I tugged gently on the line, and the mare's head

rocketed upward, eyes rolling. She wasn't going to make this easy. Part of me wanted to drop the rope and beeline it for the house, but I couldn't leave her—no matter how she acted. The road wasn't far from my property line, and I didn't want her wandering off and getting hit by a car.

My phone chirped with a reminder of my meeting. I slid it into my back pocket and clucked to the mare. This time, she followed, jumping around but moving forward. The closer we got to my neighbor's, the quicker her steps became, until she was jigging and trotting sideways, head held high.

The barking hadn't stopped, and as we neared, the whinnies of horses joined it. The mare answered, ears twirling like helicopter blades and her nose flaring. I jiggled the line a few times, trying to keep her attention on me, my heart pumping crazily. I loved horses but hadn't had much contact in the last twenty years.

"Easy, girl. You're okay." I kept my voice steady and low despite my nerves. Paddy, my slightly nutty thoroughbred jumper, used to calm down with my nonsensical murmurings. My eyes stung, and I blinked quickly to clear them. Memories of Paddy always did me in.

Despite the calling of dogs and horses, my neighbor's place was quiet and smelled of fresh-cut hay. The house was a rustic A-frame with a large wooden deck, a well-cared-for yard, pristine flower beds, a separate garage with several cars parked out front, and a faded-red storybook barn. Between the barn and one of the pastures, a shaggy black dog stood over a prone figure. *Shit!*

I wasn't sure what to do with the red mare, who

was now almost doing wheelies around me. So I corralled her into the barn, opened the first vacant stall, and dumped her in it. I checked to make sure she had hay and water, secured the lock, and ran back out.

Stretched out in the dirt, mumbling something I couldn't make out, lay a man. Blood oozed from a gash on his head and ran down into the scruff covering his jawline. Among his gibberish, I caught the word Elliot and maybe Owen. I leaned over him, and two things hit me: he smelled like mint and coconut, and he was a good six feet tall with a broad chest.

"Hello? Can you hear me?"

His mouth stopped moving, but his eyes remained closed. The dog switched from barking to whining, tail swiping through the dirt.

"Are you okay? Can you hear me?"

He didn't respond except to moan, head lolling back and forth. This was bad. Dirt coated his jeans and black T-shirt. His hand clutched a fierce knife, and next to him lay his cell phone and the severed end of the lead line. He'd either been kicked, dragged, or both.

Fingers shaking, I yanked out my phone and dialed 911.

"911. What's the emergency?"

I opened my mouth, but nothing came out. Ambulance sirens and medical personnel would definitely not help me keep a low profile. What if they asked for personal information? The dog whimpered, pawing gently at his shirt. I gulped and tried again. "I'm here at my neighbor's. I think he's been hurt by his horse."

"Is he breathing?"

His broad chest rose and fell smoothly. "Yes."

"Okay. Don't move him. Give me your location, and we'll send someone."

I spit out the information, thankful I remembered our new address, and hung up. I sat back on my heels, a pit in my stomach. Oh, God. Sick, hurt people were not my thing. I could barely take care of Jazz and Cody when they had the stomach bug.

"I don't know if you can hear me, but an ambulance is on its way."

For a second, I thought maybe I could cut out, sneak through the bushes, and get back to my desserts and private life.

The dog whined again and nuzzled him. His hand tightened on the dog's head just a fraction. "Good girl, Ellie." His voice was barely a murmur.

He was coming around. I touched his shoulder but quickly withdrew my hand. "Help is on its way."

Eyes closed, he mumbled something I didn't catch. I leaned forward to listen. "Need…to…lock my house."

"Lock your house?" I echoed dumbly. *He couldn't be for real, could he?* That wouldn't be my first thought when regaining consciousness, but I was a paranoid mom running from her past.

As if regaining all sense of where he was, he struggled to sit up. "Yes. Before anyone gets here."

I placed a hand on his chest. "You can't get up. You're hurt. Just wait for help."

Half-sitting up, he twisted away from me, cursing as he did so. His face contorted in a grimace. "I have to lock my house. If I don't, they have a right to just waltz in." He strangled out each word, his voice raspy and rough, all the while pulling his limbs into a sitting position as if he might attempt to stand. Blood coursed freely from the open wound on his head. It leaked across his forehead, painting the side of his face in dark red, and ran in rivets into the ground.

"Are you insane?" My words came out shaky. Great, really sounding tough.

He raised his head to me, and I gazed into green eyes, the color of beachgrass—full of pain but also hope. Michael, my ex, had eyes like that.

"I can't lose this farm. Can you do it for me?"

"Uh—" Despite soulful eyes, this guy was a complete stranger. Maybe he was the nicest person on the face of Earth, but then again, maybe not. Either way, it was too risky for me to get involved in anyone else's drama. Besides, I had enough heading my way with Michael soon to be released. I used to be mesmerized by the sorrow in Michael's eyes, wanting to fix it all for him, and in the end, I almost lost everything because of him. I had no intention of repeating that mistake.

"Please. Promise me you'll lock the door."

The timing on this was impeccable, in a not-good way. I had desserts to plate and pack up for work. Not only this opportunity, but my job also hung in the balance. Nobody appreciated a late employee, and with the kids and traffic, I cut it close enough most days. But there was something in the way he said *please*, or maybe the loss and defeat so evident in his rugged face. I knew both—well. There wasn't a day that went by that I didn't miss my parents or the farm I was raised on. I glanced between the house and him, my walls of detachment crumbling with each second. "Where are the keys?"

He swiped a palm across his forehead, smearing

blood into his nutmeg-colored hair. Breath wavering, he sized me up. "Kitchen table." He closed his eyes and collapsed back into the dirt.

Sirens wailed in the distance. Against all better judgment, abandoning my ingrained motto of always playing it safe and keeping a low profile, I ran to his house. I stepped through the open front door and froze. What lay inside was much worse than the bleeding man outside.

Chapter 2

CJ

What a dumbass I was, thinking I could handle that mare. I tested my ankle, rotating it around; a shot of pain rocketed up my leg where the lead line had wrapped around it. I bit back a groan. Rookie move. After years of SEAL training, I knew better than to be anything less than vigilant about my surroundings. Thank God for my switchblade. I slid the ivory handle through my fingers and clicked the blade shut. It'd saved my life on more than one mission, and it did no less today, cutting through that line before I got dragged around the property.

Something dripped into my eyes. Head wounds sucked ass, bleeding way more than necessary. I swiped a hand across my forehead. It came back sticky and coated in blood. The metallic scent sent me reeling. The world tipped sideways and back, and my heart thudded in my ears. I rubbed the silky strands of Ellie's fur and tried like hell not to let the memories of J-bad drag me back there. But my brain froze like a rusted M16. Trigger stuck, springs creaky and glitched, pulling me back to a place both dreaded and familiar. The memories played as if it had only been a day ago:

The sun had disappeared behind a cloud. Sweat trickled down my side. The bitter tang of blood and desert sand filled my nose. Voices jumbled with shots echoed in my ears. I swiped left and then right, searching for the shooter. Elliot lay sprawled in the dirt, blood seeping into the ground.

"Blue Two is down. I repeat Blue Two is down."

Jack Thompson's deep voice rang in my head. "Do you have the HVT?"

I didn't, did I? Why couldn't I see anything? I swept right again. Where was the high-value target? Had I missed him?

Sandpaper rubbed my face. Wet sandpaper. *Where am I?* A whine and a lick. Ellie. Another lick. *Farm. North Carolina, not Afghanistan.* I tightened my hand on her coat, the fur soft against my skin. She nuzzled me again.

You are not there. You are here. On your farm. Stay awake so you won't lose it.

Fingers touched my face, pushed my head to the side, dabbed at my forehead. Something sweet and spicy floated over me, bringing back memories of Christmas mornings at my grandparents' farm. Cinnamon maybe. A hand fluttered along my chest. I cautiously opened my eyes, praying to God the vision of Elliot was gone.

The woman leaned over me. Her blonde hair, a mix between honey and straw-colored, fell forward across the side of her face. Keys dangled from her hand. "Where do you want them?"

Sirens whistled. "Keep them." My words came out in a croak.

She shook her head. Doors slammed. Where was my phone? I dragged my hand through the dirt, searching until my fingers touched metal. "My phone.

Griff."

The woman bent over me again, lifting the metal from my fingertips. She stood, and three men replaced her image—two chunky men, emergency kits in hand, and a taller balding one dressed in a blue uniform. Troy Eastley.

"How we doing, CJ?" Condescension dripped from Troy's voice as if he knew every detail of what had happened. If there was one thing I could count on, it was Troy jumping to the wrong conclusions.

I closed my eyes, not bothering to answer. He wouldn't listen anyhow, and I didn't want his ugly mug imprinted in my mind.

If my teammates could see me, I'd never live it down. Beaten by a horse, helpless on the ground, at the mercy of a jerk of a town cop. I prayed I would find the cinnamon woman when this was over, that she kept her promise and told Troy what was on my kitchen table. I assumed the odds were not in my favor.

Chapter 3

Finley

I had this idea when I decided to move us here from D.C.: a picture of me becoming a different person—perky, punctual, impeccably dressed in crisp capri pants and a fashionable shirt, put together with sleek hair perfectly coiffed. Fantasy-me was even friends with the other moms and not worried about staying hidden and safe. How quickly did that disappear? Instead, here I was—worn T-shirt, flour in my disheveled ponytail, running late with some stranger's keys hidden in my hand and his cell phone and switchblade in my pocket.

Granted, he was good-looking. Despite the dirt and blood, his chiseled jaw and soulful eyes shone through. But even good looks couldn't balance out a handgun and plastic baggie filled with pills and what looked like joints on his table. After seeing that crap, I'd almost tucked tail and ran away. But I put a lot of stock in promises, so I threw a kitchen towel over the stuff and locked the damn door on my way out. I'm not sure that would hold up in a court of law, but after being married to a lawyer for fifteen years, I knew something about objects in plain sight.

The picture in my head of my new life definitely didn't have cops swarming around twenty feet from me either. The last thing I wanted was to be caught up in some scandal of drugs and guns. I could just see the headlines in this small town: *Woman from D.C. Involved with Local Drug Ring.* Talk about coming full circle after twenty years. So much for lying low and flying under the radar. Jack always said, "If you don't want people in your bullshit, knowing about what happened to you, then don't be friendly and definitely don't get involved in their lives."

What was wrong with me? It would have been easier to just say no or, better yet, not catch the mare in the first place. The prone guy mumbled something, and my heart softened. If I hadn't caught the mare and if I hadn't brought her back, then who knows what would have happened. I'd seen enough death and dying in my life. I didn't want to be responsible for another horse or person losing their lives.

My watch vibrated against my wrist. If I left right now, I still might be on time for work.

The EMS guys worked fast, passing medical paraphernalia between the two of them. They strapped my neighbor to a gurney. A mud-covered, black pickup truck roared up. The driver exited—with closely cropped hair, a wrinkled gray T-shirt, and well-worn jeans—and strode past me. Politely pushing the EMS worker aside, he volleyed a string of curses at my prone neighbor. "Candy ass" was one of them. My neighbor's eyes opened, and his lips twitched into a half-smile. EMS rolled the gurney to the ambulance. The pickup-truck guy patted my neighbor on the leg. He murmured a response and closed his eyes again.

The pickup-truck guy advanced toward me. The black dog, who had been keeping a vigilant eye on her owner, followed closely behind.

"I'm Griff"—he held out his hand—"CJ's business partner. And this is Ellie, CJ's service dog." The black dog wiggled next to him.

I tucked the keys farther into my palm and grasped his outstretched hand with the tips of my fingers. If he noticed, he didn't show it. "Finley Thompson." I jerked my thumb at the nearby clump of trees. "I just moved into Mattie Bennett's house." With my free hand, I reached out to pet Ellie. She responded immediately, brushing up next to me.

He nodded. "Do you know what happened?"

"His horse came running onto my property. I found him when I brought her back." I edged away. Better to leave before he asked more questions. I did my neighborly duties, even more than I should've done if I counted the stuff on his kitchen table. I needed to get out.

He angled his body closer and petted Ellie, effectively blocking my path. Now it would be more obvious if I cut and run. "Did he say anything?"

The cop standing across the way perked up, head bent as if listening for my response. "No." My voice shook a bit. I sucked at lying. "Nothing I could understand. I did hear him mumbling something about blue two."

Griff's eyes softened. "Teammate. Died a while back. CJ had a TBI, so sometimes his memories get a little—well, a little wonky."

"Traumatic brain injury?" My heart squeezed again. I needed to get rid of that habit if I wanted to make it on my own.

"Yup, in A-stan." He must have seen the horror on

my face. "He's fine now, but if he hit his head or that horse kicked him, it's enough to have some effects. More than if it happened to you or me."

A kick to the head would be enough to give anyone side effects. Death was one of those pesky side effects if delivered to the right spot. Ellie pushed her head into my hand, and I kept petting her. The motion alone calmed my frayed nerves.

I nodded. "Do you live here too?" Maybe I could dump the keys and switchblade and get back to my desserts. If I drove really fast, I might make my shift.

"No. This"—Griff waved his hand around—"is CJ's place."

"Looks just like him," the cop said. "Run-down, broken, and desperate." Bitterness echoed in his words.

"Screw you, Troy. Go bother some other unsuspecting citizens."

"Just doing my duty, Griff." The cop headed for the house. "I'm going to take a stroll around and make sure everything's in order."

Griff stepped into the cop's path. Ellie followed suit, ears at half-mast as if she wasn't quite sure how she felt. "Duty is exactly what I'd call that bullshit line. All you're going to do is see if you can write CJ up on some bogus charge. The house is locked, so back off. You have no right to do anything else."

"That's not a threat to a police officer, is it?" He glared at Griff, his hand gracing the gun hanging at his hip. Ellie's ears slid farther back.

The charge in the air was almost palpable. What the hell had I wandered into? I fought the urge to run back to my house, but Griff was the best chance I had of unloading CJ's stuff.

"Troy." Griff mock-bowed his head and stepped back. "I wouldn't dare threaten you." He over pronounced every letter.

Troy, apparently satisfied, walked toward the house. Griff turned his head to watch the EMS guys. "You self-serving prick."

A nervous giggle threatened to escape my mouth, and I clamped down on my lip. Troy tried the front door, and I instinctively gripped the keys tighter. The door didn't open, and he stepped off the porch and went around the side.

With Troy out of eyesight, I opened my hand to reveal the keys and yanked out the cell phone and switchblade. Griff raised his eyebrows, and as smooth as silk, he slipped everything into his pockets before Troy circled around to the front of the house.

The EMS guys slammed the ambulance doors. "We're leaving!"

Griff glanced their way, back to Troy, and then last to Ellie and me. He cocked his head sideways in Ellie's direction. "You seem to have hit it off."

I stroked Ellie's head. When I paused, she nudged me with her nose. My throat tightened. Sarge, my yellow lab growing up, did the exact same thing. "She's very sweet."

"Can you keep her for the afternoon?"

"Uh. That's…"

Appeased by my lack of words, Griff backed up in the direction of his pickup. "She'll be lost without CJ."

"You don't even know me!"

"I know Mattie, and that's good enough for me. Her food's in a big plastic bin in the barn. Thanks for helping, Finley. CJ will come by and grab her as soon as he can."

Before I could protest further, he climbed into his pickup and maneuvered around to follow the ambulance.

So much for keeping a low profile. I stared at the empty driveway for a full five seconds until the beep of my phone broke my reverie. My alarm set for the time to leave. I hurried to the barn with Ellie hot on my heels. Her plastic bin full of food was right where Griff had said it would be. I grabbed it and peeked in the red mare's stall. Content, she munched on hay, her water bucket still full. A shadow fell across the barn aisle, and the mare and Ellie jerked their heads up at the same time. I jumped. Troy stood at the doorway, his arms crossed over his chest. Thank God I didn't have the keys anymore.

"You should be careful," he said—his body, uncomfortably close.

I adjusted the bin, hefting it farther up on my hip, and edged out into the yard. "She's okay."

"Not the dog. With the guy who lives here. Be wary of him."

He needn't worry. I lived that careful creed ever since Jack died. My recent actions this morning, a great exception to that mantra. "Okay."

As if my tacit acceptance wasn't enough, he stepped forward, again too close. "This guy, CJ, he's bad news. He's on the edge."

My eyes drifted from the A-frame house to the flowerbeds and cut lawn, to the old but well-kept barn and wooden fences gracing the land. Despite Troy's earlier jab, nothing here screamed rundown or dangerous. Not that looks couldn't be deceiving. I, of all people, knew that.

Troy took another step forward, crowding into my space. "Drugs, alcohol, he's into it all. Such a shame. A promising career in the military. A SEAL, in fact, but don't let that persuade you. He's fallen off the path."

Ellie pressed against my knee, one ear cocked forward and one back, tail still. She didn't like Troy in my space any more than I did.

Troy leaned closer. "Where do you live?"

For a second, I had the urge to lie. "I'm renting. Mattie Bennett's place."

He scrunched his bushy eyebrows down. "What's your name?"

I held my hand out. Maybe this wouldn't drag on too long if I was direct. I had to get those desserts to Peak Coffee House and find a place for Ellie to camp out in my house. I silently cursed Griff. I didn't have time for this—not *any* of it. Most importantly, I wasn't following Jack's advice at all here. This time around, it was more than people not knowing what had happened; it was about staying hidden and staying safe. "Finley Thompson."

He took my hand and held it for way too long. "How did you wind up out here?"

Great. A nosy cop poking around into my life was the last thing I needed or wanted. But I couldn't afford to piss him off. "Mattie's a friend. She gave me a good deal."

"I'm sure she did with a madman as a neighbor."

I motioned in the direction of my house. "I better go." I backed away from him, pivoted, and hurried for the break in the fence. How long would it take for him to trace my name? One minute? Five minutes? Jack had managed to erase a hell of a lot when I married him, but I still didn't need anyone searching into my past. I shivered and ducked through the gap in the fence between our properties. Troy made me want to run away more than CJ. Of course, CJ had been compromised, unable to rise from the ground, whereas Troy was able-bodied with a gun.

"Make sure you lock your doors!"

Little did he know I had plenty of reasons to lock my doors, none of which were my madman neighbor.

Chapter 4

CJ

Hospitals were one step away from hell for me. After months spent doctoring my injuries from A-stan, I vowed never to return to one. So following a long night of countless medical tests and little sleep, I phoned Griff to pick me up and cajoled the doc in charge into releasing me before Ashley showed up and gave us both the ninth degree. My sister was a neurologist and, as usual, would be full of opinions.

Griff rolled up outside the main doors right on time. He didn't wait for me to close the pickup door before handing over my cell phone and switchblade. He motioned to a cup of coffee, chicken sandwich, and hash browns sitting on the console.

I pulled out the wrapped sandwich and nearly moaned at the heavenly scent. "Thanks."

"Best hangover cure."

"If only."

"What'd the doc say?"

"Concussion. Take it easy for a week or two. Come back to get checked. I feel like hell, and my leg fricking hurts." My leg, scarred from combat, usually gave me enough trouble as I worked among the garage, the barn, and the pastures. Now, it really throbbed. The doctor had offered painkillers, but I turned them down. That road led nowhere good.

"You're lucky you weren't hurt worse." He didn't bother hiding the reproach in his voice. Griff wasn't a big fan of all my rescued animals, especially the horses. He had valid concerns because our newly opened garage business couldn't afford for one of us to be hurt. But he wouldn't tell me to stop; he knew how important it was to me.

"Don't get your panties in a bunch. I'm fine." I took a sip of coffee, relishing the burn down my throat. The pain reminded me I was alive—or at least that's what I told myself most days.

"Do you remember Troy showing up? He's vindictive. I guarantee he was looking for anything on you, snooping around your house. You're lucky the house was locked."

I couldn't disagree there. Troy's competitive streak from high school, which had us battling it out for spots on sports teams, had transformed him into a superior asshole after high school. Determined to "beat" me financially, he and his brother, Wade, a local realtor, had teamed up to buy and develop land.

"Troy's looking for a reason to get my land," I said. "As long as I'm soluble and not in bankruptcy, they don't have a claim."

"I went into the house to feed the dogs—do you consider throwing a towel over your handgun and drugs being careful?"

I had no idea what he meant by a towel. "I was trying to get them in bags for Ashley to donate to that program she works with."

Griff slanted a look my way. "If you're not careful, Troy will have you in handcuffs in a New York minute.

You know I can't run that business alone and take care of the boys."

A little bullet of pain ricocheted across my chest, as it always did when kids came up. Conversations about kids hurt my chest more than a nasty cross-check during the final seconds of a Navy lacrosse game. Add crappy sperm to my bum leg and scarred face and throat—well, it wasn't pretty. Some days the list of things I couldn't do loomed over me. This was where my rescue animals helped.

"Were the dogs okay?" Where Griff had boys and an ex-wife, I had a collection of lost and abused animals. Not that they were equal.

"Yes. I sent Ellie to your new neighbor's. The one renting from Mattie Bennett."

"What?" I almost choked on a bite of biscuit.

"You know she doesn't like to be alone." Griff was right. My other rescues didn't mind bunking in the barn at night, but Ellie was a house dog all the way. Most nights, she wound up curled next to me on the bed.

I bit the bullet. "So that blonde woman wasn't made up?" I sighed in relief. "I thought maybe I was seeing things."

Griff grinned. "I wondered if you remembered her. Found your horse and then you. I think she may have saved your life."

She did more than that if she locked my house. She saved my stupid ass.

"Ellie liked her, so I asked her to keep her until you got out."

A twinge of jealousy sparked through me. Ellie was my special dog. She knew me better than people, always there when my flashbacks thundered in. She instinctively knew when I was on edge and needed an extra nudge or lick. I wouldn't have made it these last few months without her. "I hope this woman is taking good care of her."

"I'm sure she is." Griff side-eyed me. "Jealous your dog will like the hot woman better?"

"No." That came out too quick and loud not to be defensive. "And she wasn't hot."

Griff snorted. "Said the guy with the concussion."

The throbbing in my head rushed back with a vengeance. Instead of arguing, I leaned against the window, the cold glass a welcome distraction. An image of my new neighbor floated into my mind. She had beautiful blue-gray eyes with dark rims and honey-blonde hair. When I asked her to lock the house, she gazed up at me, and those beautiful eyes filled with something—fear, worry, remorse maybe. I wasn't sure. As with most things with my brain, it was better not to think too hard. My memories came quicker and with better clarity when I didn't concentrate or try to pull them up. I closed my eyes. When she brushed my hair back, her bare leg had touched my arm and the scent of cinnamon floated in the air.

As a general rule, I kept away from people I didn't know. With a body covered in scars and a mind that sometimes chose to malfunction, it was easier to keep to myself and avoid people who didn't know me. People, especially newcomers to town, meant questions. And questions came with answers that dove into memories better left alone. There were some things that no amount of time or a hospital could fix.

Chapter 5

Finley

"Some guy in a truck is in our driveway!" Cody called from the stairs, his feet stomping up the steps, echoing through the house. Mattie had warned me about the sound of this old farmhouse as well as its "quaintness," as she called it—*cute from the outside, falling down on the inside.* I hadn't cared, and I still didn't. Jack made me promise that if he ever died, I'd leave D.C. Mattie had offered me the perfect way to make good on that promise. A falling-down house was better than a dangerous address and waiting for a schizophrenic killer to show up and get his revenge.

The doorbell rang, and I dropped a bag of flour on the counter. White plumes floated through the air. *That will be a bitch to clean up.* Ever since I went to my neighbor's, I'd been jumping at the slightest sounds expecting somebody to show up demanding answers as to how my fingerprints got on that guy's phone or knife or door. I prayed it wasn't the cop, Troy, standing on our dilapidated front porch. I had a distinct feeling I'd be hearing from him. I pulled a batch of peanut butter chocolate chip bars from the oven, slid in an apple tart, and headed for the front hall, which in this house was about ten steps from the kitchen. *Please, please don't be Troy.* There was something just a little skeevy about him. Ellie shadowed me, her nails scratching on the floorboards. I peered out the window. It wasn't the cop.

This guy was tall and well built, not overly muscled like he pumped iron but rather like he got fit wrangling cattle or maybe alligators. He resembled a man in a tough-guy truck or whiskey commercial. His head was tucked down, and the edge of a bandage was visible on his forehead. Along the side of his face ran a grisly-looking scar. I cracked the door open.

"Hello?"

He lifted his head and speared me with his gaze. His eyes, green with specks of brown and a darker green ring around them, held a touch of sadness, something deep, something missing. The corner of his mouth edged up into a crooked smile, softening the lines of his face. It was just enough to tug on my heart.

"I'm looking for Finley Thompson?"

His voice was how I remembered it exactly—mid-range but raspy, like he'd been up smoking and drinking way too much. It was a voice that matched the scruff that covered a pronounced jawline and evoked images of cowboys and warriors. At the sound, my already bucking heart ran off with the air in my lungs. He twisted his head a bit but not before I got a good look at his scar. How did I not see it yesterday? Angry and red, the mottled skin ran down the side of his face, marring an otherwise near-perfect silhouette. As if someone took a broken bottle and tried to etch something into the side of his face. *Where did he get a scar like that?*

Ellie whined and pushed her nose through the crack, her tail wagging furiously.

"Hey, girl." His eyes softened, and he reached out,

petting and scratching her head. She busted through the door, her body wobbling from side to side from enthusiasm.

I used the distraction to whip my ponytail holder out of my hair and finger comb it. I couldn't do anything about my yoga pants and pink T-shirt, clothes fine for baking in and helping the kids with homework but not for seeing people, especially not a hot military guy.

Standing and able-bodied, he made a much more formidable picture than yesterday when he was sprawled flat in the grass. With one hand still on Ellie, he turned his attention back to me and held out his hand. "CJ Sinclair. You helped me yesterday."

Light brown hair, overgrown and tousled, slightly crooked nose, and a jaw with an edge that screamed: "stroke me." A tattoo peeked out from under his T-shirt sleeve. His name fit him, like the broken-in jeans that hung from his hips. And those eyes.

Despite my jumping heart, I hesitated. This was a guy who had both pills and a handgun lying about in his house—and judging by his reactions, both were probably illegal. I wondered what else he was hiding. Ellie's wagging tail whacked my leg. He also had a dog who loved him. But of course, Michael had loved animals, and they loved him too. And look where that got me. That relationship destroyed everything I had at the time.

I realized I was still holding his hand. He released it and picked up a pot from the ground—a lavender plant. "I want to thank you. From what everyone says, you saved my life. The lady at the hardware store told me to plant lavender for good luck, so I figured since you just moved in…"

Manners told me to take the plant and ask him in. That's what you did with neighbors who bought you stuff as thank you gifts. But what was the protocol for neighbors with bags of pills on their table? *Don't forget the handgun on the table, too.* I smushed my lips together, searching for the nerve to let him take Ellie and just close the door in his face—politely, of course. But I didn't want him thinking I was shutting the door in his face because of the scar. Besides, I had Ellie's food. He needed that.

Jazz barreled down the stairs, Cody right behind her, and ran into me like a train into a station. "Is it the pizza? I'm starving!"

"Where's Ellie going?" Cody asked, his forehead furrowed.

"Home where she belongs." I felt my own twinge of remorse. I hadn't had a dog in the house since my yellow lab, Sarge, and I had enjoyed Ellie's presence. But I didn't want to let on. The kids would be after me for a dog, and I couldn't do that kind of commitment while trying to get my business off the ground. Besides, what if we had to leave quickly? A dog would just complicate things.

"You're not the pizza guy?" Jazz's voice dripped with disappointment.

The corner of CJ's mouth twitched. "Nope, afraid not. I'm the lavender-plant guy."

"That blows." She turned away.

"Jasmine!" I cringed and pressed my fingers to my forehead. Her manners had disappeared since Jack's death. Of course, my hiding didn't help things. Dropping my hand, I motioned between them. "This is our neighbor, CJ. This is my daughter, Jasmine."

"Hi." In true-teenager style, she placed a hand on her hip and sized him up from head to toe. "Are you going to come in or just stand there blocking the door? We want to play lacrosse."

CJ hesitated a moment, checked out the smile I plastered onto my face, and then crossed the doorway, limping as he did so. The kids headed outside, lacrosse sticks in hand. They didn't get along most of the time, but when it came to avoiding homework and playing sports, they seemed to miraculously put their differences aside.

"Excuse my daughter. She's all teenager and not very happy we moved."

"How's that going?"

His hair was wet, it glistened more than it did the other morning, and he smelled like coconut.

I motioned to boxes waiting to be unpacked. "Not very well."

"What brought you to Davidson?"

"Work and kids." It was my pat, evasive answer, which seemed to work well with most people.

"A job transfer?"

Figures he would ask more questions. Although I avoided disclosing information at all costs, I also hated spinning a web of lies I wouldn't be able to keep track of. "My husband died nine months ago. We needed a change from D.C." It was a version of the truth that helped me deliver it without my voice shaking or hitching, which happened when I outright lied.

His eyes widened just a bit. "I'm sorry."

I held his gaze, and for a moment, time seemed to stop. Thankfully, the timer from the kitchen stove went off.

"I have to get some bread out of the oven." I headed down the short hall to the kitchen, calling over my shoulder. "How's your leg?"

He followed, Ellie glued to his side. "Okay. It was injured before yesterday. The run-in with the mare just made it worse."

Horses were a safe topic. "How is she?"

"She's fine. Tried to bite me today."

"Have you had her long?" Please say no. I didn't want to think that she was underfed because of him. I turned off the timer and removed an Irish soda bread from the oven. Its scent of butter and sugar floated out and filled the kitchen.

"No. I rescued her from an auction a few weeks ago. She's having trouble coming around." CJ checked out the room, his gaze traveling from one filled counter to the next. "Wow."

"I know it's dated." I swung an arm around, motioning to the green-colored cabinets and pink Formica countertops. "I'm trying to bring it into the twenty-first century, but I'm afraid I'm failing miserably."

"I meant the desserts. Did you make all these?"

I half-laughed. "I've gone a little overboard. I work at Peak Coffee House in town, and I asked my boss—"

"I know him. Small town."

"Yes, well, I asked him if I could bring some samples of my baking to convince him to sell them in the coffeehouse. I'd been too late yesterday, and my boss had already left. But after a lot of apologizing and a little begging, he agreed to give me another chance tomorrow." *Why am I telling him all this?*

He wandered over to a batch of cookie bars. "What are these? They smell delicious."

"Peanut butter chocolate chip bars. You want one?" I held one out for him. "They were my mom's favorite." The words slipped out before I could stop them. *Shut up, you idiot.* He didn't need to know that. Just saying the words made my heart ache. My mom was the reason I knew how to bake. Winter snow days, stuck in the house, she taught me her favorite recipes. I'd stopped after she died. But when the kids were little and Jazz came home from preschool asking to bake cookies, I'd gone back. Dragging out my mom's cookbooks and sharing those old family recipes with her—well, after that I never stopped baking. Even when the memories of her and me baking overwhelmed me and made the tears slide down my cheeks. Somehow, I felt like baking brought me closer to her, that she'd be proud of me for sharing our thing with the kids.

CJ placed the planter on the counter, popped a small piece in his mouth, and motioned to the chair shoved under the back door. "What's with the chair?"

My heart fluttered. *Was everyone in this town so nosy?* This was why it was better not to have anyone over, especially someone with drugs and a handgun. I didn't want anyone knowing I was scared or the weird precautions I took. "The lock isn't very strong. The chair gives back-up."

Limping over, he jiggled the simple slide-and-twist to test its strength. He furrowed his brow. "I see your point, but I don't think that rickety chair is going to do much to help."

Despite his injuries, he seemed to take up all the available space in my small kitchen. I'd managed to

31

squeeze a portable island table in there to prep my baking. But combined with our kitchen table, it left little room to maneuver. It occurred to me I was rarely in close quarters with guys. Jack died almost a year ago, and the only man who had visited us since then was— one of Jack's best friends, who the kids called Uncle Ian. Since moving here, none. Until this night. My heart pounded at the thought.

I took a deep breath. I needed to get rid of this guy. Politely if at all possible. I wasn't looking for friends here. If he took offense, so be it. Better to be safe and alone than exposed to whatever this guy was into. The kids didn't need anything more in their lives. And I certainly didn't need some guy asking questions. I glanced at the picture of Jack and the kids pinned on the refrigerator.

His gaze flicked to the kitchen window and back. "I'd like to explain some things."

Oh no, he was going to confess or, worse, lie to me. I held my hands up. "You don't have to explain anything."

He played with a spatula on the counter. "I think I do. Those pills on the table—"

"It's fine. Please. It's none of my business." At my interruption and tone, a dark pall settled over the room.

He glared at me across the island, his eyes hard and piercing. "I'm not a drug user."

I laid my hands out, palms up. "I don't think you are." I lied.

He leaned forward. "Or a seller."

"Fine."

"Did Troy say something about me?"

"No." That may have come out a bit too quick. I

slid the Irish soda bread off the pan onto a cooling rack.

"Because he's a liar."

His voice was tight and clipped. Great. An angry ex-SEAL, maybe a druggie, in my kitchen. I better fix this. "Listen, it's fine, you're fine, I'm fine. Don't worry about it."

I dropped the pan in the sink, where it clattered against the ceramic bottom and made me jump. When I turned around, he was staring at me, forehead furrowed.

"You don't look *fine*." He twanged the word fine and, if I didn't know better, added a touch of sarcasm.

"Neither do you."

His face had gone white in the minutes of standing in my kitchen.

"Leg's a bit banged up. I need to rest it." He swayed, and I had visions of him splayed out on my kitchen floor. I grabbed a chair and brought it to him.

"Sit." Perhaps one shouldn't command a SEAL. "Please. Before you fall down."

"I won't fall—" But he sat, and when he looked up at me, he gave me a half-smile. "—I promise."

I smiled back despite myself, despite all my fears. "I'll take that promise."

I handed him a bottle of water from the counter, and he twisted off the cap. His Adam's apple bobbed with each gulp, and I followed that line to the collar of his T-shirt. He had really nice shoulders that sloped to sculpted arms. I bet his abs under that shirt were equally as nice. When I snapped my gaze back to his face, he was staring at me. My cheeks flamed. What was I doing? This guy seemed to sap all my resolve to stay aloof.

He scrunched the bottle in his fingers and stood up.

"I better go."

"Yes." Did that sound breathless? Wonderful. Twenty years after Michael, and the bad boy still appealed to me. Hadn't I learned anything in my life?

The front door slammed, and the kids crowded into the kitchen.

"Jazz cheats," Cody said.

"It's not my fault you suck at ground balls." She turned to the two of us as if we hadn't heard her the first time. "He sucks at ground balls."

"Enough, Jazz."

Jazz twisted her black hair into a ponytail. Born brunette with beautiful shades of red, she'd dyed it black in the last few months. I hated it, but I knew arguing about it wouldn't help. Since Jack's death, our relationship had been strained, especially since the recent move forced her to give up her spot on her lacrosse team in D.C.

"It was one thing when the coaches knew him and us," Jazz said, "but now he's an outsider. He's got to be better than everybody. If he wants to make a team, he better fix his ground ball problem—maybe you should have thought of that before we moved." She smirked at me, grabbed a raspberry cookie, and waltzed out of the room.

The urge to throw my spatula at her flitted through my mind, but I didn't want to look like a total crazy mom. Besides, she wasn't wrong. My past was littered with unsuccessful impulsive decisions.

Cody, used to his bossy sister, ignored her outburst and sized up CJ. "Is that your business on the side of your truck? The garage?"

"Yes. My best friend Griff and I run a body shop

and garage out of my property."

"Cool—" Cody nodded to me. "—you should have him take a look at dad's SUV."

Cody's response to Jack's death was to assume that he needed to take over certain aspects of our life, like car maintenance. It was cute but no less concerning than Jazz's behavior. Both kept me up late at night worrying if I was doing an okay job at helping them cope with the loss of their father.

"Cody. It's fine." I waved my hand through the air as if that motion could make the issue go away.

He swiped a peanut butter chocolate bar off the plate and ran out toward the stairs, calling back as he disappeared around the corner. "Something's not right with it. You told me that on the drive down. When's the pizza coming? I'm starved."

CJ returned his gaze to mine. "Is something wrong with your SUV? I'll take a look at it."

"It's fine. Really. Cody gets overly worried. His dad died in a car accident. It was sudden, unexpected." I sucked my lip in and bit it. I didn't want to be rude, but I didn't need a favor from this guy. The less contact we had, the better.

He squeezed the half-empty bottle of water; the crinkling of the plastic echoed in the quiet. "I'm sorry."

"Me too." CJ had no idea how much I meant that. According to the report, Jack had been drunk as a skunk. It's a miracle he didn't kill anyone else. Thank God, or I'd have more people's deaths on my hands.

Another crinkle. He tipped the bottle of water up and finished it off. He dropped his hand down to the counter and gave me a small, crooked smile. "Can I have another one of those bars?"

The death mood broke, and against my better judgment, I smiled. I loved it when people liked my baking. "Sure." I grabbed the plate and held it out to him.

He took one and popped it into his mouth. "How'd you catch the mare? She won't even let me near her."

"I used carrots and patience." I shrugged and rearranged the cookie bars on the plate so that the empty spot wasn't as obvious. I licked a dab of chocolate off my finger. "She was pretty jumpy, but she calmed down—a little."

His gaze—the heat in his eyes almost palpable—flicked down to my lips and rose slowly back up.

My pulse spiked, my mouth instantly dry, just the way I got right before I went into the show ring to compete. Great. I wanted to slap myself in the face. *Get a grip!* He was my neighbor, a guy with drugs and a handgun. I needed to politely turn him down, make an excuse that I didn't need his help, and get him out of my house. I grabbed Ellie's food bin from the corner and held it out to him.

He tucked it under his arm. "If you change your mind on the car, bring it over. Griff or I will look at it. For free, of course. A return of the favor."

Now only a total witch would turn him down, and I hated being rude. "Okay. Thank you."

His phone rang. He pulled it from his pocket, checked it, and slid it back in. "Thanks, Finley—for watching Ellie and for earlier. I better go. Come on, El." Ellie, sleeping in the corner, jumped to her feet and padded after him.

I followed too, staring at the way his T-shirt fell from his shoulders to his jeans. In the hall, he paused before the side table. On it sat an eight-by-ten of Jack and the kids, taken last fall at the kids' homecoming fair. Having returned just a few days earlier from the Middle East, his eyes were dark and haunted as they often were when he came home from overseas.

CJ turned to me; his face had changed. It was empty of what it had before—and expressionless. "Is that your husband?"

"Yes." I half-laughed, which came out sounding a bit more like a sob. "Normally, he was a clean-shaven kind of guy, but whenever he came back from Afghanistan, he always had a full beard—and a full mind. Reentry was always a bit rough."

That last time was especially bad, and the picture showed it—Jack looked depressed, his eyes dark.

CJ cocked his head to the side, examining Jack's face. "Military?"

"No, nothing like that. State Department. More like support work. We snapped that picture right after he returned from Afghanistan. The kids took him to some car race in the hopes of pulling him out of his mood."

Geez. What the hell is wrong with me around this guy? I was like a geyser but, instead of water spewing forth, it was personal information. Some of it wasn't even entirely true. Jack worked for the CIA as an analyst. I rarely divulged that info to people because they always jumped to the wrong conclusions believing that Jack was a spy. Either way, there was no reason to spill family secrets. I didn't need a new best friend as a neighbor, especially one I felt the need to tell stuff to.

He nodded but didn't say anything else and instead opened the front door. Halfway through, he stopped abruptly, and I almost collided with him. His fingers wrapped around the door jamb—large and capable and ready to crush the wood beneath them.

"I don't know what Troy said to you, but I'm sure it was something along the lines of 'He's crazy, he uses drugs, he's dangerous.' And although he's not right on everything, he is right that I'm dangerous. But I'm not the only one. Make sure you lock this door, and if it makes you feel better, stick a chair under this one as well."

Is he making fun of me? There was a huskiness to his voice. His eyes were hidden from me, and for a brief second, I wanted to slide my fingers underneath that chiseled jaw, pull his face around, and look into them.

He dropped his hand from the door, and I closed it behind him. I peeked out the side door window. At the bottom of the steps, he paused, waiting. As soon as I turned the bolt, he limped toward his truck. He threw the food bin into the bed and opened the driver's side door. Ellie jumped up. He hoisted himself in, and they eased on down the driveway.

I returned to the kitchen. The space was empty and still without his presence. Even injured and limping, he had an energy to him. I dropped my head down. I made a promise to Jack to keep the kids safe. I didn't need complications or distractions, and if there was one thing I knew, it was that this guy was both.

Chapter 6

CJ

A trace of vanilla, butter, and cinnamon followed me to my truck, reminding me of the freshly baked coffee cake my grandmother used to make on Saturday mornings. I wanted to wallow in it—sit in my truck and examine every minute in Finley's house—except that I couldn't. I punched my console twice, three times. Jack Thompson's widow is my new neighbor? Talk about a whole lot of screwed-up mess.

Why was she lying? Jack didn't work for the State Department. I'd eaten meals with him, shared beers, killed and captured men the CIA valued as targets on his say-so. Hell, he was the voice in my last flashback barking about the HVT. When he hesitated on that last op, I was the one who convinced him to do it. I punched the console another five times before I reached my house, which was saying something since we lived about one minute from each other.

Ellie whined, pushing her head under my hand, trying to steady me. Rusty, the beagle my neighbor Hank Bennett gave me, met us at my truck's door. He and Ellie exchanged sniffs. I tried petting them to calm me down, but it was useless. Nothing could break through the racket going around in my head. I'd been dreading this day, expecting it. I'd kept everything I knew, everything I remembered under wraps, and now some lithe widow with stormy eyes had the ability to blow it all out of the water.

It was dinnertime, and the horses whinnied expectantly from their stalls. They were more exact than alarm clocks and didn't like dinner being delayed. Griff had brought them all in from the pastures for me, but when he offered to feed them, I insisted I could do it. Stupid dumb pride. My leg throbbed marginally more than my head. The horses' buckets were lined up outside the feed room door. I pressed McDavies's number on my cell and waited for him to pick up.

Scooping out the horses' grain, I dumped the specific amounts into each bucket. The sweet smell of the grain wafted out of the buckets, and despite my churning emotions over Finley and my aching body, I smiled. Feeding time, with its set rituals of grain, hay, and water, had a way of smoothing out the edges of a rough day.

On the fourth ring, he answered.

"Hey, McDavies."

"Si-in. What's up?" He broke my name up into two syllables—his trademark way of calling me—but his voice trailed off, lacking his usual enthusiasm. My instincts shot into focus, and I tamped down my own emotions. If McDavies was in a bad way, he didn't need any more problems.

"Nothing." I lied, hoping my voice didn't betray anything. "How ya doing?

"Okay." Exhaustion dripped from every syllable of that four-letter word.

Throughout our military careers, we were taught to push our bodies past all normal levels of pain, sleep, and physical and mental output, but that didn't mean we weren't affected, especially once we were done with a mission. He didn't sound good at all. "You sounded better that night in BUDS when they tried to drown us."

Basic Underwater Demolition SEAL school is a six-month SEAL training course in California. The beginning of a journey and a brotherhood that withstood all the crap life had to dish out.

"Can you specify which night you mean?" A shadow of his normal cocky-self broke through, his voice steadier.

The plaintive wail of a baby filled my ear. "What's going on?"

I dropped some cut-up carrots in each bucket as treats, pausing to pet each one, except the red mare who pinned her ears at my approach. I dumped her bucket quickly and beat it out of there.

"The baby's sick. Again. Up all night. They think she might have some kind of blood disorder."

I stopped and rubbed the back of my neck. I couldn't imagine what I'd do if my nieces or nephews got sick. I'd wanted kids. But Trish had been the only woman I'd had a long-term relationship with, and she ended our marriage by hopping in bed with the golf pro. An image of Finley in her kitchen grew steady: her blue-gray eyes holding mine, lips full and pursed, her honey-blonde hair brushing the opening of her V-neck T-shirt. I shook my head, trying to banish her image. There was no way I could go after her. She was Jack's widow. "Sorry, Mac. That's horrible."

"Laney gets no sleep. We're taking her for testing this week."

I dropped the buckets back in the feed room, closed

the door, and leaned against the wall, exhausted. I was about a minute from falling down. But I couldn't rest before I threw each horse some hay. "You know—anything you need."

"I took two weeks off when she was born, but I think I'm going to ask for another four weeks off."

"Are you sure you should?" McDavies had suffered from depression since he'd come back. The job was the only thing that helped. I pushed off the wall and rolled back the hay stall door.

"I'll be okay."

"I can fly out there." We were connected and always would be. All of us. That's what the teams did for us, gave us a brotherhood that didn't end, even if our careers had.

"Nah. I'm fine. We'll be okay."

"Keep me posted. Remember, yesterday was the only easy day."

He half-laughed. "Don't I know it."

I clicked off and stared at my phone. Asking for help was never an easy thing, especially as frogmen. We were trained in highly evolved and effective military warfare—trained to lead when no one was there to lead, to finish what we started, and to succeed no matter what. It was great for combat, but the problem was fitting into civilian life. There was no outlet or calling for our skillset in the everyday world. I made a mental note to call him in two days.

I threw hay into each horse's stall and uncoiled the hose. Horses consumed five to ten gallons of water a day. Without it, they could get sick. I turned on the hose and pressed Owen's number.

He picked up on the second ring—standard

procedure.

"Ridding the world of bad guys one computer key at a time?" I asked. Since retiring, Owen started a consultant security company which was code for digging up dirt on people for whoever paid him and testing out people's security systems. He had a few corporate clients who were paying him nicely to keep their businesses safe and the employees they hired on the up and up. I peered into the stall of my gray-dappled horse, Storm.

"Maybe. How about you? You keeping your shooting skills sharp by taking out local bad guys?"

I turned off the water and slowly coiled up the hose, my cell phone nestled in the crook of my neck. "You forget where I live. The only targets I have here are rats the size of small dogs."

"Actual or figurative? And don't give me your small town, Green Acres bit. There are bad guys everywhere. Did you get any this week?"

Unable to sleep most nights, I used the spare time to wage battle on the rats scurrying in and out of the barn from my front porch. Afterward, I'd send the body count to Owen. "Five."

"Not bad."

I snorted. "I'd like to see you make that shot." Maybe I'd lost most of my skills in that shitstorm op, but I was still a better shot than Owen. And he knew it.

"My weapons are more delicate. Right now, I'm running some shit for Rivera at the Bureau."

Rivera was another of our SEAL brothers. He'd landed a government job after retiring from service. Since Owen wasn't constrained by pesky laws like a government employee, I think Rivera used him plenty to run down leads.

"McDavies is having trouble," I said.

"Yeah, I heard about Mac. What's up with you?"

I paused. Once I said the words, there was no taking them back. "Did you know Jack Thompson died?" Finished with coiling the hose, I contemplated collapsing onto one of the trunks outside a stall to catch my breath, but there was the distinct possibility that I wouldn't be able to get up again.

"No. When?"

I hesitated to answer. I re-checked the stall latches to make sure everything was secure and no one would be escaping late at night. Then I turned out the light and hobbled outside.

"CJ, what happened?"

"A car accident." I stared into the dark night. "A few months ago."

Owen knew me well. "Sin—what's going on?" His tone had turned from friendly to complete businesslike. In two more seconds, he'd be master chief again.

"I met this woman today. She's renting my grandparents' old house. The one next door to mine."

"And?"

"She's Jack's wife. Told me her husband worked for the State Department and died in a car wreck nine months ago."

"Understandable why he wouldn't tell her he worked for the CIA."

"Maybe. Said his last trip overseas, he came back depressed."

"Didn't we all."

In the moment of silence, I wondered if Owen was thinking about Elliot like I was. He didn't come back from that mission at all.

"Do you think she knows, or is she playing you?"

"She's hiding something. I just don't know what." My guess was she wasn't hiding anything as big as I was. "Did you see Jack after that op?"

"Nah—everyone was too busy adjusting, retiring, or recovering. Did you tell her you knew her husband?"

"No. I didn't see a picture until on my way out the door."

The silence was palpable. "Was that door tonight or this morning?"

"Tonight. Give me some credit."

"I am, Sin. I know you. I've seen you in action."

I was a player or had been. I liked women and they liked me, and all of it came easily. Of course, that was before marrying Trish and before my injuries. None of it came easily now, and Trish was long gone—married to a successful banker who could give her everything she wanted, especially a fancy house, a big paycheck, and kids. "That guy is long gone."

"Are you going to tell her the truth?"

I snorted. "Not about Tajikistan. But I do want to know why she's down here and the specifics of his accident. If he was killed, if someone's cleaning up that mess, I don't want to be here sitting out like a duck in open water."

"What about the wife? You going to leave her as a sitting duck?"

"I'm not leaving anybody open, but I'm hardly the one to help her. Some days I can barely get out of bed." I rubbed my forehead, trying to extinguish the faint pounding of an oncoming headache.

Owen, never one to indulge my whine-fest, cut

through to the chase. "If someone's gunning for her, are you going to let this thing lie? Because the SEAL I knew had a problem walking away when innocent people were on the line."

"The SEAL you knew had four working limbs, a brain that could remember every minute detail, and a voice that could shout louder than anybody. That guy is long gone, blown to pieces in a hell hole of a shit town. This *ex*-SEAL wants no part of anything complicated, and that woman has complicated written all over her." Of course, complicated or not, she was beautiful. *That's the last thing I need to be thinking about.*

"You want me to look into it?"

"Yeah. If you can."

"Sure. Stay out of her pants."

"I'm not going after his wife." I didn't bother hiding my growl.

"Your nickname's Sin. Aptly given if I remember correctly."

"I know that. And your memory's crap. Sin's short for Sinclair."

Owen's cackle reverberated in my ear, and I held the phone away, hoping he heard my answering curse.

Lights bounced down the drive, and a minivan pulled to a stop: Ashley, my older sister.

"Got to go, O."

"You owe me."

The car door swung open, and Ashley stepped out with a tray in her hands and a plastic bag swinging from her arm. My older sister was half my size, but that didn't daunt her and never had. She'd inherited my mom's Southern self-assuredness and confidence, and there wasn't anyone she couldn't talk to or convince to like her. She reached into the back seat of her minivan—her wavy brown hair threatening to escape from her hair tie—and returned carrying groceries and a tray covered in tinfoil. "Aren't you supposed to be resting in bed?"

"Hi, Ash." I grabbed the tray. The smell of sausage floated up.

"Lasagna"—she held out the plastic bag—"and lettuce for a salad and a loaf of bread. Where have you been? I've called you, like, five times. I was scared you were unconscious somewhere."

"I'm fine. Thank you for the food, but you didn't have to."

"You are my little brother, and you spent the night in the hospital. Of course, I did." She cocked her head sideways, eyeing me. "Honey, you look better than yesterday but not by much. If I'd have had my way, you'd still be there."

"If you had your way, I'd be wrapped in bubble wrap."

"Exactly." Ashley hadn't been thrilled when I joined the military and even less so when I became a SEAL. "Have you thanked the woman who helped you? Griff gave me a quick rundown."

Of course, he did. Some days I had the distinct feeling that Ashley and Griff kept tabs on me through each other. "Ash, leave it be."

"Little brother, I haven't even said anything."

"I know, but I know you and where you're going." Ever since Trish ran out on me, Ashley had made it her goal to find me someone else. I think she convinced herself that if I had someone new, then that meant I was healed. I didn't have the heart to crush her dream and tell her not everything healed with time.

Never one to drop anything, my all-knowing older sister barged ahead. "Griff told me she was pretty."

I pushed away the image of Finley's shirt hugging her curves and the surge of anger toward Griff. What was he doing talking about her looks? "Not particularly," I choked out.

"Really?" She shook her head. "Not even a spark?" Her voice held a hopeful note.

There was only one way to handle my sister: crush any wayward thought she had about Finley and me. There were so many things I could say, but I picked the most obvious and the one that twisted my heart when I really thought about it. "She's living in Mattie Bennett's house."

Ashley's chipper demeanor closed up in one second flat. Years ago, when my grandparents ran into financial trouble, they sold most of their acreage along with their farmhouse to Hank Bennett. They retained the four acres I lived on and put a small A-frame cottage on it. After a few years, Hank in turn sold the acreage to his niece, Mattie, and her husband, now soon to be ex-husband. I'd had my eye on the place ever since we lost it. Troy and Wade Eastley had their eye on it, too. They were buying up all the neighboring land to put together a large and ugly subdivision. It was a race to see who could get the most money together the quickest.

Ashley, like me, loved my grandparents' farm. We had a lot of great memories there. "Granddad and Nana's house?"

"Yes." That kitchen that Finley so casually labeled as "dated" was the last place I'd seen my grandparents together: vibrant, joking around, and full of love. It was in that kitchen where my granddad and I had hatched the plan for an equine rescue farm. Both of us animal lovers, we'd had dinner together, hashing out the details, before I'd shipped out. By the time I got released from rehab, my granddad was wheezing his last breaths from lung cancer and my grandmother was in a nursing home for Alzheimer's.

"How do you feel about that?"

I swallowed the lump in my throat and shrugged. There were so many things to be upset about, and the exhaustion I'd held at bay through the horses feeding threatened to overwhelm me. "I'm just trying to stay upright here. Ask me tomorrow when it has all sunk in."

"Maybe with a renter, Mattie won't sell it."

I ran a hand through my hair. "Maybe."

"You could ask Dad again?"

Six months ago, when Mattie first mentioned putting it up for sale, I asked my dad for a loan to buy it. He promptly lectured me on what constituted a good deal and refused. As far as he was concerned, unless I wanted to develop it, it shouldn't be bought. Land strictly meant money and development to him, not nostalgia or for pleasure. He should have been Wade and Troy's dad. They seemed much more alike. Wade and Troy probably would have turned out better too. "I'd rather get dragged by the horse again."

I resumed walking toward my house. Ashley fell into step beside me.

"Where's the new neighbor from?"

"Up North, and she has kids."

"A Northerner with kids? She'll fit in well. How

old are the kids?"

I couldn't tell if Ashley was being facetious. There's been so much development and so many transplants from up North that half the time I didn't recognize the town I grew up in. "Teenagers. Twelve and fifteen?"

"Ugh. No wonder you don't like her."

"I don't *not* like her." In fact, there'd been nothing not to like. Blue-gray eyes, full lips, sculpted cheekbones. Pink T-shirt and yoga pants, annoying on so many of the moms in town but had fit her well, outlining her curves. Her honey-blonde hair piled messily on top of her head, strands poking out here and there, curving around her neck. The endearing way she smiled, motioning to all her desserts.

As if she could read my thoughts, Ashley's concern morphed into a knowing smile. "Really?"

"Knock it off, Ash. She's off-limits. And that's fine by me. I'm sure we have about as much in common as me and the Pope."

"Why's she off-limits? Because she's renting Mattie's house?"

I hated when I went too far. Ashley wouldn't understand the whole code of not getting involved with another veteran's wife or widow, much less one involved in our last op. She had no idea what happened over there. Finley, on the other hand, might hold information that could lock me up.

"She's not for me. Let's just leave it at that. I got to go. My head's killing me, and my leg isn't far behind."

Finished, I spun on my heels.

Ashley caught my arm and pulled me into a hug. "Hang in there, little brother. It'll get clear. It always does." She released me and backed up toward her minivan.

Ashley had an entirely positive view of life. Unfortunately, whatever optimism I had, I left on the bombed-out, twisting streets of Jalalabad.

I raised the tray of dinner in her direction. "Thanks for dinner."

She waved from her van on the way out. "Anytime. Love ya!"

My mangy crew of four dogs rushed me. Three too many, but I couldn't stop picking up strays. There was something about their sad, soulful eyes that always did me in. Finley had eyes like that. The thought shot in from left field.

I petted each one, roughing up their hair and rubbing their ears. They returned the affection with licks and sniffs. I tried to give each their equal time and equal love. They deserved it. The hell some of these dogs had been through made something we shared in common.

I dropped dinner on the kitchen counter, swallowed Tylenol and Motrin, and despite all my aches and pains, I returned to the porch. Dusk had given way to a surprisingly warm evening for October. I took in the clarity of the stars, remembering my therapist's advice. *Just look up*, she had said. *Wherever you are, the night sky shows you how infinitesimal we are in the grand scheme. And yet part of it too.*

I tipped my head back and stared at the lit sky, but all I could see was Finley's face and hear her words. A lawyer with the State Department. Why would Jack lie to his wife about where he worked? And if he didn't lie and she knew, why was she lying to me?

Excepting the recent purchase of the rescued mare, I'd lived a quiet life for the last year—trying to leave the past behind, trying to plan for the future, trying to make that dream of my granddad's a reality. In just one day, this woman had thrown everything into jeopardy. Yes, she had saved me, but if she really didn't know about her husband and I told her the truth, what would she do with that information? And would that endanger us all?

Chapter 7

Finley

I turned off Greenway Road and onto Creek Road. Focused on the three mailboxes that delineated my driveway, I pressed the brakes to slow down for the turn. Nothing happened. Crap! I pressed harder, my foot hitting the floor—still nothing. I yanked the wheel left. *Make the turn, make the turn. Please.* Unlike the brakes, the wheels cooperated. Jack's decrepit SUV grazed off my mailbox, slid across the gravel and bounced into a pine tree, and came to a stop.

I dropped my head onto the steering wheel, gulping the air. The blast of a horn jerked me upright. I pushed the door open and peeked out.

A white minivan idled on the curve of the road, its driver halfway out. "You okay?"

My voice croaked. Licking my lips, I tried again. "Yeah, I'm fine."

"Need help?"

I assessed my predicament. I was halfway across my driveway and in the ditch that ran between mine and CJ's. There was a dent in my door from where I hit my mailbox and a dent in the hood from the pine tree, but otherwise, I was fine. The mailbox, on the other hand, lay flattened in the ditch. I could call triple AAA or just try CJ. I waved to the driver. "I'm good."

She nodded in answer and accelerated away. I turned the car off, grabbed my bag, and jogged down CJ's driveway. Hopefully, he meant what he offered last night.

CJ's driveway was longer than mine and lined with pink crepe myrtles. Halfway down, I determined I needed a more vigorous workout plan as I was sucking wind as if I'd just run the Kentucky Derby. Unlike the other day, today the property bustled. Several cars were parked outside the garage area. Griff was busy talking with a customer, but CJ came from the garage. His limp was less noticeable today.

He made a striking picture: dark T-shirt, well-worn jeans that hung from his hips, hair at just the right length with a messed-up sexy look. Did he roll out of bed looking like that? Already beating like a maniac, my heart did a little extra dance. Wonderful. This day was trying to kill me. In my life experience, good-looking guys and I didn't mix well. It hadn't just been Michael; Jack and I hadn't made the best couple either. Great in pictures and on paper. In real life—not so much.

CJ met me as I panted to a stop. "Are you okay?"

I shook my head. "My car. I couldn't stop it."

He reached for me but halfway stopped, his hand hanging in the air, brows drawn tight together. "What?"

"When I turned for my driveway—luckily, I wasn't going fast—the brakes wouldn't work. I plowed into a tree at the end, near the road." I waved my hand in the general direction.

CJ pivoted on his good heel and limped back to the barn, emerging on his ATV seconds later. He roared to a stop next to Griff, who shook hands with the client and climbed in next to CJ. They raced back to me. "Stay here—" CJ pointed into the garage. "—and we'll bring it back."

I wanted to fight him on it, but suddenly I was overwhelmed and tired. I nodded, not sure I could manage any more words. I pressed my keys into his palm, and a zing surged up my arm. *Seriously?* That was the last thing I needed.

He jerked his head in the direction of the barn. "Drinks are in the barn." They accelerated down his driveway, rocks spewing from the tires.

His driveway and mine ran parallel. We were kind of like the sides of a U-shape, but then my property opened in the back to a lot more land. Mattie told me she and her ex were arguing about whether to sell to developers because the land was so valuable now.

I decided to take him up on his offer and grab a soda from the garage. A faint pounding radiating through my head was becoming a steady throbbing; if I was lucky, the hit of caffeine would keep it at bay. I didn't want a mild headache to morph into a full-blown, incapacitating migraine. Since Jack's death, my occasional migraines had become regular visitors, popping up at the worst times, like during Cody's baseball games or Jazz's plays. Eight ounces of caffeine wasn't a foolproof cure, but sometimes, if taken early enough at the onset, caffeine worked. Besides, it gave me an excuse to look in the barn and find the red mare. So far, I hadn't seen her in the pastures flanking the barn.

The fridge in the tack room at the edge of the barn held plenty of drinks: sodas, teas, bottles of water— something called cheercola. I cracked it open, and the first sip bubbled and fizzed in my mouth, icy on the edges—some type of soda, nectar to my head.

A soft nicker echoed from the barn aisle. I followed it and found the red mare, head hung over the stall door, eyes wide, checking out what was going on. I balanced the can on an available board and went over to pet her. I knew CJ had said he had problems with her, but to me she didn't seem as far gone.

I lifted my hand slowly and touched her wide cheek. She didn't move away. Her big brown eyes vacillated between trusting and being wary, but she stayed where she was, accepting my strokes, which I took as a good sign. I rubbed her nose gently and then scratched up to her ears. She pushed her head into me, clearly enjoying the attention. Her stall was the only one without a wooden nameplate hanging over it.

I murmured gently to her. "You need a name, don't you?"

The Monday Horses had been a favorite book of mine growing up, but none of those horses' names fit. An image of my mom reading *Black Beauty* to me in bed filled my mind. She'd cuddle up next to me, her voice soft but clear in the dim light before I went to bed.

The mare twisted her head to give me better access to a spot right behind her ears. I dug my nails in and gave her a good scratch. She grunted in appreciation. "If you were mine, I'd call you Ginger. It might sound boring, but you're a red, saucy mare, and it was Black Beauty's best friend. Besides, *Black Beauty* was my mom's favorite book. She would adore you."

My throat tightened. There were two things my mom loved: red horses and mares. She always said, *if you can ride a chestnut mare, anything else is easy as pie.* Ginger swung her head away, done with my ministrations. So like a mare. Willing for attention but only on her terms. I fed her a mint, which I had shoved in my pocket at work, and stroked her nose. Unlike the place behind her ears, this spot right there was as soft as cotton and as smooth as silk.

The crinkle of the mint wrapper brought the other horses to their doors. There was a really cute brown and white paint, a little red roan pony, a glossy round gray, a bigger bay horse, and another chunky chestnut. CJ had a full barn. I hadn't noticed all of them the afternoon he'd been hurt. Roaming from stall to stall, I petted them all, but I returned to Ginger and spent the most time with her. I rested my head against the post next to her stall door. For the first time in as long as I could remember, the weight pressing against my chest eased just a bit. I rolled my shoulders back.

The nonstop racket in my head vanished. I didn't hear the guys outside working. I didn't have kids calling for me, or customers asking for coffee and staring at me as a stranger and wondering where I'd been and how I'd landed in North Carolina. There was only me, the swish of tails, and the quiet munching on hay. The sweet aroma of fresh-cut hay floated in the air, mixing with the scents of dirt and leather. Years ago, these aromas and sounds were—my favorite place on Earth.

"You really are a risk-taker, huh?"

I yelped and nearly jumped a foot. In response, Ginger bolted to the corner of the stall. Her tail thrashed back and forth. CJ leaned against the door of the barn, his legs crossed at the ankles. I wondered how long he'd been there. The jeans that hugged his ass so well looked equally nice falling from his hips.

"Not really," I replied.

Maybe I had been once a long time ago when I piloted thousand-pound animals over four-foot jumps. But that was a lifetime ago, and I paid the ultimate price for those risky dumb decisions I made back then. And those decisions still haunted me. But what was worse was that my nightmares might come true when the psychiatric hospital released Michael.

I searched for a safe topic. "You sure have a bunch of horses here, don't you? Do you have—"

"No—" CJ frowned at me. "—I don't." His tone matched his frown.

Oops. That wasn't the right thing to say. I meant to say nice horses because they were. They were round and fat and well cared for, and I knew from experience how much work it took to keep them that way.

Levering himself off the door jamb in one fluid motion, he approached the stall. Ginger stood in the corner, ears pinned and tail swishing against the wall. His eyes softened when he got close enough to peer inside. "She hates me."

"You know what they say about chestnut mares?" My voice shook a little. Why couldn't I stay calm around this guy?

From the blank stare he offered it was clear he didn't.

"Chestnut mare—beware," I said.

"Really?" He ran a hand over his brow and eyes. At this range, I could see some grays dotting through his hair. It tempered his toughness, adding depth, and made him even more attractive.

"Yeah. It's pretty common. Of course, if you can get on the good side of one. They're incredibly loyal."

He fixed those soulful eyes on me. I traced the line of his scar with my gaze. What could've happened to give him that? I'm sure whatever I imagined was ten times less than what actually happened. Jack hadn't divulged a lot when he came back from overseas, but sometimes when he was drunk, he'd muttered about throats cut, bodies blasted to pieces, drops from helicopters, and treks through desolate unforgivable land where all that stood between a SEAL and death was a mere second or fraction of an inch. Jack didn't do any of that dangerous stuff, but he had a front-row seat to witness it.

He tunneled his fingers through his hair. "Are you speaking from experience?"

I thought of Inca, the Belgian Warmblood that my dad had imported from Europe for me. A world-class jumper. When she was on her game, she could clear five feet. On a bad day, though, I couldn't force her to do anything she didn't want to do. She'd run me into the fence and dumped me plenty. I had scars on my calves as evidence. I avoided answering his question and directed the conversation to him. "Why'd you pick her?"

"The kill buyers were bidding for her. She was in desperate straits. Tucked up, skinny. Misunderstood."

I swallowed the *aww* that threatened to escape. "No good deed goes unpunished, huh?"

"Guess so. She's got stripes across her back where someone whipped her."

"I noticed that." I clenched my fists, fighting the bile that rose in my throat. The abuse of animals was so disgusting.

"I'm impressed she lets you get so close."

"Well, I'm a woman."

He furrowed his brow. "What's that mean?"

I shrugged. "She's a thoroughbred. Most likely came from some second-rate track, didn't get bid on in a claiming race. The owner probably fell on hard times, sold her to some auction, and she wound her way down until she fell into an auction with kill buyers. Odds are she was mistreated by someone along the way, and good odds are that someone was a guy. Someone who didn't have the patience and ability to give her the time to process demands and who didn't understand how to get the best out of her. Probably at the track, but who knows where else."

"They told me she was a quarter horse at the auction."

I snorted. Quarter horses were stocky workhorses of the West, known for their ability to cut cattle and work a ranch. Thoroughbred racehorses, on the other hand, were sleeker, more refined, and hotter tempered. Both were good athletic breeds but had different body types. Ginger had thoroughbred written all over her long legs, lean body, and nervous temperament. "If that mare's a quarter horse, I'm a Danish model."

CJ's gaze roamed over my body. "You could be."

My cheeks flushed. "Have you recently hit your head?" It was meant as a joke. But as soon as the words left my mouth, I regretted it. Shit. What a stupid thing to say. The dumbest things filled my head when I was nervous. At Jack's funeral, I spent ten minutes in the bathroom giggling uncontrollably about a floral arrangement.

CJ's face closed up, and he took a step back, throwing a wry smile my way. "As a matter of fact, I have. But it didn't do anything to my eyesight." He waved his hand through the air. "Anyway, I came to see how you're feeling after your crash?"

Before I could answer, a guy with a clipboard lumbered into the barn with Griff quick on his heels. "Are you Connell James Sinclair?" His annoying voice was high-pitched and in direct opposition to his large, cumbersome frame.

"Who wants to know?" CJ's answering tone was smooth and deep and made me think of Reynold's, the after-hours bar I loved to crash at in New York. At Reynold's, jazz pumped softly from the sound system, and people talked in whispered tones in shaded corners where nobody bothered them. Hunkered down in a booth, I could kick off my shoes, relax, and feel safe.

"Mecklenburg County Animal Control. We got an anonymous complaint from a woman stating that you're keeping too many horses on this property and some wild ones at that."

CJ shot a look my way. "Anonymous?"

"Yes. The caller indicated the number of animals exceeds your acreage, which is correct. You are only allowed four horses, and I see that you have six as well as countless dogs."

Ginger charged the side of the stall, ears pinned back, teeth bared.

"And this must be the wild horse." He jotted down some words on his pad, ripped off a few papers, and shoved them in CJ's direction. "You are in violation of both county and city codes. This is a ticket explaining your offenses and the fines. If you don't come into

61

compliance by the time we check back, the fine will be increased, and we have the right to seize the animals."

Finished, the man strode out of the barn and to his truck.

Cold and hard, CJ pinned his glare on me. "Did you do this?"

"What?" My voice squeaked.

"You. Did you call them and complain?"

I narrowed my eyes. "Why would I do that?"

"You're the only woman who's been on my property in the last twenty-four hours. He specifically said a woman." His glare intensified, and I could almost feel the heat. If he had been a cartoon character, his whole head might have exploded.

Of course, what he didn't know about me was that I had a fuse about an inch short for stupid people. I clenched my fists and stared him down. "Yes. Yes, *I* called them. I threw a towel over your drugs and handgun—probably illegal—and saved your farm from the cops, and then for giggles and kicks, I called animal control to take your horses." I stomped out of the barn, throwing some choice words in his direction.

From where I stood, Jack's SUV was visible on the lift. I couldn't care less. I knew the way home, having ducked through the break in the fence two days ago. The last thing I needed in my life was to argue over horses with some messed-up drug addict. If I knew one thing in life, it was guys with drugs spelled bad news. That lesson had been seared in my memory. The less I had to do with this guy, the better.

Chapter 8

CJ

She stomped away, her hips swaying with each step, and all I wanted to do was chase after her, grab her, and kiss her. Damn, her telling me off was the hottest thing I'd seen in ages.

Griff gave me a sideways look. "Oops."

Reining in my idiot hormones, I kicked an empty bucket out of the aisle. My orange tabby cat, lazing in the sun, jumped into the air and scurried up one of the stall posts. "She's the only woman besides my sister who's been here in the last two days."

I tried but failed to keep the frustration out of my voice. The last thing I needed was a complication with the county board of health.

"She also saved your life and kept your secrets, as she pointed out. Why would she do that and *then* call animal control?"

I ran my fingers through my hair, rubbing my head as I did so. "I don't know. Maybe she's a crazy animal activist?" *With really, really nice legs.*

"And your basis for this is…"

None. I had no basis—just a vague feeling that this woman was hiding something and an overwhelming desire to kiss her. Neither was good. I did the one thing I could do. I took aim at Griff. "Screw off."

My anger rarely fazed him. "Gladly," he said. "Now, if you're done with that hissy fit, there's something we need to talk about."

"Really? Now?" I moved past him toward the house. I was in desperate need of some kind of food.

"Her brake line had a hole in it." There was something in Griff's voice.

I paused to clarify. "A tear?"

"No. A hole. And a cotter pin was missing."

That stopped me. I changed direction and headed for the garage and her car. "How did she *not* get into an accident driving down here?"

"My thoughts exactly."

"Do you think that's a coincidence?" I surveyed Finley's SUV suspended on the lift. Nothing outwardly showed its failings.

"If it is, it's a one in a million chance." Griff slanted a look sideways at me. "You've been strung as tight as a bow aimed at a heavy-horned buck—you want to tell me anything?"

I was trained in guerilla warfare, groomed to withstand torture and extreme hostile situations, but after thirty years of friendship with Griff, there wasn't much I could keep from him or that he didn't figure out just by looking at me. I took a deep breath. "Finley Thompson's husband died in a car accident a few months ago."

Griff nodded. "Yeah?"

"He worked with me in A-stan. But she doesn't know that. She thinks he worked for the State Department."

"Are you screwing with me?" Griff's voice rose and fell, riddled with surprise, and if I wasn't so worried, I might have laughed out loud.

"She told me he worked for the State Department overseas. I'm telling you, he worked with the teams. He had firsthand knowledge of Afghanistan and all the crap that went on over there."

Griff glanced outside the garage doors, checking that no one was near enough to be eavesdropping. "Was he there when your op went sideways?"

"Yes, but I can't remember the details. My memory's a foggy hole around that op." I brushed my hair back and rubbed the knot left on my head from the explosion. My hair had grown back a long time ago, but the hard bump remained.

The truth is I remembered some details, but I didn't want to reveal them, not even to Griff. Jack had been instrumental in getting the intel on this op, but when he wavered about whether to pursue our targets, I'd been the one to convince him to send us in. Hell, I'd hammered on him to let us go. Then I'd let him down just as I'd let Elliot down.

"You better tell her."

"Yes, but what exactly? Your husband lied to you? Your car was possibly sabotaged?"

"My advice: everything."

I swiped a hand across my brow. How did things get so complicated? "And the car?"

"Put it to the side to be fixed later. Tell her to buy a new car or loan her one. Would you want to drive around in some car that's been tampered with? What if something else's broken and we don't know about it? That's an awfully big risk to take for a ten-year-old car."

Griff had a point. I waved toward Finley's SUV.

"Get it down and park it outside. We'll figure something out later. I better go find her."

"Good luck with that."

I nodded because I sure needed it. How the hell was I going to tell her the truth about her husband and the truth about her car all in one fell swoop? Neither one was going to go over well. What if she wanted more than the truth? What if she wanted the details about Jack's job? Details that could endanger me and the rest of the guys.

Chapter 9

Finley

I drove from the rental car place to work with my surly neighbor filling my head—his windblown hair, wild eyes, and the fact he accused me of turning him into Animal Control. None of it sat well with me. I tapped in Mattie's number.

"Hey, girl. I was just about to call you. How's the house?" Mattie's smooth but chipper voice filled my ear. In the background, the sound of ambulances screamed along with a jumble of voices. Mattie was a hotshot lawyer with some big firm in downtown Charlotte.

"Are you okay?"

"Yeah. A fire alarm went off in our building. I'm out on the street. What's up?"

"You didn't tell me about my neighbor."

"My uncle Hank?"

"No, not him. Your *other* neighbor. The angry one." I slammed on my brakes. Right before the geese crossing sign, a gaggle of geese stepped off the curb and waddled across the street.

"The Baker's grandson? CJ?"

"Yes." The majority of the gaggle crossed the street. The oncoming car eased forward, but in my lane, a slow straggler hadn't quite made it across. I wanted to be annoyed, but it was just so cute.

"Nice bod?"

"Yes." The word came out in a rush of breath. She didn't need to give me a blow-by-blow of his looks. I was well aware. That wasn't the problem. Or rather, that was part of the problem. I wanted to run my hands through his hair. So much wrong with that thought I couldn't even begin. I contemplated slapping myself in the face in the hopes that reality would rear its head.

"He's a nice guy."

"Are you sure about that? Seems kind of hot and cold." The car behind me honked, and I waved my hand in the air. I wasn't going anywhere until I was sure the straggler was safely across.

"Ha. He is wide open." She drawled out the word *wide*, which made me smile. "Or at least he used to be. I never hung out with him, but rumors were the more dangerous, the better, like jumping off of things, swimming across rivers, stuff like that. He joined the Army—no, wait, the Navy. Anyway, did a bunch of tours in Iraq or Afghanistan. Sharpshooter, maybe?"

More sirens.

"Got hurt. Got some awards. Wound up back at home. My uncle loves him. He's a nice guy. Just a little banged up. Why?"

I opened and closed my mouth. Did she need to know all the gritty details? That he seemed to steal my sanity when he was around? "No reason. I just can't figure him out."

"Says the woman with the changed name."

Very few people knew my real name—except, of course, Mattie. She helped me through the whole mess. After my ex-boyfriend Michael killed my parents, after he'd pled guilty by insanity and been sentenced to the mental hospital, after my face was plastered across New York newspapers, I'd changed my name. "Listen, that was circumstance, and you know that. I'm very straightforward."

"Yes, as easy to get to know as a porcupine—a porcupine hiding out from her past."

"Playing it safe, Mattie, not hiding out." Finally, the straggler was across, and I accelerated slowly.

An excellent lawyer, Mattie was never one to lose sight of the main issue. "You're hiding behind words here. Cut him some slack. He may surprise you."

"Maybe." I shrugged even though she couldn't see it. "What's up with you? You said you were going to call me."

"I have a favor to ask."

"Sure." Mattie had come through for me and offered me her house when I called her in a panic about moving. I didn't plan on refusing her any request.

"My niece Isabelle has started riding at a barn up in Mooresville."

"O—kay." My voice hitched a bit. Mattie and her husband were divorced, but I knew Mattie was trying to keep things amicable with her ex's sister and family.

"I know what you're thinking, but Isabelle really loves horses and there's not much you can do about that love." I knew plenty about that. The good and the bad. "Could you meet me there tomorrow?"

"I have work in the morning, but after that I'm free. What's up?"

"I need your opinion. Her instructor seems like a real nut job. But I don't know if I'm just being super sensitive. I need a neutral third party."

Horses again. After a twenty-year drought, it seemed like it was pouring rain now. I'd avoided horses ever since my parents died, and now I couldn't go a day without some reference to one. "Okay. Text me the address."

"You're a love. Got to go. Thanks!" The line went dead, which was just like Mattie, never big on goodbyes or wasting time.

Despite my best efforts, since moving here I'd been dragged into the horse world more than I wanted and certainly more than I envisioned when I decided upon this move. We were supposed to be safe here. The last thing I wanted was to dive into the horse world. But I couldn't turn Mattie down. She'd done a lot for me, and I was grateful.

Mattie's info on CJ surprised me as much as her favor. Nice wasn't exactly the word I'd use for him. Good looking, yeah, hot with those green eyes and chiseled jaw, totally. Waist and ass I could fry an egg on. Definitely. But don't forget the fierce-looking knife, bag of drugs, handgun, and attitude from hell. Put it together and it made for one confusing picture and a dangerous one at that. I knew danger. I'd messed in those waters twenty years ago, falling head over heels for Michael. It only led to heartbreak and disaster. My best bet was to just stay away from him. Get my car fixed and go my merry way—back to keeping a low profile.

But there was something about him, something just out of reach, that made me want to break through that tough, prickly exterior. This was a guy who rescued dogs and horses. Something told me whoever was beneath that rough voice and curt words was as lonely as me.

I parked my rental car, making sure to leave Jack's hat and boots visible on the passenger side. An old habit from our days in D.C., Jack always said I'd be safer pretending I wasn't driving alone. Of course, now I was really alone. I pressed my hand to that place between my ribs, trying to ease the knot there. My stomach always acted up when I was stressed. My thoughts jumped back and forth from Jack to CJ, and I headed for the coffeehouse. The problem was, I'd been down that road before, with Michael and even with Jack. We didn't need more of that chaos. It was better to put my neighbor out of my mind and concentrate on my desserts and work. Besides, the fewer people I got to know, the easier it would be to remain low and well-hidden. And the less I had to do with him, the less I had to tell him. Odds were some ex-military guy was going to ask questions, and who needed that? If I could stay hidden long enough, until I was sure Michael was locked away for another twenty years, then maybe I could really get my business up and running—not just isolated in this small town—but expand and stand on my own two feet. Save some money. Put my kids through college. In the grand scheme of things, my neighbor wasn't important.

I jaywalked across the street, and traffic in both directions slowed to let me pass. My heart lifted a bit. Doing that in D.C. would have meant a trip to the emergency room. Things were a little bit slower here, which was fine by me because included in the slow lifestyle were friendly, laid-back people—except my neighbor, of course. But I didn't have to talk to him just because our homes were within walking distance. The less we talked, the better. My goal was to keep everyone on a superficial, friendly level anyway. I was good at that; I'd been doing it for twenty years. I just needed to keep doing it.

A small town with one main street and lots of out-of-town college kids was a perfect place to hide out. Maybe it was slightly boring, as Jazz had claimed when we drove here. Who cared that the town only had one main street? That one street had charming brick sidewalks and was filled with eclectic shops and good restaurants. So far, the midday rush hour—when the local preschools let out and the streets were filled with moms, strollers, and toddlers—seemed to be the most dangerous aspect. Second most dangerous. CJ taking the number one spot.

Hopefully, the small town of Davidson was our safe haven.

Chapter 10

CJ

I called Finley three times that afternoon, but each time it went right to voicemail. *Why doesn't she pick up her phone?* Done with work and feeding the horses, I hopped in the shower and headed over to my grandparents' house. After thirty years, it was hard to think of it as anyone else's, even Mattie's. The lavender plant I gave Finley was planted close to the porch, and its sweet scent filled the air. Maybe it was a good sign that it was planted and not in the trash.

I rang the doorbell and practiced the speech that Griff and I had hashed out. The lock slid back, and Jazz stood there. Her dark hair was pulled into a ponytail, and in her hand, she twirled a lacrosse stick. "You again, huh?"

"Yep."

"No plant this time?" She gave me a crooked sly smile, and an image of a young Finley crossed my mind.

"Nope. Your mom here?"

"Nope. Works in town."

"I tried calling her."

"Yeah, her phone's crap. It's old and doesn't work half the time, but she refuses to get a new one."

"She's old school, huh?"

"More like totally paranoid. Insists a new one could be tracked. Her current one is ancient. No GPS. No camera. Sucky antenna. Useless."

I motioned to her stick. "You any good?"

She snorted. "I used to be until we moved to this damn place. I missed all the tryouts here."

I raised my eyebrows. "I have a good friend who coaches at Carolina. I might be able to pull some strings, maybe get you a try out with a team around here?"

"That'd be awesome." This time when she smiled, it lit up her face.

"Okay then. I'll let you know." I trotted down the porch steps.

"Hey, do you own guns?"

That was from left field. I clamped my mouth shut and swung back around. This was an easy question to answer, but not to a teenage girl whose mom probably hated me. I tilted my head and waved her on for more info.

"I got invited to some bonfire party at a friend's farm out in Albemarle. They say they're going to shoot stuff. I've never shot a gun. I don't want to be the only one who doesn't know what I'm doing. Can you teach me?" Her voice shook just a bit. High school anxiety. I wouldn't wish that sucker on anyone.

"Yes. But only if your mom says it's okay."

"Okay, thanks. She's at Peak Coffee House. But she's in a mood. Be careful."

It was my turn to ask for help. "Words of advice?"

Cody, chomping on some sandwich, appeared next to Jazz. "Buy her desserts."

I chuckled. "Got it." I pointed at the door. "Lock

that."

They shut the door behind me. I waited to hear the loud click and the slide of the bolt. With a mix of relief and anticipation, I headed for my truck and town, my heart thumping, which was so stupid. Even if she wasn't married to Jack, there were major issues. That attitude she gave me this afternoon for one. Hot yes, but it didn't erase any of the other reasons standing between us. I had no business wanting to see her.

As soon as I crossed the coffeehouse's threshold, I knew I didn't have to worry.

Her gaze shot to the open door. "Hey, welcome to Peak—" The greeting died on her lips. She grabbed a bottle of beer and returned to the counter, handing it over to a Davidson student. Behind that student stood Troy Eastley's brother, Wade.

I couldn't catch a break.

Taller and slimmer than Troy but with less hair, Wade leaned on the counter, chatting up Finley, something about baseball. He had a whole Mr. Clean vibe going with his shaved head, but when he wanted to be charming, he could turn it on. Finley laughed, which was more than I could say for what she did with me. My green-eyed jealousy monster living in my gut, and especially susceptible to Wade, gnashed his teeth.

Wade grabbed his coffee and turned halfway around. A sly smile graced his mouth, and he winked at me as if he knew I'd be bothered by his flirting with Finley. "Sinclair."

Grinding my teeth, I eked out a smile in his direction and nodded my head. *Stay away from her, you son of a—*

I buried my emotions. If Wade knew it bothered

me, he'd only try harder for her. Who was I kidding? No matter what my insides said, there were several valid reasons as to why Finley and I wouldn't work. Of course, that didn't mean I wanted a scumbag like Wade after her.

"Can I get you something else?" Finley asked him. Her voice was full of more sugar than my Nana's sweet tea.

"No. Thanks," Wade said. He muttered something as he passed me; it took a moment for the words to make sense. "Screw off, Sinclair. I got here first." I glared at Wade's departing back, wishing that I could throw daggers with my eyes.

"Can I help you?" Finley's voice lacked all warmth. The sweet tea tone was gone, replaced by sour lemonade.

With my mind still caught on Wade, I jerked my head toward the door. "Do you know who that guy is?"

She frowned. "Know him? I've lived here two weeks. I don't know anybody."

"That's Wade Eastley. His brother Troy was the cop on my property."

"He comes in and gets coffee. Are you ordering anything?" Her tone was just shy of snapping. Her one finger tapped lightly on the cash register.

"He's a jerk. Just like his brother." I fought the urge to look toward the doors again. She raised her eyebrows, clearly unimpressed with my deduction, and waited for my order. "Coffee—black. Please."

"Coming up." Her short dress swished around her legs, right below mid-thigh, and she glided between the coffee machine and the cash register, filling my order. "So?"

"Don't fall for his charming crap. It's all a farce."

"Is this a common thread with you, trouble getting along with people?"

I intercepted the cup from her hand, our fingers brushing as I grabbed it. "Maybe," I said and shrugged. "But with the Eastleys, it's well placed."

She leaned forward and dropped her voice to a stage whisper. "I will take the warning and make sure I withstand his evil plotting. But then again, I'm evil, so maybe we're both plotting against you."

Oh good, sarcasm. I tightened my fingers on my cup, trying to ignore her vanilla and roses scent, and plowed ahead. "I may have jumped to conclusions today."

Her eyes held mine. "May? You accused me of something I would never do."

"The animals. They mean a lot to me. When I see someone I love in danger—well, I get worked up. And go off half-cocked without thinking through all the scenarios. It's a flaw."

She nodded. "Since you don't know me, let me give you a clue. Despite my husband working for the government, I'm not a huge fan of law enforcement, so you don't have to worry about me calling someone."

Her eyes slid a bit left of mine. Interesting. There was something there, something she was hiding. I reached across the counter but stopped and curled my hand into a fist. "Listen. I need to talk to you about something."

Someone placed four bottles of beer on the counter.

"I can't. Not now. Call me. Or swing by the house. I've got to go." She motioned behind me. "Other customers besides you." Her hand whipped through the air as if dismissing me, and she turned to the guy next to me. "Do you want anything else besides the beer?"

"Nope. Great earrings."

She flashed him a smile, open and inviting, and one I'd never seen. "Thanks. I got them here in town."

I checked out her delicate ears. Her earrings were cascading loops of silver with some kind of colorful stones interspersed. Intricate and bright, they matched the bracelets sliding on her wrist. My gaze followed her long silver necklace down to the slight show of cleavage.

The guy stuffed a five in the tip jar and smiled at me as he walked by. He was younger by years, and his cocky swagger made me want to reach out and hurl him into the wall.

I ground my teeth together and stalked out as best I could. Call her? Did she know her phone barely worked? Maybe she should try getting a phone made in this decade.

I couldn't want her; my brain knew that. Unfortunately, other body parts weren't quite on board with the order. More frustrating and annoying was that she wouldn't even give me the time of day. She was like a moving target in high winds, and I was aiming with a scopeless shotgun from the last century. I couldn't hit it no matter how hard I aimed.

I plowed through the door and nearly bumped into Wade. The last thing I wanted was to deal with him. I was clearly off my game tonight.

"You have no idea what you're messing with, Sinclair."

I rubbed my scar, willing the itchy skin for once to just give me a break and stop. A mix of spiced rum, smoked barbecue, and wet cobblestone hung in the humid night air. In the spring, spiced rum was traded out for blooming flowers and margarita limes as the families congregated on the green, enjoying warm spring nights. It didn't matter. I'd know Davidson even if my eyes were blindfolded.

"Hello to you too, Wade." I let the door fall from my fingers and sidestepped him. There was no way I wanted to deal with him tonight.

"You're in over your head," he said.

What the hell was that supposed to mean? Besides, I didn't want her, not that Wade needed to know that. "I doubt that."

"You just want her because you're hoping she doesn't know all your shit, Sinclair."

"I don't want anyone." I limped off toward my truck.

Never one to give in, Wade followed. "That's good because a fine piece of ass like Finley Thompson wouldn't want your damaged face and wounded psyche anyway."

I took a breath and slowly counted to ten. Ignore him. The last thing I needed was to lose my temper around Wade. He rattled on.

A catalog of instances from our childhood and high school years filled my mind. Growing up, thrown together in the same sports and schools, we always had a natural competition between the two of us. But I'd excelled under the pressure, and Wade had not. The widening gap during high school fueled Wade's animosity to me. Of course, his daddy and his verbal beatdowns hadn't helped. Where my dad was merely selfish and self-centered, Wade and Troy's dad was a total jerk. Since combat and my injuries, Wade was on a mission to prove he had the upper hand.

I opened my truck door and focused on my fingers wrapped around the handle and not in a fist connecting with his face. "Wade, I envy people who haven't met you."

"Whatever." He lifted his chin in my direction. "Hey, I heard you had some trouble out at your place. Better be careful. I wouldn't want you to lose it. Then you'd wind up at that hospital your daddy wanted to ship your sorry ass off to."

I dropped the door handle and took two steps toward him. He backed up, which gave me both a flush of pleasure and a twinge of guilt. "Stay away from me. Stay away from my farm—and stay away from her."

He sneered at me. "What are you going to do about it?"

I could seriously hurt him, even disabled as I was. The thought flooded through me, but I pushed it down and unfurled my fists. Neither one was worth going to jail over. I knew that.

A cop car approached down the street. Troy. Always keeping an eye out for Wade and vice versa. Perfect timing. Screw them both.

"Someday, someone's gonna put you in your place, Wade, and if it's not me, I damn well hope I'm there to see it." I backed off and swung into my truck.

"I'm going to win this, Sinclair!" Wade's nasal voice floated over the hum of my truck.

Was he talking about Finley or the land? Maybe the odds were stacked against me with the land, maybe I'd never get it and never open that animal rescue center my granddad and I had planned. But I thrived on bad odds. Bad odds had been my profession for ten years.

My phone rang through the cab of the truck. Ashley.

"Hey CJ, I'm standing in the barn, and Griff says I have to move my horses? Is this right? You know my barn's not ready for another month."

"I'll be right there, and we can talk about it." I pressed the gas pedal down and accelerated. Ashley was not going to be happy with what I had to tell her.

Chapter 11

Finley

At the horse farm in Mooresville, I pulled down a long tree-lined paved driveway in the early afternoon. Two large pastures flanked the drive on each side, and the driveway itself ended at a beautiful stone barn. There was a jumping ring to the left and the small white fence of a dressage ring to the right.

More accustomed to flip-flops and sneakers these days, I wiggled my toes in the paddock boots I'd dug out of my trunk early this morning. I probably didn't need them, but I refused to show up to the barn without the proper equipment, and thousand-pound animals could wreak havoc on one's exposed toes. I parked and headed over to the ring where jumping lessons were being held. Mattie stood on the side, one foot propped on the lower fence rail, her long black hair spilling down her back and glistening in the sun.

I leaned on the fence next to her. "Hey."

Mattie, forehead furrowed, didn't break her gaze from the activity in the ring. "Is it just me, or is this lady a moron?"

If I closed my eyes, I could be a teenager again in the warm-up ring of a horse show on the East Coast. The instructor's voice was just the right pitch and grating volume of any number of trainers I encountered.

The worst were ones that always hogged the rings and acted like their students were the only students warming up or showing that day. In jeans, boots, and a tank top, with a frizzy, mousy-brown ponytail hanging through her dark blue ball cap, she waved her arms at the students, impatience coloring her voice. It was the last thing flighty sensitive animals and novice students needed.

"She's something all right."

Mattie choked back a laugh. "Bring back memories?"

"Too many. Though I was lucky. My instructors never rushed me or berated me like that. You?"

Mattie didn't answer except to shake her head. A truck and trailer rumbled down the driveway and pulled up next to the barn. I could see why someone might board here, but I didn't understand why anyone would take lessons with this trainer.

She raised the jumps and barked out a command to the four girls and their horses. The first three, including Mattie's niece, navigated the higher jumps fine. But the last girl clearly lacked some of the basics, and her horse was a nervous type. Three strides out, it was obvious they were in trouble.

"He's going to refuse," Mattie said, her voice barely a whisper.

I gripped the fence, hoping she was wrong. But sure enough, the bay gelding slammed on the brakes. His poor rider tumbled over the jump, and the bay took off at a gallop, reins flying in the air. Mattie and I ducked through the fence at the same time. At the far corner, another woman ran toward the fallen rider. The little girl got up, clutching her arm.

"You get the horse!" Mattie ran for Isabelle, whose horse was spinning in circles.

The bay horse slid to a stop in the corner, head as high as a giraffe's. I approached cautiously and scooped up the loose rein.

"Hello there. It's going to be okay." His breath came hard and fast. Despite his wild eyes, I rubbed his neck, and he slowly dropped his head. I clucked, and he followed. Halfway back to the group, the instructor intercepted me and yanked the reins from my hand, jerking them down. The bay's head shot back up, and his eyes rolled, showing the whites. The instructor dragged the horse over to the jump and hit him wildly on the chest with one of the student's crops.

My adrenaline, already running high, surged. I bounded over and grabbed the woman's arm before it descended a sixth time.

"That's enough. You're not teaching him anything except to be scared of the jump."

Surprised, she dropped the crop. "Who the hell are you?"

I fought the urge to push her into the dirt. Instead, I yanked the reins out of her frozen hand. The bay, happy to be free from her grip, twirled around me, almost knocking into her. She jumped out of the way, and I used the distraction to spirit him away and over to the brick wall jump. Mattie sprinted to me, Isabelle's helmet clutched in her hand. She proffered it like it was a great gift.

"Here, take this for your head."

"Mattie, I'm not getting on. I haven't ridden in twenty years."

"You have to. Otherwise, she might." She patted

the bay's bouncing neck. "You'll be fine."

The barky instructor headed our way. In the past, whenever I dreamed of riding again, it did not play out like this—hyped-up horse, crazy instructor, bystanders milling in the ring. I jammed the helmet on my head, fit my foot into the loose stirrup, sent a prayer to my mom, and hoisted myself up onto the bay's back. *Oh God, Oh God. Please, little bay, don't dump me off.*

The instructor reached for the bridle, but the horse wanted nothing to do with her and spun away. I slipped my other foot into the stirrup, and we rocketed off at a trot. Although I was as loose as a wet noodle, my legs bouncing against his sides, I hadn't forgotten how to post or stay with a horse. He didn't seem bothered by it, and after a round or two, he settled into a lovely floating trot. The power from his trot and his flexing muscles seeped through the saddle and into me. My blood was on fire. I squeezed, and he responded by surging forward into a canter. Mattie dropped the suspect jump down as low as it could go. I had no business jumping, but all we needed was one good effort, and I could retire knowing he ended on a good note, not on the sour revengeful beating of the instructor.

We headed up toward the jump. He hesitated for a second, but I squeezed and gave a good loud cluck, and he popped over. I circled him around and did it again. This time he didn't hesitate. I patted him furiously and slowed him to a walk. This time it was I who was breathing hard. Breathing hard and smiling. Why had I ever waited so long?

A woman in boots and breeches stood next to Mattie, frowning. "I'm the owner of this establishment, and you need to get off. You don't have permission to ride, nor have you signed a liability waiver."

"Sure." I swung a leg over and slid to the ground. I ran my stirrups up and patted the bay's neck. "He's a lovely horse."

"That may be, but you had no right to get on." She held her hand out for the reins, and I handed them over—reluctantly.

He was a really sweet horse. I played with his mane, and he dropped his head. "Well, your instructor was beating him, and I wasn't going to stand by helpless."

The barky instructor barreled across the ring. "Are you kicking her out? Did you see what she did? Who the hell does she think she is?"

The well-dressed lady held up her hand. "Enough. We will talk about this later." She nodded at me. "If you ever want to come back, get my number from Mattie." Then she pivoted and left the ring, the bay horse following dutifully behind.

I handed Isabelle's helmet back to Mattie. "I better go."

Mattie smiled and walked with me across the ring. "Nice piece of riding. You could have jumped it without me dropping the rail down a hole."

"Ha. My legs feel like rubber. I'll be sore tomorrow." I ducked back through the fence. "I guess you have your answer to the whole instructor question."

"That's for sure. That lady's a loon. I better go find Isabelle." Mattie lifted her chin in the direction of the barn. "Did you see CJ?"

I followed her motion. Sitting in the metal stands was my neighbor with sunglasses on. I gulped down the golf ball in my throat. "How long has he been there?"

"Sat down just before the whole fiasco. I think he trailered some horses. Going to say hi?"

"Not a chance in hell." My legs were already weak and shaking from the ride, and the last thing I needed was to confront him. "I'll call you tomorrow."

"Sure thing, Velvet Brown."

I choked back a laugh at her reference to National Velvet, another of my favorite horse books, and skulked off to my car. What was I thinking hopping on that horse and making a scene? I couldn't seem to stay out of trouble. Truth be told, I was intrigued he was there, and that alone had me running for the hills. I had no business making personal connections with anyone in this town or any town, most of all not him.

Chapter 12

CJ

I was used to a dry throat. It came with the territory of my scars. But this time, my throat was parched because of her. It had been a mistake to shoot my mouth off and accuse her of calling Animal Control. Deep down I knew it. But after watching her wade into a ring of strangers and swing up onto that horse and calm him down, it confirmed my misjudgment and stupidity. It was obvious she wouldn't mistreat animals. How I hated it when the Eastleys jumped to conclusions with me, and here I'd gone and done it with her. She headed for her car, and I stood up to follow. I needed to apologize, especially before I hit her with stuff about her car and Jack. I still didn't know how to tell her without spilling the whole truth about Jack—and me.

A white SUV pulled in, blocking my view, and out stepped Hayes Donovan, fellow SEAL and teammate. I might as well have been kicked in the chest by one of the horses. All the air left my lungs, and my throat closed to the width of a straw. How the hell did he know I was here, and what did he want?

"We need to talk." Donovan didn't bother with formalities, not that I cared. Although I worked with Donovan for years and trusted him implicitly as a teammate, we'd never been the best of friends—

probably because we were both too alpha. Donovan spent a lot of time contradicting any of my ideas. Somehow his plans always seemed like a better idea than mine. At least in his mind. In any tricky situation, he wouldn't be the first person I turned to for help.

"Is this on your route from New York? Seems like quite an area you manage now." I tried but failed to sound funny. Instead, all that came through was the jealousy eating at my gut. I knew it wasn't his fault, and I wouldn't wish bad shit on him. Still, it pissed me off. He rankled me with his able-body and unscarred face because Donovan returned stateside in one piece, unlike me, and now worked for some private security firm doing God knows what. Donovan's father had been some big wig in the federal government, which certainly helped Donovan in his moves up the political ladder, connecting him to all the right people. From what I knew about his past, he hadn't lacked in money or connections. Meanwhile, I limped around a farm and a garage, fighting tooth and nail to keep both.

"I've got a few questions for you, and then I'll get out of your hair."

Donovan always had an arrogant part to him, and it was usually on display when telling someone what to do.

"Is that a promise?" Finley's earlier comment about me having trouble getting along with people flashed through my mind. Maybe she wasn't wrong.

"Don't be an ass, Sin. I'm here as a friend, and you are on the brink of making a bad decision."

I flicked my gaze to the cola can in my hand. "You think I should do diet?"

He stepped closer and whipped his sunglasses off.

"I think you should think about what you're doing here and who you are doing it with. I got a call recently about Jack Thompson's death. Are you messing in those waters?"

"Maybe."

"Drop it now, Sin. For everyone involved or someone's going to get hurt. Badly. And you don't want that."

"I'm already hurt."

"This is a powder keg ready to explode. All it needs is the right spark. Back away."

"What the hell do you know?"

"This is what we both know. Jack died on a wet stormy night when his car sped off a dark country road and down an embankment. Let it go."

"I don't know that. In fact, up until two days ago, I didn't even know the guy died. Besides, I'm not doing anything."

"Owen made some calls. The only person Owen ever goes out on a limb for is you."

"Jealous?"

"Yeah. Like a horse is jealous of a mule."

"Are you calling yourself an ass? Because if the shoe fits—"

He grabbed my arm, glowering at me. "Back off. You're asking for trouble. This goes way higher than you or me."

I yanked my arm from his grip. "Don't get your panties in a bunch. I had a few questions. That's all. I'm not doing anything else." That might have been a lie.

"Good. I've got to go."

"Long drive home?"

He shot me the bird. "Keep your distance."

"Always."

He snorted and strode off. I gave him a thumbs up and headed for my own dented truck and trailer. He pulled out, and I started my engine, letting it idle there for a moment. This was the second time in twenty-four hours that I'd been warned off Finley Thompson, which confirmed my suspicions that she was hiding something. And also that she might be in danger.

The smart thing would be to follow Donovan's advice. It was heartfelt. He meant it, and he was worried. And when he got worried, his asshole meter rose about a hundred times.

I drummed my fingers on the steering wheel.

"Screw it."

I threw the truck in reverse. I was never good at listening to advice, especially advice from Donovan.

Chapter 13

Finley

One of the benefits of my old farmhouse was the water pressure, which I had an inkling it hadn't been regulated by the county. Ever. It made for a really good shower. The water blasted out of the showerhead, rinsing away the sweat and dirt from the horse farm and easing my sore muscles. The kids had both gone straight from school to sleepovers, which left me with a whole night ahead to relax. I combed out my hair, threw on a shirt and shorts, and strolled down the driveway to get the day's mail. I fought the urge to whistle. It never did good to be too happy or too content—that's when the other shoe always dropped. My impromptu ride had not only given me sore muscles but a smile I couldn't wipe off my face. It was like a piece of me lost had finally fallen back into place. I tossed the mail pile on the kitchen table and grabbed the bottle of white wine chilling in the fridge. Carrying my wine glass in one hand and a takeout food container in the other, I kicked out the kitchen chair and plopped down, ready to relax. A plain envelope fell on the floor. Its yellow sticker faced up with my forwarding address. Long, white, and generic, it resembled a charity mailer except for the return address printed in bold: *Flower Hill*. My chest tightened, and a wave of nausea crashed over me. I should have known. Things were going too well. I steeled myself, slid a finger under the flap, and pulled out a one-page letter.

Dear Ms. Thompson,

As we indicated in our earlier correspondence, upon his last evaluation, it was determined that Mr. Michael Davis is rehabilitated, poses no threat to anyone nor himself, and is ready and able to resume a normal position in society. Therefore, this facility and the State of New York have all intentions of releasing Mr. Davis on or about the first of December.

Thank you,

Erin Brown

Case Manager

A date. In black and white. Confirmation of the psychiatric hospital's plan to release him.

I squeezed my eyes shut, but it was useless. Some memories never dim, no matter how hard you try or how much time passes. On a normal night, my parents' spacious foyer was bathed in soft warm light from the sconces suspended along the curving staircase. But that night, the harsh light of the emergency vehicles had flooded the open door, illuminating the blood that had seeped across the black and white tiles. My mother's body in an awkward, uncomfortable pose. My father slumped over her as if he had been trying to protect her. Three neat bullet holes through their heads. Had they been scared? Had they thought of me?

Had they blamed me? I did.

Breathe. In and out. In and out. I pushed back from the table and shook off the memory.

I knew there was always the possibility that Michael might one day be released and considered rehabilitated, but I tried not to think about it. When Jack and I married, he promised he would protect me, promised that Michael would never hurt me, promised we'd be safe. He seemed so sure of himself, and I believed him.

Our lives went forward—kids, bills, lacrosse games—until we'd received the first notice about Michael's possible release. Jack didn't seem so sure anymore. He had come home one night, reeking of cigarettes and too many beers.

"Fin?" he had said. He'd shaken me lightly to wake me up. "Remember that promise I made to you on our wedding night, the one about keeping you safe or moving when Michael got out if we had to?" His voice was thick and wobbly and faded off.

"Yeah?" I grabbed his hair and tried to pull him down for a kiss, my eyes still closed.

He resisted. "If something happens to me, promise me you'll still do it."

"Move?"

"Yes. You must move if something happens to me. You and the kids. Don't tell anyone where you're going. Leave it vague. Don't make friends. Forward your mail. Get a post office box. Forward your mail from there. And keep moving, if you have to. Promise me."

"Nothing's going to happen to you." I threw him a sleepy smile, not opening my eyes. "Why are you so serious? It's too early in the morning."

"Promise me." His tone had been full of warning as if I hadn't been taking him seriously enough. I hadn't.

We never talked about it again. A month later, he was dead.

Scrolling through my phone, I found Ian's number—one of the detectives assigned to my parents' case, Jack's oldest friend, and the reason Jack and I had ever met. I pressed call. It rang three times before he answered.

"Yello," Ian said. His voice flowed in a deep New York accent. In the background, someone cursed. Jack and Ian had grown up together in a suburb in New York. They were as thick as thieves, roaming far and wide and raising hell. When Jack had gone to college and then night law school, Ian had joined the police force and risen through the ranks from street cop to detective. Their friendship had endured through marriages, divorce, job promotions, and relocations.

"Hey, Ian."

"Whitney. How are you?" He loved to use my old name as if it gave him a previous claim and brought us closer. It didn't. That girl was gone. I wasn't her anymore and would never be again. Jack had helped to bury most of the old information on me anyway. I didn't appreciate the reminder.

Gritting my teeth, I plowed on. "I got another letter today from Flower Hill. They're going to let Michael out December first."

Ian had been one of the arresting officers on my parents' murder case, testifying on behalf of the police. "I know," he said. "I meant to call, but I'm deep in some case and haven't had time. How's the move? If you send me your address, I'll send you a house-warming gift."

I skipped answering his question. I hadn't told Ian where we were going, just as I hadn't told anyone else in D.C. I had all my mail forwarded from a post office box, just as Jack told me to do. "It's…hectic—" An image of CJ flitted through my mind. "—and stressful."

"I told you to wait." I could almost see his smirk. When I confided in him that we were moving, he'd told me to hold off, but I didn't listen. A promise was a promise.

"I can't believe they're going to let him out." I tried to keep my voice level. The last thing I wanted was Michael Davis out. How long would it take for him to find us? Deep down, I convinced myself that the hospital would never release him. We had talked to the doctors. They had seemed receptive, acknowledging the lunacy of releasing a murderer. Of course, I was wrong. Thank God I'd listened to Jack.

"It sounds like they think he's paid his debt to society and is ready and rehabilitated."

I snorted. "How can anyone pay a debt for a double murder, especially under those circumstances?"

"He's been in a mental hospital—not a prison."

A faint throbbing pulsed behind my eyes. *Please, not now.* "I don't think that's a good enough reason to let him out."

"It's government bureaucracy. He's been there a long time. Honestly, they probably have no more room to keep him." A trace of bitterness laced his words.

I didn't want to talk about it anymore. I changed the subject with the first thing that came to my mind. "How's your brother?" It just popped out—the question I always dreaded asking, and I braced for the worst.

"My brother?" The bitterness was no longer veiled. "My brother is the same. Too damaged to be a functioning adult, not damaged enough to die. Existing. That's what my brother is—existing."

Ian's brother, Steve, had been a detective too. But he had an accident that had left him too hurt to live with his wife and kids and left Ian struggling to support them.

I stared out the window, searching for the right words. A robin flitted around our shell of a deck, alighting on the railing and taking off again, which was a smart move since that railing looked like it couldn't support a fly. In some ways, my problems paled in comparison to Ian's.

"Whitney?"

"It's Finley. And has been for a long time."

"Well, *Finley,* if you want to fight the release, you can contact them."

"I figured Jack would take care of that for us. But now. I don't know. It depends on the kids, school—work."

"Oh, right. Are you still trying that baking thing?"

Was that condescension in his voice? His tone stirred a little pit of fire in my gut. "Good. It's good. Slow start. I'm working at a coffeehouse, first trying to learn—"

The name Davidson almost slipped from my lips, but I swallowed it down.

"—stuff."

Ian wasn't a threat. But Jack's voice in my head held me back from telling him where we were: "Promise me, Fin. No one is your friend."

So, I kept silent.

"Anyway, *Finley.*" Ian's tone was back to brusque. "If he gets out, you have no idea what he might do. Come up and meet with Michael's doctors. Besides, I'd love to see you."

For twenty years, I had lived with the fear that Michael might get out and come after me. But the last thing I wanted to do was talk to his doctors or see him in a courtroom and have him know I was fighting his release. "I'll think about it."

"Okay. Good. Let me know when you land. You can stay with me. How's Jazz and Cody?" So like Ian to assume that was a done decision.

"Good. They're good." With as much as he had on his plate, Ian still had always cared about my kids, even in the last few years when we hadn't spent as much time together with Jack's job moving us to D.C.

A ruckus erupted in my ear. "I gotta go," he said. "Don't be a wimp about speaking with the hospital."

"Okay."

I dropped the phone on the counter and grabbed a glass of water. My phone vibrated again, dancing across the worn Formica. *Damn it. He never could take a hint.*

I picked it up. "Ian, I'll call them, I promise. But can we leave it alone? I'm tired of talking about it."

"Who's Ian?"

The breath left my body. I gulped, trying to force liquid and air around the lump in my throat, praying that I was wrong about who was on the other end of my phone. "Who is this?"

"I don't think my voice has changed that much, Whitney."

He was right on that. His voice sounded exactly the same. I imagined him as he'd been one of those last days in court: sober, his long hair cut military short, dressed in some dark suit that hadn't fit him well. Awkward and miserable, not anything like the smooth surfer boy I'd fallen in love with. But then again, I'd probably looked different too. Shock and death had a way of aging a person overnight.

"How—" My voice caught in my throat. I punched the counter, and the pain shot up my arm, steadying me. "How did you get this number?"

"That's not important. You *need* to listen to me. We have to meet when they let me out."

"I don't ever want to see you again. Besides, they're not going to let you out." I spread my hand out on the counter, trying to get it to stop shaking.

"Yes, they are, and when they do, you and I are in danger. We need to talk. They think one of us knows the offshore account or the safety deposit box number, and they're going to put us in the same room until we crack."

"My dad lost all his money. I saw the statements— there was nothing left."

"You're wrong."

"How do you know? You didn't even remember killing him."

"Listen, ten months ago they changed my meds. I remember a lot more now than I ever used to. One of those memories is the cops dropping me at the drug house and talking the whole way there about what they were going to do with the money from your dad's business."

"You're crazy." I pulled my hair around my shoulder, trying to get some air on my neck. The already-too-small kitchen had shrunk to the size of a postage stamp.

"Ask your husband."

"Ask him what?"

"He came to see me. He told me he had evidence—

bank account numbers. Ask him."

He had no idea how much I wished I could do that. Bitterness filled me at the unfairness of life, and I clenched my fists, trying to keep control. "I can't ask him."

"Why not?"

"He's dead."

I blurted the words out and instantly regretted it. The last thing I needed was Michael knowing I was on my own. Maybe the only thing keeping him away from me was the threat of Jack. Oh, God. How stupid could I be? Screw being calm.

"Michael?" His name squeaked out, past the elephant that had suddenly descended to sit on my chest, the same one that came to roost in the middle of the night when images of my parents' foyer pressed down upon me in the darkness of the night, making it impossible to breathe, much less sleep.

There was complete silence on the other end, and my screen lit up with *call ended*. I placed the phone on the counter and backed away, staring at it as if it might come to life like one of Cody's old transformers. When it didn't ring again, I grabbed a chair, climbed up to reach the top cabinets, and pulled down a bottle of whiskey. I lowered it to the counter and was halfway down, teetering on the edge of the chair, when someone knocked on my back door—and opened it.

The tip of a baseball bat cleared the door, and my foot slipped off the chair.

Chapter 14

CJ

I dropped Cody's bat and dove for her, catching her around the waist. I couldn't stop her fall, but I slowed it, using my body to cushion her as we both fell sideways to the ground. If I thought that was the end of it, though, I was wrong. It was like holding onto a wet bar of soap. She struggled and flipped, squirming in my grasp.

"Geez, woman, what do you do to stay in shape?" I gasped, searching for something soft to sink my fingers into and stop her frantic thrashing. She deposited a well-aimed kick into my shin and scrambled away.

In the tiny kitchen, her screaming reverberated as loud as ten Apache copters on a military training exercise. She pulled herself up by the cabinet handles and backed against the fridge. Panic mode was an ugly thing—PTSD was even worse. It wasn't hard for me to recognize it in others. Whatever had set her off, she had yet to come back to reality.

"Finley!" I used the voice I saved for when Ellie ran off the farm wholly focused on hunting some skunk.

She stopped, but now her mouth opened and closed, sucking in air like a fish on a hook, gasping its last breath. I snatched the bottle of whiskey, twisted off the cap, and poured a healthy three fingers worth into a nearby glass. I eased her hand off the fridge handle and pressed the glass into it. "Drink."

Her eyes were unfocused and glazed, and I wasn't sure if she even saw it. I wrapped my fingers around her own and guided the glass to her lips. The liquid spilled over the rim and into her mouth. She swallowed and coughed. I repeated the motion, but this time her own hand took control. She gulped, closed her eyes—and took another swig. Her chest heaved, but the whiskey worked, breaking whatever reverie she had been in. She placed the glass unsteadily on the counter, keeping her head turned, her eyes hidden from me.

"Finley?"

"Air. I need air." Her voice was so soft, I almost didn't hear it.

Leaning her body into mine, I directed us out the kitchen door and onto the porch. She collapsed into a chair, pitching forward, head between her knees.

"Can you find me a soda and a beer in the fridge?" Her voice was breathless, her face hidden by her cascading hair.

I found both easily, grabbing a beer for myself as well as the whiskey. My heart thumped along at a good clip as if I'd just finished a practice maze and decimated all the targets. Clearly, she'd had some kind of shocking incident. And here I was about to add to her troubles with talk of her sabotaged car, and in the process, implicate myself. What if she wanted more answers than I could give? I handed her the cola, and she knocked back half the can before sitting up. Calmer and more in control, she pushed her hair behind her ears and motioned for me to put the beer on the ground next to her chair.

"What the hell happened?" I shook the porch railing to make sure it wouldn't collapse under my weight and leaned back against it. Her face was no longer white as chalk, although her eyes still looked like dark sunken pools. Most of my brain cells screamed at me to get out after that scene in her kitchen, but the other ones rooted my feet to the porch floor. Complicated or not, I wasn't leaving now.

"You surprised me."

"Surprise is a yelp and a jump." I raised my eyebrows, waiting. I wasn't sure she'd cave, but if ever I might break through that cool exterior, now was the time.

"I got a call from someone—someone I never planned to talk to again." She waved a hand at the bottle of whiskey balancing on the porch railing next to me, beckoning.

I lifted it up. "Seriously?"

"Yes."

I poured a shot into the glass and held it out to her. She downed it in one gulp, grabbed the beer, flipped off the tab, and guzzled half. Whoever had been on the phone, they must have done some number on her.

"Do you want to talk about it?"

A faint shake of her head. On the upside, that was a good thing because I wasn't very good at talking or coddling. But on the downside, I wasn't leaving her sitting out here alone, so I'd better come up with some kind of plan. My eyes skipped around the porch and yard, searching for a distraction.

She broke the silence before I did. "What—" Her voice caught on the first word, sounding almost rough and unused. Her chest rose and fell in a deep breath, and she tried again. "What are you doing here?"

I had been dreading this conversation all day, and that was before the scrap on the kitchen floor. I wished to God I didn't have to say anything. But if Donovan's visit did anything, it confirmed I couldn't let this go on any further. She had a right to know something wasn't right or that someone was after her.

"We need to talk about your SUV." I waved in the direction of the kitchen. "Also, I found Cody's bat outside. That bat will get as crooked as a chicken's foot if he doesn't keep it inside at night. I dropped it in the kitchen."

"I didn't know chickens had such crooked feet." A smile played around the corners of her mouth.

It was way too enticing. "Incredibly so." I held her eyes, and for a brief second, the connection was palpable.

She nibbled on her lower lip. "Good to know." Snapping her gaze away, she tilted her head back, eyes focused on the night sky. "The nights here are so different from up North. They're sultry and warm, even now in October."

There were plenty of ways to make the nights even warmer. The thought crossed my mind, and I wanted to punch myself. Thank God I hadn't actually said those cheesy words out loud. I shifted against the porch railing, and it creaked. Wonderful. Maybe I could go tumbling off her porch.

"What's wrong with it?" She hadn't brought her eyes down yet, keeping her gaze firmly up at the sky.

"You had a hole in your brake line. That's why it was hard to stop. On top of that, you were missing a cotter pin."

"What's that?"

"Holds the wheel in place."

"That sounds bad."

"It *is* bad. Two things that if they malfunctioned could cause a really serious accident."

She lowered her gaze, her forehead furrowed. "Are you saying something?"

I wanted to brush my fingers across her forehead, see if I could ease those worry lines. But I rubbed a hand behind my neck instead. "Yes. Those two things don't just happen. Not together. Not like how we found them."

I waited for the truth of the words to hit her. Her eyes roamed over my face, left to right, up and down. Maybe she was looking for me to crack a smile, but I didn't. The irrefutable truth was that someone tried to kill her or at the very least cause an accident. Donovan's visit only hammered that home. The question was who did it and why? My money was on someone connected to Jack, and by default me and the rest of my crew. We all could be implemented—Owen, McDavies, Donovan, Nash, Fox, Rivera, and me. My stomach turned over at the thought.

"Are you serious?" She tipped her head to the side as if she hadn't heard me correctly. "Are you saying someone tried to kill me, tried to kill my kids?" The edge of her voice wavered. She was holding it together but not by much.

I poured myself a shot and downed it. "I'm saying that your car had two serious life-threatening things wrong with it, and the odds are, they didn't happen themselves."

She bolted out of her chair. "You're saying my car

was tampered with?"

"Was it malfunctioning when you left D.C.?"

"Yes. All the way down, I had trouble braking."

"Why didn't you take it in before this?"

"We just moved. I kept thinking it would get better on its own. I was trying to get settled." She collapsed back into the chair and slumped over her knees, hands gripping her head. Through the curtain of her hair, she kept an ongoing stream of words. "I suck at car maintenance. I procrastinate with everything. Oh my God, what am I going to do?"

Screw Donovan's words about keeping my distance. Fighting the urge to touch her, I crouched down and grabbed the armrest of the rocking chair for balance. My leg never let things be easy. "For starters you're not going to panic. You've been here only two weeks. Has anything else strange happened?"

She sat back and pinned her gaze on me. "I met you."

Her stormy eyes—part blue, part gray—held mine, and I smiled.

"And I rode a horse today. I haven't ridden in twenty years."

My gut tightened up recalling her ride. She'd been sexy as hell. "Besides that?"

She shook her head and pointed to the whiskey bottle. "I need another one of those."

I stood up, trying hard to ignore the pain shooting through my leg. I filled the shot glass but kept it in my hand. "Let me have this one."

Narrowing her eyes, she pursed her lips as if to argue.

"You can't shoot whiskey alone. It's unhealthy for

you and ungentlemanly of me."

"At a time like this, that *is* what's most important." Sarcasm dripped from her words. She must have been feeling better.

The second shot went down even smoother than the first, and the fire in my gut sparked a little higher. I took a swig of beer. Besides the scene in the kitchen, it seemed strangely quiet here. "Where are the kids?"

"Sleepovers." She shrugged again, a wry smile playing at the corners of her mouth. "My kids are pretty good at making friends. Two weeks and they've both got places to go on a Friday night."

I hated to drag the conversation back to serious matters, but I wanted more information. "Was the SUV your main vehicle?"

"No. It was Jack's. I had a leased car. I turned it in when we were moving down here and took his SUV. It seemed strange to waste money with a lease when Jack's was paid for and sitting in the garage."

So Jack was the main target. This filled me with equal parts dread and joy. "When was the last time you drove it—before coming here?"

"Never. Jack drove it on weekends. I didn't drive it until after he died, and honestly not until we were moving. It sat in the garage the last few months."

There were good odds that it was only Jack they were after. Slightly less disturbing. I waited for her to connect the dots, but she didn't. Instead, she twisted her wedding ring around her finger, the lines between her brows deepening. I wanted to smooth them away, ease her worries, protect her. But why? Why now? Why her?

"What car was Jack driving the night he died?"

"He had a car through work." Her eyes widened.

"Somebody meant that for him. They were covering their bases. Two cars messed up, and they knew he'd drive one of them."

I shrugged. "It would seem."

"Why would someone want Jack dead?" Her eyes glistened in the night light.

I had a distinct feeling I might know why, but I didn't volunteer it. Not until I was sure. "I don't know."

"Jack was drunk. That's what the report said. Maybe it's all a coincidence."

"It could be. Did he drive drunk a lot?"

"No—" She blew her breath out in a huff. "—but he came back really messed up from that trip."

"How so?" Did I really want to hear this answer?

"Angry, depressed, more than usual. He drank a lot." She snorted. "His idea of normal consumption and others was probably skewed, but after that trip it was even worse."

She was staring at me again. Of course, maybe that was because I kept dragging my hands through my hair—a stupid stress habit that seemed ten times worse around her. This was bad. What would she say when she found out I was part of that reason? "All I'm saying is it's suspect that he died in a car accident, and his remaining car shows signs of tampering."

"Should I call someone? The police, his old office?"

I almost blurted out, do you want to die? But I bit my tongue at the last minute. "I think you should just forget about it."

"What? You want me to forget about it?"

"I told you because I think you should know. But I want you to think long and hard before you go running off calling the authorities. Some things are better left in the past."

"Not if he died *not* in an accident." She stared off into the night. A minute later her gaze snapped back to me as if something clicked inside her. "I have boxes of his office stuff. Maybe there are clues in there. We could go through them and figure it out. You served over in the Middle East. You might know things that could help."

"I'm not the person for that." I almost barked the words out. Nice. Real heroic to tell a widow to forget why her husband was killed.

As if my words punched a hole through her, she sank back down, shivering. With just a T-shirt and jeans on, I didn't have anything to give her. I swung the door open and hobbled into the kitchen—it always took a while for my leg to work after prolonged sitting. A blanket lay draped over the edge of the living room couch. I grabbed it and couldn't help but notice a picture of Jack and the kids sitting on the side table. He was smiling, arms draped over his two kids' shoulders. When I'd asked him to, Jack had put it on the line for me, and I failed him. I still was.

She was hunched over when I returned, rubbing her hands over her legs, her whole body shaking. Shock. I threw the blanket over her, squeezing her to warm her up. My hands traced the edges of her arms, trying to generate some heat without being the creepy touchy guy. I tried hard not to feel the outline of her biceps and shoulders through the thin blanket. I wished to God there'd been some fluffy thick one hanging there instead of this thin polar fleece one. After two rubs, I couldn't take it and stepped away. Jack's face fixated in my mind, and I could almost hear him talking: "You're touching my wife, but you don't have the balls to help her. What kind of SEAL are you?"

"The lame-ass kind," I muttered.

She jerked her head up. "What'd you say?"

"Nothing."

She stood up and frowned at me. "You said something. I heard it."

The blanket fell from her grasp, and her chest rose, the buttons on her white shirt expanding a fraction of an inch. The cotton shirt molded to her chest before dipping into her waist. She was built more like a runner than a lingerie model, but it didn't matter. She was hot, and I was drawn to her. *Keep it together, idiot.* That's not going to help. I jerked my eyes away, searching for anything else.

She needed a distraction from her rigged car and whoever had surprised her on the phone. I probably needed the distraction even more. I looked across the yard and motioned to her half-fallen-down barn—its doors flung open and a ping-pong table inside. "You play ping-pong or just the kids?"

She grinned. It was shaky, and there was a wildness to her eyes as if she wasn't quite sure if she should leave her panic or indulge it, but it was a grin nonetheless.

I could either come clean or double down. I went for it and nodded. "There's nothing we can do tonight about the car. You any good at ping-pong?"

"I can hold my own." Cocking an eyebrow at me, she poured another shot and followed it with a slug of beer. So much for the shakes and shock.

Her whiskey-covered lips molded around that

110

bottle, and all the blood in my body flowed south.

I slapped my thighs and stood up. "Let's play a game then."

She took another long swig of beer, eyeing me over the bottle. "I'll only play if we bet. No reason to play without something at stake."

If I wasn't attracted before, I sure was now. "A challenge, huh? Fine, if I win, you have to come over and work with Ginger."

"Okay." She held her hand out to me. "But if I win, you help me go through Jack's files."

I hesitated, wondering if it would really be dangerous to just look through his files and see if there were any clues. "If you don't tell anyone," I said. "No alerting the authorities. Deal?"

She was cagey, ballsy, and beautiful. In the faint light, her hand trembled just a bit. She wasn't completely over the news, but she was putting on a brave front. I raised my eyes to hers, and she smiled and bit the side of her lip. A faint flush of red colored her cheeks.

She was a mom with two kids, and a husband who more than likely was killed in some way and for some reason connected to his work and to me. Maybe she relocated to start a new life, maybe for another reason. Either way it couldn't have been easy. I *couldn't* have anything to do with her. According to Donovan, I was messing with a powder keg. But if someone was after Jack, if it was connected to our work overseas, then any kind of research into him and his job would not only connect us but would let her know what happened over there. But if she could relocate and strike out on her own as she had done, then I could stop being a grade-A wimp and help her.

Demons from my past be damned. I slid my hand over hers, stilling the shake with my fingers.

She raised both her eyebrows, her hand still clasped in mine. "I thought you didn't get involved in people's business?"

"There are always exceptions to the rule. Besides, what makes you so sure you'll win?"

Her answering laugh broke the night sounds. It rose and fell in sweet tones and, like a knife, cut through my protective armor. For a brief second, it occurred to me the stakes were far greater than old files and a misunderstood horse. But I never backed down from a challenge. Or at least that's who I used to be.

She slid her fingers out from mine and half-jogged down the steps, heading toward the ping-pong table in her barn. Glancing back, she smiled, and this time I got the smile she had sent the college boy at Peak Coffee House. "You coming?"

Yes, but not before I made sure we were safe. I knew this property well. I'd spent more than half my life here, dodging around trees with Ashley and Griff, playing cowboys or the bionic man, but I'd never looked at it as a place I might get ambushed, somewhere I would need to keep someone safe. The farmhouse was sideways to the main road, with the driveway looping around and arriving between the house and the barn. The barn in its condition wasn't the best cover, but it would do. I adjusted my shirt and checked for my handgun tucked in my jeans. Nothing there. A force of habit. Ever since my run-in with Troy, I felt better with my firearms at home, secure under my bedroom's floorboards. I didn't know Finley well enough to trust that she wouldn't say something—even if by accident. I had permits, of course. But I wouldn't put it past the Eastleys to give me trouble. They were looking for anything to hang on me.

I bent down and flicked open the ankle pouch that held my knife. I didn't need a firearm to be deadly.

Chapter 15

Finley

My mind spun in ten different directions, but CJ wasn't wrong. Ping-pong made me focus and forget the phone calls and his recent revelation. It kept me half-sane and occupied when all I wanted to do was run around screaming my head off. Luckily for me, ping-pong had been one of my dad's favorite pastimes, and he had taught me well.

CJ pounded the ball, and I returned it smoothly.

"So, why did you move here?" he asked.

More scruff grazed his jaw than when he'd stopped by the first time. He wore a fresh scratch across his cheek, which I'd given him in our struggle on the floor. He emanated toughness and a stay-away attitude, yet when he peered at me next to my rocker, there was a vulnerability there. My stomach fluttered. *Moron.* Don't soften now—on anything.

I drummed my fingers on the table, picking through various memories. There was so much I couldn't say, so much I didn't want to say. If I told him the real reason for our moving, then I'd have to tell him the truth behind Michael—and my parents. I had no interest in doing that. "It was a bunch of things. The kids were struggling, and I thought a change might be good. When I spoke to Mattie one night, I told her what was going on, and she offered me the farmhouse."

"How do you know Mattie?" He stood poised, paddle in the air, ready to toss the ball.

"College." I motioned for him to serve. "Did you grow up here?"

He regarded me over the net, eyes narrowed in contemplation. "Technically, I grew up in Charlotte. Down in the Myers Park area. But my grandparents lived here forever, and my sister and I spent a lot of time up here living with them. Some of my happiest memories were here." He cocked his head sideways. "You?"

I pursed my lips together and shrugged. "New York, then D.C. with Jack, now here."

"Do you like it?"

"Yeah, the kids seem better." I slammed a shot with spin. There was no need to dwell on specifics like Jazz's anger or my past. Some things were just better left unsaid.

"Eight to five." He pitched the ball to me. "Your serve. And you?"

Happiness wasn't a term I'd use for myself. Especially not tonight. The only thing that stopped my hands from trembling when I thought about Michael was the whiskey and the ping-pong. "I'm good. I never really liked D.C. Too complicated. I only moved there for Jack's job."

He got one by me. I needed to start concentrating. I threw the ball at him, and he caught it mid-fly, serving it in one fluid motion.

"Complicated?"

"I could never figure it out. Too much traffic, too

much politics, who worked for whom, who was connected to whom. Complicated." I tapped a return, and it died over the net.

He smirked, tossing it over. "Favorite sport and team?"

"Hockey." I served it across and missed his return.

"What team?"

"Rangers." My heart gave a little squeeze. Rangers had been my dad's favorite team. "You?"

"Football. Panthers. But I follow the Hurricanes too."

"They stink."

It was his turn to serve, and he stopped mid-throw. "Panthers or Hurricanes?"

I tightened my grip on my paddle. "Both."

He shook his head. "Should I remind you the Hurricanes have a cup?"

"Rangers won a cup."

"Not in this century."

I hunched forward, readying for his serve. "What's a Southerner doing liking hockey?"

"I can't tell if you're kidding or serious."

"I'm serious." It was a bit of an exaggeration, but I liked taunting him. It flustered him a bit.

"Plenty of hockey in the South. Florida has two teams. Besides, I had a roommate who played. We spent a lot of time following it when we weren't out on assignment. What's a horse girl doing liking hockey?"

I waved my paddle at him. "My dad's favorite sport. I watched a lot of games with him. Are you going to serve?"

"Is he a Rangers fan too?"

"He *was* a Rangers fan. He's dead." My insides

twisted just saying the words, even after all this time.

"I'm sorry."

I shrugged. It was a diminutive action, but all I could manage when someone asked me about them and the crushing weight of their loss hit me anew. "It happened a long time ago." As if that could make it okay or erase what had happened.

He dropped his paddle hand by his side. I knew where this was going—more questions I didn't want to answer. I'd come to the conclusion years ago that nothing could ever make it right. I'd never stopped missing them, never stopped wanting to pick up the phone and hear my mom's singsong voice or my dad's gruff hello, never stopped wanting to tell them all about their grandkids. "Serve," I said.

"Happened? How'd he die?"

I waved my paddle at him, urging him to serve, but he didn't move. Jack's warning echoed in my head: *don't make friends.* I took a deep breath. "Car accident. With my mom." It was a lie but better than the truth, and it was one I'd been telling for years because nobody wanted to know about an accident with a loaded pistol and a psychotic boyfriend strung out on drugs—the same maniac who was being released in a month. I grabbed my beer and downed half of it; waves of anger and frustration crashed over me.

"How old were you?"

"Twenty-two. Right after college. Now serve."

His arms sagged down.

Don't say anything. I silently prayed as I chugged the remains of my beer. It was people's niceness sometimes that was hardest to take. And their stupid comments. He cleared his throat and served. I missed.

"Eleven to nine," he called.

"I should get one point just because of what we were talking about."

He paused and smiled slowly, one corner edging up before the other. "Not a chance in hell, DC."

"DC?"

"I may not know a lot of things, but what I do know is that you are complicated."

He had me there.

Chapter 16

CJ

Sometime between game four and five, when we were tied in wins, we split her Italian takeout dinner, which helped to soak up some of the booze. Even so, by eleven, I was done in. I'm sure my doctor wouldn't have approved of boozing with a concussion. I set my paddle down, trying my best not to sway.

"You okay?" I asked as we walked back to the porch. Her stride was straighter than mine. Impressive, given her size and the earlier scene in the kitchen. I tried not to stare at her, but it was hard to drag my eyes away. I'd met tough, aloof women before. My mother was the epitome of Southern propriety covering a sharp-shooter badass, but Finley was different. Hers was a combination of a tough, formidable woman and someone with something to hide—and hide it deep. A dangerous combination. And I couldn't help but want to figure her out.

"Yes."

"I can't tell if you're lying."

She cocked one eyebrow. "I'm not. I'm not great, but I'm better."

"Will you be able to sleep?" The circles under her eyes were more pronounced under the porch light. She set her empty beer bottle on the porch railing, her hand shaking just a touch. I could offer to stay, outside on the porch, so she didn't have to worry. So she could get rest. Sleep was elusive for me, and I'd never needed much anyway. Maybe it came from missions where we slept on aircraft carriers flying across the world. Or from keeping watch in desolate, dangerous places where one false move, one casual nod off, meant the difference between walking out or being carried out in a body bag. Maybe it came from memories that liked to rear their ugly head in the darkest hours of the night. Either way, I didn't need much sleep.

"With the lights on."

I hesitated outside the front door. Truth be told, I wanted to touch every inch of her, which was really bad news because she was off-limits. I couldn't keep my past life a secret and sleep with her—even if every cell in my damaged body wanted it. Besides, even if I could, why would she want me? Wade hadn't been wrong. I was hardly desirable with my injuries and my screwed-up head.

Headlights bounced down her driveway along with the crunch of car tires on gravel. We both turned our heads and waited. The car stopped, reversed, and then disappeared back onto the road. Slowly. I tracked the lights until they disappeared around the bend.

"Someone must be lost," she murmured.

"Yeah." Though we had more traffic than ever before on this road, being lost this late at night seemed suspect. I turned my gaze back to her. "I should go. Lock your door."

She leaned against the jamb. "You are obsessed with doors. You might look into a support group for that. Doors Anonymous."

"Very funny. I'll wait out here while you lock it."

She slanted a grin my way and closed the door in my face. "Is that good?" Laughter colored her voice. She was feisty to the core.

I placed my palm against the worn wood. *I want to be on that side with you, right now.* "Did you lock it?"

The deadbolt turned, and with it, my breathing eased. I leaned forward, my forehead resting on the door. "And the chair?"

"You're incredibly bossy."

I waited for the scrape of the chair legs and the wedge of it under the knob. "Good."

But this was so *not* good. I shouldn't be this worried about a woman with whom I should have nothing to do with. I left my head resting against the door, dizzy from the booze and dreaming of her in various stages of undress. The last remaining frogs of the season started up a croaking chorus. "Thanks for the game, DC." That's not what I wanted to say. What I wanted to say was let me stay—with you.

"Thank you, CJ."

It was the first time she'd used my name, and a zing surged through me. I pictured her standing in that small front hall. Jean capris. Pink tank top. Sweater that hugged her curves.

"Will you come over tomorrow?" My words tumbled out before I knew what I was saying. It was as if another person was doing the talking. "Bring the files and anything else you want me to look at."

Booze. It always made me impulsive.

I waited for her answer, and the frogs hummed along like ominous background music.

"I only won two games," she said.

"You fought like hell in the others." *And that only made me want you more.*

"Thanks. I'll see you tomorrow."

"DC?"

"Yes?" Her voice was close to the door as if she too was leaning into it, wanting me to be on the other side with her. Doubtful.

"You're one hell of a ping-pong player."

She laughed. It floated through the door, and my heart stuttered at the sound. "Now I know you've had too much to drink. Good night. Careful getting home."

"Good night." I stepped backward, hesitating with each step.

Careful? I passed careful four hours ago when I saved her from crashing to the floor, entangling the both of us in a mess of limbs on her kitchen floor. I placed the bottle of whiskey next to her front door, picked up the remaining empties, and limped toward the road. Reaching it, I glanced right and left.

A car idled about a quarter of a mile up on the right. Lights still on. I couldn't see the license plate. I wished I had more than my switchblade. There was no way I was approaching that car unarmed. After a minute, it pulled out on the road and drove away. Teenagers searching for a place to hang out? Not likely.

Was I right when I told her that whoever was after her husband wasn't after her? Maybe not. Maybe she was in danger. Maybe I was, too. Donovan certainly made it seem so. From my front porch, I could see any lights that went down her driveway, and I could get to her in less than a minute. It wasn't a foolproof plan to keep her safe, but it was something—and better than nothing.

Chapter 17

Finley

My buzzing phone jolted me awake. Eight am. Who was texting me this early?

—Coffee—

I groaned and flopped back down. Even three glasses of water didn't fix the amount of booze I'd consumed. I kneaded my eyes with my fingers as if that could calm the gathering headache-storm.

—Nonfat mocha latte. —

—Beautiful day out, DC. See you at the barn.—

I padded to the bathroom and let the water in the shower run super-hot, hoping to steam away my hangover. It didn't work, but it did wake me up. I got out and stared at myself in the mirror. Was it just me, or did he feel it too? That feeling that there was something there, between us. Was I off my rocker to think this guy—a good five years younger—would be attracted to me? Yes, he had that scar and sometimes a limp, but it only made him look tougher. I, on the other hand, was over forty. I'd been blessed with a relatively thin body of good proportions, but at forty, an extra piece of cake or ice cream produced evil results on my figure. Still, my legs and arms were nice and lean, even if I had a little extra skin hanging around. No amount of working out stopped the sagging, it seemed. I thought of Jack as

I stood there assessing myself. Jack, who for all his faults never critiqued my body. Whenever I commented on an extra pound gained and hips that expanded no matter what I did, he'd wrap an arm around me and say, "You look good to me." I missed him and the routine of our lives. We'd had our problems, but I knew them, and up until a year ago, I had an idea of what the future held. Now, it all seemed a mystery.

I grabbed the empties CJ had left at the door and carried them over to the recycle bin in my barn. My old tack trunk sat next to the bin. It had been a Christmas gift from my parents when I was fifteen. I ran a finger over the top. Despite the years, the dark stain of the wood hadn't faded, and the brass nameplate on the lid read: *Whitney and Paddy*. My father had made the trunk for me right after we bought Paddy. The night our barn burned and my parents died, it was in the dressing room of the horse trailer safe from the flames. It was one of the only things that escaped the fire set by Michael. I'd hauled it with us from house to house despite Jack's complaining. I just couldn't part with it.

Of course, up until the day before, I hadn't been riding since that night, so why I kept it made no sense. Although sometimes I opened it up and looked inside as if somehow what I lost that horrid night was buried deep in there, as if I could turn back time and be that girl again.

Nestled within the trunk were leg bandages, brushes, Paddy's leather halter, and my saddle. I pulled my saddle out and checked it for mildew. Rich chocolate brown, the expensive leather soft and pliable, it still smelled like a dozen tack stores I'd ever been in. My mother's round face, flushed with joy, filled my mind. How proud she'd been the Christmas morning she handed me that saddle as a gift. My heart twinged. Had I appreciated everything they'd done for me? Tears welled up, and I clenched my fists. I'd been a stupid teenager, and there was no way to go back. The bold headline tumbled in: *Did Horse Princess Kill Parents for Drug Money?*

I shook my head to stop the tears and put back the saddle. Wallowing in the past, wishing for a do-over that wasn't possible, was no way to start the day. I grabbed the leather halter. It would fit Ginger perfectly and be better than the dirty red one she currently wore.

CJ's truck in the driveway told me he had decided to walk home last night. He left his keys on the seat. I started it and called Ian as I drove over to CJ's. This phone call wouldn't help my headache, but it needed to be done.

"Twice in twenty-four hours," Ian said. "Missing me?"

I cut to the chase. "Michael called me."

"What?" His voice rose and fell, filled with surprise. "When?"

"Right after you."

"Why didn't you call me?"

"I had a panic attack. Don't you think it's weird he called me? I don't even know how he got my number."

"What did he say?"

"Oh, he rambled on about new medicine and remembering things, cops framing him, and some crazy stuff about finding some lost account or safety deposit box."

"What a shithead. Trying to stir you up."

"Maybe. But it got me wondering what he meant.

Do you know anything about this?"

"No. Why would I?"

"I don't know. He made it sound like he had told people about these things."

"He's locked up in a loony bin. I'm sure he says a lot of off-the-wall things."

Over the pasture fence, the horses were playing. Ginger and Storm, chestnut and dappled gray, the two of them grabbing each other's halters like two toddlers yanking a toy back and forth.

"But—" I hesitated, suddenly unsure of whether I should say anything. That last night with Jack kept playing through my mind.

"Whitney?"

"He said Jack went to see him. Did he?"

"I don't know. Why would Jack go see him? What else did he say?" Ian's voice was tight and hard.

"He said to ask Jack, and when I told him Jack was dead, he hung up."

"What a psycho."

"I know. But they're planning to let him out. What if he comes after me?"

"That's why you need to come up here and make your case in person. Tell them about the call. Come stay with me. Look, I gotta go. I'll call you at the end of the week. Call his caseworker."

He hadn't sounded crazy, though—I realized for the first time. Only scared. "Okay," I said.

I wanted Michael to stay locked up, but I didn't want to go up there and rehash it all, bring up all those memories. I fought the urge to pummel the steering wheel.

Ginger, done playing with Storm, whinnied from

the field. I grabbed the halter and headed for her, taking some deep breaths along the way. *Clear your mind. You can't change the past.* If I wanted her to interact with me, I needed to focus on her and not my past. Holding out a mint, I clucked to her. She eyed me suspiciously but took a few steps closer and reached through the fence to nibble it from my palm. I stroked the side of her nose, the spot where the skin was super soft, and all the noise in my head dissipated. It was just me, her, the sweet smell of hay, and the calls of the birds in the trees.

Contrary to CJ's beliefs, I wasn't any horse expert. My jumper days of buzzing stop clocks, tight turns, and hang time at the top of a four-foot oxer were long gone. And I'd never worked with an abused horse. But CJ was right about one thing: I loved horses and had for as long as I could remember. That love had come with a high price, though, and even now, I wasn't so sure I could enter that world again. It was one thing to hop on that frightened horse in the spur of the moment, but it was another to make the conscious decision to get emotionally involved with horses again. Yet I couldn't let anyone take Ginger away. If there was one thing I knew, it was that she was a misunderstood horse, and if she got shoved anywhere else, it only spelled disaster for her. She'd spiral down through the cracks and most likely wind up on a cow trailer headed to Mexico for slaughter.

I ducked through the fence. She took a few steps away but stopped when I patted her side. I stroked my way up to her head and slipped the leather halter on. The dark leather contrasted nicely with her chestnut coat. She'd been trained plenty at some point because she allowed me to do stuff like lead her and groom her. It was also clear from her interactions with CJ that someone had manhandled her and broken her trust. She needed time to gain back that trust. Baby steps.

Despite the chill, the sun warmed me up quickly. I shed my jacket, slung it over the fence post, and got to work doing some basic natural horsemanship. When I asked, she stepped away from me, which meant she respected me as if I was the herd leader. She was reluctant to come to me though, and that was the bigger problem. A trust issue, like I'd suspected. I stood still. Waiting. Letting it be her choice. Even a tiny step closer would be positive.

"Hey, girl," I said softly, leaning back on the fence and assuming a relaxed stance.

She watched me warily, but after a minute or two, an ear flicked forward and back. I kept up a steady stream of mindless conversation until one of her front hooves moved an inch, and she edged closer. I praised her some more. She took another step. I reached out my hand and waited. A breeze ruffled the edges of the leaves, and in the closest tree, a cardinal hopped from branch to branch. Cody once told me that cardinals were a symbol of a deceased loved one coming to visit. Maybe my mother was watching. What would she think of me twenty years later? Ginger touched my hand, and my eyes welled up.

I let her sniff and bump my hand, never moving. Her normally hard eyes held an interesting light. I rummaged in my pocket and pulled out another mint. I clipped the lead line on her halter and clucked to her, and she willingly followed me. Halfway around the small pasture, firecrackers exploded. I shrieked, and

Ginger jumped, spinning sideways and kicking out. The lead line slid through my hand. I tried for a moment to gain control, but it was useless. Another round exploded. The line burned through my fingers, and I let go. She raced away to the corner, snorting.

Who the hell set off firecrackers in October? Over the hill behind CJ's barn, I could see people moving in camouflage, rifles balanced across their arms as they walked. Hunters. Those weren't firecrackers but gunshots. I squashed down my own flight instincts and hurried across the pasture, thankful for the last mint in my pocket. When I got closer, I wrinkled the wrapper and Ginger's ears pricked forward. I fed her the mint and unclasped the lead line. She head-butted me gently as if to say sorry.

I rubbed her neck. "I know. Self-preservation is first and foremost on a prey's agenda." It would be wise to remember that for myself. She dropped her head to graze, keeping one ear cocked toward the hills. I didn't blame her. I felt the same unease. I stepped away. She stopped eating a moment, staring at me, her eyes soft and warm, and then she dropped her head down again.

My heart lifted, and with it, my headache eased. I didn't know when the county agent was coming back, but he'd have to take her over my dead body.

Chapter 18

CJ

Coffees balanced in hand, I limped across the driveway, gritting my teeth with each step. The chilly morning plus that leap and fall in her kitchen last night made my body ache more than a ten-mile run followed by a five-mile swim in the freezing Pacific. It would take a day or two to straighten out.

Of course, I'd never get back to who I was before that op, and some days the frustration over it made me want to spit nails. But I was grateful I was alive. Some guys, like Elliot, didn't make it back at all—or worse, came back like Jack, drinking themselves under the table. I scratched my scar. Although healed, the rippled skin still itched like hell. Of course, some days gratefulness was like a mountain to scale, and my scars were a daily reminder that I wasn't the same able-bodied SEAL I once had been.

Finley had just got done working Ginger in the pasture. Ginger's willingness to let Finley close to her amazed me. All she ever wanted to do was bite me—and up until last night, Finley didn't seem too eager to be friendly with me either. She approached the fence. Ginger walked easily behind her.

"How'd it go? Did she try to bite you like she does me?"

Finley held out her hand as if she was waving hello. Deep-red spots dotted the tips of her fingers and the top of her palm.

I balanced a coffee on the fence post and pulled her hand closer, trying to ignore the little zing of pleasure that shot through my arm. "That's not good."

I knew what rope burn felt like. I brushed my thumb across her palm. It reminded me of the soft part of a horse's muzzle. I raised my gaze from her hand to her face. Her eyes were more gray than blue this morning. Ten seconds passed. Did she feel it too—that little hum in the air?

She slid her hand from my grasp and opened and closed it a few times. "Yeah. Some hunters were firing on the hills, and she got spooked."

Hank rarely went hunting without his beagles, but he usually gave me a heads up first. "Did you hear any dogs?"

She shook her head and leaned on the fence. Her attention focused on Ginger. "Nope. Just a few guys in hunting gear—I think."

"What do you mean?"

"They were kind of far away, but the shots sounded close."

My gut twisted a little. It's probably nothing. I'd have to call Hank later and double-check.

She gingerly picked up the coffee cup from the fence post. I bet the rope burns hurt more than she let on. She raised her cup to me. "This mine?"

I nodded in answer. She took a sip, her lips pursed. They glistened in the sun. I wanted to kiss her, but maybe she felt differently—if she didn't, she would once she found out the truth.

I got closer and leaned on the fence. Ginger trotted off and dropped down to roll. The mare grunted, flipping from side to side and covering herself in as much dirt as possible. Well, I'll be—I think she was actually happy.

I suddenly felt self-conscious and didn't know what to do with my hands, like some awkward high school kid. I ran them through my hair. "New halter?"

One hand around her coffee, she folded the other across the fence post and leaned on it. Ginger leaped up, let out a buck, and trotted off in search of more grass.

"You can't put a chestnut horse in a red halter," she said. "It clashes. Besides, the other one was too big for her."

"I'll take your expertise on the colors. Another hundred pounds, she'll look as good as new."

"Yeah." There was a wistfulness in her tone.

But judging by her tense body language, she seemed guarded. Maybe the booze last night had made me think she felt something for me when she didn't. The sun filtered through her hair, making it shine golden like straw. She reached up and pushed it behind her ear, giving me a great view of her profile. She leaned her chin on her one hand, and her face softened in the sunshine. *Wow, she's beautiful.*

"It's so pretty here," she said. "Nothing beats an early morning watching horses roaming and grazing."

"That's for sure." Truer words were never spoken. I never took my eyes off her. Trish, my ex-wife, wouldn't have understood. She'd have complained about the smell, the cold, the dirt. She wouldn't feel the peace or see the simple beauty.

Finley took another sip of coffee. Her stormy eyes gazed at me over the lid. "Thanks for the coffee."

"You're welcome. Thanks for the hangover."

"Ha. Don't blame me. You did that to yourself."

"Where'd you learn to drink like that?"

She turned sideways and leaned her hip against the fence, her brow furrowed. "You make it sound like a skill."

"It is if you can put it away like that and not feel it the next morning."

She took a swallow of coffee and squinted at me. "One, I feel like complete crap. And two, in my twenties, I could drink guys under the table."

"Really?" I leaned against the fence and angled my body toward her. "A lot of guys?" A spark of jealousy coursed through me, which was ridiculous. *You cannot be with this woman.*

"No." She threw a wicked smile in my direction. "Only the ones that challenged me."

For a second, I wished I had known her then. Before I was injured, before she married Jack, whose death may or may not have been my fault but at the very least was connected to me. In a different time and place, there wouldn't be three feet between us.

She stretched out her fingers, opening and closing her hand. I knew those burns hurt even though she tried to brush it off and make light of it.

"I brought Jack's files and computer," she said, "and some Irish soda bread."

My ears pricked the most at the bread thing. "Okay"—I pushed off the fence—"I'll grab the boxes from your car, and we can get started."

Going through those boxes should have been the

last thing in the world I wanted to do. But against all better judgment, I was picturing her in my house across the table from me, and it made my heart beat just a little bit faster. This was a bad sign. Whatever we found in those boxes might be enough to damage me and crush her belief in her husband. On top of all that, what if whatever we found just raised more questions for her. How much was I willing to compromise my vows and provide confidential information. Information I knew I was not allowed to disclose. Or worse yet, information that would make her hate me.

Or if Donovan was right, information that could put both of us in danger.

Chapter 19

Finley

Evergreen and mint wafted over me. Pleasant and unassuming, like a Christmas tree chewing spearmint gum. A combination of log cabin and farmhouse style merged through the eclectic furniture and appointments. Polished wood beams were interspersed throughout the ceiling and complemented the wide plank wood floors. A white-washed brick fireplace was the focal point in the main room. A simple leather couch. Blue-striped chairs. Nothing overdone. Just simple and clean with a modern open feel. I hadn't noticed before when I was covering up his pistol and pills. It seemed like the home of a man who was, well, maybe not the man I thought he was.

I paused in the doorway, and he almost banged into me, coming through backward, arms grasped about one of the boxes.

"What?" His eyes darted right and left. He looked nervous, which was different than his normal confident manner. Was he nervous about his house or having me in it? He shifted the box in his arms.

"Nothing. Just checking out your place."

Maybe he had a decorator—or a girlfriend? My heart lurched, which was really stupid. What did I care if he had a girlfriend?

He brushed up against me as he passed and deposited the box on the large farmhouse table halfway between the kitchen and the couches. "Don't worry. No drugs or handguns."

"Hiding them?"

"Absolutely."

He threw me a grin, and I couldn't tell if he was serious or not, which was not a good sign. Normal people didn't joke about either. Ignoring the doubts circulating through my mind, I followed him to the kitchen. He handed me a cutting board and large knife and returned to the table.

"What's his password?" He opened Jack's computer.

I shrugged, handing him a piece of bread. Jack had no trouble keeping secrets, and the access codes to his computer and phone were no exception. Maybe we were married, but that didn't mean we shared everything or even a little. I figured that's what all military guys were like, including this one. Secretive to the end at all costs.

He took a bite, widening those green eyes at me.

"This bread is as good as those chocolate chip bars you gave me. Have you gotten anywhere with your boss? Is he going to let you bake for him?"

I shook my head. After our meeting and tasting, my boss had been nonchalant, promising to give me an answer at some unspecified future date.

"He'll come around." He took another bite and followed it with coffee. Dusting his hands off on his jeans, he focused on the computer. "Okay. Pet's name?"

I rattled off our cat Scottie's name, the kids'

birthdays, my birthday. Nothing. CJ pulled out his cell phone and called someone. He punched in keys on the keyboard, his phone wedged between his shoulder and ear. His conversation was little more than nods and short-clipped yeses and noes. I stepped a little closer to make out the voice on the other end. CJ paused and looked up at me. He winked. I blushed and stepped back.

I rummaged through the file boxes. File folders and yellow pads galore. Bills from our house, rental car agreements, closed credit card statements. Was anything we needed actually in this junk? Was this what a normal widow would do, or would she have just gone straight to the police?

"Are you sure I shouldn't just call the police?"

CJ hung up the phone and kept pecking at the computer keys. "What would you say to them? And who would you go to? I don't think the Davidson police would be the answer."

He had a point there. Of course, when I really thought about it, I didn't want to go to the police anyway. I had no real proof besides the car, but most of all because I didn't want the questions and the subsequent digging into my life. With enough digging, someone would uncover the truth about me, which was the last thing in the world I wanted. I was in this town trying to hide from the truth and from Michael.

I took a seat across from CJ at the table and peeked at him through my hair. He hadn't lost his looks overnight. Not that I expected him to, but part of me definitely hoped it was just the booze talking. Chiseled jaw covered in scruff, slightly unkempt hair, intense eyes focused on Jack's keyboard, all still there. His forearms rested on the table. He lifted one of his hands and rubbed his scar. *Did it hurt? How did he get it?*

He jerked his eyes up and met mine. "What?"

Shit! Did I say that out loud? I cleared my throat. "Did you get in?"

His hands dwarfed the keyboard. "Did Jack tell you what he did—at the State Department?"

To be honest, I wasn't even sure of the details of Jack's job with the CIA, which was embarrassing to admit. But I'd been caught up being a mom. I pushed my hair behind my ear. "He told me he worked on Middle East relations. But he also told me that there would be details he couldn't reveal."

I pulled out a stack of folders from one of Jack's boxes and flipped open a folder labeled *car*. Titles and insurance policies. Nothing more. I looked up, and CJ was still staring at me.

He nodded as if he understood. I'm sure he did, being a SEAL. From what I knew from Jack, they too were held to a code of silence. I had never pried into Jack's work life and never pushed to get more info. Now I wish I had. The questions left unanswered were growing by the minute, questions I wasn't sure we'd find answers to—and part of me wasn't sure I wanted to.

CJ's phone rang. His brow furrowed, and he pushed his chair back a bit.

"Sin." The voice came through loud and clear. Is that what he was called? Sin? That's fitting—me being attracted to a guy with the nickname Sin.

"O," CJ said. He stood up and wandered down the hallway.

From there his conversation was unclear. He

leaned against the wall. He had nice lines. If he was a horse, my mother would have given him a ten for conformation—put together really well, no obvious faults in his body parts, good lines, and good looking. He glanced my way and gave me a small smile. My stomach fluttered. What would he do if I walked over, pushed him against that wall, and kissed him? Not a nice peck but really kissed him, the kind of kiss that meant drop your clothes and screw me against the wall. Heat surged into my face, and I fought the urge to grab a file and fan myself. *Get a grip!* I cannot sleep with the guy helping to solve my husband's murder.

He hung up and returned to the table. My gaze followed him.

He glanced up at me, and I quickly looked away. I lifted the file of our heating bills out of the box. Underneath was the mugshot of Michael with a sticky note attached. What the hell was that doing in there? I shot a glance at him. His attention was back on the computer screen. Heart pounding, I grabbed the photo, folded it, and shoved it into my back pocket. *Phew.* I'd take this home, hide it in some distant corner, and forget about it. The last thing I needed was a whole lot of questions about something I didn't want to talk about. Ever.

A wave of nausea crashed through me, and my toes tingled. I needed a place to regroup before I passed out. "Where's your bathroom?"

Chapter 20

CJ

Her phone buzzed across the table. I waited for a few seconds, but when she didn't come traipsing down the hallway from the bathroom, I picked it up. The word *Bug* lit up her screen. Who the hell was that? Something sparked in my gut, which was really stupid on so many levels. I wanted to know more about her, but I couldn't because then she might ask to know more about me. I stood up and turned to deliver it to her.

Halfway down the hallway, we nearly collided. I held out the phone. She grabbed it and answered, pushing her hair behind her ear and biting her lip all in one motion.

Her vanilla scent filled the hallway. How much fun would it be to press into her, lean down and kiss those pouty lips, and see if I could tease a smile from them? Instead, I backed away, giving her space. Her voice was clipped, her answers into the phone short and brisk. She'd been distracted since she put that piece of paper in her pocket. What had been on it that she felt the need to hide it?

I left her in the hallway and retreated to the table, snatching a piece of Irish soda bread.

Done with her call, she stopped in front of her chair and finished the last of her coffee. "I've got to go. The kids have been home alone for a while now. I need to check on them."

It was easy for me to forget about kids, not having them. It made me out of touch with almost everyone in my generation. I didn't have homework to oversee, games to go to, or carpooling to do. "Which one is Bug?"

"Jazz. When she was a little girl, I called her my cuddle bug. She loved to cuddle in bed. Mornings when Jack wasn't around, she'd climb into bed with me, and we'd snuggle together."

For a moment, everything went silent. I could see that picture in my mind. Of course, what I really wanted to know was what Finley was wearing at the time. A T-shirt? A pair of those little, snug shorts?

Rusty, the beagle, barked, thankfully, breaking the silence and my stupid thoughts.

Finley sighed. "We're a long way from that now. She hates when I call her Bug, but I can't quite delete it from my phone. I better go. I've been gone long enough." The lines around her eyes suddenly seemed more pronounced. She patted her back pocket and swiped her keys off the table. Whatever it was in her pocket, she didn't want to lose it.

"Okay. I'll keep going." I walked toward her, and she turned quickly, stumbling over one of the boxes. She half-shrieked, and I grabbed her elbow to steady her.

She pulled away from me.

I stepped back. Her face was hidden. She straightened up and pushed her hair behind her ear.

"Sometimes I can be a klutz."

"You don't look it to me."

She shrugged but then took a deep breath and raised her eyes to mine. "Thank you for the help. It would be a daunting project alone."

"No prob." Of course, it would be nice if she would tell me what she shoved in her pocket.

She curled her lips in. "Listen, I just want to make sure this thing with working with Ginger and even today, it's just a friend thing, right?"

I leaned on the door jamb. "A friend thing?" I had an idea where she was going with this, but I certainly wasn't going to fill in the blanks here. What was holding her back? Not that I should care. But I did, and that ticked me off as much as anything else.

"Yes. After last night maybe you got the wrong idea about me."

I wanted to tell her I had no fricking idea about her at all. Normally I was a good read on people, or at least I had been. I glanced out to my barn, where I imagined Ginger was busy nosing through her hay for the choicest pieces. "I think you're jumping to conclusions."

"I am?"

I hoped I heard surprise in her voice. "Yeah. I always play ping-pong with widows in the middle of the night. It's like a welcome strategy of mine."

She narrowed her eyes. "I bet."

"Ask anyone in town. There's a whole group of women I've ping-ponged." That was a slight exaggeration. My past was littered with the women I'd slept with, but being with anyone, *really* being with anyone, meant showing my scars, physical and otherwise, and who wanted to do that?

"Uh-huh."

"Absolutely. It's like Doors Anonymous."

I fought the urge to reach out and brush a hair away from her mouth. That would definitely cross the friend barrier. Three feet separated us, and despite knowing I couldn't be with her, that it made no sense and put myself in danger, despite all that, I hated every inch.

I held the door open and motioned for her to step through.

She hesitated for a moment. I slightly laughed. "Well," I said, "and this is meant in only a *friendly* kind of way—want to make a bet?"

"We already made a bet. I lost and have to pay up by working with your crazy horse. I don't need any other things to do."

"I thought you were a gambling person."

She snorted. "You thought wrong. I'm a very boring play-it-safe kind."

I know she may have wanted to be that, and she wanted me to think that, but the vibe I got off her was quite different. "Come on, DC, one small little bet won't hurt."

"Does it have to do with my door?" A glint sparkled in her eyes.

"Not today, but don't tempt me."

She sucked her lower lip into her mouth. It made it hard not to stare at her mouth and think of all the things I'd like to do to it. "Okay. What's this bet?"

"Your Rangers are playing the Hurricanes tonight. Rangers win, you choose."

"And if the Hurricanes win?"

"You and the kids come boating with me tomorrow. I saw the wakeboard in your house. It's supposed to be a beautiful day tomorrow."

I liked her, more than I wanted to, and definitely more than I should have, given who Jack was and who I was. I needed to keep this strictly professional. But all that aside, boating on the lake was one of my favorite activities, and for some weird reason I wanted to share it with her. Besides, she needed someone keeping an eye on her, making sure she was safe.

She wrinkled her nose and raised an eyebrow. "My kids' wakeboard. They'd love it, but I don't know."

"The lake is one of the best things about this place. You won't regret it."

"Fine." She held her hand out. "I want a bottle of whiskey if my team wins. You drank mine."

"*We* drank yours. And no problem." I grasped her hand and shook it, fighting the urge to yank her forward and plant a kiss on those pouty lips.

She turned and started for the driveway.

"I'll pick you up tomorrow at noon!"

"In your dreams, buddy. We have Smith in goal tonight." She flipped her hair over her shoulder and gave me a parting grin.

Friends, she'd said. I didn't think there was a man on this Earth who wouldn't want more with her. But I didn't—More importantly, I couldn't have her know the role I played in Jack's life and death.

I closed the door and limped back to the table. I was a complete and utter moron asking her out on the boat. What was I thinking? I grabbed the next folder and flipped through it. Menus. Wonderful. Paco Taco, Thunder Boys, Bagel Bonanza. My stomach rumbled. Great. Hungry already. The last was Royal Siam. A plate of Pad Thai sounded great right about now. Too bad this place was about three hundred miles from here.

I opened the menu up. Cursive curled between the lines of the food listings. What the hell? Sandwiched between Moo Goo Gai Pan and Pad Thai were names of companies, with arrows pointing to scribbled names of countries in the Middle East. I'd seen action in almost every one of them. I flipped it over, and on the back was a list of people's names. Owen, McDavies, Donovan, Nash, Fox, Rivera, Elliot, and lastly— Sinclair.

Son of a bitch.

I threw it down and stood up, my leg buckling from the speed. I grabbed the edge of the table to stop myself from falling.

Why the hell would he write all that stuff on an Asian food menu? I'd assumed Donovan was exaggerating. He always had a dramatic flair about him. Sweat trickled down my back. Ellie scrambled to her feet, her nails scratching on the wooden floors. She must've sensed my alarm. *Don't panic. Don't panic.* Ellie pushed her head up into my loose hand and whined. My mind whirled. Jack was hiding information. He probably figured no one would glance at restaurant menus, and he was probably right. He must've been scared that someone would go through his office files. He knew he was in danger. I grabbed my phone, and with shaking fingers, took a picture of it. I hesitated. *Owen or Donovan?* I hit the send button to Owen. I could rip it up and pretend it never existed. It might not even mean anything to anyone else, but the unavoidable fact was it meant something to me—and it would mean something to Owen.

I didn't know exactly the consequences. But what I did know was once I showed it to her, once I let the cat out of the bag, I'd never get it back in and nothing would be the same. She'd have questions and expect answers. Although I might be able to elaborate on some of it, the full answers were either classified information or locked inside my injured brain. Neither would give her any satisfaction, especially once she realized her husband had been lying to her the whole time and that he worked for the CIA and not the State Department.

The question was, how long did I have before I had to tell her?

Chapter 21

Finley

Ten seconds after Smith let in the winning goal and the buzzer rang, my phone beeped. A text from CJ.

—*How's 11? We can grab sandwiches for the boat. Should be warm, but bring a sweatshirt*—

The kids, in true form, were more than up for a boat ride, knowing that they could put off chores and homework. I didn't fight it. It was a beautiful fall day, and since Jack had died, we hadn't done many fun things. We drove over and followed behind him into town. Unlike weekday mornings, Main Street Eggs was quiet, the church crowd not yet out and about. We placed our order, and the kids ran to the pharmacy to get some supplies. CJ and I drank our coffee outside and waited for the food.

He drummed his fingers on the table and shifted in his chair, checking behind his shoulder two or three times.

"Is everything okay?" I'd read once that a lot of veterans returning from war had problems with public places. Davidson wasn't crowded like a city street, but it wasn't a secluded farm either.

"Yup." His voice hitched just a bit.

Was he lying? God, military men were the worst. Always hiding something, never letting on when something was bothering them.

"Do you go through more files? Find anything interesting?"

His jaw tightened. "Other than you paid a lot in heating bills?"

I made a face. "I hate being cold."

"Duly noted." He threw a wry smile my way, and my heart tripped a beat. *Don't be attracted to him.*

He drummed his fingers some more. "I did find some names of companies and stuff scribbled on a menu."

"Really?"

He pulled out his phone and scrolled through some pictures before handing it over. Sure enough, it was Jack's chicken scratch. I enlarged it, twisted my head, turned the phone. The writing made no sense to me. "I don't recognize anything."

"Is it Jack's?"

"Oh yeah, that's his handwriting. And just like him. He was always writing important stuff in the craziest of places. One time he wrote a best man speech on the back of some flyer from the kids' school. What are the numbers?"

"I don't know. I tried calling one of them, but it went nowhere." There was an edge to his voice, and he checked behind him again.

"Are you sure you—"

He brushed away a strand of hair caught on my bottom lip. It was unexpected and intimate and so unlike Jack, who after fifteen years of marriage had rarely touched me. CJ's touch, despite his stay-away attitude, was surprisingly soft. My stomach fluttered.

Suddenly nervous, I grasped for something to say.

Anything safe that didn't have to do with my dead husband or the fact that CJ just touched me. "How was Ginger today?"

"Not bad." He grinned and raised his arm. "No new bites today." His tattoo slid out from under his short sleeve, revealing a frog—the signature sign of frogmen, Navy SEALS.

My gaze lingered on his arm. "Did you get hurt in combat?"

He tilted his head to the side, his face guarded. "Yes."

"Middle East?"

"Afghanistan, Iraq, Pakistan, Central America, South America, Sudan. We go wherever the fight is, and we bring that fight to the enemy."

"Did you like it?"

He fiddled with his cup's top and took a long pull. "The best damn time of my life. I was the luckiest guy alive."

I opened my mouth, but he held up a hand.

"Now you're going to say I was injured," he said, "but let me set you straight. I was doing my job. Defending my country. Created out of necessity. Forged through hell. SEALs are the best damn fighters there are, and we don't give up. Ever."

He didn't yell the words or even raise his voice, but somehow his quiet, clipped delivery revealed the strength of his convictions and his loyalty. It drew me to him and backed me off in equal measure because I knew that life, or at least part of it. The secrets, the travel, the danger that was never talked about—it all ran like an undercurrent. I didn't want any of it. Not for me, not for my kids, not again. Even if my stupid hormones

149

said otherwise.

"I've been—" He stopped short and cursed under his breath. Wade Eastley sidled up with a smirk.

"Look what the cat dragged in. The almighty CJ Sinclair. Going boating or doing the right thing and going to church?" Wade waved his hand in the direction of the church across the street. His voice was overly loud and had a grating quality to it. A few people nearby turned to look at us.

I frowned and scanned the street for the kids.

"Wade, God doesn't have time for my sins. He's too busy shoveling the bullshit you throw his way."

I whipped my head back at the tone of CJ's voice. In all my dealings with him, I'd never heard that one: low, rough, and menacing, like a Doberman stalking along a fence.

"Boating it is. You always were a selfish bastard and never prone to making the right decision." Wade rubbed a finger over his eyebrows and turned his focus on me. "You know, there's more to this town than rednecks like this guy."

I wanted to mutter, you mean jerks like your brother? But I kept my lips firmly closed. The people watching us moved farther down the street.

CJ's chest rose and fell in a deep breath. "Don't turn her off this town, Wade."

"*Don't* let this guy—" Wade gave CJ a once-over from his T-shirt to board shorts to flip-flops. "—show you around. Let someone with the right connections and class do the honors."

CJ stood in one quick motion, drained the rest of his coffee, and bank shot the paper cup into the wastebasket at the edge of the door. "My flea-ridden shelter dog has more class than you. You only have money because you're ripping off old ladies by selling their farmland and not paying your wife alimony."

"Those ladies get more than enough, and the farmland gets developed. A win-win for all parties."

"Yes, especially for the town." The sarcasm dripped from every word out of CJ's mouth.

"The next parcel going is the one right next to you."

"Not if I have anything to say about it." CJ almost growled the words out, and I had the urge to step out of the fray.

Wade plunged ahead. "But you don't, do you? Your daddy made sure of that."

A cloud passed over CJ's face, and his pulse throbbed along his jawline like a drumbeat. "Screw off. You know that land shouldn't be developed."

"I know nothing of the sort—" Wade laughed loudly. "—and unless you find some money soon and beat me to it, you're SOL."

CJ leaned forward, his face inches from Wade's. My stomach fluttered. I hoped he wouldn't hit him. I'd never seen him this angry. "You wouldn't be such a tough guy if you didn't have your brother sticking up for you."

"You're just pissed off because for once I'm better at something than you are."

"No, Wade, you greedy bastard, I'm pissed off because you're taking advantage of people who don't know better or don't have the means to get help."

"Don't get on your high horse CJ. Even before you were a SEAL, you used people plenty"—Wade cocked his head in my direction—"but now you're just better at it."

CJ's face closed in one fell swoop, and he broke his gaze from Wade's. His chest rose and fell in shallow breaths. He flung open the door to the Main Street Eggs and strode in.

Wade's gaze turned to me and lingered. "Well, nice to see you again." He smoothed down his tie and waltzed off down the street.

CJ emerged with the food. Anger still vibrated off him.

"Do you want to put this off?" I asked. Maybe today wasn't the day for a boat ride. The kids headed our way from the store.

He frowned. "Absolutely not. If I stop doing something every time the Eastleys are up in my shit, I'd never go anywhere." He threw me a cocky smile. "Don't worry. I'll take care of you guys."

****

I was glad we hadn't changed the plan. The lake was breathtaking and peaceful. CJ's boat cut through the water, quick as the Carolina sun burning through the morning fog. The trees were a glorious dark green, the leaves' edges tipped with gold and red.

CJ pointed at a large display of hulking buildings. "That's the energy plant. All of the lake gets its power from there. If it ever blows, we'll all be dead."

I whipped my sweatshirt off. With the sun beating down, the air felt downright hot. "That's a cheery thought. Is that what those evacuation signs are for?"

CJ snorted. "Yes. But with the way traffic is here, you'd never get far. I, for one, don't put a lot of stock in it."

Jazz, busy braiding her hair, lifted her eyes from

her task. "You mean you wouldn't evacuate?"

"I've already almost died stuck where I couldn't get out. I don't ever want to be in that position again."

We headed away from the plant, passing a few fishermen along the way. I lay back on the bench seat, relishing the sun on my face, and thought of him. He wasn't all tough, all SEAL with honor, code, and fight. Something had happened to him over there, something that had left scars on more than just his body. My eyes filled with tears. He was just like Ginger. The lash marks across her back were nothing compared to her broken trust in people. It was the inward scars that were the hardest to heal. I, of all people, knew that.

Water sprayed over the bow and drenched me. I yelped and sat up. Jazz laughed, handing me a towel. CJ's chuckle reached me.

All tension gone from earlier, he sat tipped back in a plastic chair at the wheel. The wind whipped his hair around, giving life to each strand. His sunglasses blocked half his face, but the chiseled part left exposed was mighty fine. Butterflies stirred in my stomach. On the one hand, he was like Ginger—wounded on the inside. On the other hand, he reminded me of my childhood horse Paddy—calm and cool on the outside, but if challenged, he would find another level within, a level that gave him the ability to jump four-foot fences and not touch a single rail. Those rides, the ones where I rode a fire-breathing dragon and balanced on his back like a leaf on the wind, had been the best of my life.

There was more to CJ than met the eye, more than I knew, and maybe more that he hid. There was something there when he showed me the pictures of the menu—something in his voice. Maybe that menu he found with the company names meant more to him than he let on.

If I wanted answers, if I wanted to find the things he hid, then I was going to have to push him. I would have to poke the fire-breathing dragon and hold on tight.

My phone buzzed in my jacket pocket. Ian's name popped up on the screen. I didn't want to hear from him badgering me about coming to New York. A police boat passed us and circled into one of the coves. CJ's gaze whipped back to trace its course. It turned around, and he shook his head.

My heart picked up its pace. I stood up and went closer to him. "Is that a problem?"

"Maybe."

"Is that Troy?" My voice squeaked above the motor of the boat.

CJ grimaced. "Probably not. But it may be friends of his, keeping tabs on me. Wade probably called him about our run-in in town."

"Should we go back?"

"I'm not going to be chased off this lake by Troy or Wade. I've been coming out here since before I could walk. Why do some people with power feel like they can push around everyone else? As if it makes them better when more than likely it just makes them corrupt?"

There was steel in his voice. Was he just talking about Troy and Wade or someone else?

Ian crossed my mind. Always pushing me, proclaiming it was for my good. How did he know what was better for me? Of course, Michael getting out wouldn't be good. So maybe Ian was right. I closed my eyes and wished away the faint pounding that always started when I thought of Michael. I had the overwhelming urge to touch CJ's arm. I curled my fingers into a fist and moved away instead.

CJ steered between two islands and veered the boat right into a side cove. The police boat zoomed past us and headed into the main channel. Behind us, one of the fishing boats from the energy plant chugged along. Could fish actually be biting at this hour?

Chapter 22

CJ

The police boat wasn't the problem. The fricking fishing boat, chugging steadily behind us and showing up in each of the coves—that was a problem. *What do they want, and is it her or me?* I hated when Donovan was right. My scar tingled and itched; I rubbed a hand over it. I cut the boat right, trying to get closer to the fishing boat but without putting Cody in danger boarding behind. If they were really fishing, they'd be pissed off about a boarder being so close to them.

Nobody was visible from the deck. This got fishier by the minute. Do I tell her about the boat or pretend it wasn't there?

As it was, I'd already lied to her. And I wasn't a liar. I hated lying. It made me all itchy and jumpy. Maybe it wasn't an outright lie, but it still was something. More of a lie by omission. Still a lie. But I couldn't let her see my name scribbled in Jack's handwriting. I wasn't ready to be an open book, expose my mistakes, especially not my role in that holy mess over there and my part in Jack's demise. Part of me wasn't ready to kill this thing between us either.

She was hiding something, too. Not the info on the menu, on that she was genuinely surprised, but there was something else going on, something I couldn't put my finger on. Not that I had time to figure it out now.

I circled around to pick Cody up. What difference did it make to Troy that we were out here? And if it wasn't Troy that had sicked the boat on us, then that was even more disturbing. Who was it and why? I glanced at my cell phone perched next to the steering wheel. Could the picture I sent to Owen be ricocheting back on me already? Maybe it was time to activate the bag of burner phones in my closet.

Cody bobbed in the water, his wakeboard propped up.

He pulled up the ladder and collapsed on the bench, smiling. "That was fun!"

Finley tossed him a towel. "It was, but we should head back. It's getting late." Her voice wobbled just a bit. Was she worried about something? Did she notice the boat following us? Maybe it wasn't following me— maybe it was following her.

"If we get back early enough, I can fix that door of yours," I said. "Someone could knock that thing down in one kick."

Maybe that same someone was following us around.

"I doubt that."

"I bet so." The words were out before I could stop them.

"Do you like to bet on everything? Is this a problem I should know about?" She raised her eyebrows slightly, her tone matching the incredulous look on her face.

I thought of McDavies, Owen, and Elliot. We played poker every night we could. "Kind of."

"Well, I hope it doesn't ever come to it, but my bet

is it'd take at least two good kicks."

Her stormy gaze met mine and held, and for a fleeting moment, the rest of the world fell away. Missions gone sideways, dead husbands, mysterious boats, they all vanished in the heat of her eyes.

"We should head back." She looked away. "The kids have homework, and I've, well, I've got stuff to do."

What kind of stuff? Was that guilt on her face? What was she guilty about?

Despite my paranoid concern over the boat that seemed to be following us, despite my simmering attraction to her, despite my resolve not to get too involved, I wanted to know what was distracting her. I turned the boat around and headed home, checking in the mirror as I did so. Sure enough, the fishing boat also started moving. Great. When we docked, it stopped about two hundred yards away. The supposed fisherman came out on the deck and threw in a line. From where I stood, I could just make out a tall figure. At this point, I'd have felt better if it was Troy. Anyone else meant bigger problems.

Finley came to get the coolers and towels. "Is everything okay?" Her cheekbones were flushed with color, and the setting sun shimmered off her skin.

I debated my answer because three things currently bothered me. One, we spent the entire afternoon under surveillance by an unnamed party. Two, there was some strange shit going on during the last few months Jack was alive, which most likely involved me. And three, the cold wind and the waning sun had caused her nipples to pebble. I wanted to drag her bathing suit down and set my mouth to each one and see if I could make her knees buckle. Out of all my emotions, it was desire that was the strongest, which was freaking me out more than the mysterious boat.

I swallowed, trying to regain my composure and control of my errant body. "How's it going with your boss? Did he agree to your desserts?"

She half-laughed. "No, he said something about too risky with homemade desserts. So I'm back to the drawing board. Got to come up with some way to make more than ten dollars an hour. As a single mom with two teenagers, I don't have the luxury to indulge in fantasies. "I'm trying to get an office job."

"You want an office job?"

She shrugged. "I have to take what I can get. *Want* doesn't really get to be a factor." She leaned the wakeboard on the dock railing, grabbed a bunch of towels and a cooler, and headed back up to the cars.

Jazz climbed out of the boat. "She was really excited about the business."

Finley trudged up the dock, overladen with towels in one arm and a cooler swinging off her other shoulder. She stopped, dropped the cooler for a moment's rest, and took a deep breath. She picked it back up and mustered on. I thought about my dad criticizing me, saying that I'll never make my business work, never get my life together, and therefore, he would never lend me money. I had been an excellent SEAL, but since being injured, I knew what it was like to always feel like I was balancing on the knife's edge of failure.

I lifted the remaining cooler out of the boat and handed it to Jazz. "Maybe I can help?"

She shrugged in a totally teenage dismissive way.

"Maybe."

Out of the corner of my eye, I caught the fishing boat slowly chugging away. I wish I could have gotten more information or a good picture of the guy. I was running blind here, and I hated it. What if the Eastleys were messing with me or something even more serious? I needed to find out who it was and take care of it.

When I got up to the parking lot, Cody and Finley were having words. Cody gave one glance his mom's way, his face screwed into a scowl, and then scrambled into the rental and slammed the door.

"What's wrong?" I piled the coolers in the back of my truck.

Finley sighed, brushing her damp hair back from her face. "He wants to drive home with you."

I closed the cover of the truck bed. "That's fine."

She shook her head. "No. It's not. He has homework." She pulled in her lower lip and bit it. Her gaze roamed over my face—assessing me and uncertain about what she was finding.

I crossed my arms over my chest. "And what?"

"I just need to be careful here."

Jazz slid by, grabbed the keys to the rental car from Finley's finger, climbed into the passenger seat and started it up.

"It's one thing to be neighbors," she said, "but it's another for me to get involved and—"

"You're kidding me? We have a boat following us on the lake, and you're scared of *me*?"

She sucked in her breath in an audible gasp. "I knew it. It was the fishing boat, right? The one that appeared after the police boat left?"

She was more perceptive than I gave her credit for.

"Yes."

She glanced at the kids sitting patiently in the idling car, and when she turned back, her eyes shimmered with tears. "This is not happening." Anger laced her voice even as it wobbled. She strode around her car and flung the driver's side door open.

"Finley."

She was too quick, the door closed, and she backed up before I could even shuffle over to that side. Damn. That did not go very well.

Let her go. That was the smart thing to do: let her go and thank my lucky stars I dodged a bullet. I waited a brief millisecond and put the pedal to the floor. Maybe she'd be safer without me. Then again, maybe not.

Chapter 23

Finley

Shit, shit, shit. I should never have let my guard down. I knew that boat was strange out there. I tightened my hands on the wheel and weaved through traffic, mentally packing up the house. The kids, tuned into their phones, luckily didn't notice my erratic driving or breathing. We'd pack tonight and leave as soon as we could. Screw the lease, work, and school. I'd figure it out after we left. "Just keep moving," Jack had said. "Just keep moving."

Halfway down the stairs, dragging packing boxes behind me, the doorbell rang.

"Finley, it's CJ." His raspy voice bellowed through the door.

Great. Just what I needed. I could ignore him, but I was pretty sure he'd barrel through anyway.

"Get the door, Jazz." The boxes slipped out of my hands and slid the rest of the way, bumping down the stairs.

Jazz scowled at me. "No."

I raised my voice. "Jasmine."

"I'm not going anywhere, and I'm not doing anything you tell me to."

Wonderful. Teenage attitude at its finest. Perfect timing too.

Cody, lacrosse sticks balanced on his shoulder, threw the door open. CJ stood there, pizza boxes in one hand and a rifle in the other. I didn't want him here, didn't need his gravelly voice or his eyes that turned from sharp to soft in an instant. Eyes that held a fire, scaring me and drawing me in at the same time. I didn't want any of it.

"What do you prefer?" he asked. "Extra cheese or supreme?"

Maybe if I was tough, he'd go away and leave me in peace. "Look—"

"Now hold on. Before you go off half-cocked. The other night you asked me for help, so I'm here to help."

"Listen, maybe as a SEAL you're used to people following you and accosting you in town and all that goes along with living a life of danger. But that's not me. And I'm not hanging around to find out who that was on the lake."

"But he brought pizza, Mom," Cody said.

"The boy's got a point. You're panicking."

"She's totally panicking." Jazz motioned to me. "She makes bad decisions."

"Enough, Jazz. I'm the head of this family now, and what I say goes. So start packing! We are leaving tonight."

Cody dropped the lacrosse sticks. "I don't want to leave. We just got here, and it's way nicer than D.C."

"I'm not leaving." Jazz crossed her arms over her chest and narrowed her eyes as if daring me to contradict her.

Anger, raw and hot, bubbled up in me. I was trying to keep them safe. Why couldn't they understand this? I placed my hand on the open door and turned to CJ.

"You need to go. I appreciate your help, but I don't need it."

He shoved the pizzas into Cody's hands. "Take this, and you and your sister go set up dinner. I need to talk to your mom."

Of course, they listened. To me, hardly ever, but to some guy who they spent four hours with, they do what he asked. I let my simmering anger loose. "Who do you think you are? You can't come in here and order my kids around."

I didn't know which made me angrier, the fact he did it or the fact they listened.

"Nothing is going to be achieved by moving."

Yes, it will. I will be gone, and no one can find the kids and me. "I don't like danger. I don't like you. And I don't want either. That boat was following us, and you didn't even mention it until the end."

"I didn't mention it because I figured it was Troy being a scumbag. That's what Wade and Troy Eastley do. I told you I'd take care of you guys out there. And I did, didn't I? What are you freaking out about?"

"I'm not brave, CJ. I'm not a risk-taker. I have the kids to think of."

"Okay. I get all that."

But he didn't really. He didn't know about Michael. He didn't even know that Jack worked for the CIA. For all I knew, on that boat there was someone connected to Jack and his death or, God forbid, Michael. Maybe Michael hired someone to watch me, to find out where I was before he got out, to track me down and do what—

"You asked me for help." He stepped forward, his palms out, despite my attempts to usher him out the door. "I'm involved."

I stood holding the door open for him to leave.

He rubbed a hand behind his neck. "You can't go racing off because—well, then I'll have to go racing off after you. And Griff will really be pissed about that."

I smiled despite myself. He's right. Griff would be pissed at him. But I didn't know if I believed CJ really would chase after us.

He took the opening of my silence and ran with it. "On top of that, you can't solve problems on an empty stomach."

I tightened my grip on the one moving box that hadn't fallen down the stairs. "But you can with pizza and a gun?"

"You'd be surprised what you can solve with pizza and a gun." Using the butt of the rifle, he lifted the edge of the deconstructed moving boxes and leaned them against the wall. "Give me a chance to help. Also, the gun is for Jazz. She wanted to learn how to shoot. I took Cody boarding, so I should do something for her too."

"I'm not sure shooting is the answer." To be honest, I had no idea what the answer was, with either my kids or this mess we were in. Part of me liked that he took an interest in my kids—but the other part of me, the part that I should listen to, didn't like it at all.

"She told me she needs to learn for some party."

I blew out the breath I'd been holding. If Jazz was confiding in any adult, it was an improvement over her anger with Jack's death, this move, and lacrosse. "Fine." I stepped back. "Dinner, and then I'll decide."

He brushed by, the faint smell of coconut shampoo wafting toward me. He had changed from shorts into jeans, but that hadn't dimmed the lines of his body.

CJ's head swiveled left to right as we walked. He motioned to the bookcases lining the walls. They were a new addition to the house but necessary. I never had enough space for my books.

"Are those all your books?" he asked.

"Nope. I've got three more boxes to unpack in the barn." Of course, now I didn't have to. Instead I had to pack these up.

The kids had done as he asked, and the pizza boxes lay on the island, a stack of paper plates next to them. He propped the rifle in the corner and leaned back through the doorway as if to get a better look. "Did you read them all?"

I'm glad he could relax. I had no intention of following suit or being distracted from my job at hand. I dropped the moving box on the floor and set about constructing it. "Yes."

He chewed thoughtfully on a toothpick. "That's a lot of books."

"I was an English major in college. It was the one subject I had any talent or interest in. Why?" Box constructed, I whipped open a cabinet and started dumping the contents into it.

"No reason, I was just never one for all that writing and reading. Numbers were more my thing."

He slid a piece of pizza onto a plate and held it out to me. I shook my head. "Just put it on the counter. I'll get to it." I moved onto unloading another drawer into the box. The kids munched busily on their slices from the kitchen table.

CJ surveyed the room, his eyebrows drawn together. There was something about this house that seemed to annoy him, and I had yet to figure it out.

"Is it hard to cook in this kitchen?" he asked.

"It can be," I admitted. "If I owned this house, the first thing I'd do is gut the kitchen."

His jaw tightened. "And the second?"

"Gut the rest of the first floor."

He nodded as if digesting something serious and noteworthy. "Be prepared—I don't know what you'd find. Old farmhouses like this have lots of secrets."

There was a wistfulness to his tone I'd never heard before.

"I don't like secrets."

"You might like this one. There's a cellar that leads almost to the fence."

"Huh?" That perked Cody up, whose eyes lasered in on CJ's face like a stray dog on an old sandwich. "What do you mean?"

"Down the stairs, there's a root cellar that cuts through half the yard. A long, dark tunnel comes out by the fence. Generations ago they stored vegetables and things they needed to keep cold down there. But—" His face pulled taut as if he was about to tell a spooky story. "—I wouldn't go down there except for during the day. You never know what animals have taken up residence. It's been vacant for a while."

I slammed the lid on the box. "Well, I won't have to worry about that, and he'll never find out because we're leaving. Tonight."

Jazz jumped up from the table, her chair legs scraping on the floor. "Oh my God. You're so annoying."

"Mom," Cody whined and then turned his gaze to CJ. "You've got to convince her to stay. I'm this close"—Cody pinched two fingers together—"to making the lacrosse team."

CJ gathered up some of the empty soda cans and held them out to Jazz. "Go set these up outside. I'll be right out with the rifle."

They both did as he said.

"Still bossing around my kids, I see." I grabbed another box.

His gaze skated over my face. "Tell me why you want to leave so badly."

Because maybe the guy on the boat is my psychotic, drug-using ex-boyfriend. "Why I want to leave? You were the one who told me my SUV was tampered with? That Jack was killed." I pushed my hair back around my ears.

He smiled.

"Why are you smiling? There's nothing about this worth smiling over."

"You fiddle with your hair when you're nervous. And it's mesmerizing."

"You must have a very boring life if that's mesmerizing. Besides, I do not."

He unwrapped a mint and popped it into his mouth. "We don't know anything for sure. So, don't run off prematurely. Your kids want to stay. Listen to them. Listen to me. Besides, what vehicle are you taking? The rental company wouldn't be thrilled to find their car out of state and who knows where."

I hated when people brought up rational points in the midst of my panicking. "Here's an idea. You go do your shooting lesson, and I'll keep packing."

He just stood there staring at me and sucking on that stupid mint. Despite my best efforts, I couldn't drag my eyes away from his lips.

"You're very determined, aren't you? I don't think you should leave, but I do like that quality." He sauntered out the kitchen door, and it slammed behind him.

What did he mean by that?

On the way to get more boxes from the decrepit barn, I got to witness both kids shooting the cans clear off the fence posts. Jazz stayed for a second round and nearly glowed as she handed the rifle back to CJ.

"Thank you, Mr. Sinclair."

He smiled in return. "You're welcome. And call me CJ."

Jazz looked to me for confirmation, and I nodded. "Go pack your room. There are boxes in the front hall."

She grumbled an answer, but it wasn't hard to see the bounce in her step as she went back inside. It lightened my heart and gave me a pang of uncertainty. Maybe I was overreacting. How could I yank them away when they were just making friends?

CJ bent over and picked up the dented cans, his leg injury more noticeable. He tossed me a can, and I caught it. "You want a turn? Do you know how to shoot?"

There was a devilish glint in his eyes. *Is he flirting with me?*

I scrunched the can in my fingers. "Jack taught me. I can't shoot very far, but I can do it."

Jack's name hung between us, and the glint in CJ's eyes faded.

"Don't run away," he said. "You're just getting settled. They're getting settled."

"What?" I didn't bother disguising my attitude. It burned me that he could almost read my mind. His annoying calmness and rationale were stealing my momentum and adrenaline; and without them, my motivation was slowly leaking away. In my mom's words I was losing pace on my jumper course. And without pace, jumping was nearly impossible and at times downright dangerous.

He tossed me another dented can. "You asked for my help the other day. Don't run away before we've figured anything out."

I picked up a can near me. "We've figured some things out, like the fact someone is watching me."

The real question was, who and how were they connected? To Jack or to Michael? And would I put us all in danger if I stayed to figure it out?

"We've figured out nothing," he said. "The boat was following us, but we don't know more. It could've been following me. I was wrong to blurt it out like I did. I was just pissed off you didn't trust me."

"I want to. It's just you send me lots of mixed signals." I took a deep breath struggling to find the right words. He deserved some kind of honesty, but I wasn't sure how much.

He straightened up and approached me, and for a second, I wished to be back inside the house with a kitchen counter between us. Even with his bad leg, he had a fluidity to him and a presence that was intimidating. "And?"

Screw it. "I met you less than a week ago with drugs and a handgun on your table. It's none of my business, but I can't expose my kids to that. It's one thing for me, but another for them. I can't forget. I shouldn't have made that bet with you or gone on the boat ride. I just—I feel bad I moved them, and I thought if they had some fun, maybe they wouldn't be so mad at me."

I scanned the ground for any other targets, searching for an escape from his piercing gaze. Unfortunately, he'd gotten them all.

I scrunched the already shot-up cans in my hands and walked back to the kitchen, dumping the cans in the open recycle bin. Knowing he was hot on my heels, I grabbed another box and unloaded a cabinet, hoping to do anything but meet his eyes.

"Most of those drugs and joints were my granddad's, for his cancer. A few were mine for pain for my surgeries."

"Why do you have them?" I wrapped the utensils in tea towels. Did I really want to start over in another town? And where would I find a great deal like Mattie gave me?

"My sister is supposed to dispose of them through some recycle drug program. She hasn't taken them yet. What are you scared of?" He leaned across the island, and I fought the urge to step back.

"Besides the fact that someone's stalking me? And you think my husband was killed and not just died in a car accident? Nothing."

I lied. *Everything.* His eyes scared me—the way they pierced through to my very soul. His hands and how I imagined they'd feel on my skin. Most of all, I'm scared if I'm safe, if the kids are safe. Twenty years ago, I made the worst decision with Michael, and I was still paying for it. I couldn't afford to repeat that mistake.

He pulled his lips in slightly, and his gaze roamed me up and down. "Bullshit."

I dropped the utensils in the box and wrapped up some knives. "See, you're doing it again."

"Doing what?" He tilted his head a fraction of an inch.

"Sending me mixed signals. Being pissed off and nice. You want me to stay, and yet other times you seem mad at me. I can't tell if you like me or hate me."

"Classic words coming from someone as easy to read as a closed book. It's not that I don't like you. Or don't want to help you. That's not the problem."

I stopped packing and met his eyes, waiting. He cleared his throat.

"My life—" He rubbed the scar on the side of his face.

Did he realize he did this when he was thinking? Did it still bother him?

"I'm not a big fan of people," he said. "I have trouble with them since being injured. I just want to be left in peace with my—" He dropped his hands to the counter and curled his fingers into fists. "—animals. On top of that, you've stepped into a fight between the Eastleys and me. Each of us gunning for property. Me to save it. The Eastleys to develop it. All I see is property being sold off to developers who don't care a bit about the land except for how many houses they can cram in. Do you know the other day some guy didn't stop for the geese crossing through town? Almost ran them over. If that's progress, I'd rather not have it. Contrary to the Eastleys' opinion, that's not us, and that's not what this town is about."

"I saw that. Some guy behind me was honking for me to go faster, but those geese take a long time to cross."

"See? Years ago, no one would honk. No one would care that they had to stop for fifteen minutes."

"What's the grudge?"

He ran a hand through his hair, displacing the windblown strands even more. Something was going through his mind but obviously not anything he wished to share. "There's no love lost between us."

"I noticed that this morning when you almost lunged at his throat."

He swung his gaze to me—his green eyes softly shaded but sharp as a knife. He pulled one of the packed boxes closer to him and lifted out the utensils I had just dumped inside.

"Can you stop that?" I picked up the utensils and placed them back in the box.

He sighed, and his broad shoulders sagged just a bit, the tautness easing. "You don't need to be a part of that. It started ages ago. I shouldn't have lost it like that."

He reached for the empty pizza boxes, and his arm brushed mine. The tension crashed over me like a heatwave. The pounding in my head had yet to organize itself into a migraine, but it sat there as if it was waiting for the worse time to take over.

"Don't be," I said. "I get it."

He swiped the boxes off the counter, balancing them in one hand. "Get what?"

"Life. There's a cruelty to it sometimes. An unjustified unfairness that makes a person want to scream. Just when you think you have it figured out, accepted your consequences, it goes and turns your world upside down."

"Ain't that the truth." His gaze locked on mine, and

this time his eyes didn't hold anger but a totally different kind of heat, and all my roiled-up annoyance disappeared. He grabbed the tied-up garbage and stepped away. "I'll take all this out."

I nodded and let him go, listening to the back door slam against the wooden frame. Thoughts swarmed my head: What was I doing? Maybe he was right. Maybe I shouldn't go. I'd never find out the truth if I run, and what about the kids? They deserved a place to call home. And I'd never get enough money saved for the kids' college if I keep moving us. Jack had made me promise to leave D.C., but he never said anything about running. Did he? Is running what he meant when he said, "Keep moving if we had to"? CJ wanted me to stay and promised to stand by me—or run if I did. That was worth something. In fact, it was worth quite a lot. Even my silly dream of the bakery—that was worth something too.

CJ came back in, rubbing a hand behind his neck. "I have something else to say."

I spread my hands out on the kitchen counter. "Okay. Shoot."

"If you stay instead of running, you could get a booth at the farmer's market to help with your bakery."

A little zing shot across my chest. How did he do that? How did he know I was thinking about the bakery? "What?"

"There's a farmer's market here in town every Saturday, even through the winter. You can sell your goods there. Once you get a following, restaurants might want you." He raised a jelly cookie in my direction. "These are too good not to share with the world."

He cocked an eyebrow at me and waited. Could I be safe here? Would I be safe? What was the best decision for the kids?

Jazz barreled into the kitchen with Cody fast on her heels. Screaming in short bursts, Jazz held the remote control for the TV above her head as she circled the island. "Mom. Mom."

"Give it to me. It's my turn."

"It's mine, you jackass," Cody whined. "It should be packed with my stuff."

I plucked the remote from Jazz's hand as she ran by. "This is mine. And watch your language."

They stopped their race around the island.

"Homework. Now." I pointed out of the room.

"Homework? I thought we were leaving?" Their voices chimed in unison.

"I think we'll stay. For now." We could always leave another day—if anything changed. God, I hoped I was making the right decision.

Cody made a celebratory fist and yanked it to his side, mouthing the word *yes.* They both complied without grumbles or backward dirty looks. Small miracles. I turned my attention to CJ. "Happy?"

His gaze dropped to my lips and slowly rose back up. He grinned again, that same grin. I wasn't sure if he was making fun of me or not. "For now," he said.

My cheeks flushed with heat. I waved my hand around the chaos of the kitchen. "I should go and unpack."

He leaned on the counter, closer to me. "Want help?"

There is that moment when you're riding and the thousand-pound animal beneath you decides there is a scary monster in the corner of the ring and in a millisecond, he spins and leaps as only a prey animal can do. As a rider, if you are balanced, aware, and lucky, you move with him and don't wind up eating dirt on the ground. But even so, that doesn't stop your heart from almost beating out of your chest for the next five minutes. Somehow CJ could make my heart do the same.

"No. I'm good, but thank you." I needed some time away from him to really think this thing through, figure out if it made sense not to just pick up and leave, to not have him influencing my decision. I didn't know where Michael was, and I had made that promise to Jack.

He straightened up. Maybe he could tell my mind was undecided.

"Listen, don't freak out. Odds are it was one of the Eastleys. They've done that before to me. I can make a few calls about getting a booth. Want to come over tomorrow, and we can finish those boxes?"

I nodded, pushing my hair behind my ears. "I'm off work at one."

"Great." He pointed at the plate of cookies. "Can I have another one?"

"Of course. Thank you. And thanks for today."

He stepped away and opened the door, throwing a smile my way as he exited. "Don't panic. I'll be outside tonight. In my truck. I'll sleep there to make sure everything's okay."

And just like that, my heart calmed down and fluttered all at once. Nobody had ever offered to help me like that. But I couldn't ask him to do that. He didn't even know about Michael, the real reason I was scared. "You don't have to do that. We're okay."

"I don't *have* to, but I'll feel better if I do." He brushed his hair back. "Besides, I barely sleep at night anyway."

I rarely slept too, although I wondered if my reasons for not sleeping were different from his. "Do not sleep out in your truck all night. I'll call you—" I wiggled my phone in my hand. "—if I have a problem."

He furrowed his brow. "I don't know. Your phone seems kind of unreliable. Jazz says you need a new one. How old is that thing?"

I shook my head and laid my hand on his forearm. "Kids think everything needs replacing if it isn't the latest and greatest. It works just fine. Don't worry. I'll call if there's an issue."

"Fine." His voice was scratchy, deep and rough, and a tingle ran all the way down my spine. He jiggled the door handle. "Lock this door. And put the chair underneath it. I'll fix it this week. I promise."

"Okay." He went through the door, and I slid the small bolt into place. When I lifted my hand off the bolt, my fingers were trembling. I wedged the chair underneath and closed my trembling fingers into a fist. I lied. I was scared. For our safety—and my heart.

I surveyed the kitchen. I could finish unpacking or bake some bread and muffins for tomorrow. I pulled out my mixing bowls. Baking always relaxed me, and I needed some of that right now. Sometimes it helped me think too. I measured in flour, sugar, and baking powder. In the second bowl, I mashed up bananas and added to it some fresh vanilla and eggs. Mixing the two together, I made the batter for my nana's banana muffins. I left the mix sit for a while—all muffins were fluffier when the batter sat—and moved on to Irish soda bread. I was kneading the dough when Cody clambered down the stairs.

He tossed something, and it landed on the counter, skidding through the loose flour.

"What's that?"

"A flash drive. I needed it for school. But it's got something on it, so I can't use it."

"Okay. Well, what do I need it for?" I itched my forehead with my wrist, careful to keep my doughy hands away. The one step that was messy in Irish soda bread was the kneading part.

"It's got some encrypted file on it."

"So?" I shaped the bread into a flat disk and placed it on the baking pan.

"I'm not messing with some flash drive with an encrypted file. I'll just get another one tomorrow at school."

I made an *X* across the top of the bread and drizzled it with melted butter. "I don't get why this involves me. Do you need money for a new drive?"

"Because I got that flash drive from Dad's desk a few months ago. I figured it was one of those blank ones he kept in there. Anyway, it's not. So, I didn't know if you might need it back."

My stomach fell to the bottom of my shoes. *Move your feet.* Don't let on it could be important, that anything could be wrong. I slid the baking sheet into the oven, my eyes filled with tears. What if something bad was on that flash drive?

I carried the muffins to the counter.

"Are you okay?" Cody asked. "You look like you're going to cry."

I waved my potholder through the air. "I'm fine.

It's just the heat blast from opening the oven."

"Okay, good." He blew me a kiss from the doorway. "I'm going to bed. See you in the morning. Love ya, Mom."

"Love you too, bud."

Could he hear the wobble in my voice? I washed my hands and picked up the flash drive. It had a coating of flour on it.

An encrypted file.

I glanced at the clock. It was after eleven. I know he said he stayed up late, but there was no way I was calling him to have him race over there. Maybe it was nothing. I slipped it into my pocket. Despite its insignificant size, it felt like a dumbbell. I cleaned the counters and washed the dirty dishes. When I couldn't avoid it any longer, I opened my computer and pushed in the flash drive.

A nameless file I'd never seen before popped up. I clicked on it. The little wheely thing spun. I jiggled my leg, waiting for it to open. The word *encrypted* flashed across the screen, and an open box appeared, requesting a password. The only time I'd ever seen files with passwords were from the bank or Jack. This file didn't have the bank logo on it.

Chapter 24

CJ

There were so many issues with this night I couldn't even list them. I had been sitting in my truck for a while, rubbing my sore knee. My mind tumbled back and forth over the day. I lost track of time trying to make sense of my run in with Wade, the boat on the lake, Jack's cryptic writing, that last mission gone sideways. I laid my head back upon the seat rest. The tall pines that dotted my property line swayed ominously in the breeze. The day one of them toppled over, they'd probably all come down like dominos.

Finley had been very committed to leaving. Was it just the crap on Jack that spurred her on or something else she hadn't told me? What had he told her? What hadn't he told her?

For standing in her way, I was the northbound end of a southbound mule. Stupid of me—urging her to stay because I wanted her. I knew that if or when we solved Jack's murder, she'd discover how closely I worked with Jack, which would most likely kill any hope of a relationship. Thinking I could protect her when some days I could barely walk. She was in danger on some level. Jack worked in dangerous waters; I knew this. I had worked in those waters too. Somehow those waters had overflowed from the Middle East to here. Donovan had made that clear, and still I ignored him. I owed Jack a debt of protecting his wife and kids, but I wasn't sure he'd think I was repaying it by putting her in further danger or, worse yet, wanting his wife.

I hobbled down from my truck and slammed the door. That was all it took for the dogs to start a chorus and whinnies to echo from the barn. "Go to sleep, guys."

Finley thought the problem was that I didn't like her. The problem was *not* that I didn't like her. The problem was that I liked her too much. All I could think of as she stood there was how much I wanted to crowd in behind her and trace that line of her neck from behind her ear to her clavicle with my tongue. Brush my fingers over her nipples until they peaked, and she ached with desire. Feel my way into her jeans and stroke her until she whimpered with need. Hell, she couldn't have been more wrong. Liking her wasn't the issue. Wanting the woman whose husband's death was tied to my work in Afghanistan, wanting a woman who had no clue the extent of my injuries, those were problems.

I'm a fricking moron. The closer we got, the more we dug into those files, the more likely she was going to want the truth.

Ellie and Rusty followed me up the porch steps and bombarded me with kisses. I flung the door open, disgust and lust warring inside of me, the wooden porch door taking the brunt of both. It creaked against its hinges, ricocheting back. I poured dinner out for the dogs, turned the lights out in the kitchen, and headed for my bedroom. It was a nice cool night, and I opened the bedroom window just as my phone rang. For once, good timing on Owen's part. He saved me from imagining Finley in her bathing suit and having to take a cold shower.

"How's it going?"

I took a deep breath gathering my wits and hormones before answering. "Good. You?"

"Decent. How's your new wife?"

"You're very funny. *Jack*'s wife is—interesting." I stretched out on my bed, settled against a pillow, and flicked on a sports channel. Little did he know how loaded a question that was.

"I found something."

Owen's tone jerked me out of my prone position. "Really?"

"After they broke us up, Jack moved over from counterterrorism to straight narcotics with a focus on the Middle East and Eastern Europe. On one of his last assignments, he was tracking the Albanian mob, its connection to the U.S., its network, drug-trafficking— the whole nine yards. Remember the pallets of money and heroin when we raided those farms outside of J-bad?"

I snorted. "Yup. And even greater stores of weapons." A breeze ruffled my blinds, and the scent of freshly cut hay overrode the burning leaves. Hank must have been cutting today.

"He ran with that contact and info we retrieved. Used it in a later op with Echo team. Those HVT's were moving drugs up thru Tajikistan."

"Albanians are fricking hard-core. They'd have taken him out just for sport. She was asking me about combat today."

Ellie, done with dinner, sauntered into the room

and hopped onto the bed, curling up beside me.

"Did she ask you how you got hurt?"

"Yup." I rubbed a hand behind my neck.

"Did you tell her?" Owen's tone was tight and hard, and even across the wires, the tension was obvious.

"When was the last time you told anyone about what happened over there?" I met his tone, biting off each word. He didn't have to answer. I knew it was never.

"Do you think she's after something?" His voice was softer. Owen rarely lost control, especially not if he wasn't one hundred percent sure our call wasn't being monitored.

"Besides answers about her husband? No. Of course, maybe she's just after my body." I scratched Ellie's head, who in response stretched out, taking up more than half the bed.

Owen coughed into the phone. "Does she seem mentally unstable?"

"Funny. Like moths to a flame, buddy. It's like clearing a house in Ramadi. Remember how I'd get to the roof before you?" I smiled as the words slid from my mouth, a shade of my former cocky SEAL self still there. My injuries had robbed me of most of that confidence.

"I just puked over the side of the bed. You want the rest of the details, or are you going to keep stroking yourself?"

"You're just jealous."

He chuckled.

"Go on." I punched my pillow to fluff it up and leaned back. The last of the cicadas were making quite a racket outside the window.

"Okay, so three interesting things. A week before he dies, he goes to see some retired police chief in New York. On that trip, he also stops at some mental institute in upstate New York. Flower Hill. Ever heard of it?"

"No. Did you get the records?" A squeal and a *thunk* against wood floated through the window. Wonderful. It was probably Ginger giving attitude to her barn mate.

"Waiting on the transcript from the mental hospital and still digging for info on the police chief. Rivera is getting me some phone records. If he bothered to see him in person, the odds are that conversation was the important one."

"What's the third thing?"

"On the night he died, he had dinner with an old childhood friend. Some guy named Ian Monroe."

"You think it's worth digging into?"

"Yeah. Anything else new on the widow?"

Ellie bounced up, ear pricked. I jumped up, staggered on my leg, and grabbed the window frame to steady myself.

"Sin?"

I bent the blind and peered out the window. Nothing moved outside. "I had her out on the boat today."

"Making the moves?"

"Her kids were with us. And just to be clear, she's pricklier than a porcupine and as cuddly as a skunk." Of course, she smelled a lot better—like vanilla.

Rusty barked, and my other rescues joined in. Ellie scooted off the bed to stand beside me. Something was riling them up. But it could just be a skunk or coyotes. Some nights the coyote's yipping could be heard for miles. "We were followed, too."

"Shit. You got anything?"

"Nope. Not close enough." A new round of barking started up. I'd never sleep now. I grabbed my rifle and left the bedroom. Ellie padded faithfully behind me. "I think it's the local cop I told you about."

"What's he want from you?"

"Besides more money than God and rewriting his high school experience, I don't know. He likes to bust my balls." I slipped my boots on in the kitchen.

"Speaking of busting balls, have you heard from McDavies recently?"

I snatched my backpack I kept ready at the door, grabbed my small cooler filled with drinks and snacks, and left. "No. Must be at least a week."

So much for my resolution to stay in touch more. As SEALs, we tried to keep each other above water, and we had better exit rates than other branches of the service. But PTSD could be wearing on anyone—SEAL or not. My brothers in arms had been there for me on more than one occasion when I needed a pick-me-up.

"Yeah, me neither. I'll call him tomorrow. You want me to update you, or will you be too busy dodging cops and romancing the widow?"

"Screw off." I could hear him laughing even as I ended the call.

Romancing the widow? Judging from today my odds of romance were about as high as my odds of running a marathon. I had a better chance of winding up in jail thanks to the Eastleys. One of these days, that whole situation was going to explode. I just hoped I'd fare better than the last time something exploded.

I checked the dogs on the porch to make sure their doggy door worked and that they had plenty of water. They wouldn't wander away in the dark and had settled down by now. I bypassed my truck and headed for the break in the fence. Ellie followed me. I'd promised Finley I wouldn't sit in my truck all night, and I meant it. But I never promised anything about her decrepit barn, which she used as a garage and for ping-pong, but where I used to roam high and wide as a kid. I knew its crevices like the back of my hand. I firmly believed she was hiding something from me. But then again so was I, and what I didn't dispute was that she was in danger. I found the outside ladder to the hayloft, spread a blanket for Ellie on the ground, and then climbed up. Ellie whined a bit and then lay down. The ladder creaked but held me. I pushed out the hayloft door, set a bottle of water and my rifle next to my thigh, and settled back against the post. From here I could see the area surrounding her house, and if anyone ventured close, I'd have the perfect view. I was a mule's ass, but I was also a mule's ass that wasn't going to let someone get hurt.

Not on my watch. Not this time—and definitely not her.

Chapter 25

Finley

Ginger was out in the pasture but trotted to the fence when I called her. She'd really made some progress. I fed her mints and stroked her nose, trying to push Ian's last voicemail from my mind. I found some solace in her big brown eyes and the way she gently nudged me with her muzzle. When my supply ran out, she wandered back to the grass, and I headed for the house. Halfway there, CJ intercepted me from the barn.

"Hey, DC."

I jumped back and nearly screamed. "Every darn time, CJ."

He cocked his head to one side, his eyes roaming up and down. I was wearing jeans and a black T-shirt. I couldn't have looked that good.

"You okay?" he asked.

An image of the encrypted file crossed my mind, and I checked my pocket where the flash drive was stashed. "I didn't sleep much last night, and we were slammed during the breakfast rush. You?"

"I didn't sleep much either." He smushed his lips together as if thinking about something. "Beautiful sunrise this morning."

"You watched the sun rise, too?" We were probably both up at the same time. My heart pounded at the thought, which was really stupid.

He nodded. "My favorite time of day. Everything is just starting to stir and wake up, and it's more light than dark."

"I love that time. When I was horse showing, we'd leave the barn in the dark and drive to the show. You'd get there to the show grounds and get ready all the while the sun was slowly starting to come up and everything around was coming alive. Sometimes I'd get on my horse, and the mist would be covering the ground, and I'd ride through the mist—the beat of hooves, the snorting of horses, and the call of birds the only sounds."

A quietness filled the space between the two of us. His gaze skated slowly over my face.

You cannot do this. He doesn't know you. I snapped my attention away and pointed to the brush in his hand. "That's *not* a file box."

He smiled, one side of his mouth tilting up. It gave warmth to the lines etched across his face. "Very observant. Neeley, Hank Bennett's wife, called. Hank's out of town fishing, and the cows have gotten through the fence. I usually have Griff here to partner with me on the ATV, but he's off at some school function for one of his kids. Care for a ride to get them back?"

"Instead of digging through Jack's files?"

"I'm at a standstill waiting on my friend to get me some info, so yeah, might as well have a ride." He shrugged. "It's a great day for it."

He wasn't wrong on that. The sun was out, and a slight breeze swayed the gloriously colored leaves. I glanced at Snickers and Storm standing on the cross ties in the barn, already tacked up. My heart kicked into overdrive thinking about it. Horses had been linked to my parents' deaths for so long now it was hard to split the two, and difficult to remind myself that I wasn't that horse-crazed girl anymore so focused on horses and her boyfriend that she put her parents' lives in danger. I needed to convince myself that just because I threw a leg over a horse's back didn't mean I'd suddenly revert to that selfish person. But the guilt was hard to shake.

"Okay. Not long," I cautioned. "And not fast."

"Do I look like I'd go fast?" He gave me his cocky smile that lit up his face and quickened my pulse. He looked like he'd do everything fast, except for the things that he would do insanely slow. My cheeks flushed.

"I promise, whatever you want." He held his hands up.

This only made me flush more, which was really embarrassing. I was forty, not twenty. I glanced down at my flip-flops. "I need boots."

"My sister always keeps an extra pair in my trunk." He waved toward the trunk. "Probably will fit."

Storm nickered to me as I ducked under the cross ties. I opened the trunk and lifted out the dusty black paddock boots. A pair of socks lay on the top shelf. I pulled them on and then slipped my feet into the boots. Breathing deep, I zipped them up, and my stomach joined my heart in doing jumping jacks.

CJ smiled at me and tightened Storm's girth. "Nervous?" he asked

"A bit." I rubbed Storm's face. He dropped his head, pressing it into my hand.

"I saw you ride. You'll have no problem. It's like riding a bike, right?" CJ gave Storm a gentle slap on the butt and moved on to Snickers.

I smiled despite my butterflies. Jack used to say that all the time, but he used it when referring to our sporadic sex life.

"That was different. It was a horse emergency. Besides, I've never ridden Western."

"Nothing to it. Ready?"

I nodded and followed him out of the barn, conscious of Storm's body moving next to me and even more so of CJ's in front of me.

CJ mounted in one fluid motion, which only added to his hotness. He looked back at me from Snickers's saddle. "You good?"

Inhaling deeply, I gathered all my strength and will. I knew how to do this. Hell, I'd been on horseback only a few days ago. I just didn't want the flood gates to open and all the good memories along with the bad to come tumbling in. I'd locked them away as best I could, and I didn't know if doing this would somehow loosen the bolts. *Here goes nothing.* I swung up, settling lightly in the saddle. I wiped my sweaty palms on my jeans and picked up the reins, imitating his one-hand hold. Shifting my weight right and left in the saddle, I familiarized myself with it. Western saddles were substantially bigger than the jumping saddle I'd been used to. If I did this again, I'd bring my saddle. A gift from my parents when I turned twenty, I'd always taken good care of it, even though I tucked it away for two decades in my tack box.

Storm twisted his head to look at me. Big brown warm eyes met mine before he sniffed at my foot as if to say, "Don't worry, I've got this." I leaned forward and gave him a pat. The peculiar and heavenly scent of dirt, horsehair, and leather floated over me. Most of my nervousness evaporated. I exhaled my breath and shot CJ a small smile.

Taking my cue, he turned Snickers and headed for the gate behind the barn. Storm knew his job and followed.

CJ pointed in front of him. "If we go that way, we can take the path around the woods and up to the pond. I'm sure that's where the cows came through."

"Okay." Storm's muscles flexed. Despite the bulkiness of the Western saddle, his power was evident. I'd forgotten just how strong it could be, forgotten the connection. A shiver ran through me. "Do you do this often?"

He clucked to Snickers again and directed him off the grass and down a path that cut into the woods. "About once a month, the cows get out. Hank and Neeley's neighbor on the other side is a real witch too—always complaining about loose animals. So the Bennetts try to round them up as quickly as possible. I think Griff likes it. Gives him an excuse to run the ATV without the kids."

"How many kids does he have?"

"Two boys. He's divorced."

"And you?" God, my legs were like wet noodles. *Heels down. Remember your basics.*

He squinted at me. "Married or kids?"

The wrinkles edged out from the corner of his eyes, and the warmth in my face traveled down to my belly. "Either."

"Divorced, no kids."

"What happened?" Breathe. Any tension I held onto could be felt by Storm—riding 101. My trainer always liked to remind me of that. She'd said that my very last ride, that Saturday morning before all hell broke loose, before the fight, before I'd come home to a burning barn and my parents shot dead. Was this a smart idea? Riding again, especially with someone I didn't want to get to know.

He threw me a cockeyed grin. "Trish didn't like the new version."

"Excuse me?"

"Trish and I were high school sweethearts. I came back from combat very different from when I went in. She didn't like it. How about you? Were you happily married?"

I shifted in the saddle, uncomfortable in more ways than one. This was definitely not a good idea. "I met Jack when I was bartending, through a mutual friend."

Jack had been a safe choice—a lawyer wanting to work for the government—or so I thought. Smart, focused, dependable. The opposite of drugged-up Michael. And he was—for the most part.

The path veered right and then down a hill. With the surrounding woods and the tree branches creating a heavy canopy, the path was fully shaded. It reminded me of the path between my house and the barn growing up. For a moment I panicked, thrust back into that horrid night when I couldn't see five feet in front of me but could hear the screams of the horses as the fire consumed the barn.

"You doing all right?" he asked.

"Uh huh." I lied, gulping in the fresh scent of fallen leaves and hoping to blow away the memory of smoke from my burning childhood barn. At the bottom of the hill, sun broke through the heavy foliage dappling the ground. Storm navigated the decline, and I leaned back and out of his way. I focused on what was right before me to remind me of where I was, that I was safe. The woods opened up at the bottom of the hill and into a field. In the distance, a pond glistened in the sun. But I could still hear the horses' screams and picture the flames licking at the barn roof.

I needed more. Maybe moving quicker would blot out these memories. "Let's go faster."

"Want to trot?" There was a challenge in his voice.

"Sure. You go first." I didn't want him to see me bouncing around like an idiot if I couldn't figure out how to post in a Western saddle.

He gently kicked Snickers, and off they went. Storm didn't need any urging from me, and he quickly followed.

I jiggled around, feeling loose and inept. I sat a bit, squeezing harder, and Storm moved out into a canter. Now that was better. As long as I remembered to breathe, I'd be okay. We swept by CJ, Storm's smooth canter strides eating up Snickers's little trot steps.

"Really? You're on, girl!"

I glanced back and smiled.

Behind us, Snickers's hoofbeats moved from the two-beat trot to a three-beat canter. I loosened my reins and gave Storm his head, enjoying the rush of the wind on my face.

Freedom.

That's what existed on the back of a horse: possibility and a sudden unexplainable connection to all things. I wondered if that connection is what had helped CJ heal, if that's what he had found in the barnyard and in the quiet nature of the horses.

Storm broke back to a trot, and we approached the pond, which was good because I was huffing and puffing like a runaway train. Apparently, my daily run wasn't prepping me for riding. The surface of the pond rippled from dragonflies touching down, reminding me of days my mom and I would trail ride together around our farm and through the neighbor's property. We had a fountain and a large koi pond that sparkled in the sun. My mom always said still waters run deep, that it was okay that I wasn't outgoing and bubbly like some of my friends growing up. Of course, in this instance my still waters now hid secrets I didn't want anyone knowing. Secrets of my drug days, selfish decisions, killer boyfriends, burning barns, dead parents.

A wave of anger—anger from the futility of trying to keep these secrets and protect my kids—swept over me. I kept my face hidden, trying to get my breath and keep my eyes from overflowing. Snickers pulled even with us, and I busied myself with the reins.

"You okay?" he asked.

When I knew I'd gotten control, I turned to him. "Oh yeah. Just out of shape, you know." I took a deep breath and blew it out, willing my voice to stop shaking.

"You didn't look it."

"Looks can be deceiving."

He fixed with his gaze—his eyes shifting colors. One minute, dark; the next, light. "Truer words were never spoken, DC."

Chapter 26

CJ

Something about riding opened her up and closed her off all at the same time. For a moment, she'd been a different person—carefree and smiling, racing across that field. But then she'd all but disappeared, her face hidden. And when she did turn toward me, her eyes glistened. I wanted to tell her not to worry, and whatever it was, I could help. But who was I kidding; I had enough trouble getting out of bed every morning. Besides, I had to protect my team. There were things she didn't need to know—things I didn't want her to find out. How the hell could I help her and keep our secrets?

So, I didn't ask, and she didn't tell.

We found the cows where I predicted. Finley didn't know much about herding. But she listened to my calls, moved her body with Storm's, and let him do his job of pushing them back through the broken fence. Her horse sense was as high as any horseperson I'd ever met, including my sister, Ashley. Once the last cow was across, I hopped down and grabbed my work gloves. She followed suit.

I held out the clippers to her. "Hold these. If you don't mind?"

Our fingers brushed in the transfer, and a zing

surged through me. Why did she do that to me? I dropped my head, concentrating on the fence and not her body five inches from me. I needed to splice the broken ends together and make sure they were strong enough to hold the cows this time.

She held the cut strands so I could work on them. "Was it hard coming back home? After life in the military?"

I settled my gaze on the line of trees and the hills that rolled away from them. The air brought the call of a hawk. Her question was getting near dangerous waters. Something could slip. Something that she wasn't prepared to know, and I wasn't willing to risk.

I changed the subject. "I love this place, the space, the fields filled with cows or horses or both, the warm nights and autumns that last for months, the years that we go to Christmas in Davidson in shorts, and the fact we can swim in the lake in May or September."

"You didn't answer my question."

"I need those." I nodded my chin at the clippers. "I loved my life as a SEAL, and I'd be lying if I said I didn't miss it."

"What did you love about it? Isn't it like the toughest post in the military? It was brutal and deadly, right?"

My heart jumped a bit, and I paused to think about my answer. I didn't plan on divulging too much to her. "It was a calling for me—protecting our country and our brothers and sisters fighting the war."

With a twist of the clippers, the wire strands meshed together. I picked up the next strand and held it out to her.

She grabbed it without meeting my eyes. "Okay. I

think I meant, not being in combat. I would think what you do now is very different than what you were trained to do."

I knitted the open wires of the last two strands together. Sweat dripped down my forehead. Once I secured the new ends, I lifted my ball cap, brushed my hair back, and fitted it back on my head. She wasn't wrong, so I thought about my words carefully. Patiently, she waited for a more direct answer, reaching out her hand and petting one of the cows.

"I'm lucky—I came home. But yes, that's the part I miss most.

"Your unit?"

"No, my brothers." I gave the fence a little shake. "I think that will hold it."

Her eyes met mine for a fraction of a second and then settled on the horses hobbled and grazing nearby. "Did you ever have to do something you didn't like?" she asked. "You know, something you didn't agree with? Did you ever go against what you thought was right?"

How did she know? Anger white and hot surged in my gut—not at her, at the memory. Ghani's face flashed through my mind, the feel of his small hand in mine transferring the flash drive to me, what we had come for.

"How about Jack?" I asked. "Did he love his job? Did he go against his principles?" My tone sounded more defensive than I had meant. I wasn't sure I really wanted this answer.

She hesitated a fraction. "He was committed to it. I think sometimes it weighed on him—the decisions he made that affected innocent people. Near the end, one or two of his last trips overseas, he came back torn up. But he liked it. He certainly never confided in me that he wanted a different job."

She was right about him liking it, but it wasn't that simple. He was devoted to it. If anyone knew that fact, it was me. He'd taken the fall or part of the fall for my actions. I walked back to Snickers and slid the pliers into a pocket hanging off the saddle. Should I tell her now that I knew what he did, what he sacrificed, that maybe I was the reason he was in the ground?

"Not that his job was anything like yours," she said. "From what I understood, he did a lot of research—or at least that's what he told me—relations in the Middle East, between the military and the local tribes. Also, something having to do with the drug trade. He said a lot of the drugs were coming in from the Middle East." Her face held a pensive expression like she was trying to figure something out.

I snorted a half-laugh and swung up into the saddle.

"What's so funny?" She pulled Storm over to a fallen tree and mounted.

I loved the way her jeans molded around her ass and legs. I cursed under my breath. I was a jerk. *What am I doing?* I couldn't help myself, but I knew I shouldn't be attracted to Jack's wife when I was possibly a cause of his death and most definitely a contributing factor to his drinking and demise of his career.

"Not funny," I said. "More like pathetic. Some of my work was in those mountains in Afghanistan and Tajikistan. You should have seen the fields of poppies and the amount of opium coming out of those countries.

Their two biggest weapons are their terrorist ideologies backed by stolen Russian arms and drugs. And they'll do anything to further both." Ghani's tortured corpse, severed extremities, and dead family filled my mind. "They don't care who they use or kill to further their agenda."

"Is that what it was like? Watching people use other people to get what they wanted?"

There was horror in her voice, which didn't bode well for the truth about Jack or me. Hell would freeze over before I answered that question. I sorted my reins and rubbed Snickers's withers. "Let's head home."

"CJ?" Her tone had morphed into annoyance. There was nothing I could do about that. I wasn't answering any more of her questions.

I turned Snickers toward home. "You want to race again?"

Her gaze skated over my face. Could she tell I was done sharing my secrets?

"Fine," she said.

A breathlessness tempered the annoyance, so that was good. Maybe I could distract her with speed.

I let Snickers move out into a canter. When Storm's hoofbeats sounded next to us, and Finley flashed me a come-and-get-me grin, I urged Snickers faster. Finley took the bait, and we raced stride for stride. The wind whipped through the horses' manes, and Snickers snorted as he pushed his head forward, trying to get ahead of Storm. Finley's laughter carried backward, the sound warming me. I didn't want to be the one to give her the bad news, to ruin what she knew about Jack. I didn't want to do anything that would ruin this moment.

We approached my backfield and slowed down. The other horses raced across the pasture to greet us. Storm jigged a bit, picking up on their energy. Finley patted him gently, not the least bit disturbed. We left the edge of the pasture and wound back up to the hunting cabin on the edge of the property. From there, we could see clear down to Finley's house and even catch a glimpse of mine. We stopped for a minute.

"Great view," Finley said.

The green and brown fields rolled away from up here, dotted with cows and fences. The trees were a mix of fiery reds, golden yellows, and bright oranges. There was no place on Earth I'd rather be.

I breathed deeply, my eyes taking in all the colors, relishing the sprawling space. "It's what I need to see and hear when the world gets too much, when I can't keep out the memories of war. It gives me peace."

What I didn't tell her: It helps me stay sane, keeps me connected to the world here and not the overwhelming pain or, even worse, the void of nothingness that resided within me after combat.

Finley's gaze held mine, her eyes shimmering in the afternoon sun. A hawk circling above cried. She broke her gaze and nodded toward the cabin—a little ramshackle wooden hut. "Whose is that?"

"Hank and Neeley Bennett's. It's right on the property line, but he never uses it." I glanced down. As if mocking me, footprints dotted the ground around the falling-down porch. My heart lurched. I jerked my eyes away and scanned through the trees, searching for anyone or anything suspicious. I'd give good odds that Hank hadn't been up here in weeks. I prodded Snickers forward toward the cabin porch. Cigarette butts littered the ground as well as scrunched up cans of cheercola. Hank didn't drink it anymore, not in years, not since his diagnosis of diabetes. Someone was trespassing. Both the Easterly's brothers favorite drink was cheercola. In high school they drank it by the case, and not much had changed about them since then.

"Do you just toss your cans on the ground?" Disdain colored her voice.

"What?" She was as changeable as the little lizards that dotted my front porch. "No. Those aren't mine."

"You had cheercola in your fridge."

"You're in North Carolina, sweetheart." I drawled it out just to annoy her. "Everyone drinks cheercola. It's our drink. That and moonshine." That may have been an exaggeration, but her accusation pissed me off, which was probably good. There was no point in deluding myself and getting wrapped up in the beauty of her, especially in this place.

I swung Snickers's head toward home, still scanning the horizon. Finley and Storm followed suit. "Has Wade or Troy been into the coffeehouse recently?"

Finley shot a look my way. "Wade comes in every day. Why?"

"Were they asking any questions?"

For a moment, I wondered if the Easterlys were using her to spy on me. In a perfect world, we were two people becoming friends, maybe more, on an innocent trail ride. But the world we lived in was far from innocent. It was filled with real estate sharks, power-hungry cops, drug dealers, and killers. People tried to get ahead at all costs. I'd found through the years that nothing ever was what it seemed. She was keeping secrets. And Jack had enemies—so she did, too. I'd agreed to help her, but nothing more, and I needed to remember that.

She speared me with a sharp look. "What happened between the three of you?"

This was just as off limits as my past career, so I parlayed. "Do you know Ian Monroe? He was a friend of Jack's."

She pulled her bottom lip in and bit down on it.

I hoped this wasn't a mistake.

"What is it?" she asked. "How do you know Ian?" Her voice fluttered at a higher octave than normal.

"Jack met him that last night. Before he drove home."

"He did?" Her voice rose with surprise.

"Yes. I take it you didn't know."

"Jack did lots of things I didn't know." An edge replaced the surprise. Her eyes darted around the yard.

"What about Flower Hill?"

She shifted in the saddle. "What about it?"

"Do you know what it is? Why Jack might have gone there?"

"Ian had a perp in there from a case years before. Why are you asking about all this stuff?" The edge had morphed to panic or maybe anxiety.

I reined in Snickers in front of her and inspected her face. Panic—definitely panic. "Listen, I know this isn't easy. Reliving the days before he died, but you asked me for help, and help means dissecting everything that happened near Jack's death."

She smiled at me, but the warmth didn't touch her eyes. "It's very interesting how you want to dive into my life, and yet you can't give me answers to my questions, not anything with some meat to it."

"What does that mean?"

An errant bug landed on her arm, and she brushed it away. "You're vague. Guarded. Friendship requires an exchange of information, some kind of trust. It's not a one-way street."

I laughed. "That's like the badger talking to the coonhound."

She frowned at me. "I have no idea what that means. And you know what? It doesn't matter. I can't do this again. I have kids to take care of." Her voice was clipped and tense, full of anger. I'd gone too far, which was just like me. So much for the heavenly day I'd been blathering on about in my mind.

I reached a hand out to place it on her saddle, but I thought better of it and patted Snickers's neck instead. "What do your kids have to do with this?"

"I'm a mom. Alone. My kids have to do with everything. If you don't get that, you don't get me. At all."

The anger was gone, replaced with bitterness. I touched something, got closer to the center of her own lies and secrets. And she didn't like it.

She pulled Storm's head around, bypassing Snickers and me, and slid off. Watching her walk him into the barn, I had the distinct feeling that, like Ginger, she was back against the stall wall and trying to decide if she should charge at me or make a run for the gate.

We untacked and groomed the horses. The silence was palpable. Every now and then, she murmured a word or two to Storm, but otherwise we were quiet, just the swish of brushes against the horses' hair. I threw her a lead rope, and we walked the horses outside to their pasture.

I hated that our ride was ruined, but I couldn't share too much with her. Once I started, I wasn't sure I could stop, and disaster lay in that direction. Maybe she felt the same way. "Can't you just let it lie and take it for what it was, a great day for a ride?"

She huffed, which was actually cute and annoying all at the same time.

My insides tightened, and I grabbed her arm. "What's that supposed to mean?"

She yanked her arm free. Shit. I was an idiot sometimes.

"I'm sorry," I said. "I didn't mean to grab you."

She glared at me. I just didn't want her to leave while still angry with me. Sometimes I let my past, all my baggage, get the better of me. Sometimes tweaking people was just easier than dealing with my own feelings.

"Didn't mean to grab me? People don't grab other people just by accident."

"You're right—I know. I'm sorry." Damn, the fire in her eyes was sexy. "I'm an idiot. Look, we had a good ride today. Can we just enjoy it?"

"Guys don't have guilt or responsibilities like women. They wreck your life and leave you stranded at the world's mercy. But oh no, they had a good time, so everything's okay. And you're left to pick up the pieces—to make something out of nothing."

"Are you talking to me or Jack?"

Her eyes glistened. "Does it matter? He wasn't Mr. Open Book either. And where am I left? Wondering if he was killed. With two kids to raise. Wondering if I'm in danger from someone in his past. I'm in enough trouble. I don't need his shit, which I know nothing about, haunting me and messing things up. And I don't need you asking me questions about him. It's none of your business."

I reached out to gently touch her arm. She jerked away.

"I promised myself when I moved here that I'd stand on my own two feet and do something for myself by getting my business up and running. Getting sidetracked by you is the wrong thing." Pivoting on her boot heel, she strode back to the barn. Her shoulders slumped, but her stride was purposeful.

I called out after her: "Why am I sidetracking you? You asked *me* for help."

She threw her arms up in the air as if I should know better and kept going. I stared after her, completely dumbfounded. Then I picked up the lead ropes and walked back. Every sane part of me said to let her go and be done with her because she was right— I couldn't level with her.

Of course, the other part, the part that hated losing, the part that reveled in that vanilla and cinnamon scent, that part wanted to pull her closer and tell her all my dirty secrets. Secrets that no one needed to know.

Chapter 27

Finley

With shaking fingers, I unzipped his sister's boots and placed them in the trunk. I hadn't been fair. I knew that. He didn't know the full story. I hadn't been anymore truthful with him than he with me. He didn't know how freaked out I was by all those questions, that maybe not only did I have to worry about Michael coming after me but also maybe some crazy jerk that Jack messed with. The last thing I wanted to do was tell this guy about my sordid past and all my stupid mistakes. Maybe I shouldn't have let him talk me out of leaving. Maybe if we moved, we could put everything behind us. Of course, if Jack was really killed, would his killer want to come after us, too? Did Jack know, and that's why he told me to keep moving? My stomach turned sour at the thought. I swallowed the bile rising in my throat and pulled the flash drive from my pocket. I glanced CJ's way, changed my mind, and shoved the drive back in my pocket.

CJ met me at my rental car. I unlocked the door and pulled it open, but he wrapped his hand around the door frame, tapping his index finger. The color of his hair on his arms was less like nutmeg and more like brown toast. It matched what I saw on his chest when he hooked his sunglasses on his T-shirt. Strange how I could notice such simple and pleasant things when my life felt out of control. My stomach tightened—and so did all my muscles below. Part of me wanted to freeze the moment and the delicious throbbing and heightened sense of touch and time that pervaded every bit of me when I was near him. The other part—the sane, controlled part—told me to get out now. Nothing good came from feelings like this, and my life was living proof of it.

He still held my door. I motioned to his hand, but he didn't move it.

"I'd like to think—" He cleared his throat and tried again. "I like to think I didn't distract you as much as relax you."

I huffed at that. He looked utterly complexed, vulnerable even.

"I get that this business is important to you," he said, "and that you're not sure how to get it off the ground. I'm not like an asshole guy trying to discourage you. In fact, I think it's great. I know what it's like starting a business, and I want to help, even if that is just going for a ride or crushing you in a game of ping-pong."

I gave him a sideways glance. "You didn't crush me. We were neck and neck the whole time."

His lip quivered just a smidge. "Look," he said, "when you showed up here, you radiated stress. Two minutes riding and you were a different person." He held out a business card.

"What's this?" I dragged my gaze upward. His face was inches from mine. My heart ricocheted around in my chest.

"I'm doing a session at this equine therapy place

tomorrow with a whole bunch of vets. The owners of the farm are friends of mine. They cater in sandwiches but never have much for dessert. Bring a host of your desserts for the luncheon. If Annie likes them, you could become a regular supplier. People under stress love to gorge on desserts."

I thought of how he looked talking about the war and being a SEAL. Hard, rough, and demanding. But he was more than those prickly, rough edges.

I took a deep breath. "I'm sorry. I just got—" I paused, searching for the words. "—frustrated and overwhelmed. I'm not sure staying is the right decision for us."

"Please take the card and come. Please. Not for me. For the rest of the guys—my brothers."

I pulled out the flash drive and gave it to him. "This is partly why I was so stressed today. Cody found this in Jack's office and tried to use it but discovered it had some kind of encrypted file. I tried to open it too but with no luck. I can't tell who it's from. I don't even know if it's important, but it seemed so strange. I thought maybe you should look at it."

He took it, his forehead furrowed. "I might need to send it out."

"That's fine."

"Listen, I know you're scared and worried, but we'll figure it out. You've got this. I think you're way tougher than you give yourself credit for. Have some faith."

I got in my car, and he closed the door after me. Leaning in, he reached out and tapped my sunglasses down onto my face. His knuckle grazed my cheek. "I see you, DC. I *see* you. Don't sell yourself short. I sure as hell wouldn't."

I didn't know what to say. All the words, all the anger, all the frustration slipped from my mind, and all I wanted to do was kiss him.

He tapped the roof. "Bring those chocolate chip cookies and the peanut butter bars tomorrow."

I almost laughed out loud. Those bars were my dad's favorite. "The butt bars?"

He peered back in the car window, amusement crinkling the corners of his eyes. "Is that what you call them?"

"They have graham cracker crumbs, a stick of butter, and chocolate and peanut butter chips. They don't make your butt smaller."

His answering laugh echoed in my ears as I drove away.

Chapter 28

CJ

The small flash drive weighed a thousand pounds in my hands. What could Jack have hidden there and why? Something he didn't want other people to see. I had a few ideas but hoped I was wrong. I limped back to the house and inserted the flash drive. The file was just as she told me, and it wouldn't open for me either.

I called Owen. "I've got a flash drive here that Finley found. It's got an encrypted file on it."

"Send it to me." He rattled off an address, and in seconds a copy of the flash drive was on its way to his computer.

"You want the actual drive too?"

"It wouldn't hurt. Overnight it to me when you get a chance."

"Okay. It might be nothing."

Owen snorted. "Yeah right, and Gretzky isn't the greatest hockey player."

"I know." I fought the urge to punch the wall and went out to feed the horses. I had a long night of staking out Finley's house ahead of me.

****

The next day, I waited for Finley at Annie's horse farm. I wondered if she would back out, but she showed, looking hot as hell. She emerged from the back seat of her car with platters of food. I grabbed one of them. The scent of butter, vanilla, and cinnamon floated up and dragged me back to the day Ginger had kicked me and I met Finley.

"What's in this pan?"

"Butter tarts."

"Were you making these the day Ginger got loose?"

She smiled. "Yes. Good memory."

My memory was anything but good, but the sight of her leaning over me was the best image to fill my mind in years and one I revisited all the time.

We carried the platters into the pavilion set up for group meetings. Finley arranged the platters, trying to put forth what side showed the best. It didn't matter. The vets swarmed around. One guy, balancing on his crutches and his remaining leg, swiped one from each plate. "These are really good," he said, a cookie in his mouth. A few others, munching away, nodded their approval and gave her thumbs up.

She smiled back, her eyes sparkling. "Thanks."

My gaze drifted over her. She wore jeans and a deep wine-colored top that draped across her front, slipping off one shoulder as she moved.

For all her prickliness and toughness, there was a vulnerability that came through, especially when she talked about her baking. As if she didn't want to dare to dream too much because odds were, it wouldn't happen for her. I wanted her to succeed. I wanted for everyone in this town to taste her genius desserts and bang down her doors for them.

And that bare shoulder peeking out—I wanted to kiss it. Maybe I shouldn't, maybe I even couldn't, but that didn't mean I wanted anyone else to either. I could be a jealous jerk sometimes. I stole one of her butter squares and popped it into my mouth. "Want to take a walk?"

"Sure." She sure didn't sound so sure. Her head swiveled around. "This place is really nice."

"Yeah. It was all Annie's doing, you know. She merged her two passions, horses with psychology and therapy. Her husband totally supported her in making this place and getting all the accreditations and credentials and what she needed to run a licensed equine therapy program. It's about twenty acres total."

"That must have taken a lot of work."

"Annie's a go-getter. She had a friend with an injured son who could never get the right care. Annie always said she watched her friend struggle, and she wanted to help her and others like her."

Finley reminded me of Annie. There was the same quietness and strength to each of them.

We took one of the paths that cut off from the lot. "They opened up five years ago, and they've really done some great things. They work with people with all kinds of issues, from teens with eating disorders to veterans with depression and PTSD. The barn holds eight horses, and they have a few fields with run-in shelters. That building next to the barn is their meeting center."

"What's over there?" She pointed toward a smaller barn and enclosure.

"Two pot-bellied pigs, four goats, and two bunnies. They use all the animals for therapy." The sound of barking filled the air. "And, of course, cats and dogs."

She cast a sideways look at me, a small smile

playing at the corners of her mouth.

"What?"

"I've never heard you sound so excited."

"I love it here. I think what they're doing is really important." I glanced at her and tried to figure out if now was a good time to tell her some truths. "That house you're in is actually my grandparents' old house. I spent a lot of time there growing up. When they ran into some financial issues, they were forced to sell it and the land and move into the parcel I'm on now. I want to buy it all back—for them, even though they're dead, and for me. We'd always planned to open up an equine rescue center to help all those horses who wind up in auctions, and I want to do that still and maybe also equine therapy."

"That's why you know so much about the house?"

I nodded. She didn't say anything for a bit except to chew on her lip.

"What?" I didn't know why I cared what she thought but I did.

"Interesting. And impressive. To have goals like that." She nudged me with her hip, her smile wider now. "And cute."

Nobody had ever called me cute. Never. And for a minute, I enjoyed it and the way she said it.

Before us, the path wound its way along the perimeter of the farm, all twenty acres with benches and tables dotting the way. I stopped at one of my favorite spots. A little higher up than the rest of the property, it gave a good view of the fields sloping off and horses grazing. To the right, I could see the veterans I had spoken to earlier eating Finley's desserts before their afternoon session. From the smiles on their faces, they were enjoying them. She could make this business work. Here. With me.

Finley immediately went to see about the horses. They came to the fence, searching for attention. She murmured to them but stopped when I came up and handed her a sandwich.

She motioned with her sandwich in the horses' direction. "What's with these guys?"

"I don't think Annie needed them for today's session. We can groom them if you want." A grooming box with brushes hung on the fence.

"I'm not exactly dressed for it but sure." She adjusted her shirt, pulling it over her exposed shoulder. If I flicked one of the sleeves slightly, her shirt would slip back down. Clavicle to shoulder. I wanted to trace my fingers over them. What was wrong with me? If I was in the field, I'd have gotten us shot and killed by now from lack of focus.

I dug in my pocket and handed her the list I had been working on.

"What's this?"

"A list of the events in town throughout the year. I'm sure your boss has his hands full running the coffeehouses and just isn't sure about making the jump with you. If you sell your desserts at the farmer's market and other events, that may sway him enough. Or else you can build your business up enough not to need anything. You could get your own booth. It's how Griff and I spread the word when we started. Then your own farm—like Annie if you want."

She half shook her head. "I don't—"

"There's no reason you couldn't do what she did."

"No. There are a million."

"Are any of them valid?"

Lips pursed, she perused it up and down, and lots of nice and dirty thoughts flooded my mind.

"Thank you. I've never had anyone who actually believed in my ideas. Not since my parents—" She raised her eyes to mine, and they glistened in the sun. "I appreciate it more than you know."

She tucked the list into her back pocket and ducked through the fence. The horses had wandered away but came back in search of treats. Clipping lead shanks to each of their halters, we loosely tied them to the fence. I handed her a brush, our fingers touching, and that warm zing zipped up my arm. It was that same feeling I got when I balanced a rifle on my shoulder and took aim, or from the satisfying *thunk* of my ax connecting to a log—it was focused, peaceful, nothing else existed in that moment.

She smiled, and her eyes lit up. I wished for more because it filled me with peace, the way she looked. She turned away and whispered a few words to the golden-colored horse she was brushing.

For a few seconds, the only sound was the scratch of the brushes against the horses' coats and the light breeze through the trees. I concentrated on the motion of the brush, on the soft feel of the coat of fur beneath my fingers, in the rise and fall of horses' breath. And with it, the rest of the world and all the tension from this morning faded away. Maybe I could tell her about Jack, about that last op. Like me, she was scarred too— but her scars just weren't as visible.

Without even thinking, the words tumbled out of my mouth. "What is it about horses that helps?"

Finley shook her head. "I don't know. But I've

always loved them and been drawn to them ever since I can remember. Maybe because when you're with them, you must be in the present, you must be present for them."

There was a few seconds of silence and the swiping of her brush. "Did you need it after you got hurt?"

"Yes." I brushed out a patch of dried-on mud. I owed her some honesty, and I didn't want to ruin the time we had. "Life without being a SEAL was hard for me to do. I had a lot of injuries and flashbacks too. Stuff I'd always been able to do, I suddenly couldn't."

"Jack didn't have flashbacks." Her voice wavered. "He didn't do dangerous stuff, but he definitely was changed when he came back from overseas."

A pang of guilt stabbed me. He didn't do the ground maneuvers, but he had the dangerous knowledge. He came back different in part because of me. She paused her brushing and locked her gaze on me. Those steel-colored eyes, seemingly wanting more, pierced right to my soul. "I can't—" I paused. "—I can't be in crowded places. Or tight places. I was trapped once. And now the anxiety. It almost kills me."

"Does Ellie help?"

I brushed vigorously at a spot for a minute even though the dried-on dirt was brushed out. "Yes, and coming here. It helps to share my story with other veterans and hear theirs. It keeps me sane and focused on moving forward. Maybe it helps to share with you too."

She tilted her head sideways and regarded me. "My mother had a saying when I got hung up on finding jump distances on a course. If you move forward with enough momentum, you won't need the perfect spot, the distance will come up naturally. Always think forward."

Her cheeks flushed pink, and she grabbed her horse's tail combing it out gently.

It was sweet, and the urge to kiss her nearly overwhelmed me. "Yeah, well, sometimes it's easy to get stuck in the past. If I don't focus on the now and make the garage business work, I'm out of ideas."

She paused again. "That's what Wade Eastley was talking about the morning we went boating?"

"Yeah. He loves dredging up the past. That guy's a real prince."

She went back to the tail. It nearly glowed from all her attention. "How does he know?"

"Grapevine. His old man and mine are business friends. Charlotte and its surrounding areas are pretty small, especially at certain social levels."

"I'm sorry."

"I shouldn't have been surprised. I love my parents, but placing things above people is not a new thing for them. They're into their social status and their money. My father has never liked anything I did. He's not going to start now." The words were out before I could take them back. A light above my head was either flashing *danger* or *idiot* or both. If we were on a practice maneuver, this was the moment right before the terrorist jumped out and nailed my ass.

She dropped the tail and straightened up, leaning an elbow on her horse's rump, and focused on me. I probably sounded like a bitter, entitled jerk. Anger flared in my gut for sharing such a personal story. I knew better than that.

She reached out a hand and touched my arm—just

a slight brush. I fought the urge to grab it and hold her fingers in mine. She broke her gaze from mine and rubbed her fingers through the horse's hair. "Jack was a drinker, you know. Even before he started going overseas."

The words reverberated in my head, and I almost missed the rest.

"High functioning and high achieving, but still a drinker. He could do his job, and he was super smart. But when he drank, *he drank,* and everything and everyone else faded away. He loved the kids and me, but he loved booze more."

She shrugged, but her lower lip trembled. The guilt seeped deeper.

"And maybe his job too," she said. "Those two things took all his time. He loved me when I had nobody, but it didn't come without sacrifice. I gave up a lot for him, walked away from things that were important to me. And in the end, he couldn't walk away from the booze. It doesn't make for the happiest marriages."

"I bet not." My voice broke her reverie, and she swung her gaze back to mine. Blue-gray eyes, flickering in the sunlight, locked on mine. For a long moment, everything around us stilled. I could almost touch the air between us.

She smiled and patted her horse gently before moving closer to his head. "I better go. Did you get anywhere with that flash drive?" She unhooked her horse and ducked through the fence.

"Yes. It's definitely encrypted. I sent it off to a friend to unlock it."

Her smile disappeared faster than a raccoon with

garbage. "Will it take long to break?"

I gathered up our lunch remains and pitched them into the trash. "I doubt it. Owen said he'd have an answer for me by tomorrow."

Despite her question over the encrypted file, a calm of peace settled over me. There was something about her and the horses that did it for me, helped me find peace amidst chaos. Maybe it was the way she accepted things, willing to embrace the moment offered, not fazed by sharing lunch with a bunch of dirty horses.

We walked back to the parking lot together. She motioned to the meeting place. "Do you have more to do?"

My eye caught a new car parked next to her rental: a police car. I scowled and scanned the yard for signs of the cop, hoping it wasn't Troy.

"Nah. I've got to head home." My ex was stopping by to have her car serviced. I looked forward to this as much as a root canal, but Trish seemed oblivious to my feelings toward her and her husband. Boyd indulged her in whatever she wanted.

Finley fiddled with her keys. "Great day today. Thank you."

What would she do if I reached out and kissed her?

Troy strolled out of the meeting center. "Just the people I was looking for."

Finley stepped back and with her went all my new-found peace.

"What do you want, Troy?" I tried and failed to keep the irritation from my voice. If I quit showing how he pissed me off, then he might lose interest in screwing with me. But I'd failed miserably in that task.

"Well, that's the funny thing." He pointed his cola

can at Finley. "I'm here looking for her."

"Me?" Finley's voice nearly squeaked in surprise. "Why?"

"I got a call from Dana McIntyre."

Finley stared blankly at Troy.

"She's the nice lady who owns Fair Acres Farm in Mooresville. Seems like they had a break-in two days ago and a whole bunch of saddles were stolen. And when I went there to talk to her about things, she told me about a run-in she had with you."

"A run-in?"

"You caused some trouble there with one of her instructors."

Finley pushed her hair behind her ears. "It wasn't really trouble."

"I think she'd dispute that. The only occurrence she could come up with since the farm opened was this run in with you, so that makes you a prime suspect."

"In a robbery?" There was an unmistakable shake to her voice.

"You are new here. Aren't you?"

"I didn't rob any barn or steal any saddles."

"I guess we'll see about that. Where have you been the last two nights?"

"Home with my kids."

Troy leaned in toward Finley, too close, and she backed up a step. "Is that the only alibi you have?"

What a bully. I stepped in between them. "Troy, this is ridiculous. We're going."

I all but propelled Finley to my truck and nearly threw her inside of it. I cranked it; it sputtered. Not now.

Troy approached.

I tried again, and this time it caught. I reversed out of the parking lot. "He's a jackass."

"I don't think he was done." Her eyes were shiny.

"Well, I was. He was trying to strong arm and intimidate you. I can't stand people in power manipulating others. It's bullshit."

She rocked forward in the seat. "Why would he think I stole saddles? Why would anyone accuse me?"

"I don't know. I don't even think Dana was that upset that day. I talked to her after."

"I can't be charged with stealing saddles."

"No one's going to charge you with anything. They don't have any proof. How can they charge you with a crime you didn't commit?"

Her eyes widened like saucers, and a tear spilled over the edge and slid down her cheek. She whipped her head right and stared out the window.

I slipped my hand over hers and squeezed. "Hey, it's okay. It's a misunderstanding."

She swiped at her cheeks and turned back to give me a lopsided smile. "You didn't say goodbye to the owners. And my rental, we left it there."

"We can pick it up later. I'll send a text to Annie. She'll be fine with it."

She was silent on the way back to my place. I fought the urge to reach out and give her neck a rub.

I pulled down my driveway and turned off the truck. "He's just a jackass. Always has been. Just ignore him. He's more bark than bite." I hoped that was true—for her and for me.

She nodded. "I'm going to check on Ginger. Then I'll head home. I don't want to be late for the kids."

"Sure." I motioned to Trish's fancy car pulling in.

"That's my three o'clock. I'll come find you after."

She hopped down and strode toward the barn. Her jeans and shirt hugged her just right. I didn't think I'd ever get tired of that view.

I rubbed my scar. I wasn't as sure as I had acted with Finley. Troy could be a scumbag when he wanted to. My head ached. I took a swig of cola, exited my truck, and steeled myself for the coming storm of Trish and her new husband, Boyd.

Boyd stood outside his car, and Trish sat in the passenger seat. She unfolded herself from the car and came toward me. "Hey, handsome."

Screw her, cooing like I still wanted what she was never going to offer. She wore a bright-blue sweater that brought out her eyes and skin-tight leggings. Trish had a nice body. Since hitting her thirties, her boobs had increased generously in size, thanks in part to a doctor in Charlotte.

Trish wasn't entirely fake. She just knew what she wanted: marriage, kids, a golf club membership, and friends in all the right places. I'd wanted none of it except for the kids, and when I couldn't give her those, she traded me in for someone who could. Of course, it would have helped if she'd leveled with me instead of hopping into bed with the golf pro at our country club. There's nothing like hobbling in after a day of rehab to find an able-bodied man, ten years your junior, screwing your wife doggy-style.

"Trish." I tried to muster some enthusiasm.

Boyd padded behind her, and I couldn't help thinking he was used to that position. Right down to his name, Boyd oozed good breeding and money. Of course, I knew him—we'd attended the same schools early on, then rival schools later. Population aside, Charlotte heralded a small-town attitude, especially the established upper echelon.

Boyd and Trish had met and gotten married just under a year after we'd split, and they already had twins, a boy and a girl.

"Where are the kids?"

"Oh, we left them with Mama." Her accent was drawled out. "It's like a dream come true for her to have them to herself. You know me, I'm all about my daughterly duties." She pushed her designer sunglasses up on her head and gave me a dazzling smile.

Yeah, I knew her. Trish possessed the impressive ability to turn anything selfish into a selfless deed. She threw a bright smile Boyd's way before turning it back on me. "Besides, Boyd and I needed some time to ourselves."

I waited silently, but she didn't say anything more. Instead, she perused the yard—eyes narrowed, disdain evident.

I didn't want her here tainting my refuge. "What's up?"

Boyd stepped forward. "Our car's making a suspicious noise. We thought maybe you could check it out before we trek all the way up into the mountains."

Trish pushed one of the dogs away and brushed off her pants. "I'm going to get a cola." She headed for the barn.

It ticked me off the way she still acted like she knew everything around here. Including me. The sooner they were gone, the better. I tapped the hood for Boyd to release it. He did and then joined me at the front.

"I heard the Eastleys are buying up all the land

around you," Boyd said.

"How do you know that?"

A guilty look flitted across his face. "Trish saw your dad the other day. Bumped into him and Wade's dad at the club, having lunch."

Just like my dad. Business above all else.

Boyd went on. "Apparently, Wade's got some big-time builder interested in the land. Hopes to close the deal soon."

As if conjured by words alone, Troy's cop car slowly drove down my driveway and came to a stop a few feet away. Wonderful. Why couldn't he ever let anything go?

I glanced at the barn. Trish hadn't come out, and neither had Finley. If I knew anything about Trish, it was that she was never okay with another woman. She didn't want me, but she didn't seem to want anybody else wanting me. She'd been playing that game since high school. For a day that had started with such promise, it was turning sideways quicker than a torpedoed submarine.

Chapter 29

Finley

I turned Ginger out, and she bolted, almost knocking me down in her rush to get past. I spun around to see what scared her and spied a tall, slender woman yapping on her phone on the other side of the pasture fence, gesturing with her hand in the air.

Sides heaving and feet dancing, Ginger glared at the woman. Ignoring her antics, I slipped off her halter and rubbed her face. Ginger calmed down and then wandered off in search of hay. I ducked back through the fence and headed for the barn. Hopefully, the Animal Control guy would consider her tamed and trained. At least she hadn't kicked anyone or run away recently.

The stranger gave me a half-nod but still had her phone attached to her ear. I smiled in return as I walked past. When I came out of the tack room, the woman stood in the doorway. She eyed me up and down.

"Who are you?" Not exactly a warm southern greeting.

I held my hand out. "I'm Finley. You?"

She gave it a limp shake, after which she inspected her own hand for dirt. "Trish. You're new."

The ex in the flesh. I glanced out the barn doors, searching for CJ. A fancy car sat in his driveway with its hood propped up.

"CJ's working on my car," she said. "My husband and I are heading up to the mountains, but it's making a funny noise, and you know, CJ always does *all* my work."

There wasn't much to answer to that. I grabbed a soda out of the tack room and popped it open. "Would you like a drink?"

"I know where it is. I'm fine." She waved her hand in the air. "I used to live here."

According to CJ, they'd been living at their old house in Charlotte and renovating this place when he'd caught her in bed with another guy. He'd told me she had fought with him about moving here; she hated it so much. But far be it from me to tell her where anything was.

She surveyed the barn area, wrinkling her petite nose. "Do you work here?"

"No." I tried to sidestep around her, but she didn't move. I resisted the urge to knock her out of the way.

"Oh." She dragged the word out, her tone dripping with contempt. "You must be the new one."

Screw manners. I pushed past her, but she grabbed my arm.

"I have no idea what he's told you, but let me save you the time and trouble. He can't have kids—you know that, right? And all the money's tied up too."

I studied her face—not a single wrinkle.

"Bless his heart, but he's infertile. Has been since high school."

He wasn't an open book, but today I'd gotten more info than ever before. Yet I was still in the dark about this guy. The expression on his face whenever anyone mentioned kids now made sense.

She stared down her perky nose at me, a look of superiority and pity all wrapped into one. "Oh my, does he have you snowed? Do you actually believe this whole redneck blue-collar mechanic gig he has going? That boy grew up in one of the nicest neighborhoods around Charlotte. He went to all private schools and would have inherited his daddy's real estate business—if he didn't have it in his head to follow his granddad's footsteps and go into the military. Threw his whole future away for what? Came back ruined. Couldn't take his daddy's position for anything."

She was a total piece of work. I smiled and leaned forward as if imparting some secret. "Listen, don't feel threatened. I'm just using him for sex."

I don't know what came over me to lie like that—except for the overwhelming need to protect him and tick her off. She'd hurt him. I could tell, and I didn't like it one bit.

She dropped my arm like it was a hot poker and stepped back. Even with the Botox, the horror and anger were evident on her face as if she'd just swallowed glass. She took a deep breath, gathering herself.

"I'm not threatened," she spat. "It's you with your smug attitude who should be worried about the things he hasn't told you and all the things he can't do. At one point he was an all-American lacrosse player. Now he can barely walk a mile. I can't even imagine"—she waved a hand through the air in the direction of CJ's house—"how all *that's* working out for you. Well, I'm going to the house. I left something of mine there and I want it."

She raised her chin at me as if challenging me to answer her, turned, and headed out the door.

I brushed by her, but my laugh was short-lived as soon as I saw Troy standing near CJ.

CJ lowered the hood, his jaw clenched. Troy, scowling as usual, jabbed his finger in CJ's direction. CJ turned toward him, his eyes flashing with warning.

I fought the urge to fold myself into his side.

"He's not going to let it go," he whispered. "How's it going on your end?"

Ellie positioned herself next to me. I reached down and stroked her head. "Fine. Just fine."

"All done, CJ?" Boyd called from the driver's side.

"Yep. Just a loose valve. You're good to go."

"Great." He came forward and shook CJ's hand and then held it out to me. "Boyd Bradford."

"Finley Thompson."

Miss Superiority had regained her composure by now and strode out of the house as if she still lived there.

"CJ, doll—" She raised a bottle of top-shelf vodka into the air. "—this is mine. But this must be all yours." She tossed the plastic baggie containing the drugs in our direction. It hit the ground and busted open, scattering pills and joints everywhere. "I found it in your freezer."

I wasn't sure if she meant to cause him harm or maybe it was her way of trying to drive me off. For a moment, everyone froze, except Troy. His eyes lit up like a snake on the hunt for a frog but luckily stumbled onto a mouse. He closed the distance to the spray of pills and joints in two steps, grabbing for his handcuffs as he did so.

I knelt and quickly gathered up the evidence. "These are mine."

Troy was quicker and glowered at me. "Step away from the evidence."

"I'm sorry. I stashed them in CJ's freezer." My hands swiped through the gravel.

"Finley—" Filled with barely suppressed anger, CJ's voice was quiet but firm. "—don't."

I met his eyes from my bent position, and he shook his head. I hesitated, and my heart twisted with fear for CJ. Hadn't he just told me about crowded cramped spaces? What would they do with him if he got arrested?

Troy's eyes gleamed. "Do you want to be a thief and a drug addict? Don't you have kids? Besides, unless you can prove to me you're Connell James Sinclair or Henry Baker, that's not going to work."

Troy's words hammered home what I knew CJ had been thinking. I had more than myself to think about. I stood up slowly, leaving the drugs strewn there.

Troy clasped CJ's hand behind his back and slapped the cuffs on in two quick swoops.

"Connell James Sinclair, you're under arrest for violating the NC General Statute 90-95(a)(3), possession of more than half an ounce of marijuana, and 90-108, possession of a controlled substance without a valid prescription."

"Troy, this is a bogus charge, and you know it. Give me a ticket and be done with it."

"Fat chance, Sinclair. My discretion."

Trish bounded down the steps, hands clasped. "CJ—"

His glower cut her off. "Save it, Trish. I'm

officially firing you as a client. I would say, always a pleasure, but it never is."

She shrunk back against Boyd, which was lucky for her because I wanted to skewer her.

I followed them to the patrol car, my fists clenched so hard they ached. Before he ducked into the back seat, CJ met my eyes.

"Call Griff. He'll know what lawyer to call. And if I can't get out tonight, tell him to stay here. I don't want you alone."

Every part of me wanted to run screaming at Troy and beat him senseless. Owen was supposed to call about that file, and even more importantly, CJ wouldn't be able to handle where Troy was taking him. But I rooted my feet to the ground, knowing that reacting would do nothing except get me thrown in that car next to CJ.

Troy smirked at me as he walked around to the driver's side. "I told you he was bad news. You think you would have learned by now."

There was something in the way he said it with that smug smile. Chills ran up my spine. Troy knew something about me.

Chapter 30

CJ

I'd been locked up before. During SEAL training, we were routinely forced into small, cramped spaces to test our abilities to cope. I hadn't had a problem with it, or if I had, my desire to win outweighed my claustrophobia. This time was different. This time was post-injuries, and I was without Ellie.

I dropped my head in that crowded cell and employed every mental game I could muster to be somewhere else in my mind. I prayed that Finley and Griff pulled whatever strings they had to get me out of this hell hole in the quickest amount of time, but I knew there was only so much that could be done. Troy had known that too. Whether or not he knew the true torture it was, this was by far the most evil thing he'd ever done to me.

By the time morning rolled around, I was a wet sopping mess of nerves and had exhausted all my mental resources for tight locked-up spaces.

A lawyer friend of Griff's sprung me at ten o'clock in the morning. The clerk returned my personal effects, and the lawyer led me back out onto the street. I'd never been so happy for fresh air.

"I'm sorry it took me so long. A crowded courtroom this morning." He smiled, white teeth in a dark face. "The charges won't stick, but we do have to go through all the required hoops."

I shook his hand. "Thank you."

"I'll be in touch. Griff told me he'd meet you at the corner of Trade and Fifth."

Every muscle in my body ached from dozing on a hard metal bench. I walked the few blocks to the corner of Trade and Fifth Street, but it was Finley who pulled up, not Griff.

Ellie sat in the passenger seat, and relief flooded me. I hauled myself inside, and Ellie nearly climbed into my lap, tail wagging and tongue lolling. I let her cover me. Spreading my fingers through her fur, I concentrated on holding onto my last thread of sanity. *Don't lose it.* I repeated the mantra to myself as Finley negotiated the downtown streets and got us on the highway heading north. I knew I needed to say something, but all my energy was going toward holding it together.

"Get off at twenty-eight." I pointed to the right side of the highway.

She glanced my way, forehead furrowed. "Okay…"

"I'm going out on the lake. You can come, too. Whatever you want." The words came out harsher than I meant them, but I couldn't sugar coat anything right now. I needed space and air.

She just nodded and followed my directions back to the bungalow my sister and I owned on the lake. She pulled down our gravel driveway and stopped.

"Are you going for a boat ride?"

"Yes. With Ellie. Don't come if you don't like to go fast."

By the time I unfolded myself from the seat, Finley was already heading for the dock with Ellie by her side. I messed with the boat lift while Finley stood beside me.

"Are you sure about this?" I barked the words out and regretted it instantly. I knew what Troy had done wasn't her fault. It hadn't been her fault at all, and yet I had nowhere else to turn my anger, and it spilled out.

"CJ, I'm not sure about anything."

"Well, don't come if you're scared of speed."

"Listen, what I do for fun is climb on the backs of thousand-pound animals, and twenty years ago not only did I do that but also sent them over four-foot jumps at breakneck speed"—she pointed a finger in my direction—"so don't expect me to cower in the face of a fast boat ride."

Admiration and desire rushed through me. She was tough and fearless, and she wasn't going to put up with my bullshit. I lifted Ellie in the boat, lowered the boat lift, and we both climbed in. When I turned the key in the ignition, the first spark of peace since my arrest floated through me.

Chapter 31

Finley

CJ didn't say anything else except to murmur some instructions as we putted past the no-wake zone. Ellie found her spot and lay down, her head on her paws.

"You ready?" He locked his gaze on me. I nodded and tightened my grip on the side. CJ popped the gear into place, and we roared out of the cove, flying across the lake faster than I'd ever been. With each incoming wave, the bow leaped out of the water and plunged back down. Ellie didn't move a muscle; she must have been used to speed. Despite my best efforts, I squealed almost every time. After a while, he slowed and pulled into a vacant cove.

Without a word to me, he ripped his shirt over his head, emptied his shorts pockets, and dove in. He floated to the surface and struck out swimming, arms whipping over his head in sleek strokes. Fifty yards out, he slowed and reversed back to the boat. He floated on his back for a minute or two, staring at the sky, and then he hauled himself up the ladder and came on board. The water glistened on his torso and ran in rivulets down into his shorts' waistband. I couldn't help myself but follow their path. He shook his head like a dog, spraying water droplets everywhere, and collapsed on the seat next to me.

"When I was a teenager," he said, "my dad and I used to get into it—you know, teenage stuff. He'd lay into me. And when he was done, I'd sneak down to the dock, unhook the boat, and take it out here. Other than my granddad's place, it was the only place I've found peace."

He rested his head on the back of the seat, staring up at the sky. I leaned back next to him and tilted my face up to the sun.

"It's crazy how some things change so much and other things don't change at all," he said.

He was right on that. No matter where I went or who was in my life, Michael and my parents seemed to always be there. "Are you going to be okay?"

"With the law? Yeah. Griff's lawyer friend thinks he can get me off. It's really only a misdemeanor. Troy arrested me just to be an ass."

I snorted in answer and sat back up, but CJ kept his face averted, eyes focused on the sky.

"Wade and Troy have a reason to hate me. I don't like it, but I understand."

We didn't talk for a little while, and the only sound was the quiet lapping of the water at the sides of the boat. Seat-cushion filling threatened to escape from one of the rips, and I played with the cotton, pushing it back in, pulling it back out, pushing it back in again. "You can tell me," I said. "I can take it. Whatever is weighing you down, I can take it."

When I raised my gaze from the rip, his green-eyed gaze met mine. Behind them, he was grappling with whatever was eating away at him. But he leaned back again and tilted his face to the sun.

"We were all friends, you know? Years ago. Me,

Griff, Troy, and even Wade. We all grew up together, running wild as kids. Wade and I were competitive as hell with each other, but we were still friends."

His accent twanged on the last sentence, and I smiled despite myself, despite my dread. Although I didn't know what he was going to say, I knew it wouldn't be good.

"We were cocky, rowdy jerks in high school. We used to go out after games, just itching to start trouble. One day that trouble we were looking for found us. We got into it with a bunch of locals in a small town outside of Charlotte. We got outnumbered. Wade got the brunt of it. He had a mouth on him, and when they came looking for a fight, they really ganged up on him. We did our best, Griff and I, but by the time we got to Wade—" His jaw tightened. "—they messed Wade up and he missed the season. Things were never the same after that."

He blew his breath out.

"He'd been a really talented lacrosse player before it happened, but after that…" His voice trailed off thick with emotion.

"I'm sorry."

"He never forgave me. I was a chicken shit for not wading in there and helping him."

"Weren't you fighting your own guy?"

"I was, but still I had one and there were like four guys on Wade. I knew we were in trouble, overmatched. When I was done, I went for help."

"You went for help. You didn't run away—" He didn't wait for me to finish my thought.

"Wade has hated me ever since. Troy too. And I don't blame them. I became an All American and

Wade's plans evaporated." He leaned forward and ruffled his hair, spraying water everywhere.

"So you signed up for a job in which no one was ever left behind? No matter what." He didn't answer me or deny it. I let it sit for a while until I knew he wouldn't. "What's going to happen now?"

"With Wade and Troy?"

"Yeah. And the land?"

He slid down off the seat and onto the floor stretching out his legs. He folded his arms behind his head and closed his eyes. "I don't know. With a pending criminal case, it's doubtful I'll get financing, which was what they were counting on." He shrugged. "Some days I just want to come out here and forget everything."

I slid down to the floor, next to him. "I have some money saved. I could buy the land if that would help." The words flowed out as if they had a mind of their own.

He opened his eyes and stared at me for a moment. "You're impulsive as hell, aren't you? Besides, that's a lot of tip-jar money."

I backed up a few inches. That was stupid. Jack's life insurance policy was helping keep my kids and me afloat, and I hardly knew this guy. Still, I wanted to help. "I'm sorry. That was a stupid thing to offer."

He slipped his hand over mine, stilling my backward movement. "I don't mean to be mean. You act from a good place, saving Ginger and me that day, jumping on to that horse, trying to take the fall for the drugs with Troy, here with me now. You have a good heart."

I shook my head. He had no idea about me. I had

lied to him. If I was a decent person, I'd tell him the truth about me, about Jack, and even about Michael. Now. "CJ."

His hand felt warm and comforting on my own. He squeezed my fingers. "I can't accept your offer, but it's very kind."

He was right, of course—not about kindness but about acceptance. We barely knew each other. I wanted him to buy that land though and get his dream of an equine therapy place, and even more, a place for rescued horses to find sanctuary. Of course, I was ignoring a large problem, but it was easier to do that right now, easier to pretend I could make a life here, easier to think I would never have to pack up and move again.

He brushed his thumb back and forth across my knuckles, and heat pooled in my stomach. "I lied before. I find peace on the water, with the horses—" He paused. "—but also with you."

"Me?" My voice squeaked.

"Yes, you. There's a lightness in you."

I couldn't tell him the truth about my past. It was too complicated and, like his own decisions, maybe unforgivable. There was no lightness in my past. In fact, it was dark and murky. Of that, I was sure. But the last thing I wanted in the warm autumn sun was to shatter the peace of the water and ruin this moment with the baggage I carried. Instead, I told him the truth in my heart because in the moment—overlooking the fact he made me angry and frustrated and so mad I could spit nails—he made me feel right, like I was doing okay in this messed-up world of my life. "I don't know about light, but when I'm with you, I find peace too. As if who I am, is good enough."

He lifted his hand from my knuckles and traced my cheek. "It's more than good enough." My heart thundered in my chest in a way it hadn't in decades. And then his phone rang.

He groaned, threw a crooked smile my way, and reached for it resting on the console. "This better be good."

Whatever whoever said, it wasn't good because CJ gathered himself up and hobbled to the end of the boat. He sank down on the bench, listened for a minute, growled an answer into the phone, and disconnected. Head down, eyes on the ground, he rubbed his hands through his hair. He raised his gaze to me. For a brief second, they glistened in the sun. Then he pressed his lips together, and as if a mask dropped over his face, his eyes turned dry and hard. "I have to go. Now."

I pulled myself back up onto the boat bench.

"Okay. Is everything all right?"

He shook his head but didn't bother to elaborate. Instead, he fired up the engine, and we were back skipping across the water, heading home as fast as we had come.

He was silent in the car, drumming his fingers on his knee. I pulled up his driveway and parked next to Griff's black pickup. He turned to me.

"It's a SEAL thing. I've got to go out of town. I shouldn't be long. Griff will be here if you need anything."

Always secretive, even retired. This was why I was supposed to stay away.

"What about the Eastleys and the land?" I asked.

"I'm just going to have to take my chances on that.

I shouldn't be more than a few days."

His lips curved up into a half smile, and his eyes softened.

"Thank you for today. You were a godsend." He cupped my jaw, and his mouth brushed mine. Briefly.

Then his lips were gone—he was gone.

I drove home, my mind in a fog. Had he really kissed me? Did he mean it? It was so fast, so soft. Maybe it had all been in my head.

I called Mattie when I got home.

"Hey, girl. What's up?"

"Do you know anything about residential real estate?"

"Some. Why?"

"You know that landlocked parcel behind your house?"

"Yeah."

"CJ wants it, and there's a big mess with the Eastleys over it. I was thinking maybe I should put in an offer."

"Well, I know the sellers. I could represent you. You want me to contact their realtor?"

"That's the problem. It's Wade Eastley. I think he's got the inside scoop."

"Well, he's required to bring any offers to the sellers. Let me see what I can do."

I hopped in the shower replaying the entire afternoon. For a day that started out pretty shitty, it had definitely picked up. I got dressed and checked my phone—a text message from CJ.

—My contact said the file had info on drug dealers in New York. I'll see if I can find anything else out.—

What the hell was Jack doing investigating New

York drug dealers? He worked on things overseas, not domestic. I threw on some clothes and headed back to CJ's place.

Chapter 32

CJ

I shoved my suit into my duffel bag. *How stupid am I for kissing her like that? So much for staying away.* Griff watched me warily from the door. He had come to get instructions on taking care of the animals while I was gone.

"I'd tell you it's not your fault, but I doubt you'll listen to me."

"It's a bullshit statement, and you know it. I promised to keep in touch with McDavies, and now he's missing."

My phone buzzed. Owen. I held it up and motioned to Griff. "Give me one minute."

He nodded, and I turned my back on him and walked down the hall. "O. My flight lands at five."

"You gonna be okay?"

At his words, the butterflies I'd been tamping down for the last fifteen minutes multiplied by one hundred. I didn't know how I'd handle an enclosed steel contraption filled with people thirty-thousand feet in the air. *You can do this. You have to do this. For McDavies.*

Sweat trickled down my back. "Yes." I lied.

"Okay. I'll see you at the exit."

I hung up and glanced at my dresser. The menu from Jack's stuff sat there, guilting me. In the kitchen,

Griff rummaged through the fridge. I grabbed the menu. A soda can halfway to his lips, he stopped when I shoved the menu toward him. "I found this in Jack Thompson's stuff. Keep this while I'm gone, in case something happens to me."

He eyed the scribbles cautiously. "A bunch of names, company names, countries. So?"

I flipped to the page I'd conveniently hidden from Finley. As he skimmed it, his brow furrowed. "What the hell is your name doing on here?"

"He worked for the CIA. Our paths crossed." Although I never lied to Griff, I also wasn't sure how much I wanted to disclose. The less he knew, the better off for him.

"Did you see the numbers here?" Griff turned the menu sideways and pointed to a row of numbers. "Does Finley know this?"

"No. Hell, she doesn't even know her husband worked for the CIA. She thinks he worked for the State Department."

The screen door flew open, and Finley strode in, eyes blazing. In three quick steps, she was beside me. She yanked the menu from Griff's hands and scanned it.

"Why didn't you tell me about this?"

She planted her hands on her hips, and with the motion, a waft of her perfume floated over me—vanilla, some flower, and the scent of baked sugar.

"I don't know why my name is on it." That was a bit of a lie. I didn't have concrete evidence, but I had an idea.

"Really?" She waved one hand through the air. "You must have had some idea, or you wouldn't have kept it a secret. What are you hiding, CJ?"

That was a loaded question and one I had no intention of answering. "We ran in the same circles."

She narrowed her eyes at me. "Bullshit."

She didn't move an inch, except maybe to squint her eyes some more.

"Can we *not* do this now? I've had one hell of a twenty-four hours, and I need to be on a plane in two hours for New Mexico."

"You said you would help me. Why didn't you tell me you worked with Jack at the Agency?"

"Why did you tell me Jack worked at the State Department? You're not the pillar of honesty here."

"I've known you a week. In that time, I've found out my car was tampered with, my husband's accidental death was probably not so accidental, and I've been accused of robbing a local barn. And *you* hardly tell me anything personal. Why should I be the only open book?"

That stung. Did she not realize how much I'd shared with her? She practically knew more about me than Trish ever did, and we dated since high school.

"Not personal? You know about the Eastleys, and my dad. And my favorite sports teams. If you want more than that you, better go looking elsewhere for someone else."

As if I said the most enlightening statement ever, she lifted her hands up in the air. "Exactly. That's exactly right."

On her way out the door, she pivoted around. "And just to be clear, I'm not looking for anyone *and* I don't need your help. Stay out of my business, baking or otherwise." She threw the screen door open and let it slam behind her.

Griff glanced at me. "Damn."

Damned wasn't even the start of it.

Chapter 33

Finley

I'd gone over to CJ's house to tell him the truth. The truth about Michael and me and Jack. Instead, I'd gone off on him, furious that he kept the truth from me. I had no right though. I was keeping plenty of truths myself.

I strode across CJ's porch and ground to a halt. *What the…?*

Dressed in jeans, a T-shirt, and hiking boots, Troy Eastley sneaked from CJ's garage, pausing along the way to take pictures. His car, police or other, was nowhere in sight. Hadn't this guy done enough damage sending CJ to jail overnight and accusing me of doing something I would never do? Troy disappeared around the corner of the garage. I crept after him, keeping a good distance. The last thing I wanted was to be discovered. But information could be power, and with it, maybe I could force him to back off from me and CJ. A long shot, but I'd take anything right now. If CJ knew this guy came on his property, he'd freak out. And rightly so.

I ducked around the corner of the garage. Troy was heading toward the hill. Jazz was right—I needed a new phone. I couldn't even snap pictures on this thing.

Wade's nasally voice floated out of Troy's phone:

"The guy wants to see the hunting shed. Take some pictures of that."

"I'm breaking the law here," Troy said. "It was bad enough when you convinced Trish to call Animal Control. What's so important about this?"

"Do you want to close this deal or what?" Wade asked. "This is millions to us. The guy asked for the pictures. Let's just give him what he wants."

"We don't own this land, Wade."

"We will. If I have anything to do with it."

Troy shoved his phone in his pocket and climbed the hill behind CJ's barn. What the heck was Wade up to? *I shouldn't care. I shouldn't even bother with it. I should do what I told CJ to do. Stay out of his business and move on with my life.*

Of course, I was never really very good at moving on or forgetting.

Chapter 34

CJ

For all of my travel as a SEAL, I still hated the smell of jet fuel. I swiped a hand across my brow. I was grateful to be out of the plane but not so happy for the desert heat of New Mexico. The sun here was even stronger than in North Carolina. A black minivan pulled up to the curb. The window rolled down, and Owen's fiery-red hair was visible. "Your chariot, princess."

"Nice wheels." I tossed my bag in the back and folded myself into the passenger seat, thankful to be able to finally relax and breathe. Absolutely exhausted, the only thing that kept me going through that flight in an enclosed space was focusing on McDavies and how we would find him.

Owen smiled weakly.

My heart fell to my boots. "Where?"

"A lake about fifty miles away. Some campers found him."

I exhaled slowly. "How?"

"Bullet from his gun."

"Damn it." I slammed my hand against the dashboard, and when it didn't do a thing to the pain tearing me up, I tried my other hand. Owen passed me a silver flask, and I took a deep gulp, the whiskey burning. He didn't ask for it back, so I kept it. "What now?"

"Donovan got us a house. Some billionaire golf digs. Where the hell does Donovan meet these guys?" Owen rubbed his nose. He did that when he was working on a problem. "Anyway, Laney's planning to have the funeral tomorrow or the day after."

Owen's cap was pushed back, and his fiery-red hair looked about the way I felt—pulled in twenty different directions with no real purpose.

I rubbed my forehead. Could I have done something different with McDavies? Anything that would have changed the course he was set on?

Owen reached behind him and dug through a backpack. An angry trucker next to us honked.

I grabbed the dash. "This isn't J-bad. Stay in your lane, O."

He tossed a manila envelope in my lap, threw me a devilish grin, and accelerated past the tractor-trailer. He loved speed and danger and always had.

The second swig of whiskey went down easier. "What's this?"

"A list of ops Jack was connected to after we split up, also a list of companies he was investigating in New York. Some of those same companies listed on that menu of yours."

I broke the seal on the envelope and pulled out the documents. "I wonder why New York?"

"From what I can tell, he was chasing down Albanian connections to New York companies. You ever come across an Albanian named Ahmeti?"

"No." I flipped through the stack of papers. Names I knew jumped out at me, but the rest of the words blurred and ran together. Suddenly, the whole morning—hell the last thirty-six hours—became too much. My heart rate rocketed up, my mouth went dry, and my head throbbed. I opened and closed my hands, concentrating on the details of the papers in an effort to calm down. "What is this, Owen?"

"Proof of a connection between this Ahmeti guy and Asllani."

Asllani was one of the most brutal terrorists and drug dealers we dealt with. He had ordered the hit on one of our informants and his family, a hit our SEAL team was too late to stop. Images of the mutilated bodies filled my mind. "Pull over."

"I can't."

"Do it or the inside of this car is toast."

Owen yanked the wheel right and cut swiftly across three lanes, accelerating onto an off-ramp. A motorist laid on the horn, and Owen hung his hand out the window, waving his middle finger.

He rammed on the brakes on the side of the road, and I catapulted out of the car onto my knees, heaving up the whiskey.

He passed me a water bottle, and I swished my mouth out and sat back on my heels. I squinted up at him. "Are you telling me Asllani is connected to Jack's death?"

He shook his head. "I'm telling you that Asllani is a shareholder on some of those corporations. Originally owned by his second cousin Ahmeti. It's a tangled web as it always is when we involve the Middle East and drugs. I've hit enough roadblocks to know that Jack didn't die in some random accident."

I stood up and brushed my knees off. "Sorry for the pansy-assing."

Owen shrugged. "No apology needed except for the waste of my whiskey."

"I've had a hellish two days, and Asllani is the icing on the top."

The icing on the top that might be dripping all the way through. What if Asllani was after Finley? And I left her, angry with me and exposed? I could call her, but to do what? Warn her after I didn't level with her? Asllani wasn't known for targeting extraneous persons, but there was a first time for everything.

"Ever feel like you can't leave the past behind?"

I snorted in answer and took another swig of water. "The past is like the fricking dust of the desert—it's everywhere no matter what I do." My gut twisted, gnawing itself from the whiskey or stress I didn't know.

"How's Jack's wife?"

I ran a hand through my hair. "I had it out with her earlier." *Boy, do I regret that now.* "And then I left her, and she could have a madman after her. You should have told me about this before I got on a plane. I need to be there, not here."

Owen adjusted his ballcap. "I would have told you if I thought she was in real danger. Hell, if Asllani was actively involved, she'd be dead already and you know it. Something else is at work here."

He wasn't wrong. Asllani was hardly the type to leave loose ends hanging.

He walked back to the driver's side and got in. I picked up the fallen flask and climbed into the passenger side. Owen rubbed his nose again, and I waited for him to talk. He wasn't a man to rush.

Owen negotiated us back onto the highway. "Jack was running down companies twenty years old. I'm missing something, but I don't know what."

"Can anyone else help like Rivera? Or Donovan?" I choked out his name. Despite the fact Donovan and I weren't related, sibling rivalry ran deep with us.

Owen cracked his neck. "Maybe. I'd rather keep it between us for a few more days. But if I can't figure it out, they would both be a good resource. Can you talk with the wife again?"

I took a swig from the flask, testing out my stomach. "Maybe."

"Do you want to?"

That was a stupid question. As much as I shouldn't want to talk with her, or think about her, I wanted to do all that and more. I didn't answer. Her eyes were seared in my mind, smoky and perceptive, meeting mine over the back of the horses, her hair falling into her face after our ride, the way she jutted her chin and glared from the door, giving back the crap I was throwing her way. She had this innate ability to knock me off my feet, turn me around, and ground me all in one. But if I let myself do what I wanted, then I was exposing myself and everyone else to danger, to letting her know the truth about Jack's work over there and that last mission that went sideways. I would be in danger, but so was she. I rubbed my scar. What if Owen was wrong? What if Asllani was after her? I wouldn't leave her unprotected, but protecting her and getting involved with her were two different things.

Owen pulled off the highway, through some development gate, and five minutes later into a driveway of an unassuming, two-story Spanish-style stucco house. Like the other houses in the development, its yard was well cared for, and the surrounding golf course could be seen rolling beyond the edges of the yards.

Despite its nondescript tan stucco facade, the front hall opened to a cathedral-styled living room with a wall of windows that overlooked an outdoor grill area and sparkling pool.

I whistled. "Boy, Donovan really moved up in the world. What friend is this?"

Owen nodded at me. "You know Donovan, his old man is loaded and connected. He actually came to me with two houses. I picked the one with the pool."

There it was: the understanding of a brotherhood. The guys all knew how important being active was to me. Swimming was the one activity left to me that my injuries didn't slow me down.

Various members of my team greeted me. Nash picked himself up off the couch, and Fox and Rivera came from the pool table, sticks in hand. Donovan half-waved from a patio chair outside the glass doors.

"Si-in." Fox drawled out my nickname in perfect imitation of McDavies. My throat tightened, and I clenched my jaw to keep my emotions in control. It wasn't the same without McDavies being here.

I shook hands and clapped backs wordlessly. Under different circumstances, the excitement to be reunited would be palpable. Now the air was heavy.

Donovan came in from the patio. His jaw looked as tight as mine felt. I shook his hand. His eyes held mine and a second of understanding passed between us— about why were we here and who we were mourning. I should have known that would be all I'd get from him.

"You take my advice and stayed away from Jack's wife?"

I dropped his hand. "You said, stay away from the case." I kept my voice low.

"I saw a picture of her. She's a nice-looking woman."

Now I wanted to beat him. I clenched my fists.

Owen stepped in between us, hands up. "All right. Easy. Donovan, give it a rest. And Sin, Donovan likes dark brunettes, not blondes. He has no interest in her."

"Yeah." Owen was right. I knew he was, but somehow Donovan could always rile me up. I swallowed the lump in my throat. "What was a northern boy doing way down South anyway?" I drew out my words in an exaggerated Southern accent just to get under his skin. "There's no way in hell it was just to warn me."

Donovan's eyes flashed in anger. "I've got some contacts in that area. The rest you don't need to know." He sidestepped us and was gone up the stairs.

"What is it with you two?" Owen shook his head. "You do know that the war between the North and the South ended two hundred and fifty years ago, right?"

"He thinks he's better than me," I said.

"In his defense, he is better than everyone. And you've got a chip a mile wide."

"He blames me for Elliot's death. Hell, he blames me for the whole damn fiasco over there."

"No, he doesn't. You're reading into it. He's more cautious than you, but that doesn't mean he blames you."

I snorted. "Doesn't mean he doesn't." I pulled up short when we entered an impressive fully-equipped kitchen where Nash was busy prepping T-bone steaks for the grill.

"Whose house is this?" I swiped a roll of salami off a plate. Rarely did military men have this kind of money.

Owen slid open the doors onto the patio. "I told you already. Some connection of Donovan's."

I stepped outside. "Did you know Donovan's working security?"

"Yeah, that's what he told me, but—" Owen shook his head, following me through the doors.

"What?"

"Nothing. Just a feeling I have."

I frowned at him. Owen's feelings were notoriously spot on. In the field, we relied on them like the Bible. "You think he's hiding something?"

Donovan and I had always had a tumultuous relationship, both of us tough and competitive as hell. But I never doubted his loyalty to the team—until recently.

"I know he's hiding something. Just not sure what." Owen waved his hand about. "Let's just call it nothing for now."

I doubted that, but Owen wouldn't share anything until he was sure. I turned my attention to the outside. My eyes slid from the pool to the card table and back to Owen.

He lifted a shoulder. "You up for a game of cards?"

It was the first good idea I'd heard all day. I dropped my bag, swallowed the lump in my throat, and grabbed a chair. McDavies had loved poker.

Owen went to round up the others, and I shot off a text to Griff. Finley had told me to stay out of her business, but that didn't mean I couldn't check on her through Griff. I had no plans to leave her in danger or to stay here longer than necessary.

The crew traipsed outside. Nash carried the steaks. Fox: eight beers. Rivera: a bottle of tequila. Donovan: eight shot glasses—six for the living and two for the dead.

I shuffled the cards, and Donovan poured the shots. Like the riderless black horse in funeral marches symbolizing his fallen rider, a full shot and a beer were placed in front of McDavies's and Elliot's empty chairs.

"All right, let's lock and load." I dealt the cards out, concentrating on where they went to focus on anything but the empty chairs.

"You've been busy, Sin." Rivera stared intently at his hand of cards, not bothering to look in my direction.

"Maybe. You going to warn me off like Donovan?" I pitched my chip in.

Donovan glowered at me from his chair, threw in his chip, but didn't open his mouth.

"Nope. But I'd watch your six. There's something funky going on there."

I rearranged my cards. It was a crap hand. "You find anything out you want to share?"

Rivera slid two cards over to me. "Two. Not yet, except to let you fuckers know you're going down tonight."

Nash, beer in hand, cackled from the grill. "You'd have more luck getting a blow job from that lizard in the corner than winning this game."

We all knew Rivera sucked at cards. He winked at me and threw a chip in the pile. I downed my shot, grabbed my beer, and smiled despite the empty chairs and the pit in my stomach.

****

A day later, hungover and miserable, we stood at McDavies's grave. Rifles fired, and two uniformed soldiers folded the American flag into a neat triangle. We knew that we'd lost a piece of ourselves we'd never get back. Shortly after the funeral luncheon, we packed our things and said goodbye.

Owen and I left together for the airport. We passed security, grabbed some snacks, and walked to the junction of our two flights.

I held out my hand. "See ya, buddy." My voice crackled, thick with emotion after the last few days.

Owen shook it, his forehead furrowed. "Did you ever think that maybe if McDavies hadn't been so set on lying to us about being fine, we wouldn't be here? We all knew on some level that he was struggling, and we let him pretend that everything was okay."

"I don't know." I dropped my head and rubbed behind my neck because the truth was, I really didn't.

Owen kept going. "I've been thinking about what I'd change if I could go back, what might make a difference—and I wouldn't have bought into McDavies's bullshit. I should have called him on it and flown my ass out here. I messed up with him, but I don't plan to do the same with you."

I narrowed my eyes on him. "What's that mean?"

"Don't lie to me about Finley, and more importantly, don't lie to yourself."

"She's Jack's wife. There is no way in hell we should have anything to do with each other, much less get horizontal."

"So? He's not here. News flash, he's never coming back. Sometimes it's those people, the ones you shouldn't have anything to do with, who are the best damn ones around. Do you know how many times in the last ten years you've spoken to me on the phone about a woman?"

I wanted to bark back, but he plunged ahead.

"Zero. And now every time we talk, you mention her. Think about that."

Thinking about her wasn't the problem. Hell, I'd called her twice in the last two days and she hadn't answered. But I kept my mouth shut.

He punched me in the arm. "Don't be bullheaded, Sin. I know you're worried about her finding out about the op, and that what we did contributed to Jack's death, but it's not a reason to wimp out here. If that shit is meant to come out and fuck us, it'll come out no matter what. And don't use circumstances as an excuse. Are you gonna ring the bell or get in the freezing water and swim?"

He smiled his shit-eating grin and sauntered off for his gate, fiery-red hair sticking out askew from under his ball cap. I jealously watched his effortless stride for a minute and turned and headed in the opposite direction.

Once the wheels of the plane had touched down in Charlotte, I called Finley. It rolled to voicemail. Again. God, what if she wasn't okay? I sent a text. Got no response. I called again. A ton of noise filled my ear.

"Hello?" Her voice was just like I remembered, smoky to match her eyes with a touch of hesitation. I didn't blame her. The last time we talked hadn't gone well. At this point, I wasn't even sure who had yelled more or been more annoyed.

I gulped. In my head this call was much easier.

"Can I come over and see you?" I hoped she couldn't hear any desperation in my voice. *Please say yes.*

"I'm not home."

My gut plummeted. "Are you working?" I could barely hear her through the background voices.

"No. I'm at some party off Grayrock Road."

"The Wallaces' costume party?" My voice actually broke with surprise. Ashley was close friends with them, so I was invited every year. That party was notoriously large with tons of people dressed in elaborate costumes. Since returning from Afghanistan, I avoided it like the plague. "What's your costume?"

"Listen, I can barely hear you. I'm around tomorrow. Just call more or come over then."

The line went dead.

Adrenaline coursed through me. I pressed the accelerator down and hoped I had some kind of costume I could rummage up in my closet.

****

Cars lined the street, parked haphazardly on lawns and driveways. I left my truck a hundred yards out and hoofed it the rest of the way. Years ago, I had actually got myself to go, at my sister's urging, but I made the mistake of parking close and getting boxed in. With the mobs of people and the late-night fireworks, by the time I was able to leave, I was a shaking puddle of sweat and fighting off flashbacks so bad that Ashley had to drive me home. I was in no mood for a repeat.

The music hit me before I reached the Wallaces' house. I passed the open iron gates and headed for the coolers. A beer would help me deal with all the people.

I didn't get five steps before Grace, the hostess, spotted me.

"CJ!" she called, giving me a big kiss hello. With flouncy skirts, half a shirt with her midriff exposed, some kind of lacy bow in her wavy hair, and a shit ton of bracelets jingling on her arm. "Your sister's here. Have you seen her? I think she's on the back porch, or maybe down by the pool house."

"No. Not yet." I dragged my fingers through my hair. Where was Finley in this mob of people? I had to find her before the end of the night because I had to leave before the fireworks.

"So glad you could make it. Dennis is by the grill with the guys and a bottle of scotch." She offered me her full flute of champagne. "But start with this."

Dennis Wallace and I had about as much in common as the pig he was roasting on the spit. I respectfully pressed the glass back into her hand. "Thanks, Grace, but I'm good." I waved at the coolers parked along the edge of the porch. "I know the drill."

She smiled, gave an appreciative squeeze to my arm, and floated away to greet someone else.

I leaned down for a beer, and my heart did a tumble in my chest. I'd underestimated Finley. Again. Every time I thought I had her figured out, she threw me a curveball. She stood near the outdoor fireplace. Flames from the fire reached high, giving her a glow and accentuating her silhouette. Unlike Grace's flamboyant costume, Finley's was more understated—with a stark-white sleeveless shirt, black mini-skirt—and when she turned, I saw a bright magenta apron. Her hair fell loose, wavy instead of its normal straight, and disheveled around her face. I had no idea who she was supposed to be, and it didn't matter. She was beautiful—and all I really wanted to know was if the lace peeking out from her skirt was garters.

Wade was next to her, gesturing wildly through some story he was telling. My gut churned at how close he stood to Finley, leaning in even when she backed away. I wanted to squeeze his annoying head until his eyes popped out. The people in the small circle were all paying rapt attention—all except Finley, who kept glancing around.

Her eyes caught mine and held. I smiled. Perfect was an understatement. I raised an eyebrow, and as if she could read my mind, she shrugged in answer. It was enough to set me forward. I was halfway across the yard when Wade finished talking and everyone laughed. I bet the story was about some fantastic house sale that Wade pulled off or the latest triathlon he ran. Most stories Wade told had to do with one thing: Wade. I found him dry as unbuttered toast.

"Well, look who it is!" Wade eyed me up and down as if I might be gum stuck to his shoe. "Is that a costume?"

I wore a white button-down and blue jeans because I couldn't rummage up any kind of costume in my closet. I shrugged. "Costumes aren't my thing."

Wade opened his mouth to say something obnoxious, but someone grabbed his arm and dragged him off before he could. The other couple turned away, and Finley and I were left standing there alone.

"I tried calling you a few times in the past two days." I tried to temper my edge, but it didn't work.

She squinted at me. "I've been busy. And you know my phone. It chooses when it wants to work."

"Are you here with Wade?"

"Yes. As soon as you left, I dove into his arms the

261

first chance I got."

"Is that bitter sarcasm, or are you trying to make me jealous?"

"Whatever. I drove by myself. Speaking of which, do you think my SUV will be ready soon? I can't keep renting."

I took a deep breath, opening and closing my hands. I had no right to be angry with her, even if she was standing here with an Eastley. "Do you like him?"

She smoothed down her skirt, which came a good four inches above her knee. "Does it matter?"

"I can guarantee he sure as hell wants more than a date with you." One drunken night in high school, Wade stood around the bonfire and did his best impression of his mean ass, drunken father: "Son, when you choose a woman, make sure she looks as pretty as a shiny sports car with an engine to match the curves and can screw you like a bunny. A few connections don't hurt either. No point wasting money on them unless you get an equal return." Or something like that. And Wade has followed his daddy's advice to a *T* ever since.

Finley shook her head and headed for a vacant patch of grass closer to the driveway. I followed.

"You're jumping to conclusions," she said. "The wrong ones, I might add."

"You told me we should just be friends. Then as soon as I'm gone, you go out with him." I tried and failed to keep my voice from sounding bitter and angry. What a shit week this turned out to be.

She reached out and grabbed my arm, dragging me across the yard to the edge of the house. Tucked behind the porch and some well-placed rose bushes, we were effectively hidden from view from the rest of the party.

Her fingers sent electric shocks up my arm.

"You are a grade-one jerk. You know that?"

I was well aware of it by this time, but I'd set my course and couldn't see my way out of it. "I'm a jerk? That guy's goal in life is tripping me up. Him and Troy. Don't get me started on how Wade ripped off my grandparents."

Wade's father's life lessons not only included what women to bed but how to cheat old people out of their money. Such a stand-up man.

Still seething over her decision, I plunged forward. "You're just mad because I didn't tell you about your husband working for the CIA. It's not my fault he lied to you."

Her head snapped back as if I'd slapped her. "No, it's your fault you lied to me about the menu. When you spend time with someone, it's called being friends. Though it usually involves talking and sharing stuff. Something as big as that, you don't hide."

"Look who's calling the kettle black?"

"What's that supposed to mean? I've been nothing but truthful with you."

Of course, Owen and I knew that wasn't entirely true. She was half in the shadows, the moonlight slanting over her features. I knew them by heart because at night I played them over and over in my mind, traced her brow bone, down her sharp cheekbones, across her full lips.

Done with words, done with fricking emotions I had to hide or control, I covered the three feet between us in one stride. "I don't want to be friends."

She stepped forward, her chin up.

Is she daring me or confronting me?

I risked it and slid my hands through her wild hair. "I don't want to *be* anything. I don't want to *do* anything, except kiss you."

Her eyes, like liquid steel, held mine. "Then do it."

I crushed her mouth to mine. Her lips, full and hot—and like whiskey on a smoldering fire, all I wanted was more. She let me in, and my tongue twisted with hers. I ran my hand over her back, sliding across the fabric of her skirt until it ended, her skin smooth and soft. She pressed herself into me, one thigh sandwiched neatly between my legs. I trailed my fingers up and under her skirt and touched the edge of lace—garters. *She's going to be the death of me.*

She nipped at my bottom lip. For a second, I contemplated laying her down right there in Wallace's flowerbeds.

She reared her head back and looked me in the eyes. "I came here tonight because—" Her voice turned husky and low. "—the day you left, I saw Troy lurking around your farm. I thought I might be able to get some info from Wade. See where they are at on your granddad's land you want back."

I stared at her, dumbfounded.

Wade's voice, nasally and distinct, filled the air like an alarm clock beeping after only an hour of sleep. "Grace, have you seen Finley?"

Fricking Eastley.

"I haven't, Wade. Have you tried the pool house?"

Finley widened her eyes, and I pulled her farther into the shadows, the thorns from the rose bushes prickling my back. In the light of the porch, her stormy eyes challenged me. "You tell me I have faith issues. Well, you should learn to trust the people in your life a little more."

She stepped away. "By the way, I knew Jack worked for the CIA. It's one of the reasons—" She gulped and shook her head. "This was a mistake. You are the kind of man who sees a burning building and rushes in, not away. I just can't. I can't do this again."

"What if that burning building is you?" The words slipped out, but in the slanting moonlight, I meant them. I didn't want to walk away.

Her big blue-gray eyes filled with tears. "It's just that—" She shook her head. "—I gotta go."

She faded into the dark, leaving my fingers holding air.

What the hell was she going to say? And why didn't she say it? Among the milling guests dotting the yard, I couldn't find her. I needed to because I owed her an apology, and she owed me an explanation.

Chapter 35

Finley

What was wrong with me, asking him to kiss me. *Am I that much of an idiot?* Clearly, I had no backbone. A SEAL? Really? They thrived on danger—the baddest of the bad. These guys were dropped into war-torn areas with nothing but a knife and a shoelace, and they made it out alive. On the scale of safe boyfriends and those who wouldn't break my heart and life apart, they were in the negative numbers. Jack always said I made the worst decisions. He might actually be laughing in Heaven.

Besides, if CJ really knew me, who I was, what I had done. If he found out about my past, a past riddled with drug use and a drugged-up psychotic boyfriend, he wouldn't want me. Good lord, I was an idiot and asking for trouble on all fronts. And I probably wasn't the nicest person after giving him a hard time about not telling me about Jack being in the CIA. But what was I supposed to say? *Hello, my name is Finley. I'm responsible for my parents' deaths.* CJ was right about the pot calling the kettle black, but that wasn't even the half of it.

I ducked out of the party and hurried across the yard and through the massive iron gates. My mission of going with Wade to get information had failed anyway.

All I'd gotten out of him was that he was going to be hugely successful by developing farmland into subdivisions. I wanted my house and my bed and to forget everything else. The wind, warm earlier in the evening, now had a biting edge. I yanked the car door open and collapsed against the seat.

Damn, did he kiss nice.

Why was it when I was around him, I was a mess? He stole my focus and purpose. I was a quivering idiot who either divulged her life story or argued with him. What was wrong with me? I went to that party intent on finding out info from Wade and now here I was escaping in my car, my lips burning from CJ's kiss.

I touched them as if they might not be there and pulled the rearview mirror down to check. Bright red. I swiped my tongue across them, tasting cherry lip balm. My whole body ached for more. I shook my head and drove toward home. His distinctive scent of woods, leather, and Ivory soap lingered on my shirt.

A set of headlights appeared in my rearview mirror. Up close. These were backcountry roads. How fast did this person want me to go? I fumbled for the can of soda I kept in the car for when I panicked and needed a sugar rush. In a pinch, caffeine could prevent a stress headache from turning into one of my vision-blurring migraines. I flipped the tab, took a sip, and dragged my cell phone into my lap in case I needed it. Although who I would call, I wasn't sure. I'd just run out on CJ, and anyone else I might call lived about a thousand miles away. The road twisted left and right. I pressed the accelerator, and my car responded. The speedometer climbed to sixty. The lights didn't fade away. If I went any faster, I might misjudge a curve.

But I pressed the accelerated down again, and as the needle passed sixty, flashing blue and red lights filled my mirror. "Oh, crap!" I slowed and yanked the wheel to the right, pulling onto a side road.

Breathe, breathe, and calm down.

I pulled over and parked. Troy approached my driver's side. Somehow, I should have known.

"Do you know how fast you were going?"

"No. You were on my tail." It sounded lame even to me.

He raised an eyebrow. "No I wasn't. You have a vivid imagination if you think I was on your tail." Troy leaned in the open window, so close I could smell his bad breath. "Have you been drinking?"

"What? No." I shifted my body away from him as far as I could.

Troy's gaze moved down to my legs.

I fought the urge to pull my ridiculously short skirt down. It would only draw more attention to its length and the fact the garters were starting to creep out. What was I thinking, letting Jazz help me with my costume?

He straightened up and held his hand out. "License and registration, please."

Troy returned to his vehicle. Its intercom beeped and cackled.

I rolled up my window and yanked my skirt down. Leaning my head back, I closed my eyes. In a flash, I traveled back in time to a darkened parking lot: documents laid out on the hood of a car, two men flanking me, their bodies effectively blocking my escape, one man's hand resting on my ass. The underlying threat had been as obvious as the papers I signed with a trembling hand.

Troy's loud tap on my window startled me. I rolled my window down, and he handed over the ticket along with my documents, his fingers grazing mine. I fought the urge to cringe.

I wanted to roll my window back up and get out of there, but he wanted to talk. "All alone tonight?" he asked. "How'd my brother let you get away? I'd never let anyone as good-looking as you drive home alone. My little brother never learns."

I choked out a laugh. Keep it light. Don't make him mad. "Your brother was super sweet. I just have a bad headache. Need to go home and lie down."

"Well, then I best not be keeping you. But just remember we got a small town here. People around here all know each other and we're all friendly."

"You're not all that friendly to CJ." It just slipped out.

"Aww, that goes way back. Now you best slow down and not drive like some crazy New Yorker."

A pit as heavy as a ten-pound weight opened in my stomach. "How do you know I'm from New York?"

"Your driver's license. Now drive safe now. You got two kids—I'm sure you wouldn't want to wind up in a ditch." He winked at me and sauntered away.

Was that a threat?

He pulled around me and took off with a screech of tires.

I rolled up my window, locked the doors, and eased the car back onto the road. He lied. My license plate didn't say New York. What else did he know about me? *Just get home.* The rear-view mirror stayed dark the whole way. My hands shook so badly the steering bounced right and left.

I stopped at the split with CJ's driveway and coasted down to mine. Running to him wouldn't help matters. The last thing he needed was to get angry with Troy. Besides, hadn't I told him I didn't need his help? Until I told him the truth, if I told him the truth, he didn't need to be bothered by me.

My house sat empty with the same lights on as I left it. Something about Troy's words and the way he looked at me made me queasy and scared. I gathered my stuff and dashed for the house. I slammed the front door behind me, double-locked it, and jammed a chair underneath the doorknob. I did the same with the back door. I closed my eyes and sighed with relief. Troy was an ass, but it could've been worse—some stranger could've been following me.

Heavy footsteps sounded up the porch steps. My heart jumped into my throat. I lunged for Jazz's lacrosse stick. If I swung it with enough force and caught whoever it was by surprise, I just might be able to temporarily take out whoever had followed me.

Michael crossed my mind. Is it possible that he was released early? Would he come here? He didn't know my address. The hospital didn't even know my address. But then—he did find my number.

Chapter 36

CJ

I rapped on the side of her door. *Come on. Get a grip.* This was not the first woman I'd ever gone after. I opened and closed my hand to stop it from shaking

"Yeah?" Her voice wobbled just a bit.

"It's CJ. We need to talk."

A scrape across the floor—probably the chair. The door swung open, and stormy eyes met mine. "We do?"

I took a deep breath. I was a former Navy SEAL. I hadn't gotten to where I was by cowering in the face of danger. "Can I come in?"

She stepped back, giving me room to walk in. I brushed by her, and that faint scent of vanilla wafted over me. God, she smelled good. She stared at me, eyebrows knitted together. Clearly, she wasn't going to make this easy. But it didn't matter because I wasn't going to be easy on her.

"Why didn't you tell me that you knew Jack worked for the CIA? Why didn't you tell me from the beginning where he worked?"

She turned her back on me and shut the door, checking the deadbolt twice and wedging the chair under the doorknob. "I never tell anyone that. Would it have made a difference?"

I blew my breath out. "Maybe. It became my

business—"

She tightened her grip on Jazz's lacrosse stick, holding it up as if she was about to spar with me.

"Why are you holding Jazz's lacrosse stick?" I peered closer. Her eyes were taut, her forehead furrowed. "Did something happen? Are you okay?"

"I'm okay." Her eyes slid left to the lock on the door.

"Finley." I stepped closer and wrapped my fingers over hers. Her hands trembled underneath mine. I eased the stick from her grip. "What happened?"

"Someone was on my tail coming home. So, I kept going faster."

"And?"

She gave me a wry, knowing smile. "I got pulled over for speeding."

"Troy?"

She nodded.

"Did he do something?"

"No, he asked me if I had been drinking." She tugged on her skirt. "He was kind of sleazy about the whole thing."

Anger, pure and white-hot, bubbled up. "I'm going to kill him."

She grabbed my arm. "No, you're not. It's fine. I'm fine. He didn't touch me. I just got shook up."

Despite her tough tone, her eyes glistened, and one small tear tipped over and streaked down her cheek.

I swiped it away and cupped her chin in my hand. "That's the benchmark for a good person: he didn't touch me." He'd shaken her up; he'd probably even liked it. I wanted to hit something, or better yet, hit him. I shouldn't have let her storm away from me at the party. "Did you check the house since you got home?"

She shook her head. "No."

"Come with me. I'm not leaving here unless I know you're safe." I slid my fingers over hers and tugged gently. Part of me wanted to make sure she came with me, and part of me just liked the feel of her skin. Her pulse hammered under my fingertips. I checked every room and corner in case someone had come in and then every door and window making sure each was locked. We ended up back in the front hall.

"Why didn't you call me?" I tried to keep the frustration from my voice. I wasn't angry with her, just with myself.

"I'm fine, CJ. I don't want to be some helpless widow you have to protect. I'm the one who chose to dig into Jack's case. I can do it on my own."

She squared her shoulders. The crisp white shirt flexed with the motion, accentuating the curves of her breasts before falling to the waist of the short black skirt. The fire in my gut morphed from anger to desire. And the reasons for coming here, my quest for answers and explanations, disappeared in the face of what I really wanted—what I'd been hiding ever since she'd found me.

I traced a finger along her knuckles. She took a step away from me, her eyes guarded.

"What are you scared of?" I couldn't keep the huskiness from my voice.

"Nothing." She jutted her chin at me as if daring me to challenge her, but her voice shook just a hair, and I knew she was lying. But more than wanting the truth, I wanted to pull her to me and taste her lips again.

"You know you give me some bogus line about

faith and trust, but you have just as many issues there."

She shook her head. "I do not."

"I beg to differ. If we're keeping score, since that's a big thing with you, faith and trust are the same things. They're homonyms."

She raised her eyebrow. "Did you come all the way here to give me a grammar lesson?"

"No." I ruffled my hair, trying to remember all the things I planned to say on the drive here. "I came to say I'm sorry. I jumped to conclusions about Wade. I was wrong."

Her eyes locked on mine, and for a long moment, everything stilled. It was probably time for more than just an apology. I needed to tell her how beautiful she was. How smart and creative and generous. How much she made my throat dry up and my heart pound. How some nights I lay awake thinking of all the things I wanted to do to her and with her. But I couldn't— couldn't get past the wall in my head. So instead, I repeated my stupid apology.

"I was wrong. I had no right to get up in your face about Wade. I had no right to stake a claim on you." But God how I wanted to. I'd never wanted a woman as badly as I wanted her.

Her face softened, and she smiled at me, holding her hands palm up. "You were, and it's not the only thing you are wrong about. Faith and trust are not homonyms. They're synonyms."

Stepping closer, she angled her head toward me and beckoned me closer.

That's all I needed. I'd had enough of words, of waiting, of everything except her. I closed the distance between us and spanned her waist with my hands.

She smiled up at me. "Homonyms are words that sound the same but are spelled differently and mean different things, like their, there, and—"

"You mean like there—" Leaning down, I kissed her collarbone, where her shirt had fallen back. "—as in *t-h-e-r-e*?"

Her breath caught. "Yes."

I cupped her face in my hands and traced the half-moons below her eyes with my thumb. "*T-h-e-y* apostrophe *r-e* beautiful."

I nibbled further across the bone, toward her cleavage, undoing a button on her shirt. It exposed the lace on her bra and the crests of her breasts. I looked into her blue-gray eyes to make sure.

"Yes," she said.

I kissed each, letting my lips linger along the fabric, bringing my fingers up to stroke one nipple and then the other through the lace. They pebbled under my touch, and I pulled the fabric down and set my mouth to one, sucking it and drawing it out. She moaned and sagged against the door.

"You're beautiful," I whispered. I moved to the other nipple.

Running her hands down my back, she pushed one leg between mine and pulled me into her. "You're, *y-o-u* apostrophe *r-e* not to be confused with *y-o-u-r* ass is damn fine. Another set of homonyms."

I was so hard, I didn't think I could last another minute. "I was never one for English or grammar."

"You don't like words?" Her breathless, questioning tone spurred me on to leave no doubt as to what I liked.

I let go of her nipple to trail kisses up her neck,

traveling slowly, tasting, exploring, listening to her breath hitch and slow. I moved over to her mouth. Her tongue tangled with mine. She kissed like she lived: defiant, determined, challenging me for more. Yet she held back a part of herself as if hiding some deep dark secret to which only she held the key. I wanted all of her, not just the parts she chose to reveal to me. I wanted to know her darkest fears and deepest pleasures.

Planting both my hands beside her head against the door, I boxed her in. Her chest heaved as fast and hard as mine.

I answered her question: "I like some words."

She lifted her chin, challenging me, a gleam in her eyes. "Like?"

"Action words." I slid my fingers down the side of her neck, pushing her shirt off to expose her shoulder. When it didn't give enough, I popped the remaining buttons open.

"Like *sucking*."

I went back to her nipple, and she moaned, hooking her leg up and around my hip. I moved a hand over the smooth cotton of her skirt down to the skin of her leg and made my way back up.

"Sliding."

With a flick of my finger, her garter clasp released.

"Teasing."

I brushed my fingers across her thong and moved to the other garter. It gave easily under my fingers. I went back to the thong, tracing its outline.

"What else?" she asked.

"Stroking."

Her body pressed into me with a shudder. "For someone who doesn't like words, you're very skilled with them."

"You have no idea." My throat was so tight with desire I could barely get the words out.

She tunneled her fingers through my hair and pulled my head down. Her voice as ragged as my breath, she whispered in my ear, "Show me." Her lips met mine, soft in texture but rough with urgency and need.

I pushed her shirt from her shoulders. It fell to the floor, and her bare skin glowed in the silver light of the moon. She released her hold on my hair, brushing her palms downward over my back.

"Please," she whispered.

She tugged at my belt buckle, and my last bit of control gave away. I cupped my hands around her ass, and she lifted herself up, wrapping her other leg around me.

"We need a bed." I panted out the words as she covered my jawline with kisses.

"Down. The. Hall." Her fingers fumbled with the belt clasp.

I would have liked to help, but I was busy negotiating the hallway and trying to stay upright. She wasn't heavy, but I wasn't exactly able-bodied. She gave up on the belt and grazed my ear with her teeth.

"First door on the left."

If she kept up with her breathless whispers and nibbles on my ear, I was going to drop her there and rip off the rest of her clothes—hard floor be damned. I found the door and kicked it open.

She let go of my ear and pulled my mouth back to hers. There was a raw need to her as if by her kisses she could find something she was searching for.

I laid her down on the bed. She backed herself up to the headboard, and I followed her. I undid the clasp of her bra, flung it off the bed, and set my mouth once more to her breasts.

"Oh my God. Oh my God." Her breath came as fast as her words. The need to see her naked, to be inside her, overrode any other thought in my brain. Mouth feasting on her breasts, I ran my hand up her leg and under the tight black miniskirt. She grabbed it.

"Wait." She sat up, scooting out from under me and off the bed until she stood on the floor.

"Wait?" I felt like a high school kid again in the back of my truck.

A flicker of uncertainty crossed her face. She covered her exposed breasts with her arms. "I'm not twenty."

"Neither am I." I crawled forward. The desire to feel her skin under my hands pulsed through me.

"No, listen to me." She put a hand on my chest, stopping me. "I'm not twenty. I don't have a twenty-year-old body. I have a forty-year-old body. I've had two kids. You're younger. I've—"

I sat back on my heels and opened and closed my hand on my thigh, trying to find the right words. This was the time to be brutally honest.

"I'm burned on parts of my body. They reconstructed my leg. I have a hole in it that's as deep as a golf ball. Those scars are who I am, how I got here. I'm not here for a lay—I'm here for *you*, Finley."

That was the truth and had been since she'd leaned over me in the grass, smelling of sugar and vanilla, and patted the blood running down my face.

The expression eased. She fumbled briefly with the

back of her skirt and then shimmied her hips. The slip of material floated like a feather to the ground. All the air left my lungs as she stood there, naked except for a minuscule piece of lace that masqueraded as panties, along with her falling stockings and high heels.

I traced the lines of her body, sliding off every last stitch of clothing. She shivered under my touch.

"Every time I think I have you figured out, think I know what to expect, you kick it up a whole other notch. It's exquisite torture." Grasping her arm, I tugged her onto the bed and cupped her face in my hands. She laughed, swung her leg over, and straddled me. She leaned forward, her hair cascading over her shoulders onto my chest. "That's good to know."

Reaching across me, she fiddled with the nightstand, and there was a crash of things onto the floor. She sat back up, a box of condoms in her hand.

I arched an eyebrow. "A whole box, huh? Is that a challenge?"

She grinned in answer.

I grabbed the box and flipped her under me. "In case you don't know, I love challenges."

She smiled slow and seductive. "I'm counting on it."

Chapter 37

Finley

It had been a long time. Maybe if it hadn't been, I would have kept my promise to stay removed, to keep that part of me, that part no one ever saw, just for me. His fingers traced my body—lightly exploring—his mouth following in its path. Every nerve ending felt on edge, ready to explode. He descended past my belly button. I tugged on his arm.

He lifted his head, fixing on me with those green eyes. "I'm taking my time." His voice husky, his fingers brushing back and forth across my hip bones.

I shook my head. "Please don't."

He leaned up on his elbows. "What?"

Heart pounding, I leveled with him. "I need—it's been so long. I just need to feel all of you now. Next time you can take as long as you want."

He cocked his head. "You sure?"

I nodded, pulling him up, meeting his mouth with mine. I needed him to blot it out, the last nine months, the pain, the fear, everything that lived inside of me. I needed it gone for just a few moments. He brushed my hair back from my face and fixed me with a crooked smile.

"Okay." He kissed me again. His lips nibbled mine, caressed up my jaw, whispered in my ear the things he wanted to do.

I reached down and guided him to me. He slid inside of me. Once, twice, and he was there filling me. He began to move, knitting his fingers through mine and raising my arms above my head. My body rose to meet his until I had no other thought except for that moment, him and me. My orgasm ripped through me. As I pulsed around him, he came too, burying his head in my shoulder and calling my name.

We lay like that for a few minutes, joined, breathless, weightless. I wanted more, more of this, of him. The thought came from left field and scared me.

He lifted his head and rested his forehead against mine.

"You good?" I asked, my words coming out throaty and breathless. It was silly to think of being self-conscious and worried about sex after all these years but maybe what was good for me wasn't for him.

He laughed. "If I was any better, I wouldn't be able to feel my body parts." He kissed my nose before rolling away. Sitting up, he ruffled his hair and glanced over his shoulder, pinning me with another crooked smile. "You?"

"Yes. Very good."

He held my gaze as if making sure I was telling him the truth and then leaned over and kissed me again. "I'll be right back," he said and disappeared into the bathroom.

I stretched out, wiggling my fingers and toes. I was content and happy, and I didn't remember the last time I felt either. Jack had never really listened all that much in bed. Our sex life had been good but nothing explosive, and the more he drank, the more it stilled until it had all but disappeared.

CJ had been everything I hoped for and everything I feared.

I was in trouble.

I knew it deep in my bones, in every emotionally and physically satisfied cell of my body. As angry as he made me, as off-kilter and off-guard, as much as I didn't want him in my life—didn't want anyone—this was more than a mindless lay. In the moonlight, the clouds raced across the sky. In my life, I'd been in love twice. Of those two men, one was dead, and one had been locked up for twenty years. The odds of this ending well for either of us were slim to none.

I turned my gaze from the open window and followed his naked body back from the bathroom. Cleaned up, he sipped from a glass of water. I took it from him, drinking deeply. He crawled into bed next to me and propped himself up on an elbow. He brushed a finger down the side of my arm. Heat surged through me. How could he do that with just a little touch?

"Tell me," he said. "Tell me what you meant at the party. When you walked away without finishing your sentence."

I was hoping he forgot about that. My eyes darted around the room, looking anywhere but at him.

His fingers reached for mine and tugged on them. "Tell me." His raspy voice was soft and gentle, and I felt my walls crumble just a bit. Traitorous damn things.

"Maybe you've given up that life, the one filled with danger and secrets. Maybe on the outside, to the rest of the world, you have. But I know it's a part of you. You *like* the danger. SEALs thrive on it and everything that goes along with it. I don't want it. I don't want it for my kids—"

My voice broke, and I swallowed the lump of emotion that threatened to overwhelm me. Jack had left us, and though I know it hadn't been his choice, his kids were now fatherless, and I was alone navigating parenthood and this world without him. Truth be told, I was scared. Ever since Jack died, I'd been scared. Pretending that I wasn't took every ounce of energy, as much energy as it took to keep the walls up around my heart, to keep me from falling for CJ. I pulled the sheet up, covering my exposed chest.

"You have that need to save the world. You flew off in a fit the other day without saying a word about what was going on. Even now you haven't told me."

He regarded me, and his eyes gradually went blank. "A teammate of mine committed suicide. But at the time when the call came in, he was only missing. I found out when I landed that he'd killed himself."

"I'm sorry."

"Me, too." He nibbled on my shoulder. "I don't mean to keep secrets. I've just practiced longer at that than not. I could learn to be better. And like I said before, what if you're the one in trouble, you're the burning building. I want to rush in there."

I tightened my grip on the sheet. "People rushing into burning buildings get burned."

He covered my hand with his and pried my fingers from the sheet. "Is that a warning?"

"Yes. No. I just—I'm not sure." I abruptly changed the subject. "What about Jack's death? Did you find anything more out on your trip?"

He pushed the sheet down and turned me over in

one motion. Hovering over my back, he brushed my hair aside and kissed my shoulder. "Right now, I don't want you to worry about anything."

I closed my eyes, feeling the trail of kisses down my back. Just like that he stole the direction of the conversation and my resolve. He was wrong, however, and I knew it. Being hurt didn't stop him from being the guy drawn to danger, the guy who'd sacrifice himself for his country or a cause. That part of him still existed—it was what drew me to him and scared me all at the same time.

He planted a kiss right by the delicate side of my ear, tracing my shoulder blade with a finger at the same time. "Finley?"

Did he know the zing he caused to surge through me at his touch? "Yeah?"

"It's going to be okay."

I nodded.

His hands followed his mouth down my back, kneading my muscles, relaxing me and heating me up all at the same time, drawing me away from my worries and to that place where touch and pleasure blotted out every other thought.

Chapter 38

CJ

I watched the sunrise through the gray haze of the morning. Finley had fallen asleep an hour before, and I drifted with her for a little bit, satiated and content. But then my mind got rocking and rolling as it sometimes did, and I couldn't sleep anymore. My alarm rang, and I dove for my phone, switching it off before it woke her.

"You want me to go with you?" she asked, her voice husky with sleep. She threw an arm around me and curled closer. My body stirred to hers. I lifted her arm off and slid out.

Despite the warmth yesterday, the temperature had fallen with the setting sun and now hovered just over freezing.

"Stay here." I leaned down and kissed her cheek. "Keep the bed warm. I'll make it as quick as I can. When I come back, you can warm me up."

She smiled, her eyes closed. "Mmm. I like the sound of that."

"I'll grab the last box on my way back over."

Her forehead furrowed. "That doesn't sound like as much fun."

I choked back a laugh. "Definitely not."

"I'll make some coffee and muffins."

She stretched out on the mattress, the sheet twisted

around her naked body. She made quite a picture. If I wasn't worried about the horses and their breakfast, I would rip that sheet off and really enjoy the morning with her. I grabbed my jeans and T-shirt discarded from the night before. My foot hit the clutter from the nightstand. I bent down. On the top was a folded sheet of paper, half undone. Jack's curly-cue writing leaped off the back: *Michael Davis.*

I glanced at Finley, but she rolled away from me and onto her side. I lifted the sheet and opened it to the mugshot of some guy.

Finley half-waved her hand through the air, her eyes still closed. "Go. I'm getting up. It will be ready when you get back. Then we'll have all morning."

I refolded the paper and placed it back on the stack, slid my jeans and shirt on, and made for the bedroom door.

****

The scent of fresh-baked muffins and coffee smacked me in the face. I dumped the final box of Jack's things onto Finley's kitchen table. She handed me a freshly brewed cup of coffee.

"How were the horses?"

I took a sip, relishing the heat. "Good." I didn't elaborate. There wasn't much to say, and even if there was, my mind was preoccupied with Michael Davis's mugshot. I'd already texted Owen with the name. If there was something on this guy, he'd find out—and the connection with Finley and Jack.

She threw a questioning look my way. "Everything okay?"

"Yeah."

She drummed her fingers on the counter, eyeing

me squarely. "Listen, I haven't done this very often"—
she shrugged—"or at least not in a really long time.
This whole morning after thing. If you regret last night,
that's fine. Just be upfront, and then we can get back to
going through Jack's things and just move on. I don't
want a lot of drama here."

I lifted my gaze and met her gaze squarely. "I don't
regret last night."

She nibbled on the corner of her lip. "You seem
pretty preoccupied."

A million images from last night crowded through
my mind. I hadn't lost myself like that in a very long
time. If ever. What did she say about trust and faith last
night? Mugshot be damned. She would tell me in her
own time. I swiped a crumb from her lip. "No. I'm
good. Let's plow through this box, and then we can get
back to more important things."

Her smile brightened, along with her eyes. She
knocked the lid off the box and picked up a folder. "We
better get started then. Kids will be home in a few
hours."

Chapter 39

Finley

The oven timer dinged, and I laid a folder of insurance policies down. To be honest, I was done looking through these boxes of Jack's. Yes, I wanted answers, but it didn't seem like there was anything of substance in them. I grabbed my oven mitts and turned the timer off. I also didn't want to find anything more having to do with Michael. The stupid mugshot of Michael had fallen out of my night table when I pulled out the box of condoms. I found it this morning when I cleaned up. I prayed to God CJ didn't see it. I knew I owed him the truth, but I just wasn't ready to divulge it all. I pulled out a hot pan of banana muffins and slid it onto a cooling rack. "You want any of these?"

CJ didn't answer. I shut the oven off and turned my full attention to him.

"CJ? You want one of these?"

He held a manila folder. Brow furrowed, he raised his gaze to me, glanced down at his hand, and back up at me. Newspaper clippings slid out of the folder and scattered on the floor, and the bold black headlines screamed out at me: *Equestrian Princess and Drug Addict Accused of Killing Parents.*

"Is this you?"

I rounded the island and reached for the folder. As

if on instinct, CJ raised his arm until it was just out of my reach. "Answer me. Is this you?"

Shit, shit, shit. I should have known Jack wouldn't just have Michael's mugshot. He was too organized for that.

"A file titled Finley slash Whitney. Is this you?"

There was no point denying it. There were no excuses to be made and most likely no explanation that would've work. I dropped to my knees and scooped up the fallen papers. When Jack had collected them, I had no idea. I shuffled them into a cohesive stack, trying to find the words to make this okay. But there was none. I held onto the papers; my sordid past was reduced down to lines in a newspaper article. A hole blasted in my life by bad decisions that would forever haunt me.

"Yes. It's me. But it looks worse than it is." Was that true? Because it probably was as bad as it looked.

"Did you do this?"

I pointed to the article in his hand. "No. As you can see, I wasn't charged. I didn't do it. My boyfriend, Michael. He did it."

He stepped away and then turned to face me as if this conversation had to be face to face. Did he think I didn't understand the severity of this, the seriousness of it? I'd been living it on a daily basis for the last twenty years. Always afraid of the truth coming out. Even neighborhood parties were torture, always sure that someone would uncover the truth as to why I didn't have parents.

He combed a hand through his hair. When had that habit morphed into one I loved?

"This is some pretty bad shit."

I choked back a nervous laugh. "You mean my

drugged-up boyfriend shooting my parents in cold blood in the front hall of their house? Yeah, it's pretty bad."

"Why didn't you tell me?"

"I just met you. It's not the thing you blurt out to a new neighbor: Hi, my name is Finley, but once upon a time, I was Whitney, and my drug addict boyfriend killed my parents. Here, try a peanut butter chocolate chip bar."

He shook his head, hurt, bewildered, maybe as if it was all too much to take in. I understood that.

He flipped the folder over where both my names were written. "Why did you change your name?"

"A bunch of reasons. I wanted to disappear and hoped that would do the trick."

"Did it work?"

"Kind of." An image of the horrible meeting I had with the guys who wanted my dad's business crossed my mind and with it a wave of nausea. "I was lost to the horse world. All my sponsors didn't want anything to do with me. And everyone else I knew through my parents—so I became someone else."

"And Jack?"

I glanced down at my hands and twisted my wedding ring. My time with Jack seemed ages ago, dwarfed by all that had happened in the last year. "I didn't meet him until later, after my name change. Jack and Ian grew up together. Friends from the time they were little. That's how we met."

"Ian?"

"He was one of the investigators on the case."

"Jack knew everything?"

"Yeah." Mostly. Even Jack didn't know about the

guys who bought my dad's business. No one knew about that.

"You stormed into my house over that menu. You went to bed with me last night. And you kept this a secret the whole time."

Put in that light I really looked like a heel. "I meant to tell you." I spread my hands out. "I wanted to tell you. But you told me I was your light, and there's nothing about my past that's light. I didn't want to ruin it."

He slowly nodded as if digesting the facts, rethinking me, rethinking us.

"Congratulations," he said. He didn't raise his voice. He didn't need to. He slapped the file down on the counter and knocked the box clear across the table. It slid off and onto the floor. "Faith and trust as homonyms or synonyms. Clearly, you don't know what either means."

He stalked out of the house. For the first time in a week, he didn't stop to tell me to lock my door.

Anger, hot and red, bubbled up inside of me— anger at the futility of my life, of trying to understand things that Jack had hidden from me, of going on when so many people near and dear to me were gone. I flew out the door behind him.

"You self-righteous ass. You don't have a right to pass judgment on me."

He pivoted on his heel and pinned his gaze on me. Those eyes, rock hard, regarded me as if I was beneath him.

I took a deep breath and tried to steady my voice. "You don't know what my life is like or was like, without my parents, without Jack. I didn't know you. I didn't know your feud with Wade or Troy when I stepped in to help you. I didn't ask for your help. You bet me, you challenged me, and if I'm correct *you* came to my door last night. There's a lot of shit in my past that I'm not proud of—" My voice cracked.

I regretted some things so hard every day that if I really thought about it, really let those feelings in, I wouldn't get out of bed.

CJ ran a hand over his face and through his hair.

I pressed on. "I wake up every day having to live with it. I don't need your smug righteous judgment. I know the part I played. I never escape those consequences. I don't need your bullshit, and I sure as hell don't need you."

I didn't wait for his response. I stomped away, slammed the door, and slid the deadbolt into place.

I also knew how to lock doors without his help. I sagged back against the locked door and let the grief overwhelm me, grief for Jack, for my parents, for what I once had and lost, and lastly for what I almost had and just let slip through my fingers by my own stupidity. Again.

Chapter 40

CJ

Part of me wanted to go after her. But the other part rooted my feet to the spot. There was not much future with lies like that. Those were big lies. Trish had lied to me, and where had that left us? I wouldn't be deceived again. I whipped out my phone and called Owen. Tamping down on any emotion, I reiterated everything I'd just learned and instructed him to find out the details.

Owen called me back in an hour. "Meet me at the usual place. I'm leaving now."

Owen meant he was flying in. His own plane. An amateur pilot, he'd gotten his license as something to do after service. This was bad news if he was coming in person. He found something that he didn't want to say over the phone.

I pried back up the floorboards in my bedroom and pulled out my handgun—and a few other favorites. If Owen was worried enough to see me in person, I didn't want to be unarmed.

The old hunting stand on Turner Road had stood there for as long as I'd been coming north to visit my grandparents. Rarely used, even in hunting season, it was an ideal spot to meet. I could access it driving my ATV down the pipeline. Owen could get there through a neighboring park made up of countless walking trails.

I parked about a mile out from the stand, surveyed the land for several minutes to make sure we were alone, and then hiked the rest of the way. I didn't spot Owen until I was right underneath. He was always good at his job. I hitched my rifle up across my opposing arm and scaled the ladder leading up to the stand. Anyone passing by would think we were two hunters out for a good Saturday.

I shook Owen's hand.

"We should have picked an inside place."

"Welcome to North Carolina."

Owen blew warm air into his hands, the white of his breath encircling them. "At least I didn't have to worry about anyone wondering what I was doing when I cut through that fence. No one was out walking their dogs in this cold."

"I bet." I pulled my wool hat off and scratched my fingers wildly over my head. I hated anything except ball caps, but sometimes the weather dictated more.

"Who owns this land anyway?" He shoved his hands deeper into jacket pockets.

"Old local family. A couple of brothers inherited it from their parents and haven't decided what to do with it yet."

"It's always something." He held out a large manila envelope, dropped it down on the small stump doubling as a table, and leveled a look my way. "I can't believe I didn't find it sooner. Jack did a good job of covering their tracks."

I tapped my fingers on the manila envelope, not ready to pick it up.

"Your lady friend was once known as Whitney

McCarney, a highly talented equestrian whose parents died at the hands of her drugged-out boyfriend. She changed her name shortly after to Finley Hoffman."

"I know all that." I tried but failed to keep the impatience out of my voice.

"My guess is here's what you don't know: The boyfriend didn't do it."

I pulled out the documents from the envelope. A picture of a young good-looking guy with long hair was on top. The same guy in the mugshot. "Why do you say that?"

Owen motioned to the picture. "Jack didn't think so either. And as far as I'm concerned, that's why he's dead."

"Holy shit. So are you saying the two cases are connected—Finley's parents and Jack's car accident?"

"Yep."

The stack of documents in my hand suddenly weighed more than a barbell. "Is this the evidence?"

"Yes—and then some, so don't go sharing that with anyone."

I exhaled sharply, and my breath curled in the air like steam off a cup of coffee. "What else?"

Owen gave me a sideways stare but remained silent. He pulled his cap lower on his head and rolled his shoulders back—bracing for a storm. Classic move for Owen before he dealt bad news.

A chill ran up my spine. "Are we freezing our asses off up here because of Tajikistan or something else?"

"Both. Neither of which I was willing to talk about in a public place, which is why we're here."

If I closed my eyes, I could see the dead bodies strewn about that room. Not all of them guilty, but all of them very dead. Round after round, I had fired into that damn room, fueled on rage. I shook my head.

"Jack wasn't investigating our op," Owen said.

"Then what were our names doing on that damn menu?"

"I think he was looking for info from us on anything we may have uncovered when we worked over there, especially on ops we didn't do with him. On any intel we might have had that could help him, that wasn't in the report. Yeah, he had already talked with Donovan and Rivera, maybe even McDavies, trying to get more info."

"You mean info on who was running the drugs?"

"Yes. Jack believed Finley's parents' murder and our op were somehow linked. He wanted info from us. Of course, he got nothing because someone bumped him off."

"What really happened?"

"The cut brake line and missing cotter pin aren't the only things. Jack had enough alcohol and date-rape drug in his system to kill an elephant."

"Someone drugged him?" The cold seeped in. I rubbed my hands together, trying to get some warmth. "Okay. Lay out what you've got."

Owen nodded. "Finley, twenty years ago known as Whitney McCarney, had a well-to-do father and mother. Father had an import/export business and dabbled in real estate. Did very well."

"What'd he import?"

"Fruits and veggies from South America, Carrara marble from Italy, gemstones from Africa—all kinds of things. Even went through a stint importing expensive horses from Germany and Holland to feed his daughter's horse habit."

"Okay. Legit?"

"Yes, very. Good reputation. But by the mid-nineties, the business starts to run into some cash flow problems. Takes on a new business partner—an Albanian guy who professes love and eye for antiques—and they begin to import from some countries very well known to us."

My heart, already bruised, sank some more. "Turkey and Pakistan."

"Yep."

"Let me guess, not antiques?"

"Antiques all right—furniture, rugs, and our old friend heroin—coming by way of Tajikistan."

"Son of a bitch. You're talking about a twenty-year-old connection."

"Yeah. Well, when we stumbled upon Asllani, Jack started digging on it and uncovered the link between the two. Ahmeti the Albanian, who was in business with Finley's dad, is Asllani's cousin, once removed. I think Jack connected the current day story with Finley's parents' murder and got himself killed for doing it."

"The boyfriend was convicted."

"He took the plea deal after two days of trial. But that's because he couldn't remember jack shit. Her parents were gunned down in that house—execution style."

"And you don't think he did it?"

"No druggie high on as much dope as they found in that kid's bloodstream could have shot them so cleanly. They let the boyfriend be the patsy, and he's so drugged up he can't remember. He's in a mental hospital serving time for killing people he didn't kill. His only crime, from what I can see, is that the dumbass was a drug addict."

I pictured Finley's face as she told me about her parents while we'd been playing ping-pong. No wonder she'd drained her entire beer. "What'd the police report say?"

"Nothing, except to pin it on the boyfriend, which is one of the problems. They should have known that as high as he was, he couldn't have done it."

"You think they were in on it?"

"His prints were at the crime scene. But he wasn't. According to the report, they found him holed up in some drug house a few miles away. In the records, there are some discrepancies in that precinct—businesses suspiciously going under, drug arrests not quite making sense. A few things didn't add up. Jack went to see the old lieutenant on the case. The guy was dying of cancer, maybe had a need to purge himself. Imminent death makes truthful men out of the biggest liars and crooks. Fear of hell and all. Jack's childhood friend worked with that guy for years."

Swallowing the baseball-sized lump in my throat, I asked the question I really dreaded. "And Finley? Anything incriminating on her?"

"The reports in the paper were ugly. In the beginning, they tried to pin it on her. Called her an opportunistic druggie turned parent-killer. It was—" He motioned to the envelope in my hands. "—absolutely brutal. The media got hold of this story and ran with it."

I brushed a hand through my hair. "But she was cleared?"

Owen nodded. "No evidence of her knowing or being connected. I don't think she used the way her boyfriend did. From everything I found, she never had another run-in with the law."

Things couldn't be more messed up. I searched for words to say, but there were none.

"I pulled the estate files too. She didn't inherit anything from her father. All the money went to creditors and, as I said, Ahmeti got the business."

"That's convenient."

Owen threw me a knowing look. "Very."

My stomach flipped over. Why didn't she trust me? "What about the ex-boyfriend?"

"He's still alive and getting released soon. Medical reports don't indicate whether he still claims he didn't do it. All the reports I have just say he's rehabilitated."

I stared out across the open field. A stag edged out of the thicket of trees and nibbled on some grass. He was the perfect distance away for a clean but challenging kill. Not that I hunted. Not animals. I probably couldn't make the shot anyway, not anymore.

I dropped my hat. The buck's head shot up.

"You gonna take a shot?" Owen asked.

"No." But I couldn't drag my eyes away. He grazed five hundred yards out.

"You'd make it."

I shrugged. "Maybe." Three years ago, I would have. I could have made one thousand yards. But now, things didn't work as well as they used to. Steady was no longer my middle name—or first or last.

Since I'd gotten wounded, there hadn't been a night I didn't think about that mission. So hell-bent on getting that kill, I'd disregarded the danger I put my team in. Elliot had paid the ultimate price. But we'd all paid for my mistake, my vengeance, my bloodlust.

Owen must have known my mind. "It was a messed-up op and not anybody's fault."

"I had the perfect shot. I live it again and again. What the hell was I waiting for? I was better than that."

"There was nothing perfect about that op." Owen's tone brooked no argument, but I knew better.

"If I'd have made it, took that scumbag out when I had the chance, we'd have packed up and gotten out. Elliot wouldn't be dead. I wouldn't be half a person." I ran my fingers over a picture of a young Finley—a young Whitney. "We lead. And if we don't lead, we follow. But we don't leave a man behind."

"And failure's not an option." Owen finished for me. "You do know there's nothing perfect in this world, right? That the only perfect thing is *im*perfection. Did I not do a better job of drilling into your head that we take the crap situations handed to us and do the best we can? And sometimes, no matter the heroics, that shit goes sideways."

"I was better than that." It came out in a snarl.

Owen wasn't ever backed off by me. His hand curled into a fist. "You are human, then and now. That so-called *perfect shot* you missed is just a screwed-up memory you concocted. Let yourself off the hook that no one else put you on. Elliot would be punching the shit out of you if he was here. All the creeds in the world won't fix a shit storm of random catastrophic events intersecting. I've seen the report."

I stared at Owen, Elliot's face and twisted corpse playing through my mind. "Were we set up?"

"Nobody's going to admit that, especially when we were in a country where we had no legal right to be in. And I'm hell sure that anything linked to that op is gone, but I'm telling you to set it down."

That lunch Finley and I shared at the therapy center filled my mind. What had she said about her mother's advice? There was no such thing as the perfect distance. Something like that. My mind stalled. Would I call her Whitney now? I shook my head, trying to banish it all. I held my hand out. "Thanks. I owe you one."

"Anytime. You know that. Watch your six. Someone wanted to keep this thing a secret, enough to kill for. If that same someone thinks Finley knows something, or you—well, you could be next. Mobsters, regardless of ethnicity, don't forget. Things could get messy."

I nodded, not saying a word.

He glanced at his phone, checking the time. "I'm going back in an hour. Let me know how it goes. Don't call me on any lines you know. I don't fancy winding up like Jack, and I've been digging around enough to alert people."

I nodded and slipped him my number from a burner phone. He reread it a few times and then pulled out a lighter and torched the sucker. We'd been trained well.

I swung out of the stand onto the wooden ladder.

"Sin?" he called. "You need to forget the past and get back on the horse."

"I'm here meeting you, aren't I? I *am* back on the horse." Five rungs from the bottom, I dropped to the ground, welcoming the jolt of pain that radiated up my leg. It didn't match the hurt in my chest, but it was a close second and reminded me to stay sharp.

What was it that Finley said that day at the horse therapy center? There was no such thing as the perfect distance. But the right distance would come up easily if you were moving forward.

Chapter 41

Finley

I guess I had something to be grateful for when Jazz and Cody traipsed through the door two hours later. If CJ had stayed, we'd probably have been back in bed, and there's no way I wanted to get caught there with my kids. I pulled a freshly baked loaf of banana bread out of the oven. In the glass of the oven door, my reflection wasn't too pretty. My hair was all askew in some haphazard ponytail, and my face splotchy from a mixture of crying and anger. Hopefully the kids wouldn't notice. I had packed up the box of Jack's files, and it stood in the corner waiting to be trekked out to our barn. I pushed a stray hair off my forehead.

"What are you guys doing home so early? I thought I had to pick you up this afternoon?"

Jazz waved her hand through the air. "Buses got in early. The Carters gave us both a ride home."

"Want something to eat?"

Jazz cut off a piece of banana bread. "I'm good." She nodded at the box in the corner. "Are you finally unpacking the books? I'll help if you are."

Cody tramped into the kitchen and dropped his duffel bag. "I'm going down into the tunnel.'

"Cody! Take that up to your room. And don't do that. Going down into some unused tunnel doesn't seem like a good idea to me."

He kicked the bag toward the front hall. "I'll be fine. I want to do this before it gets dark."

"Be careful."

He swiped a slice of bread and opened the pantry door. "I will." Before I could say anything else, the pantry door closed.

I looked back at Jazz.

"He'll be fine," she said. "He went down there last week when you were working. He followed it all the way to the edge of the property and then went and visited the Bennetts."

I didn't know if I should be angry that he hadn't asked my permission or proud he'd been brave enough to do it. Parenting was this funny balance between giving freedom and keeping from danger.

Jazz shrugged. "You want to unpack the books?"

Jack's box stood in the corner. It had to be taken to the barn anyway. I could trek it over there and pick up the last box of books. "Okay."

Jazz and I went through the books, setting them on the shelves. The irony wasn't lost on me. Here I was unpacking and maybe I should have been packing, but I was too tired to argue with her or with my head. It was nice to see the books—like long-lost friends showing up to comfort me when I needed them the most. All of them were from a time in my life when I believed in magic horses and dreams that always came true. In a few books, the pages were so worn it wasn't hard to see the passages I read and re-read.

Jazz had a lot of questions. It was as if she'd left her anger on the field trip and the Jazz of pre-Jack's death had come to visit. I reveled in it, and for a moment, I missed Jack so much the pain was tangible. We hadn't had the best marriage, at times it had seemed like the worst, but he loved our kids.

Jazz peppered me with questions about some of the books. Maybe it was her new attitude, maybe it was my argument with CJ this morning and I was tired of hiding my past, maybe it was just I was worn down. But either way, I wound up talking more about my childhood than ever before. I sat back and checked out the books piled next to Jazz and the ones on the shelves.

"What's wrong?" Jazz must have noticed my confusion.

"*The Monday Horses* is missing." One of my all-time favorite horse books.

"Maybe you forgot to pack it?"

I shook my head, a nagging feeling prickling along my scalp. *Where was it?* "I don't think so."

Jazz's phone buzzed. She typed a few minutes and giggled. Holding out for me to see "Look at this pic from the trip."

The thought thundered in from left field, triggered by Jazz—images of Troy creeping along CJ's property, heading up the hill. *I never told him! Shit!*

I grabbed my phone. Maybe this was the kind of thing better talked about in person. "I'm going to see CJ. I'll cook dinner when I get back."

Texting on her phone and walking up the stairs, Jazz nodded. "All right. See you later."

My stomach turned at the thought of another run-in with CJ. What if he was a complete ass? But jerk or not, I owed him that much. I slipped my keys off the entryway table and headed out the door.

Chapter 42

CJ

When I couldn't go out on the lake or ride, there was one last thing I did to take the edge off. Chop wood. Even as the clouds rolled in and the water hanging in the air turned to actual rain, I stayed outside and took my anger out on the wooden stump and fallen tree limbs. There was nothing as satisfying as the *thunk* of the ax into a chunk of wood. I was twenty logs in, hair soaking wet, shirt off, when she showed up.

Ellie, who had been keeping me company, immediately got up and went to say hello, tail wagging. Traitor.

Finley stopped at the edge of the clearing, petting Ellie's head. "We need to talk."

I shook my head and grabbed another log. "I don't think so." I swung the ax up and brought it down with such force the log split right into two. Damn, that was satisfying. An image of last night crossed my mind. Splitting wood wasn't as satisfying as last night, but at least the wood didn't fricking lie. I picked up the split log and tossed the two pieces onto my growing pile. Despite the lies though, despite the truth even, I didn't regret last night.

"I didn't come here to revisit that." She spat out the last word, like it left a bad taste in her mouth too. I wondered if she meant our time in bed or the morning going through the file box.

"Well, thank God for small miracles." I grabbed another log and thwacked it good. It didn't split as easily as the last.

"Listen, a few days ago I caught Troy sneaking around your property—"

"What? Something else you conveniently forgot?"

"Don't be a total jerk. If I wanted to keep it from you, I wouldn't be here. He was creeping around your barn and then went up the hill toward Bennet's place. I heard him talking on the phone with Wade."

I brushed my wet hair back and wiped the drizzle off my face. "What'd he say?"

"Something about the hunting shed." She swallowed and bit her lip.

"What else?"

She glanced away and back, uncertainty written all over her face. "He said that Trish was the one who called Animal Control."

Son of a bitch. My ex-wife was never a loyal person. Who knows what Wade and Troy promised her and Boyd. I clenched my fists.

"Did you get pictures? A recording?"

"Sorry—" She held up her phone.

"Why do you keep that ancient thing anyway?" I bit out the words, totally ticked off about everything. "And why didn't you tell me about Trish calling Animal Control?"

"I'm sorry. I forgot. Besides, I may not have been with someone in a really long time, but even I know you shouldn't bring up a guy's ex before going to bed with him." Her voice blazed full of anger. She stepped closer, blocking the chopping block. Her eyes were as heated as her voice.

For a brief second, I wanted to grab her and kiss her. I gulped the feeling down. "Fine."

I jammed the ax into the block and stalked off to the house.

"Where are we going?"

I grabbed my wet shirt off the porch railing and threw my door open. "*I* am going to find out what Troy was looking for, but *we* are not going anywhere."

"Are you going to talk to him?" Her voice rose and fell, high pitched, just like Storm when I brought in all his friends and left him alone out in the pasture.

I tossed the wet shirt into my laundry room and disappeared down the hallway in search of a dry shirt. I prayed she stayed where she was because as mad as I was at her, I still wanted her. If she followed me into my bedroom, I'd have a hard time not kissing her. And the last thing I wanted to do was kiss her. Luckily, she stayed put.

"CJ?"

I came back into the kitchen and almost smacked into her. She backed up a step, and I moved in a large circle around her, making sure we didn't touch. I grabbed my rain jacket off its hook. "No. I'm going up to the shed to see what's going on."

"I'm going too."

"No, you're not." I grabbed my handgun from the counter and slid in the loaded magazine.

"Why not? This involved me, too. Troy wants to bring charges against me for stealing saddles. I was there when he threw you into jail. I spotted him. I'm the witness. I'm coming."

Her gaze battled mine. What did she say on one of our first days? She wasn't a risk-taker. Yeah right. I tucked my handgun in my waistband. Her eyes widened, but she didn't move a step.

"Where are the kids?" I asked.

She exhaled but didn't budge. "Jazz is at home. On her phone. Cody went through the tunnel to Hank's farm."

I grabbed a second rain jacket. "Fine. You can come."

"I wasn't asking for your permission." She snatched the rain jacket from my hand and slipped it on, still blocking my exit.

I had to admit I loved her fire. "If I tell you to go, if I tell you to do anything, just do it." Maybe that sounded too harsh. I grabbed the door key and the key to my ATV. "Please."

She grabbed a baseball hat on the shelf and threaded her ponytail through the back opening. "Deal."

She spun around and strode out the door, leaving a waft of her perfume. I choked back a groan at the vision of screwing her in that hat. Ah, hell. How did I get here? Ellie, seemingly as stubborn and intent as Finley, squeezed out the door after me. We loaded into the ATV and set off up the hill, just in time for the sky to change from pissing rain to downright pouring.

Wonderful. For a day that started out with such promise, we were certainly in the weeds now.

Chapter 43

Finley

The anger rolled off him in waves, and he stared straight ahead, brows furrowed. The ATV bounced up the path behind his barn. Thank God Ellie sat between us.

"You're not going to kill me, are you?" I tried to joke but it came out flat.

He pinned those once soulful eyes on me, now as hard as rocks. "Don't joke about that. I take killing very seriously. I have a right to be pissed off."

I couldn't really argue with his point. I nodded and broke his gaze, turning my attention to just hanging on. The spitting rain made the safety handle as slick as ice. The ATV climbed the hill behind his house. It was the same path we'd ridden just a few days ago. It wasn't half as pleasant with the rain bouncing into our faces. Ellie's eyes were narrowed to slits, and her ears were blown back by the wind. Poor baby. I ruffled her fur, and she squished her head into my armpit. My eyes filled with tears at the gesture. At least she wasn't mad at me.

CJ stopped the ATV a few feet away from the hunting cabin. Ellie stood up and then immediately hunched down and whined. CJ whipped his head around, searching for what upset her. He waved his hand toward me. "Stay here."

He took his gun out and advanced forward, slowly slinking to the edge of the cabin and then around. He disappeared around the porch. "Son of a bitch." His voice, deep and hoarse, reverberated through the rain and wind. My heart jumped and then took off running.

I slipped out of the ATV. "Stay, Ellie."

CJ stalked back around and up the porch steps and with one kick blasted open the cabin door. I followed him up the stairs and into the cabin. He shot me a look and whispered, "Didn't I tell you to stay put?"

There wasn't much in the small twelve-by-twelve room except for some cigarette buts, candy wrappers, and crunched-up soda cans—cheercola. A rickety cot sat pushed up against the wall under a small window, and a tiny table and chair stood in the middle of the room. In the opposite corner, a bag of deer corn leaned up against the wall. CJ's gaze swept across the room wildly and settled on the window. Lips pressed together, face pale, he strode toward the window and peered out.

"What's wrong?"

He scratched a free hand through his wet hair, his gaze still firmly focused on something outside the window. He fisted and unfisted his free hand. Something had upset him.

I stepped back through the door. He made a grab for my arm, but I was too quick. I ran down the steps and around the corner of the cabin and slammed to a halt. Two big white mounds of fur lay on the ground.

"Oh my God." No wonder he'd look white and sick when he kicked that door down.

"They're Hank Bennet's Great Pyrenees. Good

guard dogs. The best. This one is Ollie. And Stan is the one with the black snout. Not that you can tell now. This is going to break Hank's heart."

We stood in the rain, silent.

Bending over one of them, he tried to close its lifeless eyes, but it didn't work. He swiped at some dried blood but couldn't get it off the hair. "What a waste." Disgust and anger laced his voice.

I couldn't get my mouth to move or even my brain to send any words. I just stared at those two poor dogs, their white fur matted and wet from the rain, turning muddy with red splotches from where they'd been shot. They must have been beautiful animals.

Through the cold rain, CJ squinted at the sky. It was late afternoon but felt like early evening because there was no sun, just gray clouds pressing down for as far as I could see. He pivoted on his heels and went back to the ATV. He paused to pet Ellie, murmuring to her, and then grabbed a tarp from the back.

We spread it over the dogs and secured it.

He pulled out his phone. "I'm calling Hank. Poor guy, he probably thinks the dogs went hunting. He'd never leave them out here if he knew the truth. Shot right through the head."

"Who would do such a thing?" I asked. But I knew. I knew who did such things.

"I have no idea what kind of insane person shoots dogs but when I find them, I'm going to tear them limb from limb. And then I'm going to kill them."

Sarge's stiff, lifeless body came to my mind. His yellow coat stained red where he had been shot. The night of my parents' murder, the detective had come from the study and said, "He shot the dog. Right through the head. Only crazy people shoot dogs."

This was no coincidence. Michael must have gotten out, must be somewhere nearby. Near enough to shoot Hank's dogs. I couldn't breathe. It was like a truck rolled onto my chest and stopped. CJ was oblivious, focused on his call with Hank Bennet. I backed up toward the ATV, though I'm not sure how my legs got me there.

My phone rang, jarring me. It was probably the kids wondering where I was.

CJ glanced my way but then wandered back up into the cabin, motioning to me to stay put.

I pulled my phone out. It was a New York number. The rain had lifted for a minute, and from here the lights twinkled in my house.

"Hello?"

"Finley. Erin Brown."

"Yes." My already frayed nerves unraveled.

"I called to let you know Michael was released yesterday."

I grabbed the bar of the ATV to keep steady on my feet. "Yesterday?"

He could have flown down here. He could have been here, basically in the backyard of my house, watching me over the last two days, watching the kids, killing Hank's dogs. The lights from my house wavered. In an instant, they seemed to grow smaller. The kids. The kids were alone. I let go of the ATV and broke into a full run.

I burst through the back door, my lungs on fire, covered in water and mud from where I slipped down the hill. Jazz sat at the kitchen table, munching on banana bread, her laptop open.

I doubled over, gasping for breath. "Are you—okay?"

She gave me that annoyed teenage sideways glance. "Yeah. Are you?"

"Where's Cody?"

"He came back ten minutes ago. He's in the shower."

I straightened up, my mind careening in ten different directions. I'd left CJ up there. What would he think when he came back out? Should I pack us up? Should I just go? I slammed the deadbolts closed on the front and back doors.

"You're acting weird." Jazz's face flushed with half confusion and half teenage snarl.

"Put a chair under the doorknob of the back door!"

"Mom?"

"Just do it, Jazz. Now!"

Jazz did as she was told for once, and I grabbed a chair and jammed it under the doorknob of the front door.

"Mom, what's going on? You're freaking me out."

I didn't answer, just shook my head, the words lost to me. I grabbed a bottle of water from the fridge. My peripheral vision wavered. Then righted itself. *No, not now.* I held the bottle of water out. Its outline dissolved. The words on its label dropped letters. Then whole words went missing. *Shit. Not now.*

Full-fledged migraine.

Chapter 44

CJ

I stared into the hole in the floor, speechless. Hank had reminded me of the fake floor in the cabin built into the floor decades ago by his granddad. With a little encouragement from the hammer I found on the table, it hadn't taken much to loosen the first board. In fact, it hadn't taken anything more than a slight pull. Staring back at me were boxes of ammo, an AR rifle, and several handguns. Who the hell had stored guns up here? Was this what Troy was looking for? Maybe all along he'd been investigating a case?

Ellie barked. *Shit.* I forgot about her and Finley sitting out there. I fitted the boards back in place, moved the bag of deer corn over them, and set the hammer in its spot. I needed to get out of there and make sure Finley was okay. Hank was on his way up here with his nephew to pick up the dogs and bury them. I offered to help, but he had refused, knowing the toll physically and emotionally it would cost me to move and bury them.

Ellie barked again. I locked up the cabin door best I could, banging into place the board I'd loosened when I kicked it in. Ellie sat all alone in the ATV. Finley was gone. I stopped on the porch and gazed around, searching for her. I called her name. Whatever light had made it through the overcast sky was definitely gone, and night was fast approaching.

The lights from Finley's house blurred through the rain. Even in the dim light and steady drizzle, it was obvious from the porch how clear the view was down to Finley's house. With a pair of binoculars, somebody perched up here could see directly into her bedroom. This was a good place for a stalker to get his rocks off watching Finley.

I circled the cabin and ventured farther into the woods on either side, calling her name. Nobody answered except a few of the last remaining birds refusing to vacate before winter moved in.

I returned to the ATV. Ellie whined and pushed her head under my hand.

"Where'd she go, girl?"

She wagged her tail in answer. "That's not very helpful." I called her cell phone, but nobody answered. Of course not. Shit.

I typed in a text. —*Are you ok?* —

—*Y*—

That was kind of short. No message, no call.

She was so hot and cold. I know I wasn't making it easy on her, but she could have at least told me or texted me before she took off. I shook my head, started the ATV, and headed home. The drizzle decided it was the perfect time to downpour. By the time I got back home, nearly every inch of me was soaked to the bone, even under my rain jacket.

I trudged into my house. Ellie followed me inside and shook her wet coat, shedding water all over the main room.

"El." It came out as a mutter, hardly a reprimand.

She gave me a backward glance and slunk to her bed in the corner. She wasn't happy about this outing, and I didn't blame her. I ditched my wet clothes and headed for a shower. I'd check on Finley again as soon as I had some dry clothes and a beer.

I let the shower run long and hot on my neck, trying hard to forget the vision of Hank's dogs shot through the head. Just when I thought things might get back to normal, life turned itself upside down.

Cleaned, dressed, and somewhat warmer, I went in search of a beer. My phone buzzed on the kitchen counter. Perfect timing. I tipped my open beer up for a swig and pressed the green button. "He-llo." I coughed out the second half of the word.

"CJ?" The accent twanged my name just right.

"Yeah?"

"It's Mattie." When I didn't answer right away, she kept going. "Bennett. Hank's niece."

"I know who you are, Mattie." For some reason every time Mattie called, she had to identify herself, which was ironic because she had shiny raven-black hair that fell all the way down her back. It wasn't easily forgotten. "I'm sorry about Hank's dogs. Is he okay?"

"The dogs?"

"Yeah, isn't that why you're calling?"

She paused and my heart jumped into my throat. *Did something else happen?*

"I got a call from Jazz a few minutes ago. She said Finley's down with a bad migraine, and she can't figure out how to help her. I guess she's sicker than normal. Jazz seemed scared. I can't get there because I'm in Chicago. Can you go over there?"

Well, I guess that explained her disappearing act

earlier.

"There's something else," she said. "Jazz told me Finley was ranting about her ex-boyfriend, Michael, getting out of the mental hospital and that she got some call today from a social worker at the hospital who told her that he was released early. She'll kill me for telling you all this but—"

"I know about Michael." I choked, my throat constricting to the size of a BB at the mention of Michael's name. Owen hadn't called me with this news. It was unlike him. Unless he didn't know, but that was even rarer.

"Unbelievable, right?"

She took my silence for shock, which it was.

"They let the psycho out. Just called her today and told her. No warning. You need to go over there. I'm afraid for her."

"There's no need to worry about Michael." Maybe that was a little too confident. The word on Michael wasn't in yet, but I couldn't tell her what I knew.

"What the hell are you talking about? The guy who killed her parents in cold blood just got out of the looney bin. He might come after her! There's no telling what he'll do. Rehabilitated my ass."

She had a good point. "Don't worry. I'll check on her."

"CJ, there's more. You should know."

The rain lashed against the glass doors. There's always more with Finley. "What is it?

"A few weeks after her parents died, the estate attorney set up a meeting with Finley and some guy who wanted to buy her father's company. The guy offered her peanuts, and the attorney advised Finley to turn him down. Two nights later, the guy and two goons show up after Finley gets off waitressing. They accost her in the parking lot, tell her she's going to sell her dad's business to them for one dollar, she's not going to look through records, she's not going to do anything except sell it to them and close the estate as quick as she can. Then they show her some video of a woman being raped and beaten—the estate attorney's wife. Then they said, 'That's what would happen to you if you don't do what we ask. Immediately.' "

Son of a bitch. I slammed my beer down instead of chucking it through the wall.

"Then they shoved papers at her, and she signed them all, and they left. When I found her, she was huddled in the corner of her car and could barely speak."

"Did they touch her?" My chest was so tight I thought it might explode.

"No. But after that night, she never talked about her parents again. Never, except to say that they died in a car accident. She closed that estate as quickly as she could. She moved into the city, changed her name, cut her hair, and started bartending. She's going to kill me for telling you all this."

"Did she ever hear from those guys again?"

"No. She doesn't talk about what happened with her parents because she can't. I think it might break her. But I know she carries that night with her. That's why she didn't think anything of it when Jack made her make that promise. They knew Michael might get out. They just didn't know when."

"What promise?"

"To move. And keep on moving." Another sigh.

"Anyway, I have this bad feeling. She needs you right now."

"I'll check on her. I promise. Michael isn't going to hurt her."

"She's got a good heart. She's just been beaten up pretty badly by life."

Darkness had fallen quickly. All that was visible were the rivulets of rain running down the doors. "I know the feeling."

"And CJ, when I talked to Finley earlier, she sounded pretty upset. Like someone whose heart's been crushed and who's pretty damn scared of how she's going to protect her family should a killer come calling."

"I didn't crush her heart. She—" I swallowed the words.

"Did it to herself. Is that what you were going to say? Nice. Come on, CJ. Cut her some slack. Be the goddamn hero you're supposed to be." An announcement reverberated through the line. "I have to go. They're calling my flight. Go check on her. Please. Now."

The line went dead. I set my half-drank beer on the counter. Whatever appetite I'd had deserted me somewhere around the parking lot story.

My eyes fell on a picture of my mom and Ashley out at the beach the summer before Mom had died from breast cancer. Love is about accepting, my mother used to say when I'd complain about Ashley driving me crazy. And she'd add: It's the ones that are the hardest to love that need it the most.

The thing was, Finley had never been hard to love. Not ever, not from the moment I'd first laid eyes on her. She'd been prickly and confusing, off-putting and different, hot and cold, but the loving part had been easy and natural. The easiest thing I'd done in a long time, actually. Things hadn't been so easy for me otherwise, not since I'd come back. But I had people and family—Griff and Owen, Hank and Neeley, Ashley, all of them helping me—and if I was completely honest, even dad—all supporting me when I needed it most. Some days it took all of them to get me out of bed and functioning. She'd had none of that. All of the people she ever had to count on had died.

I'd told her she could count on me and then when she needed me, I deserted her like everybody else. My phone sat on the counter, challenging me to do what I should have done a while ago. But the words that needed to be said, the ones kicking around my brain and my heart, needed to be in person. Then Mattie's words hit me: damn scared, protect her family, a killer. From what Owen told me, I knew Michael wasn't the killer, but Finley didn't, and he was still a grade-A lunatic. No telling what he might do.

I grabbed my keys, my jacket, and a new burner phone so I could call Owen and tell him about Michael being released. My old truck sputtered. *Don't do this.* I turned the key again. This time it didn't even try pretending. Nothing. "Son of a—not again!"

The rain hadn't let off, pinging against the windshield like bugs on a summer night around a zapper. I could have used the gods of weather on my side tonight. I shoved my phone into my pocket and pulled my ball cap down low.

Then I ran like hell through the rain.

Chapter 45

Finley

I pressed my cheek to the cold bathroom tile and searched for words. Two minutes ago, Jazz had left to find me a soda. Where was she?

"Jazz?" Speaking sent a wave of nausea through me.

Pelting rain. A fist pounding on the front door. A man's voice, heavy steps. Rolling my head slightly, I touched my forehead to the tile. I tried to get up. Adrenaline raced through my veins. Michael. The kids. I had to protect the kids.

Michael had been crazed that last afternoon when I went to him. He was pissed off my parents kicked him out and told me I couldn't see him anymore. High on whatever concoction of coke and speed or dope he'd ingested, he was ranting and raving about rights, about people telling him what to do. He said he was tired of this bullshit, and they're going to get theirs. I asked, "Who?" He said, "Anyone who tries to tell me what to do, who thinks they're better and smarter than me. But I'm going to take care of it." He waved a gun around threateningly and stomped out of the apartment, leaving me reeling. It had been the last time I saw him before I found my parents lifeless in a pool of blood.

Get up! Get up and protect your kids. I pulled my

legs underneath my chest and grabbed the bathtub edge. A figure appeared in the doorway. I stifled a scream, and my legs buckled. My vision went to black.

The welcome coldness of the bathroom tile against my cheek was the first thing to seep back into my consciousness.

"What the hell?" His voice ricocheted off the bathroom walls—rough, hoarse, sounding like Thor but without the accent. I groaned. CJ?

"Shh," Jazz hushed. "It's a bad one."

"Bad? She looks like death."

I feel like death.

"When did it start?"

"An hour ago," Jazz said. "I found her like this. How did you know?"

Scratching. Someone's scratching.

"Mattie phoned me. Can she move?"

No.

"She's already gotten sick. From the pain," Jazz said. "When she was still talking, she said, if I move her, the ax gets buried deeper. She wasn't making any sense."

In my head—the ax cutting open my head.

"Medicine?"

"I can't find it. I gave her Tylenol and Motrin, but neither has helped."

"What does she usually take?"

I'm out.

I peeled my eyes open. From my vantage point, CJ loomed impossibly tall and wavy. I groaned again and shut my eyes. The beginning my migraines always affected my vision, making parts of what I saw either blurry or wavy. Usually it faded away when the headache took hold but not this night. The pain, normally manageable with over-the-counter medications, had morphed into a jackhammer that was breaking my skull in two. Exhaustion had set in, but sleep was impossible.

Someone touched my cheek. I cracked one eye. At this distance, I could see the blue and brown specks within the green of his eyes.

"This is a very small bathroom. Do yourself a favor and get out before we get stuck in here."

"I have plans for this bathroom and you," he said, "and it doesn't involve getting stuck. Much."

"You heard me?"

"Yes, I heard you, Finley." His tone was much softer than yesterday.

"Are you flirting with me then? If so, it's awful timing."

He chuckled. It rumbled in the small space. "Are you surprised by that? Our timing seems off all the time. Well, I take that back, some things we had excellent timing on."

I smiled, despite the pain. "Mmm."

He stroked the side of my face with his thumb. "I'm going to get you out of here."

I tried shaking my head, which was a mistake. A burst of white-hot pain shot through my eyes. I yelped.

"Lie still."

"Is she delirious?" Jazz hiccuped out. I wanted to tell her it was okay but couldn't find the words or the energy through the pain.

Another stroke of the thumb. "Finley, what medicine do you take?"

"The empty bottle is on my dresser—" My throat

was incredibly dry.

"Okay."

I reached my hand above me, grasping for something. I caught material and closed my fingers around it, pulling with all the strength I had. He knelt back down and covered my fingers with his own.

"Don't go." I struggled to get the words out. A tear leaked from my eye, sliding across my temple and into my hair. He wiped its path with his finger.

"The dogs. My yellow lab, Sarge. I have to tell you about the dogs."

"It's okay. You can tell me later. I'm going to get you that medicine. Hang tight."

Shuffling of feet. Rummaging. Things dropping. It was so loud.

"Michael's out. They released him. Maybe he's coming here."

"He's not. But on the outside chance he is, I'm here now. You don't have to worry."

Chapter 46

CJ

If that grade-A lunatic thought he was going to get to her or the kids, he was in for it. Civilian life, relationships, communication—never strong areas for me. But fighting and protecting—all strengths. I checked my back waistband for my handgun. *Shit!* I had left it behind in the truck. It didn't matter, my knife was in my back pocket, and I had no qualms about killing someone with my bare hands. Finley had me concerned about Michael. It made me wonder if there was something more going on than Owen knew.

My heart pounded in my ears. I took a deep breath, fighting for control. It wouldn't do to lose it now. I dialed Ashley's number, never taking my eyes off Finley. Her cheeks were sunken, deep gray circles colored the skin below her eyes, yet she was still beautiful. Her one foot tapped rhythmically on the floor, barely a movement, but I could see it.

Ashley finally answered. "What's up?"

"I need a favor. Finley's having a bad migraine."

"It's seven on a Sunday night."

"I know but I am your favorite brother."

"You're my only brother. What do you want?"

"Can you call me in a prescription for Finley? For migraines."

"She's not a patient of mine."

"Come on Ash, you've done more than that for me."

"CJ?"

"She's—" I took a deep breath. *Should I admit it?* "—she's in trouble, and I made a promise." A promise I broke once, I wasn't going to do it again.

The silence was deafening, and then there was a whoosh of air. "I'll just come to you. It's easier and quicker. I've got some samples of stuff here."

"All right."

I relayed the news to Jazz and then crouched down next to Finley. "I'm gonna get you to bed."

She shook her head slightly. "I can't."

"What did I say about conceding defeat? Put an arm around my neck."

She reached up and slid her fingers around the collar of my T-shirt. God, I loved her touch. I wrapped an arm around her waist and lifted. She fit easily in my arms, and I backed out of the bathroom and into the bedroom. I laid her on the bed and pulled the covers up. A knock sounded from the front hall. Ashley must have sped the whole way.

Finley kicked the covers down, struggling to get up. I touched her shoulder. "It's okay, DC. It's okay. It's just my sister. No one's getting in here except whoever we let in."

Her gaze met mine, those blue-gray eyes with black rims, trying to muster the strength to show she could fight someone. She gave in and collapsed backward, and I tucked the covers around her.

Ashely bustled in, took Finley's blood pressure and pulse, and dispensed the pills.

After just a minute or two, Finley's chest rose and fell in a long deep breath and her eyes closed. "It's working," she mumbled. "Thank you."

Jazz stood awkwardly next to the bed, tears sliding down her cheeks, her hands visibly trembling.

I walked over and pulled her in for a hug. "Go to bed, Jazz. I'll stay with her." She struggled not to cry. "She's going to be fine. Get some sleep."

"Okay."

I took one last look at Finley lying there, and then walked Ashley to the front door. My phone started ringing before we could say goodbye. It was Owen returning my call about Michael.

"I've got to take this. Thanks, Ash."

Ashley gave me a thumbs up and ran through the rain to her car.

"Owen, what did you find out?" A flash of lightning illuminated Finley's front yard, bathing everything in an eerie blue light.

"Your information was solid. He was released. You're not going to believe what else I found."

Thunder cracked so loud the porch vibrated. "Buddy, we got a fricking thunderstorm in November. I'd believe anything you tell me."

"His application was pushed through by someone at the FBI."

I nearly fell off the porch. My heart galloped in my chest. "Are you shitting me?"

"Nope. I asked Rivera to poke around, and he just got back to me. Someone—and that someone is high up—has something they're working, and that drug addict is part of it."

"So what is it? They hoping that by releasing him,

they'll stir things up? Force the killer to make a play? But if that's it, where is he? Unless he is the killer, and he wants to finish some business." I pressed my fingers to the bridge of my nose, trying to slow everything down. In combat, on a kill, slowing things down before taking a shot was imperative. You don't shoot from adrenaline, but from a position of clarity and calmness. Better odds of finding the mark.

"I can't see it right now, the truth. But it will come. Things are going to heat up. Be careful."

"I will." Lightning forked down, and thunder cracked almost immediately following. I jumped and wished to hell I hadn't left Ellie at home. This storm was right on top of us.

"I can't believe you're having a thunderstorm in November," Owen said.

"That's the least of it."

"What do you mean?"

"In North Carolina, a thunderstorm in winter means we're getting snow soon."

"No shit."

Another flash of lightning. Everything went blue, and I glimpsed someone standing at the corner of the garage. My heart jumped into my throat, but darkness descended before I could make sure what I saw was real.

Owen yammered on, but nothing registered. I peered into the shifting rain, trying to make heads and tails out of the dark shapes, but with the wind and rain, nothing was clear.

"I'll call you in the morning—"

With Owen still talking on the other end, I hung up.

I fought the urge to jump off the porch and charge at the vision, but maybe my mind was playing tricks on me. There was more at stake here than just me. I retreated back inside, locking both doors and jamming chairs underneath each. Then I checked and rechecked all the doors and windows. Ellie wasn't the only thing I missed. My handgun was in my truck and not resting comfortably against my waist. I put in place some precautionary measures and then stationed myself in Finley's room, switchblade on my knee. I waited. Maybe my memory sucked now, and I couldn't shoot one thousand yards, but I was still deadly in hand-to-hand combat.

If someone was out there, waiting to get in here, wanting to get to Finley, they'd have to go through me first.

Chapter 47

Finley

The medicine worked as it always did. With relief from the pain and nausea, I drifted deep into sleep and wacky narcotic-induced dreams.

I dreamed of my mother. She and I walked into CJ's house. Only it wasn't his house—on the inside, it was a bank. Mom handed over two pans of brownie batter to the teller. "Please bake these at 350 degrees for thirty minutes, and I'd like to open a bank account."

"Mom, there's no money. And I don't think they bake things."

She pushed her tortoiseshell sunglasses up on her head, her dark hair spilling down around them. "They do, and there is."

"How is there any money left?"

"Sweetie, your dad was an excellent businessman. He wouldn't let those crooks take all our money. Sit on it for a while, and you'll figure it out."

The teller came back. "Ladies, there's a storm coming in, and I don't know if the brownies will be done in time." A dinging echoed. "That's them now."

Mom fixed me with a knowing smile. I reached out to touch her face, tell her I missed her, but suddenly, I was falling sideways. I yelped, and the bed caught me.

The room was lighter now. Someone had raised the

blinds. Although the sun wasn't shining, it was no longer pouring rain. CJ sat in the corner armchair. In his hands he held the picture of my parents and me at our beach house. I licked my lips. They were chapped, my mouth dried out like the Sahara.

"Want some water?" He gently placed the picture back on the table.

I nodded. He disappeared through the doorway and returned holding out a glass full of ice water. I sat up gingerly, not sure how I'd feel. I took a deep drink of water. When that slight movement didn't start the pain, I took another, straightening up a bit on the pillow.

He placed his elbows on his knees and regarded me. "How's the head?"

Migraines always left a residual headache, sometimes for a day, sometimes for longer. The top of my head throbbed but was bearable. "A five on a scale of one to ten."

"I heard about Michael."

In another world and place, the fact he knew might surprise me, but it didn't today. "I got a call from the caseworker when we were out at the cabin. The migraine hit almost immediately. How did you know?"

"Mattie called me."

I closed my eyes briefly. "There's something else."

He ran his hands down his knees. "Don't worry about anything. We can talk later, when you feel better."

He went to get up, but I waved him down.

No matter how many times I relived that night, no matter how much I wanted to change it, the outcome was always the same. I couldn't imagine he would want to stay after this, but he needed to know what we were up against.

I cleared my throat. "My parents and I had a fight that afternoon. They told me they wanted me to go to rehab and for Michael to move out of the apartment above our garage. I was furious. I stormed off in search of him. He liked to disappear when he went on a bender. I never found him. When I got back that night, it was really dark. I turned down our driveway, which was long, and all the lights were out. I should have known something was up, but we lived in a town that regularly lost electricity, so I didn't think anything of it. Sergeant, my dad's yellow lab, was nowhere to be found—another clue. I went to the back door, and then I smelled the fire. But I thought maybe a neighbor was burning leaves."

CJ raked his fingers through his hair. His stress sign. *Was it my story? Or me?*

"Then I saw the flames licking at the barn roof. I took off running for the barn. I never went into the house. I just ran to the barn and flung open the doors. The horses were screaming."

I squeezed my eyes shut.

"When I close my eyes, I can still hear them. There was so much smoke—it was black and thick. I couldn't see. I got to the first two stalls and got them open, but when I went back a third time, the fire department was there. They wouldn't let me go back in."

CJ's voice was gentle. "How many did you lose?"

I took a deep but shaky breath. "Four. My old pony called Little Love. My crazy jumper, Inca. My gelding, Paddy, the one who won me everything and taught me even more." My voice caught, but I took a breath and finished. "And my mom's quarter horse."

333

CJ cleared his throat. "I'm sorry." His voice was gruff. I wasn't sure what he was feeling, now that he was hearing the whole truth, and he wasn't letting on.

My eyes filled with tears, even as I fought it. "The thing was—my parents. I hadn't even thought of my parents. Not until the firemen came to me and asked me where they were. Then he asked if I'd been in the house. And I hadn't. They went in, and they found them. Shot. In the front hall. I wasn't supposed to go in, but I busted through fireman and policeman and saw all the blood."

He opened and closed his fists and took a deep breath. "You could've told me."

I searched for something outside the window, anything else but those eyes that seemed to no longer hold any admiration. "I could have, I should have, but I—I hate those memories."

CJ dropped his head and knotted his hands behind his neck. I wanted to reach out and touch him. Instead, I curled my hands into the comforter, pleating it and unpleating it.

"You told me that I brought peace to you," I said, "that I had a lightness. And I wanted to be that person so much more than the person whose parents were killed by her drugged-up boyfriend, that stupid girl that did drugs and chose her deadbeat boyfriend over her parents. I hate remembering."

A traitorous tear slipped over the edge and slid down my face. I let it go, concentrating on the view out my window, knowing that if I acknowledged the tear or CJ, the sobs bubbling beneath the surface would break free.

"I promised myself—after I changed my name,

after the media finally let it go, after Michael was locked up—I'd never talk about it with another person."

"What about Jack?"

"Jack knew. He tried to be supportive. When I worried about Michael's getting out, he always assured me we'd move. But at the same time, days when he was drunk, when we weren't getting along, he'd love to throw it in my face."

"Throw what in your face?"

I dragged my gaze back to his. Those green eyes regarded me softly.

I uttered the words that I carried with me every day: "That I was the reason they died."

Chapter 48

CJ

With eyes locked on mine, she delivered the words without emotion. "I brought Michael into our lives. I had the fight with them. I was part of all that happened. And I should have known something was wrong. I should have gone to the house and not the barn."

I rubbed my hands over my face—frustrated that she would think that, pissed that Jack would let her, angry that Michael would put her in that position. It curdled in my stomach.

"How would you have known?" I tried to soften the edge in my voice.

"There wasn't a light on. And my yellow lab, Sarge—" Her voice broke. She sucked in her lower lip and clamped down on it. "He wasn't around. He was always around. Michael shot him, too. He was underneath my dad's chair in the study."

Chills ran up my spine. That's what she wanted to tell me. "What could you have done?"

"I could have called the police. I could have stopped the blood. I could have done something." She raised her hands above her head. "Anything."

My heart twisted in my chest even as my frustration grew. "They were shot dead. Even if you were standing right there when it happened, you probably couldn't have saved them. And Jack saying that you were the reason for what happened is ridiculous." My voice rose, even as I fought it. How could she take the blame for this? And if Michael didn't do it, like Owen thought, then who did?

"Jack used to say I was a bad decisionmaker. He wasn't wrong."

"He used your parents as an example?"

"It wasn't only my parents. I was the one who brought Michael into our lives. I went and bought the drugs when he was too high. I was so stupid. I thought if I did what Michael wanted, got the drugs he needed, that he would love me as much as I loved him. Whenever I'd think about getting back into horses, Jack brought it up. He'd say, 'Are you sure that's a wise decision? You know you have trouble controlling that part of your life.' "

"That's horrible." I stood up just to have something to do besides throwing the chair across the room. "And not true."

"Sometimes we say some pretty awful things in marriage."

"I guess."

She raised an eyebrow at me. She was right—Trish and I had fought horribly on our downward cycle—but still, how could anyone say that to her?

"I'm sorry that happened to you, but it wasn't your fault. Any of it."

"The drugs were. I wasn't addicted like Michael, but I wasn't entirely innocent. Even if I was doing it out of some misguided idea of love, it was wrong. I should have known that."

I scratched both my hands through my hair. "What

about the men in the diner?"

She cocked her head sideways. "Did Mattie tell you?"

I nodded.

"I did exactly what they asked. I signed those papers, sold it all, moved into the city, and became someone else. And that was good because as Whitney McCarney I made some really bad decisions and everyone around me paid—my parents, the horses, Sarge." Her voice got small, her breath shallow, her fingers inching along the comforter and then smoothing it out.

"I know the feeling."

She sat up straighter and pinned those eyes on me, the ones that looked deeper into me than anyone else's. Then she waited. Every beat of my heart reverberated in my chest. I moved from the door to the window and back again. When I glanced at her, she sat patiently waiting. "Afghanistan is one of the biggest exporters of heroin. Did you know that?"

She shook her head.

"It's at a crucial position. Drugs go north through Tajikistan to Russia, Europe, and then the States, or south to Iran or East to Pakistan and India. A lot of those drugs are paid for with arms. We had an informant. Ghani. A young Tajik kid, maybe Cody's age. Very enthusiastic."

I rubbed my hand down my face as if that could erase the image of Ghani. "He was a good kid. His parents didn't want him to get involved. We made a deal. A promise. He got us information, and we'd get them out of the country, get them to the US. He wanted to help us, and he did. We got a lot of information from him, had some good kills off that info. But he got caught."

"What did you do?"

I broke her gaze and walked to the window. The window was dotted with remnants of the rain that hadn't yet dried from the new day. I braced my hands on the windowsill and watched the remaining drops trickle down. "I didn't do anything."

"You didn't help him?"

I drummed my forefinger on the windowsill.

"CJ?"

I didn't turn back around. "We had to wait until the right time, until we wouldn't compromise all our work. When they finally gave us the green light, we were too late. They tortured and killed him, and then they killed his whole family. Left them there for us to find."

Sometimes when people heard a version of this story, when they wanted to make me feel better, they echoed empty words about doing my job, doing what I was commanded to do. She didn't. I looked over my shoulder. Tears dribbled down her face and fell silently onto the comforter clutched in her fingers. She raised a hand and wiped the tears away with a jerking motion.

"I'm sorry," she whispered.

"Me too." I dropped my head for a second and turned around. Her tears had stopped falling, but her eyes still glistened. I cleared my throat. "I want to tell you that things like your parents and Jack don't happen. I want to be able to turn back time for you, take away that hurt. I want to tell you your parents' death and Jack's death are not connected. That nothing like that would possibly happen in this world, in this lifetime, but I can't."

She took a deep breath. "It's all right. All we can do is get up every day and do the best we can with what we have." She swung her legs out from under the covers and stood by the bed. Her hands were slightly trembling. She took a step closer.

I pushed off the windowsill and met her halfway. The circles under her eyes had dimmed overnight to a pale gray. I reached out and traced the line of her cheekbone. "Sometimes it doesn't seem enough."

She nodded and walked into my arms. "I know" floated out from the folds of my shirt. I held her tight, trying to soak in her warmth, chase away the chill deep inside me that some days never seemed to leave. I wanted to hold her forever, but after a few minutes, her arms loosened, and she stepped back. I didn't know where we stood after everything, so I reluctantly let her go.

She grabbed a small blanket that lay at the bottom of the bed and wrapped it around her shoulders. She straightened, her eyes still glistening but her cheeks dry and her face closed up. "Did the kids get to school? I slept right through it."

"Yes. Jazz did it all. Got her and Cody up, breakfast, books, lunches, and off they went to the end of the driveway for the bus."

"She's good that way."

"She gets it from her mother."

She shrugged dismissively and pulled the blanket closer, smiling sadly up at me. "The kids are safer at school. What am I going to do about Michael?"

I steered her toward the kitchen, one hand on the small of her back. "I'm not sure Michael is the problem."

"How can you say that? He was released early, and I saw Hank and Neeley's poor dogs shot, just like Sarge. Maybe he's come down here to finish me off, to take care of unfinished business." Her voice wobbled.

Yanking a chair out, I eased her toward it. "You sit. I'll make the coffee and some eggs, and we can talk." Of course, would talking really make things better? I doubted she wanted me to know all the info Owen uncovered or anything I had to tell her. But we wouldn't stop whoever this was until we were both honest and figured it out.

Chapter 49

Finley

He moved effortlessly around the kitchen. Even with his limp, he had a fluid stride. Watching him, my heart ached. He didn't seem angry anymore, but maybe he was hiding it. Everything I told him was a lot to take in. I knew I should have told him my story earlier, but I was entitled to some wiggle room there, some mistakes. He hadn't been Captain Truthful either.

"What happened?" I asked.

Throwing a sideways glance my way, he got two mugs from the cupboard and poured out the coffee. He set a cup in front of me and my carton of half-and-half and turned back to the eggs. "We went home after Ghani got killed. 'A needed break' was how it was phrased. But I wasn't ready to let it go. For some reason, his death was like the straw on the camel's back. We'd made a promise, and we'd failed. It bothered me more than I let on, more than I knew what to do with. As soon as they got more intel, we were deployed. To finish what was started. I was ready to take out anyone and everyone connected to Ghani's death."

I poured some half-and-half in my cup and watched it swirl. When I looked up, he was busy with the eggs. "Did you get him?"

His back was to me, and his T-shirt fell down the strong curves of his shoulders. Despite all the stress and worry, a familiar ache filled me.

"After we got to the camp, they held us up. Said we weren't going in. I convinced Jack that we could do it, to let us in, and we'd get the HVT they wanted. But things went sideways pretty quickly. We were in Tajikistan, a country we had no right to be in. Intel was compromised. I had a shot, I hesitated."

His chest rose and fell in a deep breath.

My stomach churned, and my heart beat quickened. Jack had come back from that trip messed up. He told me it had been a shit show and he felt responsible. But the fault hadn't just been with him. I wanted to go to CJ and wrap my arms around him. Instead, I stayed put, stirring my coffee.

"It was a shit storm. Everything that could go wrong did, and we didn't do what we were sent in to do—what I had promised Jack we would do. My thirst for vengeance for Ghani's death made it all the worse. They bombed the hell out of us. We did the best we could, but Elliot…"

He stirred the eggs and shook his head.

"But Elliot what?"

"All of us paid for it, but Elliot paid the ultimate price. We were split up after that. I was hurt. Elliot dead. Jack reassigned."

Adding salt and pepper, he paused before resuming his stirring. "The government doesn't take failure lightly. And rightly so. I put us all in danger, including Jack. Ready for eggs?"

Just like that, from near death back to breakfast. "Yes."

He tipped the frying pan and poured a healthy amount onto a plate in front of me. I took a forkful. They were really good. "Why was your name on that menu?"

Dumping the rest on a plate for himself, he studied me, frying pan poised in mid-air. "The HVT we were after had slipped the noose, went underground after that. As far as I know, he's still on the loose. I don't think we're in danger, but one never knows. When I saw my name, all our names, on that menu, my first instinct was to assume Jack had found evidence that we were targets for payback. But now I think he was looking for information we had—or thought we had—info on the drug cartels we dealt with."

"Why didn't you tell me any of this?" I didn't bother disguising my anger.

He placed the frying pan back on the stove, paused a moment with his hands braced on the counter, and then turned around. "You know most of what I just told you is confidential info. I'm not even supposed to tell you what country we were in, much less what we were doing. Besides, a lot of my memories around that time are hazy. The doctors say the trauma, as well as the PTSD, can do that. I knew my name was on that menu because of Tajikistan, but I didn't remember the details, and I still don't remember very clearly. I'm sorry."

"Is that where your PTSD comes from? That op?"

"Nobody can say, but it doesn't matter. To be a SEAL, we fight through the most unbelievable training that a person can endure, and we get thrown through one combat mission after another. We thrive on bad odds—on risk. We're trained for it, way more than any regular soldier. We don't get PTSD."

"But you did."

"Yes. I did. And I couldn't do a damn thing about it. I trained to be the best. These injuries—" He swiped a hand down at himself. "—I'm nothing with them. I can barely run a mile now without my knee seizing up. How the hell can I protect you?"

He glared at me as if daring me to contradict him. His chest fell in rapid successions, one hand clenched around his fork, his knuckles white from the pressure.

My throat tightened, and my heart squeezed. I wanted to say, I didn't want his protection, only his love, but I couldn't. I didn't know where we stood after everything, and I wasn't ready to bare my soul and be tossed aside. I kicked his chair out from under the table. It scraped against the kitchen floor. "I'm not trying to be a jerk, but you should sit and eat. Cold eggs suck."

My comment did what I'd hoped. He smiled at me, pulled the chair out farther, and plopped down. He took a bite and sipped his coffee.

"I know how it feels." I pushed the remaining eggs around on my plate with the fork. "To feel helpless and alone."

"What did you do?"

I glanced up, and his gaze was on me. "I moved down South, tried to start my own business, and made friends with my good-looking and slightly intense neighbor."

The corner of his mouth quirked into a half-smile. "You did more than make friends."

His gaze held mine, and the heat in the kitchen rose ten degrees. Images of the two us of together filled my mind. But where did we stand now, after everything? He gave in first and looked away. I followed his gaze.

The sky out the window had lightened even more. Maybe the bad weather was over.

"Yes," I said. "I saved you from an evil chestnut mare."

This time the smile was genuine. He pulled up his sleeve and held out his arm. Black and blue.

"Ginger?" I squeaked out her name.

"Not happy with dinner yesterday. You better come back to the barn before she nails me with a kick." He rolled his sleeve down, hiding the bruise and his well-defined arm.

"You should have that looked at."

He waved a hand dismissively and lifted the corner of the tinfoil covering a plate on the table.

"That's the last of my banana bread and muffins. I've got to make more."

He scraped his fork along the edge of the plate, rounding up the remaining bits of eggs and toast. "Sounds delicious."

"I'm glad you think so."

"I know so." He pushed back from the table and picked up my plate on his way to the sink, returning with the coffee pot to top off both our cups.

"Well?" I was hoping to prompt him. "Are we going to talk about Michael?"

He stretched out his legs and regarded me silently as if assessing whether or not I could withstand more stress. His fingers—rough, calloused, and well worked—held the coffee cup gently and reminded me of the way they'd brushed down my cheek before he picked me up from the bathroom floor last night.

He took a swig, gulped it back, and said words that shattered my remaining thread of peace. "From what we can tell, whoever killed your parents, killed Jack because he was too close to figuring it out. And Michael? We believe he is the bait."

I sat up in my chair. "Bait? What?"

He took another long pull on his coffee before setting down the cup. "The FBI released him, and my guess is it's to draw out whoever it is they're really after. Whoever set him up."

My heart raced off at a gallop. "Am I bait, too? The kids?"

"Was it Michael who called you that night you fell off the counter?"

"Yes. He told me that Jack had been to see him. That someone was searching for some offshore account of my dad's, where he hid money or diamonds or something. I had thought it was crazy then, that *he* was crazy. But now—" The migraine's residual headache throbbed with a vengeance.

CJ leaned to the counter and retrieved a bottle of Motrin. He shook one out and passed it to me. I grabbed it and swallowed, not bothering to ask him how he knew.

"What do I do?" My voice bordered on hysterical, but I couldn't calm down.

"There's nothing to do but get prepared, wait, and see what happens." He shrugged. "Or run. Which I don't recommend."

"Run seems like the best option. Jack told me to move—and keep moving if I had to."

"I understand where Jack was coming from, but if you run, whoever's after that mystery account will think you have something to hide. Do you want to run the rest of your life?"

I shook my head, unable to get words past the lump in my throat. I took a gulp of coffee and stood up. I wasn't sure who to listen to—my dead husband or this wounded neighbor I barely knew. This had to be my decision.

"That company and guys you sold the business to—were they your dad's silent partners?"

I paced around the kitchen, thinking. "Do you have any idea who it is that killed them or Jack?"

"I've got theories but nothing concrete. I've been over and over that writing on the menu, trying to figure out if I missed a clue, but I've come up empty. So has Owen."

I closed my hands around my head, determining which part I wanted to question first. "My dad had a silent partner?"

"Yes, your father may have been in some financial trouble." He drummed his fingers on the table.

"No, my dad was not in any kind of financial trouble. This doesn't make sense." I stopped and placed my hands on the back of a chair. Maybe CJ was right. He must have been in financial trouble because there was nothing in any of the accounts.

"He was," CJ said, "before he took on this silent partner, an Albanian guy, Ahmeti. Unfortunately, the Albanians used your dad's business to import heroin. Owen's guess is he refused after a few imports, and they killed him for it. We think the cops covered it up, pinned it on Michael for money or a part of the action."

"What are you saying? Michael didn't kill my parents?"

"No."

I exhaled slowly, all recent nervous energy gone,

completely overwhelmed.

"How well do you know Jack's childhood friend Ian Moore?"

"Well. Really well. He's godfather to Jazz. You can't suspect he had anything to do with this."

"Yes, I do. He's one of the cops on that unit, which seems to have been involved in some shady business. Ogilvy was the captain in charge—did you know him?"

"No." In my mind, I ran through conversations with Ian, looking for a hint, any clue he might have been involved somehow. "Ian was on the scene at my parents' deaths."

"Yes, and he was one of the last people to see Jack alive. Anyone investigating Jack's case probably has come across this fact."

Nervous laughter bubbled up and exploded out of me. "Jack has a case?"

He arched one eyebrow and stared at me. "Yeah. And it's not closed either."

Chapter 50

CJ

She glared at me from the back of the chair. "Ian's helped me countless times after my parents died. He's like family."

My chest tightened. I hated to disillusion her since she didn't have much family, but she needed to be prepared for the worst. "Family or not, he's awfully close to both cases."

"But that doesn't mean it's Ian."

"It doesn't mean it's not. Has he called you recently?"

"Yes, to ask if I was coming to meet with Michael's doctors and the board to protest him being released. When I told him no, he got upset."

"So, Michael got released and Ian hasn't called you."

"Maybe he doesn't know. Are you saying I should be scared of Ian and not Michael?"

"I'm saying that it's very coincidental that Ian's connected to both cases. Maybe Jack felt the same way and started digging."

She paused. "Do you think he found the answers and that's why he got killed, or do you think just his digging was enough?"

"I don't know."

"Oh my God." The note of panic in her voice was unmistakable. She shook her head. "No, not Ian. He wouldn't be involved in any of this. The kids call him Uncle."

I set my hands on her shoulders, trying hard not to drag her to me like I wanted to, to hold her against me and calm the vibrations of fear running through her. "I may not be a hundred percent able-bodied, but I swear to you, I'm still a hundred percent SEAL. I won't let anything happen to you or the kids. Whoever this is will have to get through me to get to you, and I'm not in the habit of letting anyone go through me."

Her blue-gray eyes stared into mine. There was heat to her gaze. Did she doubt my abilities, or was she just not sure of anything? God, she was fiery.

"And for now," she said, "until we know exactly who it is?"

"For now, I suggest coming with me to the barn. I have to talk to Griff, and you have to talk to Ginger—if you feel up to it. Odds are, at some point, that guy from Animal Control will show up."

"That's the last thing we need."

My heart lifted at her use of *we*. I pulled my hands from her shoulders, although I didn't want to. I could have stayed touching her all day.

"Okay," she said. "Let me take a quick shower." She picked up the blanket from where it fell on the floor and left the room.

My chest ached. I knew I was the one who'd pushed her away, but seeing her on that bathroom floor last night had made me realize what a stupid fool I'd been. I cleared the rest of the dishes and loaded them in the dishwasher. I wiped down the counters and checked my phones, real and burner. Nothing.

She came out dressed in jeans and a black sweater, her hair halfway dried and pushed back around her ears. Her normally rosy skin still held a pale tinge to it, but it was a marked improvement from twelve hours ago.

"Ready?" I asked.

She grabbed her keys, jacket, and phone and followed me out, making sure to lock the door and check it twice. I insisted I drive her rental car. She didn't fight me, which told me right there she wasn't feeling very well.

Griff lifted his head up from a car he was working on. He waved to Finley. "You want to stick with me or go to the barn?"

"The barn." She lifted the handle and jumped out. A small groan floated through the door.

"You okay?"

"My head hurts when I make sudden jerking motions. Nothing to worry about." She strode off toward the barn. Even recovering and nervous, she had a surety and sway to her step that I loved. I wanted to reach out, drag her back against me, and never let her go.

I dumped my stuff on the front porch and walked to the garage. From here, I had a good view of her in the barn. I had no intention of letting her out of my sight. Not for a while at least. Not until we knew she was out of danger.

Griff waltzed up, two colas in one hand and a paper plate in the other. He held out one of the cans. "Where's those chocolate chip bars Finley made for you?"

"I ate them all."

He cursed, crossing his arms over his chest. "What's going on?"

"What do you mean?" I popped open the can.

He scowled at me. "I was away for one weekend, and I come back and Hank tells me his dogs got killed by some madman stranger, that you and Finley got together and broke up all in one twenty-four-hour period"—he scrunched up his eyebrows—"and you've eaten all the chocolate bars."

"Don't strain yourself." I took a sip of cola and let the coldness fizzle in the back of my dry throat. I peered out the garage doors and caught Finley's shadow in the barn.

Griff followed my gaze. "She not working today?"

"She had a migraine. She got the day off work and she's recovering."

Griff moved in front of the door. "Give it up. I'm not moving."

"You are the biggest pain in the ass." I checked on her once more. Satisfied she was fine, I explained, as quickly as I could, what I'd learned about Finley's past. "Owen believes this whole thing, her parents and Jack's killings, is going to come to a head soon. In the meantime, she's here to see the horses and get some relaxation. She was really sick last night."

"You want her close where you can protect her?"

I rubbed my chin and met his gaze. I never lied to him, not that I could anyway. He knew me too well. "Yes."

"But you're not *together* together?"

"I found out she hid a whole bunch of her past from me."

Griff's eyes widened, and he raised his eyebrows.

"Damn. That tick you off?"

"Yeah, honesty's fricking important to me, and I let her know it."

"Now she doesn't want you?" He whistled. "How does it feel for someone to call you out on your bullshit?"

"Screw off, Griff. You tell me how it is all the time—I'm pitying myself. I'm drunk. I'm sleeping around. You have no problem cutting through the crap. And, for the record, I was the one who called it off."

He cocked his head to the side and stared at me. "Whatever you say, Sin." He dropped his arm but didn't move completely. "When you called me to tell me you were putting in to try to be a SEAL and I told you that you were out of your mind, you know what you said? 'To be the best, you have to sacrifice the most.' "

I didn't answer, and he stepped forward into my space. He was smaller than me, but his size was never an issue, not for Griff.

"The problem is," he said, "you're scared to sacrifice, to lay it on the line because maybe you're not enough this time around. Are you sure her hiding her past isn't the perfect excuse to drop her before she leaves you?"

Leave it to Griff to cut to the bone and do it with amazing accuracy. I brushed by, purposefully knocking into him. "I'm going to get some work done before she wants to go home and lie down."

"I bet that might be hard to not participate in."

"I have amazing self-control. Right now, I want to rip your ears off your head and shove them down your throat, but I'm not." I grabbed one of the car keys from the board.

He stopped me, his eyebrows drawn together, a stern, parental look on his face. "I want in. You hear me? If something's going down, let me know."

That was so like Griff: one minute scolding me; the next, on board with whatever crazy thing I had going on.

"I have no idea how screwed up it may be. You have kids."

"So does she. I. Want. In." He stared me down, daring me to contradict what we both knew: I needed backup I could depend on, and Griff was that person and always had been.

"As soon as I know something, I'll let you know." My cell phone rang. Ashley.

"Hey," I answered, walking away from Griff.

"How's the patient?"

"Much better, thanks. She's up and about today. Although I can still see it's bothering her."

"Make sure she rests at some point."

"Okay. I owe you one, Ashley."

"No, you don't. That's what family is for. That's what Mom would have said. Speaking of which, I talked to Dad today."

"Yeah?" I waited for her to drop the bomb. There was always something with my dad.

"He wants to see you and discuss this land thing."

I almost dropped my phone. The hits today, good and bad, would not stop coming. I cleared my throat, searching for words. "Did you say something to him?"

"I told him I saw you recently and that you had your life together—and that Mom would have wanted him to support you."

"Did you tell him about the Eastleys? Wade's planning to develop a whole damn subdivision on that land."

"A bit."

"Is that why he's willing to loan me the money?"

"He doesn't like to lose. He's not so different from you in that sense."

My heart lifted a bit. I'd stormed out of his house six months ago and hadn't talked to him since. We would never be close, we were too different, but I didn't want to be angry with him. Life was too short for that.

"Thanks, Ash."

"Did it ever occur to you that he's jealous of you?"

"Of me? Every decision I've made, he tells me that I'll fail."

"He might say that, but you prove him wrong every time. And he knows it. CJ, you came home a hero. Injured but a hero. Unlike him, you did exactly what you wanted with your life. Crazy as this sounds, he respects that about you, and he's proud of you. It's just that he's *Dad*. He's always screwed up about how to show those things. And too scared that you loved Granddad more than him."

My mind swirled with that information. "I never thought of that. Of any of it." Dad had always been bothered by my relationship with my mom's dad and how we connected. Even before becoming a SEAL, I'd loved Granddad's farm and chose that over Dad's life of country clubs, real estate work, and fancy restaurants. I had always thought he shut me out when I got injured because I'd failed him on so many levels. But maybe it had been more than that.

"You might try. Anyway, he's going to call you, so pick up—and be nice."

Tires rumbled on the drive. Fricking Animal Control.

Chapter 51

Finley

The Animal Control guy stormed into the barn. He was six feet and overweight, wearing stained overalls and a canvas jacket that wouldn't close over his protruding stomach. Ginger snorted and shied sideways, nearly knocking me over.

"Still jumpy, I see?" His voice was surprisingly high-pitched for his size. It reverberated in the open rafters, and Ginger quickly sidestepped the other way.

I unclipped the cross ties and grabbed the lead rope that I always left draped over her neck. "Easy. Easy," I patted her neck.

She swung her haunches around me and rolled her eyes. I moved with her, trying to disguise her nervousness and hoping she wouldn't lose all sanity and charge forward.

"She doesn't love men, probably because one beat the crap out of her at one point. She's an ex-racehorse who most likely ping-ponged from one owner and trainer to the next, each misunderstanding her and treating her harshly. She's not mean."

"Well, we can't have a dangerous animal around."

I took a deep breath, searching for control. This guy held her life in his hands and, by proxy, my heart. I motioned to Ginger, who pawed the ground. "She isn't dangerous. Nervous, yes. Mistreated—but not dangerous. She hasn't escaped in weeks. She's eating." I ran a hand down her side. "See, good coat."

He frowned and kept a healthy distance from her front hooves. "Where's the owner?"

As if on cue, CJ appeared in the doorway.

The guy motioned to the stalls. "I see you got rid of some, so you're in compliance there." He nodded toward Ginger. "But she's still a handful, and I don't like it. I'll be back tomorrow or the next day with a trailer and someone else to evaluate her. If he doesn't like what he sees, we're going to take her."

My heart nosedived to my feet, and my pent-up frustration bubbled to the surface. "You probably remind her of a past owner that beat her. That's why she acts skittish around you. You come storming in here, loud and obnoxious, making a ruckus. You spooked her. It's you! Not her."

The guy held up his hand. "It's my call. See you tomorrow." Then he snapped shut his folder and strode out of the barn.

I wanted to chase after him and stomp him into the ground. CJ pointed at Ginger's stall for me to get her in there. He turned and half-ran after the guy. I couldn't catch CJ's exact words, but the harsh sound echoed across to the barn. Part of me hoped he clocked him.

I walked Ginger in and slipped off her halter, my heart heavy and my eyes full of tears. As if she knew, she nuzzled my arm, sliding her head within its crook. I kissed the star on the middle of her head and then stepped out and rolled the door closed.

CJ paced in the doorway of the barn, his face clouded and angry.

I met his eyes, but it was too much to handle. Shaking my head, I broke his gaze. I hoped he got the message. If he touched me or said anything nice, I'd lose it.

Keeping my distance from him, clutching onto whatever control I had left, I picked up my jacket and walked toward the driveway. CJ followed, jingling his keys.

What'd you say?" he asked. "To Ginger just now."

"I told her I wouldn't let them take her." My voice wobbled.

"She say anything in return?"

"Yes. She said, 'I give you my trust and take a piece of your heart in return. You are mine, and I am yours.' "

It was a favorite saying of my mom's. A tear slipped over the edge of my waterlogged eyes and slid down my cheek. I wiped it away, frustrated by everything.

"But that trust is misplaced since now someone's going to take her away."

"No one's taking her anywhere." He nearly growled the words out.

I'd only heard him use that tone with the Eastleys—not even with me, no matter how mad he got.

"We're going to outfit that falling down barn of yours with a stall tomorrow and move her there. If he can't find her, he can't take her." He planted his feet, cocked his head, and stared at me as if daring me to fight him.

My heart jumped. "Would you do that?"

"Of course. And I'm driving you home."

I didn't have the energy to argue. "I'd like to say

no, but a locomotive's driving through my head." I opened the truck door and hoisted myself in. In the short drive from his house, my eyes closed ten times, each time longer than before. He parked and turned the engine off.

He swung his keys around his fingers. "I'd like to stay tonight just to make sure you're okay."

I nodded. "I'm not going to run as Jack wanted me to. I've decided to wait. If you want to stay here, that's fine." I didn't designate where he'd sleep. To be honest, I wasn't sure where I wanted him to be.

He gave me a crooked smile. "I won't sleep at home. I'd rather sleep out here in my truck."

The truck wasn't really what I had in mind. "How are you going to last doing this every day? We don't even know if someone will come for me."

"I have impressive stamina."

An image of us crossed my mind. "I know." The words slipped out.

His fingers moved along the seat edge, inching closer to me. I wanted to grab them in mine, but I killed the urge. It was too dangerous to risk my heart or his life any more than I already was. The truck was the best place for him to sleep. I opened the door. "Okay. I'm going to check on the kids and then go lie down."

"What's your schedule tomorrow?"

"Work and then home to bake. Maybe the store for some essentials."

"Okay. Griff and I will probably swap out in the early mornings. I'll work on the stall all day. If luck is with us, Animal Control might not come tomorrow with the storm approaching. Either way, I'll get it done so we can move her." He reached into his back pocket and pressed something into my hand. I looked down. It was his switchblade.

"What's this for?" I wrapped my fingers around the smooth ivory handle and twisted my wrist right and then left, testing its weight.

"It's for you. To protect yourself."

I shook my head. "I don't think I need this."

He grazed a knuckle down the side of my face. "For once, please just do what I ask. Take the knife, put it in your pocket, sleep with it under your pillow. I'll feel better knowing you have it."

I nodded and went inside. The kids thankfully understood the aftermath of a migraine and helped with dinner and did their homework without fussing.

Afterward, peering out the back window of my bedroom, I could just make out the break in the fence. *Left to CJ's, right to Bennett's.* It comforted me. I undressed, took CJ's switchblade out of my pocket, and slid it and me under the covers, grimacing a little at the cold sheets. I gripped the knife under my pillow. Like CJ in his truck and like the break in the fence, it was there if I needed it.

Chapter 52

CJ

Right before dawn, a doe emerged from the woods, testing the area. She signaled to her two fawns, who jumped around with childish exuberance. They picked the apples off the tree near the fence. They ate for a good ten minutes before the doe jerked her head up. In an instant, she was in front of the fawns, blocking them from whatever danger she spied. A second later they leaped back through the broken fence and into the woods.

Griff's headlights bounced down the driveway moments later. He passed a chicken sandwich and black coffee through my window and leaned on the side of my truck.

"Another storm coming in tonight. Ice, snow, and a favorite of ours: freezing rain."

"Ugh." I took a big gulp of coffee and put my truck in drive. "She's got work at seven, and the kids will leave shortly thereafter. After I feed the horses and do all the barn chores, I'll be back to work on her barn."

"Got it. Is she prepared to see me out here?"

"Yeah. I warned her."

"Did you talk about anything else?"

I shook my head, my mouth full of biscuit. I had no words to say on the matter anyway.

"Don't be bullheaded, Sin."

I gave him a thumbs-up.

****

I worked all day on the makeshift stall in her barn. Finley came by after lunch and helped, bringing supplies and buckets. Afterward, she walked Ginger over, dragging two of my newly acquired goats with her to keep Ginger company.

She stood outside Ginger's stall, murmuring to her in that soft way that seemed to soothe wounded horses—and soldiers.

"What's up?" I asked. I stopped safely outside biting distance. Ginger reached her nose toward me.

"She wants you to pet her."

"Or bite me." I cautiously offered my hand, and she let me pet her nose before resuming pacing back and forth in her stall.

"She's all keyed up. It might be the move or the storm."

I'd thought about Finley all day as I worked. She'd been at the door last night, dressed in black yoga pants and a sky-blue T-shirt that clung to her curves just right—curves I wanted to trace with my fingers, following every line of her, imprinting them upon my mind and my body. Maybe it was too soon. Maybe the timing would never be better. Maybe it wasn't soon enough.

I stepped into her space, and for once she didn't step away. I didn't know much in life, but what was clear to me in this crazy world was that she was the one that kept me sane.

She scrunched up her face, watching Ginger, thinking. "I'm going to let her out. Did you reinforce that fence? Maybe she'll do better with more space to run around."

There was an old wooden fence that ran behind Finley's barn creating a small enclosure. "Yeah. The fence isn't super strong, but it should hold her. At least overnight."

She went through her stall, pushing Ginger out of the way to get to the back. As soon as she opened the gate, Ginger rocketed through and raced away. Finley smiled and walked back out.

"It's not as nice as your place, but it works. Do you think they'll search for her when they show up at your place and she's gone?"

I shrugged. "I can't imagine they'll put that much effort in. If I tell them, I got rid of her, it's none of their business."

"Let's hope so."

Ginger trotted along the rickety fence line as we walked, keeping pace with us and nodding her head. Finley stopped once or twice to pat Ginger, but otherwise she seemed deep in thought, kicking her feet through the leaves. We turned toward the house, and I decided to take a leap of faith. I prayed I wasn't too late.

"I understand what you did and why."

She slowed and looked at me. "What?"

"I sat outside last night, and I thought about a lot of things. One year, Ashley's horse ripped up his leg and needed stitches and drains and all this stuff. My sister had ten pages of directions to care for him. The first day I go out to the barn to check how it's going, and there's my mom—white linen pants—crouching on the barn floor, shoving a drain up Rascal's leg because Ashley couldn't do it. My mom's hand was shaking like a leaf, but she did it."

"Yeah?"

"She hated blood and mess, but she did it for my sister because that's what moms do. White pants be damned, blood be damned. You moved here to protect your kids because that's what moms do. Your first priority is them. I didn't factor into it, and I shouldn't have. It wasn't about me; it was about you doing your job."

A gust of wind blew—biting, with the feel of imminent rain—and heralded the approaching storm. She stopped, and so did I. I took a deep breath and pulled a windblown strand of hair caught on her lips. I tucked it behind her ear. "I'm sorry I was such an ass."

She brushed the other side back behind her ears as she always did, a self-conscious habit I adored. "I'm sorry I didn't tell you everything. I just—" Her eyes glistened. "—it's hard to talk about it."

"You had your reasons. I understand. I'm more of a 'shoot first, ask questions later' kind of guy, which is great in the field but not in life."

She half-laughed. "Is this life? Sometimes it feels like hell."

"I think that's the definition of life—one chaotic problem after the other. But then, sprinkled within, there are moments where time stops moving and things fall into place just for a second, or maybe ten, and those moments are what makes all the hell worth it."

I slid my fingers slowly up around her face, hoping she wouldn't stop me. She didn't, and I cupped her head in my hands.

"Like this moment?" she asked.

"Yes, like this moment."
I captured her mouth with my own.

Chapter 53

Finley

My mom's words echoed in my head: *Forward, Whit, think forward. If you do that, the distance will be there. It will come up right in stride. It doesn't have to be the perfect distance just the one that works for you and your horse. Throw your heart over the fence in riding and life.* I parted my lips, inviting him in, letting him deepen the kiss until every limb was on fire.

"I missed you," he whispered.

It took all my self-control not to pull him down to the ground and show him how much I missed him too.

A buzzing reverberated in his back pocket. He cursed, grabbing his phone. "What?"

I wondered if it was Griff. His short comments only got shorter and snappier as the conversation went on.

"Are you shitting me? Right now? This can't wait? All right. Give me five minutes, and I'll call you back."

He hung up, roped an arm around my shoulder, and pulled me into an embrace.

"That was Wade. He always had impeccable timing." He pivoted on his heel and limped up the porch stairs.

"What?" I caught up to him and grabbed his arm. It slowed him down, but he didn't stop.

"Wade Eastley. He said the seller is agreeing to take offers and if I want to be considered I have to get it in now."

"But why is Wade calling you? I thought he wants the land." I jogged up the steps after him. The wind whipped my hair in front of my face. With each gust, the temperature seemed to drop by another ten degrees. Damn, this storm was coming quick.

"Apparently he has to under some real estate law thing. The seller told him they heard there was other interest, and they won't entertain his offer without knowing what the other offers are."

"Thank you, Mattie." I muttered it louder than I had meant to.

He cocked his head. "What's this have to do with Mattie?"

I pushed the front door open, thankful to be inside and out of the cold.

CJ's gaze roamed over my front hall, his brow furrowed, stopping on me briefly. "Fin?"

I brushed my hand over my forehead, pushing back my bangs. "I called Mattie and asked her about putting in an offer and if Wade had a conflict of interest because he's a realtor. She said she knew the sellers and would make some calls. Do you have a formal offer to purchase?"

"No, I don't have a formal anything. My dad wants to talk about it, but there's no way he'll commit a down payment on such short notice." He motioned with his head to the front door. "And this storm is going to hit soon."

I waved him to follow me to the kitchen and grabbed my bag by the back door. Hoisting it onto the counter, I rummaged through it and pulled out the contract Mattie had emailed me two days ago.

"Here, you can use this."

CJ glanced out the window. "This could be a bad storm. We still don't know who killed Benton's dogs. I don't think now is the time to deal with this land thing."

The mention of Hank's dogs made me shiver. *If they didn't think it was Michael, who was it?* I uncapped a pen, plopped down at a chair at the table, and got to work. "Listen, you've waited too long for this land. Let's fill this in and then we can drop it off. Mattie walked me through what I need to do. She's licensed as both an attorney and a realtor."

I scribbled in the amounts and any information I knew and pushed the sheets across to him. He scanned through them, indecision written all over his face.

"I put my name as co-buyer just so you have access to the cash. You can pay me back later, and I'll sign my portion over to you."

He drummed his forefinger on the table.

What's holding him back? Is he wondering if he could trust me now—after all the lies? "It will be fine. When your dad loans you the money, you can buy me out. This is just for now."

"How do you have this money?"

"Jack's life insurance policy."

"I can't let you—"

"Yes, you can. Now please. Sign."

Seemingly convinced, he jotted his signature and initials everywhere I pointed. I shuffled the papers back into a stack, stood up, and held them out to him. He took them and grinned at me. "Eastley's going to shit a brick."

I grinned back. "I can't wait to see his face."

The back door swung open. "Mom, we have a problem."

Words that jolt a mother's soul.

Jazz led Cody by the crook of his elbow, and Cody held one ice pack on his hand and another over his eye. Blood stained the front of his shirt.

CJ grabbed Cody's other elbow and guided him to a chair.

"It wasn't my fault." The words came out muffled by the ice pack. Another golden set of words.

A trickle of blood leaked out of one of his nostrils. I slowly lifted the ice pack on his eye to reveal a deep purplish bruise. The one on his hand was worse; his knuckles were swollen to double their size.

"Cody." It came out a cross between a scold and a cry.

"Some kid started in on Jazz."

"He launched himself over the seats in the bus and on to some kid double his size." Jazz's voice was a mix of annoyance and admiration. "I can take care of myself, Cody."

I wrinkled my nose at Cody's bruised face and hand. "It could be broken. I better call his doctor." Thankfully we actually had one local since I had needed health forms filled out before they could begin school. "I'm not much of an expert on fistfights."

CJ nodded. "I am. But still, that's a good idea." He grabbed a bag of frozen peas from my freezer and switched it out for Jazz's lunch bag ice pack. "Keep a cold pack on that hand. Can you wiggle your fingers?"

Cody groaned but took the fresh pack. "Kind of. This will make gaming hard tonight."

This was going to make everything hard, especially if I needed a trip to the emergency room. I rubbed the space between my eyebrows. "What did the kid say anyway?"

Jazz's job done, she wandered over to the counter and grabbed one of the last muffins. "He called me a slut," she said, nibbling on the muffin's top.

"What?" Now my voice really did squeak.

She waved me away. "His sister's ex-boyfriend made a pass at me. Don't worry about it. I couldn't care less what that asswipe said."

"Jazz!" There was so much in that statement to worry about it.

She hitched her backpack up on her shoulder and disappeared to the front hall. "The bus driver had to pull over. She said Mrs. Morgan would be in touch." Her feet echoed up the stairs.

The head of the middle school. My heart sank.

I scooped up my phone off the kitchen table and dialed the doctor's office. A nurse politely told me someone would call me back.

CJ placed the offer to purchase on the table. "I think it best if we wait on this."

I snatched the papers back up. "What? You can't wait."

CJ stole a glance at Cody, who groaned intermittently from his chair, shifting the bag of peas from his eye to his hand. "You can't leave here. He needs you."

I surveyed the scene before me and sighed. This was almost enough to bring back my migraine. "No, you're right. I can't." I pressed the papers up against his chest. "But you can. Run into town and come back. It shouldn't take more than an hour. By then I should have answers of what to do with Cody—and maybe talk to Jazz."

I looked forward to that conversation like a trip to the dentist.

"I don't want to leave you here unprotected."

The wind picked up and howled around the corner of the house.

I waved my hand through the air, acting surer than I was. If I didn't, he'd never go—and I didn't want to be the one who lost this deal for him. "We're fine. I'll talk to the doctor. There might not be anything to do except ice it anyway. It won't take long. Just drop it off and come home."

"That's not what I was worried about." He typed something into his phone and then regarded me, eyes narrowed. "Okay. On two conditions."

Spinning around, he swung the door open. He strode out and then returned a few minutes later, the rifle Cody and Jazz used for shooting practice in his hands. He held it out to me.

Cocking my head at him, I raised my eyebrows. "Yesterday you gave me a knife, today a gun, what's tomorrow? A grenade?"

"Whatever I need to do to keep you safe." The corner of his mouth edged up into half a smile but wavered there, concern written all over his face. "Do you know how to shoot?"

My heart, cracked and overwhelmed since Saturday, mended a tiny bit, and I smiled back. "Yes, Jack taught me. I can shoot straight as long as it's not too far. Stay safe out there, and come back to me." The words tumbled out, but I didn't regret it. I meant it. And not because I wanted protection. I wanted to see him again.

His grin faded when he opened the door and faced the darkening night. "I texted Griff. He said he'd come and take the first shift. He should be here soon." He nodded to the gun I left propped against the pantry door. "Keep that close."

I shoved his shoulder lightly. "Go. We'll be okay. Nobody knows where I live anyway." I reassured him, ignoring my doubts as I peered out into the dark. CJ wrapped his arms around me. I buried my head in his shoulder, his warmth a direct contrast to the cold, windy night.

He leaned in close, tightening his embrace, his breath warm on my neck. "Remember, you're not alone this time. And if you have to shoot, exhale first. It'll help you hit your target."

Chapter 54

CJ

Traffic slowed to a crawl through town. I turned right onto Main Street, and then inched along. My phone rang. "Griff. Tell me you are there."

"Buddy, a tractor-trailer flipped over on Seventy-Three. I'm stuck in traffic. Won't be there for at least fifteen minutes."

"Shit. This is not good." I looked behind me. I was hemmed in with traffic. Even if I could turn around, the other side was even worse. My plan had been to drop the papers off and use the back roads out of here. To get to those back roads, I had to make it through this light and past Wade's office. Either way it would take me at least thirty minutes to get home. "I should never have left. I can't get there either. I don't want to leave her alone."

"How about Hank?"

"He's stuck in traffic coming from the VA hospital. Went there for his knee."

"Damn. Can you ask her to go to your place?"

"Good idea. I'll call her now." I clicked off and dialed her phone. It went to voicemail. *When is she going to get a real phone?*

The light turned green, and we actually started moving. Thank God. I pressed redial. Voicemail.

Again.

My burner phone chirped.

"Owen."

"You are not going to like what I have to say."

"Hit me."

"Since his release, Michael Davis has disappeared."

I slammed on the brakes, almost smashing into the car in front of me. "What the hell?"

"I'm going to see what else I can find out. Watch yourself."

"I will."

I called Finley again.

"Hello?" The connection crackled.

"You need a new phone. Where have you been?" I tried but failed to keep my tone light. God, I didn't want anything to happen to her or the kids. I never should have left.

"I was talking to the doctor."

"And?" I drummed my fingers on the wheel.

"She says to stay put, ice it, and take ibuprofen. If he can move his fingers, it's probably just swollen. Call her if it gets worse."

"Listen, Griff is stuck in traffic. You should go to my place."

"I can't. Cody fell asleep. I don't want to move him."

"Fin—"

"Did you drop the papers?"

"It's not important. I'm heading back to you."

"We are fine. Drop the papers. As soon as Cody wakes up, we'll go over to your place. I promise. So do what I ask for once and drop off the papers. Please."

I half-laughed. "Okay. Okay."

"Call me when you are on your way back. I'll be really mad if you don't do it." She clicked off.

I tossed the phone aside and pulled into the parking lot. It started raining as soon as I got out. The heavy drops were halfway between sleet and snow, pinging as they hit the ground.

I ran up the stairs, no easy feat with my leg, but I was too impatient to wait for the elevator.

He greeted me at the door. "This is a colossal waste of time. I can match your offer and more. But you could never stand for me to win."

"I don't have time for bullshit, Wade. Here's the offer." I whipped out the papers I'd hidden in the folds of my jacket to keep dry. I peered around his shoulder into his office and the board room. "I thought you said the buyer was here?"

"He was. But he was so pumped to see the property, he took the keys to the gate, and went out to the property." He glanced at his phone. "Left about a half an hour ago."

My stomach flipped over. "What gate?"

"The back gate, near the cabin on Bennett's land. I showed him on the map how the land-locked piece connects to all the neighboring farms."

"You gave a total stranger access to that property?"

"I've been talking to him for weeks. A guy from New York. He just wanted to check it out in person before the deal closes."

I stepped closer to Wade, the noise in my head making it hard to even hear. "He's from New York?"

"Yeah, he's got some company, AE Imports or something like that." The awe in Wade's voice only made my stomach roil more. "Asked me all about the neighbors and for all the plats and dimensions of the land."

"You gave out people's names?"

"Of course. What difference does it make?"

"What difference does it make?" The words nearly roared out of my mouth. He'd given carte blanche to someone to go on that land—dimensions and boundaries, houses and names. Finley would be a sitting duck.

"It's a multi-million-dollar deal, Sinclair. Stop thinking like a small-town hick. Troy was right, you know." His eyes darted nervously to the side

"Troy was right about what?"

He backed up a step. "Troy told me we had to get you here before we sent that buyer out there, or you'd ruin the deal. And he's right. You'd probably accost the guy and chase him off."

I ground my teeth and tried to breathe deeply, my mind racing. "You asshole. You and Troy have no idea what's going on."

I tossed the purchase offer onto the table. Every part of me wanted to punch the shit out of him, but that would get me nowhere. I grabbed his jacket and threw him back into the wall. "If she gets hurt, even one hair on her head, I'm going to come back here and tear you limb from limb."

I bolted down the steps to the truck, knowing that my bum leg would pay for that later. A litany of curses and threats of jail time followed me in Wade's nasal voice. I swung into my truck, turning the key in the ignition in one motion, and screeched out of the parking lot.

Finley's phone rolled to voicemail, and I fought the urge to punch in my dash. I dialed Owen next as I swung through the back roads, trying to avoid the crowded main streets. I related my conversation with Wade in stops and starts, throwing in curses as cars blocked my way.

"Why can't it ever be easy?" Owen said. "I'm on my way. Donovan and Fox will beat me there."

"What? What are they doing here?" I glanced in the rearview mirror; headlights bounced behind me.

"Donovan called me ten minutes ago and let me know. He must have gotten some intel. He can be an ass, but he'd never leave you hanging and vice versa."

"I know." I swung onto 115, shooting north before hanging a left onto Spring Street. I was fifteen minutes out. "Did you hear from Rivera? Where's Michael?"

"Haven't heard anything. You know, whoever this bastard is, he wants information out of her. Otherwise, he would've killed her already. Or tried to."

An image of Ghani's tortured and executed body flashed in front of me. God, what if I couldn't do it? "O." I choked the word out and stopped.

Owen didn't need more. "Don't even think it. You'll get him."

"I'm half of what I used to be."

"I'd take your half any day over some other guy's full. Remember those godforsaken mountains with the shrapnel in your side?"

"Yeah."

"You hit every damn mark that day. Propped up, blood gushing out of you, broken bones."

The rain changed to sleet bouncing off my windshield. Great. Sleet and hail, just what this night needed.

"You still there, Sin?"

The storm's blackness seemed to increase with each twist of the road. "Yup."

"Never quit."

I pressed Finley's number again and waited to see if she picked up, my heart thundering like a runaway freight train. Nothing. It rolled immediately to voice mail as if it was turned off.

I glanced in my rearview mirror. The lights were still there. Someone was following me.

Chapter 55

Finley

I shoved bowls of pasta at Jazz and Cody and grabbed my phone as it buzzed along the counter.

"Finley?"

"CJ? Are you okay? The storm started."

"Your phone is really crackly, and it kept rolling to voice mail."

"I'm fine."

"Is Griff there? Did you make it to my place?"

"No. And no. Cody just woke up. They already packed up their backpacks. We were heading over in ten minutes."

He cursed loud and clear. "I told you to go."

I curled my hand into a fist. "I had to let Cody sleep. He's up now, and we're going to go. What's going on?"

"I'm headed to you now. It's a setup. Whoever Wade's got interested in the property is from New York. He's after you, not that property. He's out there now."

My heart jumped into my throat. "I haven't seen anyone."

"I'll be there in ten minutes. I'm going to call Hank and Griff now. Hang in there."

I went and checked the backdoor lock. The sleet

lashed against the windows. When I turned around, the kids were watching me, eyes round. Cody stood up and walked over to the sink window. A blue-black ring circled his one eye and his hand was swollen, but otherwise he was better since his nap.

"It's okay. It's going to be okay. CJ is on his way now and so is Griff." My voice shook with each word. I checked my back pocket for the knife. "It's quite a storm out there."

"Hey, Mom?" Cody called, his face pressed against the kitchen window. "Someone is out there."

"Is it CJ?" I clutched my phone in a death grip. *Please be CJ. Or the Animal Control guy.*

"Nope. He's headed for the front door."

Banging echoed down the hallway and into the kitchen. I grabbed the rifle, my feet frozen to the floor. The kids stared at me.

Another round of knocking.

"Whitney?"

I moved toward the front hall, clutching the gun. "Stay here," I whispered to the kids. In true form, they tagged along, a few feet behind and stuck to each other like glue and unwilling to let me go alone.

"It's Ian. Open the door."

My mind blanked. What was he doing here? I checked through the side window and sure enough, with his paunchy gut and corkscrew hair, Ian stood on the porch. *How did he get this address? Our mail is forwarded from a post office box.* We weren't listed in any phone books. I hadn't even signed a lease with Mattie.

I swung the door open. "Ian. What are you doing here?"

He smiled. "Checking on you. I was worried." He nodded toward the rifle. "Clearly I came in time."

I dropped my hand and held the rifle by my side—not that the rifle was hidden, but it wasn't as obvious. "How did you know where I was?"

He threw me a patronizing smile. "Come on, Whitney. I'm a detective. If I can't find you, I can't do anything."

A shiver ran up my back. I knew that in today's society, moving states and renting without a contract or paper trail probably wasn't a very effective method of flying under the radar, but hearing it said out loud was another thing altogether. Somehow Ian always had a knack for making me feel stupid.

With barely suppressed squeals, the kids rushed him and pulled him into a big hug. They didn't have the worries or the baggage I carried. Ian grinned my way. "At least some people are happy to see me."

"Of course, I'm happy. I'm just surprised." I let the door fall all the way open. "Come in before you freeze to death. The weather's awful."

He disentangled himself from their arms and hoisted an overstuffed, black duffel onto his shoulder.

"Staying long?"

"As long as it takes." He dropped the duffel in the hallway, and it *thunked* on the ground. "Is there somewhere we can talk?"

I closed the door, locked it, and flipped on all the outside lights. From here, I could see Ginger pacing in her small paddock. She didn't look happy.

"Let me get them settled in the kitchen." I nodded toward the kids. "Do you want anything to drink?"

He nudged the bag closer to him with his foot.

"Water's good."

I turned to the kitchen, still carrying CJ's rifle.

"I don't think you need that anymore."

I glanced back.

He pulled open his jacket, revealing his shoulder holster. "I'm here now."

That should have made me feel better. It didn't.

I ushered the kids back to the kitchen. "Finish dinner and then clean up. Your uncle wants to talk with me." I leaned the rifle up against the counter.

Jazz narrowed her eyes. "Are we still going to CJ's?"

"I'm not sure." Their backpacks sat next to the table, packed and ready. "Stay in here. I'll let you know."

I filled a glass with water and returned to the front hall. Ian had wandered into the small living room and was inspecting the pictures of Jack and the kids sitting on the different tables. He kept his bag close to his side. I held out the glass of water. He took a sip and set it down on the mantel.

"Why didn't you come to New York and fight Michael's release?"

"I'm good too. Thanks for asking."

"Don't be snippy. We don't have time for this, Whit. Michael has disappeared. Did you know that?" There was a trace of panic in his voice.

The unease I'd been feeling all day, jumping around in my gut like fluttering baby butterflies, morphed into full-grown butterflies running the Kentucky Derby. Oh God. *Did I make a mistake letting him in? Or am I just paranoid?*

"I knew he was released. What are you worried

about?"

"I'm worried about *you*. That's why I'm here."

Maybe, but that wasn't the vibe I was getting from him. More like nervous and edgy. Although what he was edgy about, I didn't know.

"I'm fine." That might have been a slight exaggeration, but I had CJ, and what did he say? He wouldn't let anyone go through him. Of course, I would've felt a little better if CJ was actually here.

"I think you should come with me."

"Come with you? Where?"

"I can keep you in a hotel near here. You'll be safe there until they find Michael."

"I can't come with you. I promised CJ I'd go to his house. In fact, we were just getting ready to go there."

"Who the hell is CJ?"

"My neighbor. He's been helping me." He's a retired SEAL almost crossed my lips, but I swallowed the words. For some reason, I didn't want Ian to know that.

"Why don't you ever listen to me? You are in danger, but I can protect you." He glanced at his bag on the floor.

"Listen, I appreciate it. I know something's up. Yesterday I saw my neighbor's dogs lying dead from gunshot wounds. But I told you, my neighbor CJ is helping me. I promised him I'd go to his house now. I'll be okay. We'll be okay. But we've got to go."

"Your neighbor's helping you? The same neighbor whose Great Pyrenees were shot dead? You think he can protect you better than me?" He almost sneered the words out. He was always so competitive, even in small, weird ways.

From the kitchen the kids were arguing, and the clang of dishes reverberated. Something niggled the back of my mind. I frowned when the thought slipped past as if I couldn't quite touch on what it was.

"Mom!" Jazz called.

"I better go check on them. I'll be right back."

Ian stood there scowling at me.

I was halfway to the kitchen when it hit me. The air squeezed out of my lungs as the truth galloped into the forefront of my mind. Like the time I flew off Paddy over a three-foot jump and landed on my back and busted the air clear out of my lungs. I never told Ian that Hank's dead dogs were Great Pyrenees.

CJ's words echoed in my mind, Ian Monroe is the one connection between your parents' case and Jack's case. I clenched my fists and forced my legs to keep moving as if nothing was the matter. Don't look back. Don't give him a reason to think anything's wrong. My heart thundered in my ears.

The kids were arguing over the dishes. I grabbed both their arms, shaking them to get their attention. "Don't say a word. Don't argue." I hissed out the words as quietly as I could.

I scanned the kitchen, searching for an escape, and pointed at the pantry door. "You have to leave. Now." I had no idea what might happen. Maybe I was wrong about Ian, but the sinking sick feeling in my stomach told me differently. If I could do one thing, it was to get the kids to safety.

Jazz grabbed my shirt, plowing into me as I pushed open the cellar door. "Leave? But where?"

"To Hank and Neely Bennett's place, through the tunnel."

"Mom." Her voice caught, threaded with panic. "It's pitch-black out. And raining."

"Use your phones for light."

"What's going on? What about Uncle Ian?"

I shook my head. "Move. Now. Go fast, and don't stop no matter what. When you get to the other end, run to Mr. and Mrs. Bennett's place. Don't look back. Don't come back. And call CJ. Tell him he was right on Ian. He'll know what to do."

Jazz held her phone up. "Come with us." Even in the semi-darkness of the pantry, her eyes glowed as large as saucers. She chewed on her lip, her face streaked with tears. I couldn't leave. If I left, Ian might follow us, and who knew what he had in that stupid black bag he kept eyeing. The only chance for them was for me to stay.

I pushed the rifle into her hands. "If you have to, shoot this just like you did that night with CJ. No matter who it is. Go. Now."

I swiped Cody's bat off the floor and shoved it at him.

"Stick together. I'll be okay. Just go! I love you both very much."

I closed the door behind them and rested my forehead against the cool wood, my head still echoing from yesterday's migraine. *What am I going to do?*

The air in the kitchen had changed. Something cold and hard pressed against my side.

"I heard talking." Ian's previous edgy voice had morphed into one full of steel.

"Nobody. Just mumbling to myself. I'm recovering from a migraine, and it still hurts." I stalled for time to let the kids get through that tunnel.

"Don't lie. You were always such a bad liar. Is Michael in there?"

Relief swept over me. He didn't know the kids had been here. "Michael? Why would Michael be here?"

"Turn around and do it slowly." I raised my hands and did as he commanded.

Ian stood there, pistol in one hand and an automatic rifle slung over a shoulder. No wonder that black duffel was so overstuffed.

"What's going on, Ian?" I tried but failed to keep the wobble out of my voice.

"I think you know where Michael is. Is he here? Open that door." He waved the gun at the pantry door.

I reached toward it, and someone pounded on the front door. "Finley! Open up!"

Ian grabbed my wrist and squeezed tightly. I almost yelped from the pain but bit my lip. "Who is that?" He jerked me away from the pantry door and into the front hall.

"I don't know." Although for the first time since meeting Troy at CJ's house, I was happy to see him. More pounding. Maybe if I could prolong this conversation, keep Troy on the porch and Ian busy, then the kids could reach CJ.

"Finley? Where's CJ?"

"Troy—"

Ian squeezed my wrist. I squeaked out a little yelp.

He narrowed his eyes at me. "Tell him that he's not here and to go home."

"He's—he's not here. Go home."

"I want to talk to both of you. Can I come in?"

A sheen of sweat covered Ian's face. "Get rid of him."

"I'm not sure I can," I whispered.

Ian wiggled his gun into my vision. "If you care at all about him, do as I say."

"Now's not a good time, Troy." I didn't bother hiding the shake in my voice.

"Finley. I've made a big mistake. I just got a call from some FBI agent named Rivera. Sorry I thought you were the problem. Some cop from New York had called me and gave me your rundown. But that was a setup. Rivera says you're in danger."

I didn't want Troy here. Yeah, it would be nice if he could save my ass, but I didn't want him stepping into some crazy mess that started twenty years ago. I didn't like him, and I really hated how he acted toward CJ, but I didn't hate him enough to see him get hurt by Ian.

With Ian's paunch and size, he dwarfed me and sandwiched me into his chest. I knew I couldn't escape unless he loosened his death grip. He leaned down and whispered into my ear. "You make one false move, a bullet will sever your spine, which would be very convenient for me because I'm your kids' guardian. I'll have access to everything they inherit."

My knees turned to jelly, and bile rose from my stomach.

He tightened his grip. "But I want some information, so you get to live as long as you cooperate. Nod if you understand and then open the door and let the damn cop in."

I swallowed the sickness in my throat, prayed I wouldn't puke, and nodded.

Ian peered out the side window and released me.

Moving like a snail, I slid the deadbolt back. The

door swung open. Troy barreled through.

"He's got a gun!"

My warning was too late. Ian swung hard and clocked Troy upside the head with his pistol. Troy fell back against the wall but propelled himself from it, gun drawn. He wasn't fast enough. Ian shot him point-blank in the chest from eight feet away. Troy flew across the hallway and landed near the doorway to the kitchen. I screamed.

Chapter 56

CJ

The headlights behind me followed me all the way home. I called Griff and roared into the phone. "Are you behind me?"

"Nope. I'm coming down Turner from Windy Ridge. Should be to you in a couple of minutes."

"Some asshole's following me. I'm taking him down the driveway. Pull up behind and be prepared."

"I will."

I grabbed my handgun and turned right down the driveway, accelerating the whole way before I swung my truck around. My tires spun on the gravel, and my truck screeched to a stop. The SUV behind me skidded and weaved across the gravel drive. It gave me enough time to position myself before the driver's door swung open.

"You come out with a gun, I'll blast your face off!"

Behind, Griff's pickup rumbled to a stop, effectively boxing the guy in.

"You do that, asshole, I'll blow that bum leg right out from under you."

Relief flooded through me. "Donovan, what the hell are you doing here?"

Out of the SUV piled Donovan, Fox, and Nash. "Trying to get your damn attention."

I tucked my handgun in my waistband. "Phones work well for that."

"They do if you answer, shithead."

"My plate's frickin' full right now."

Donovan slanted a look my way. "I know it. We gotta move."

I was strung as tight as a crossbow wire, and the last thing I needed was a game of cat and mouse. "How the hell do you know?"

Donovan shook his head. "Not now."

"You don't work for a security company, do you?" I barked out the question, desperately in need of information and water.

"I can't say. But what I can say is, you got a crazy guy after your girlfriend, and we better move and move fast."

I took a deep breath and looked right. Lights bounced through Bennett's field.

"Incoming," Fox yelled and took cover behind the car door, gun drawn.

I pulled out my handgun and waited. The lights slowed and stopped as if whoever was driving was deciding where to go.

"Kill the lights," Donovan said.

Immediately the headlights went off, and we were plunged into darkness except for the moving beams of lights across the field. They lit up and flicked off a few times, and even with the distance I could tell they were flashlights and not from full-sized adults.

It took a minute to figure it out, and with the revelation, all calm was shattered. There was only one thing that would make Finley send them out in the dark. I shoved my gun into the back of my jeans and took off running.

"Sinclair!" Donovan hissed into the night, but I ignored him.

I was twenty feet from Jazz's and Cody's cellphone lights. One light hit the ground, and I heard the distinct click of a rifle cocking. Shit. I took a deep breath, fighting every urge to eat dirt and grab my gun.

"Jazz!" I called into the darkness, hoping my instincts weren't wrong and I wasn't going to get blown to pieces.

"CJ?" It came out as a half sob, and then they were on me, both of them. Hank Bennett, coming from the opposite direction, ax in hand, ambled toward us as fast as his bad knees allowed. "Mom sent us—sent us through the tunnel," she gasped out.

"Who's inside?" My heart thundered in my ears like a train speeding out of control.

"Mom and Ian."

"You were right about Ian," Cody said. "Mom said to tell you."

A wave of nausea passed over me. Son of a bitch. I motioned to the kids and Hank to get in the truck. "Let's get to your house, Hank."

Griff and Donovan followed in their vehicles.

Neeley Bennett came out on the porch, shotgun in her hands. "We okay, boys?"

I shook my head. Neeley glanced from Hank to me and then dropped the gun to her side. I shoved the kids toward her. They didn't need the push, taking the porch stairs two at a time and leaping into her waiting arms. She ushered them inside and closed the door with a bang. A second later the deadbolt clicked.

I loaded my rifle and rechecked my handgun. "I've

got to get to Finley."

"You need to hear me out first," Griff said. "Davis Williams called me. He's working night shift at the airport. He said that ten minutes ago a private jet landed, and five guys exited and got into two black Escalades and left immediately."

Donovan tossed me a camo stick. "Fun. Unexpected guests. Y'all sure know how to throw a party down here." A New Englander, he twanged his words just for me.

I shook my head and then painted my face. "You didn't have to come." Of course, knowing they were here backing us up—even Donovan with his "eat shit and die" attitude—eased some of my anxiety. The rest would only disappear when I knew Finley was safe. "Do you know who's after Finley?"

"Those numbers you gave Owen took a bit, but I connected them to Jack's old friend, Ian Monroe."

I almost did a double take. "That's not criminal."

Donovan smiled. "It is when deposits come in from foreign companies linked to terrorists."

I nodded, turned the flashlight on the ground, and outlined the layout of Finley's property into the dirt of Hank's driveway. I had my army, and now we needed a plan. Quickly.

Chapter 57

Finley

Ian stood next to the fireplace, one hand on his large, menacing gun. He motioned around him. "What is it with you, huh? You always had it easy. I'm tired of playing this shit. Where's Michael?"

"I have no idea. Why would I know? And if I did know, don't you think I'd turn him in?"

"Because you guys were always thick as thieves."

"He killed my parents!"

But I wasn't sure about anything anymore.

"I think he's after the money."

"I have no idea," I said. "What money you're talking about?"

"I think you're lying."

"You think I have money? I'm a coffee server. My parents' entire estate went to paying debts. I didn't get anything. Nothing!" I spat the words out, hoping it might hide my total terror. In addition to the pistol in his hand and the huge automatic rifle slung across his shoulder, he carried another smaller handgun in a holster off his arm and a third stuck into his waistband. What was he preparing for? Ian had lost his mind.

I glanced out to the hallway. Troy's chest fell in rapid breaths, eyes closed. He hadn't been conscious since Ian shot him. I prayed he was wearing a bulletproof vest. He wasn't bleeding, but maybe that didn't matter. Maybe he was bleeding internally. Either way, he needed help. Ian probably knew that when he agreed to spare him.

I spread my hands out, palms up. Extended like that, they trembled like a baby horse's legs on its first steps. "Ian, if I had money, you could have it, but I don't. We're not rolling in it. Look around you—can't you tell. Please put the gun down. Talk to me. Maybe I can help."

My request had the opposite effect. He shoved the pistol in the back of his pants and swung his automatic rifle up.

"The only help you can give me is the money I'm owed. This gun is my insurance that I get what I came for."

"That gun is only going to get someone killed." I fought the urge to glance at Troy.

"Your dad's business was a jackpot, you know. An import business we could manipulate and use for the drugs."

"You're a cop."

"I got paid dirt. Steve was a cop too—a car accident later, and he's a vegetable with no support. You know what it takes to care for him. Ahmeti offered me a way to get paid, real money that could help my brother. Of course, he went and got killed in some mobster war, and suddenly Captain Ogilvy's sick and retires, leaving me holding the ball."

He pointed his rifle toward me, and I stopped inching along the wall.

"What did I get?" he asked. "Jack. Nosy, snooping Jack, who somehow got wind of everything and came calling."

"Did you kill him?" My knees shook so badly I wanted to lie down before they buckled. I kept an eye trained on the open front door. If I could make it, maybe I could get away, get help, but I didn't know if I could walk one step, much less outrun an automatic.

He lowered his rifle, resting the butt on the floor. "Jack should have known better than to dig around. I told him to leave it alone, but he couldn't." He raised his voice, bellowing. "Always the boy scout."

His smug satisfaction sent chills through me. "You were at our wedding. You're our kids' godfather. They call you their uncle." Then I remembered what he had said earlier: If I died, nothing stood in his way of my bank accounts. He was the guardian for my kids.

He shrugged and pointed the gun back at me. "Jack thought this was the case that was going to save his career. He thought wrong."

He grabbed my arm, shaking me so hard I swore my teeth rattled. "Where'd the money go?"

"I don't know."

"Ahmeti wanted to kill you after that attorney and you turned down his offer, but I talked him out of it. You owe me. I figured maybe you knew something, that I'd get more if you were alive. That was a mistake. Where's the money?"

Anger flared up bright and hot. "You knew about that? What they did to that woman? You bastard."

One minute, I was struggling to free myself from Ian's grip, and the next, searing pain lashed up the right side of my face. I fell to my knees, tears nearly blinding me.

Ian's finger danced on the trigger, up down, up

down. God almighty, I needed to get away.

"Come clean on the money," he said. "Do it or the next hour is going to be very painful for you."

I grabbed the edge of the couch and pulled myself up, backing away from Ian. I wiped a hand across my blurred eyes and glanced at Troy. Chest still moving.

Ten seconds. All I needed was ten seconds to clear the door.

Chapter 58

CJ

We had a few things going for us. The storm had slowed down and changed. It was no longer sleeting at a ferocious pace, and snow was falling instead. I wasn't sure which was worse. All I was worried about was if Ian would try to make a break for it and take Finley with him. The wind wasn't as constant, but it still had gusts that made the frozen tree branches bend dangerously and clink and chime. The storm was far from over, and everything could change at a moment's notice. Time was short for us; we needed to make our move.

I checked and rechecked my rifle and handgun and stuck my Gerber knife in my boot's strap.

"How are you getting in?" Griff asked, using the camo stick.

"Kitchen door."

"If he hasn't killed her already, it's because he wants information." Donovan's voice ground against my nerves.

I glowered at him, wanting to rip his throat out for even uttering those words. "And your point is?"

"You're the sniper."

"He's right," Griff broke in. I turned my glare to him. "We need to drive him out. I'm going to kick the door down. You set up for a shot."

"You think I'm going to leave that bastard to you?" Anger clogged my throat, and I could barely get the words out. Ghani's mutilated body filled my mind. I'd been too late for him, but I wasn't going to take that chance with Finley. I shook my head, frustration and hatred coursing through me.

Donovan held up his hand. "Sin, it's you and only you that can make this shot in the sleet and wind. We all know it. Let us force him out and you take it. If he doesn't come out, come in after us. To get her out *alive*, we need calculated moves here." He met my eyes and didn't waver under my scathing glare.

An image of Finley flashed: her standing in Ginger's paddock. Her hand held out, waiting patiently for Ginger to make contact. A small smile across her face, unwavering trust, and love in her eyes. What had I told her once? As SEALs, we acted from clarity, not roiled up emotion.

"Fine. I'll set up in the hayloft of her barn."

Fox tossed night goggles to the rest of the guys.

"Nash," I said, "there's a tunnel that goes straight into the kitchen of Finley's house. Hank can show you where it is. Go that way in case he tries to take her there. That way you get in the house through the pantry. Donovan and Fox—"

"We'll head up by the driveway," Fox said, "and divert the airport guys."

"Okay good. Hank, once you show Nash the tunnel, you want to drive the ATV over. Get as close as you can to the front. If anyone tries to take Finley, follow. Griff, you're with me."

I lowered my voice. "Listen—" They turned in

unison, weapons primed. "—I know you all have your own families. I'm grateful for any kind of help. I'm shooting to kill the son of a bitch but do whatever you feel comfortable with. Just be careful."

Donovan motioned to Fox and the rest of the guys, and then they jumped the fence and disappeared.

Griff and I took off. I ran hard across that land, its dips and rises as familiar as the best friend who kept pace next to me—and I realized that even though this land was all I'd wanted for the last year, now it paled in comparison to what I stood to lose if I didn't make it in time.

I matched Griff stride for stride, pain searing up my leg as if someone was driving a stake through the bottom of my foot. I gritted my teeth and pressed on, finding that other level, the one I'd used in SEAL training and in combat. It had carried me through life-threatening mission after mission, and it was the level I thought had been blown to pieces.

We slowed at the fence line long enough to check the area. The lights were on at Finley's house, inside and outside, illuminating the heavy air of the storm and the swirling flakes of snow, like a lighthouse in the fog. Griff covered me, and I barreled across the remaining yards to Finley's dilapidated barn. In my peripheral vision, Ginger twirled around her small enclosure, clearly agitated. I sent a prayer upward for the fence to keep and my bullets to find all their targets. I scaled the outside ladder to the hayloft and set up. I signaled Griff, and he disappeared around the corner of the house.

Gunfire filled the air like firecrackers on the Fourth of July.

Chapter 59

Finley

Ian sprayed bullets across the room for a second time, this time chewing up my bookcases. I screamed—my defenses destroyed. Books flew across the floor, bits of pages fluttering in the air. He pulled one of my side chairs across the floor, draped some rope from his bag across the back of it, and dropped the gun muzzle to my eye level. "Sit down."

I pressed my hands against the wall. Clammy with sweat, they slipped. "Why?"

"If you won't give me answers, I'm sure I can persuade you to remember things. But I need to make sure you stay put before we can really talk."

Bile rose in my throat. "I don't know where Michael is, and I don't have any money. Please don't do this." I swallowed hard, thinking of Jazz and Cody.

"I know Michael's here. The last time we spoke, he told me he was coming. And he knows where the money is."

A pounding noise filled the house. The kitchen door. Ian swung his attention toward it, and I ripped into my back pocket for the switchblade. There was another loud *thud*, the kitchen door splintered. The air filled with the popping of bullets. The spindles of the staircase exploded.

I edged away, but Ian caught my arm and held me in place. "Don't even think about it."

He dropped the big gun, lifted his handgun, aimed, and fired in quick succession. I glanced at Troy. My heart jolted at his still form, but then his chest lifted just a bit. Still breathing, but he needed help.

Ian threw a smoke bomb through the doorway into the kitchen. Shouts from the kitchen reverberated as people called positions.

"Finley!" It was Griff's voice, which meant CJ was hidden somewhere else, ready to take a shot. Relief swept over me. Ian dropped my arm, pitched his empty pistol to the side, and grabbed the one from his shoulder holster.

Before he could reach for me, I bolted.

"CJ!" I yelled as I threw myself out the front door. Big white flakes of snow fell steadily instead of the earlier sleet. My foot slipped on the stairs already slick from the sleet, and I flew forward across the yard, skidding to a stop on my hands and knees. I drew myself up to my feet. The muzzle of Ian's assault rifle jabbed into my back.

"She's my ticket out of here, so whoever is out there that thinks they're going to save her, it's time to give up."

In the distance, coyotes yipped and howled, and Ginger's nervous whinny filled the air.

"You mother—" My words strangled between sobs. I pressed the button on the switchblade's handle, and the blade quietly swished out.

I wanted to twist that damn knife through his gut and hear him howl in the same pain I'd felt for the last twenty years. In the snowstorm, I thought I saw Hank

Bennett crouched behind his ATV, but I couldn't be sure.

"Let her go or I'll kill you!" The wind and snow disguised his voice, but I'd know it anywhere. My heart lifted.

Ian laughed, forced and loud. "Good luck with that shot, country boy."

Ginger's high-pitched whinny filled the air again and with it the crack of splintering wood. Ian pushed me forward, lifted his rifle, and swung it down hard, the butt connecting with my shoulder. I screamed, unable to contain myself as pain rocketed down my arm. I fell to my knees—a piercing scream answered my own. Ian turned at the sound.

Through the falling snow, a big red figure galloped toward the fence, fast and furious with no sign of slowing.

I called Ginger's name into the wind. The sight of her filled me with awe and hope, and I scrambled to my feet and plunged the knife into Ian's stomach. Doubling over, he grabbed my shirt, hanging on to me. Ginger cleared the fence in one smooth stride and kept coming. I pushed the knife deeper.

Ginger barreled for us, ears back, eyes wild. I pulled away from Ian, my shirt twisting in his hand. He hung tight, his vise grip keeping me within arm's reach. I clawed at his hand, his arm, anything to get free. He tripped, the gun swinging by his side. Ginger bore down like a freight train. He let go of my shirt and raised the gun, aiming for her, but she launched herself into the air. I said a silent prayer for CJ to hit his mark, and I dove for cover.

Chapter 60

CJ

I filled my lungs with air, and time slowed down. On the exhale, I depressed the trigger and fired once for the head and again for the body. Slow, smooth, accurate. There was a red haze and his body crumpled as more gunfire filled the air.

Mouth open and teeth bared, Ginger came down, her hooves landing on his chest, and she slipped. She slid along the wet driveway, one thousand pounds of legs and body flailing everywhere. I dropped my rifle, threw myself down five rungs at a time, and sprinted across the yard, pistol drawn in case this wasn't over.

Finley scrambled to her feet. I jumped over Ian's fallen body, the knife sticking out of his stomach and the hole in his head registered, but I didn't stop, hell-bent on Finley. I crushed her to me, searching for holes and blood. "Are you hit?"

"No!" An edge of hysteria laced through her voice. "The kids?"

"With Neeley."

She wrapped one arm around me, choking back a sob. "Troy. He's shot, inside. I don't know if he's alive. He came to warn me."

Lights bounced down the driveway—SUVs moving fast, the big black ones from the airport. I desperately hoped they didn't contain Albanian mobsters here to finish Ian's work. I pushed Finley down and raised my handgun.

The vehicles slowed down, and Owen and Rivera jumped out before they stopped, guns drawn. Relief flooded me. The airport guys had been the rest of our crew.

Ginger regained her footing and galloped past us, tail flying and head high. Finley ran after her. I met Owen halfway, tucking my gun into my waistband before I got there.

"You okay?" he asked.

"I am." I grasped his outstretched hand. "But there's a cop hit in the house."

Owen called to another guy who ran for the house, punching in numbers on his phone as he went.

"Donovan knew about everything."

He shook his head. "I love him like a brother, but Donovan was always a sneaky bastard. He's working for Homeland."

"Apparently, he meant security of the country—not the mall."

Rivera came up behind Owen while the rest of their crew fanned out over the yard.

He held his hand out, and I took it. "Hey Sin, you good?"

"Yes." I motioned to Ian lying ten feet away. "Is he alone?"

"Yeah." We walked over to the body, the dusting of snow seemed to accentuate the hoofprints on his chest. He was riddled with holes, but the most apparent was the one through his eye.

Owen smiled at me and motioned to the head.

"Nice shot."

I shrugged. "I got lucky."

"Yeah, right." He punched me lightly. "Where from?"

I motioned to the decrepit second story of Finley's barn.

Rivera whistled. "In this weather. That's more than nice. Who are all the other shots?"

I glanced around. Griff, Hank, Fox, Nash, and Donovan milled around on the porch. I couldn't tell from their faces whether Troy was still alive. Sirens whistled in the night.

"Me." I lied.

Rivera snorted but knew better than to pursue it. "Who knifed him?"

I pointed at Finley, who was now doing a round of duck-duck-goose with Ginger, trying to catch her. The mare ran on pure adrenaline now. She galloped around the yard, her hooves tearing up the grass. Her back end slipped, and she slowed down. Finley made a grab for her halter and connected.

"That's a big horse." Rivera's voice was filled with awe.

Turning to me, snow falling around us, Finley yelled for me. "I need a lead line. She's going to get hurt with all this commotion."

My money was on the FBI getting hurt by Ginger, but I didn't voice it. I undid my belt and threw it to her. She threaded it through Ginger's halter and held on as Ginger spun in circles. Against the massive red horse, Finley appeared tiny but undaunted. My hammering pulse that had yet to slow down seemed to pound the words, "She's okay, she's okay," with every beat. I breathed a sigh of relief.

Rivera pointed at Finley walking in circles with Ginger. "We'd like to talk to her."

"Not a chance until she gets that horse back to the barn."

"Tell her we'll wait in the house for her to come back." If I knew Fin, and I liked to think I did, they'd be waiting for a while. She wouldn't put anything in front of that horse or her kids, least of all a police investigation. I didn't care about the investigation either. I was just thankful she'd had that knife and that I'd hit my mark. All I wanted now was to get her home and safe in one piece.

Chapter 61

Finley

When I'd been battered and bruised, Ginger had heard me scream and had come for me. I rubbed a hand over her soaking-wet face and buried my own face in her neck, needing her warmth and solid comfort.

CJ came as close as he could to Ginger without risking bodily harm. I'd always known he was tough, but his face painted with camouflage made it all the more obvious. He'd promised me I wasn't alone in this, and he made good on that promise. "Fin. They want to talk to you. And me."

"Okay. I just need to get her back in her stall. I think we should move her back to your place. She's too keyed up here without the other horses and with everything's that happened."

"I agree. No one will come looking for her tomorrow with this storm. I'll get the goats."

As we crossed the yard toward CJ's place, the ambulance careened down my driveway. The shaking started halfway to the barn. I ignored it at first, pretended that it wasn't happening, tried concentrating on something else. But it was obvious as I toweled Ginger off and doctored her scrapes that I couldn't keep my hands steady. CJ helped me as best he could and didn't say a word about it. I walked her into the stall, and CJ threw some extra hay to everyone to guard against the chill and rolled the doors shut.

He swung an arm around me, and I leaned into him. "I can't stop shaking." All I wanted was to climb into a warm bed next to him and hold on.

"It's the adrenaline, and you're freezing wet. We need to get you warm." He rubbed a hand up and down my arms.

As if reading our minds, Griff pulled up in his black pickup. CJ helped me in, and we bounced back to my house where more than ten people milled about, in and out the front door and on the front porch.

"Who are all these people?"

"FBI."

"Do they need food? I've only got one plate of butt bars and half a plate of muffins, but I'm running low on butter to bake." I creaked the truck door open. My sore arm barely worked, and the side of my face where Ian had hit me ached like I'd had dental work.

"They'll be happy with anything. Right now, either sounds good with some whiskey."

We didn't get far before I saw the body. It was lying on the ground in the same position where CJ had shot him. I stopped and stared at Ian's corpse. He'd wreaked havoc on my life for money.

CJ tugged on my arm, gently turning me away from Ian's body and toward him and the house. He tilted up my face and traced his thumb over my sore cheek. "I wish I had been here sooner—" His eyes darkened. "—before he hurt you."

He gazed down at me, and the edge of his mouth quirked up. "But watching you wield my knife was damn impressive."

I took a deep but shaky breath. "It's okay. I'm okay. We're okay. You were there when I needed you. And thank God for your knife. And Ginger. And you. Especially you."

He pulled out the knife from his back pocket, newly cleaned. "I think you should keep it."

"Really?" I couldn't keep the surprise from my voice. I knew what that knife meant to him; his grandfather had given it to him—CJ had carried it with him on every mission.

"Absolutely."

He pressed it onto my hand and bent down and brushed his lips over my cheek. I closed my eyes and breathed in his scent of pine, coconut, and mint, trying to hold onto it and him for a moment longer.

"You ready?" he asked.

I closed my fingers around the knife and nodded.

My porch was dotted with men and women in all shapes and sizes, all of them carrying guns and looking official. "They're going to break the porch."

CJ steered me toward them. "It will be fine. It's a tough porch."

"I don't know about that."

He wrapped an arm around me and squeezed. "I do."

My living room was riddled with bullet holes. Chunks of wood and books littered the floor. CJ introduced me to Owen and the rest of the SEALs and then went to find a blanket. I scooped up some bits of paper, black writing graced all of it. My poor books. *Pride and Prejudice* lay on its spine, bullet holes shot right through. *Black Beauty* had fared no better. I picked up my tattered books and righted the pictures that had fallen over in my tussle with Ian. It was a challenge with my hands shaking, but I refused to give in, no matter how long it took. I didn't want the kids coming home to see this mess.

"Your husband sent this to the head of my department."

I stopped stacking my beaten-up books. The one they called Rivera held out my lost book, *The Monday Horses*. "Jack sent this along with notes on his case. Files on Captain Ogilvy and Ian Monroe and this book, with instructions to deliver it to you." His brow furrowed, and his eyes clouded with confusion.

I took it and flipped to the end, checking for what I knew I'd find. In the first years of our marriage—before alcohol, kids, and the stressors of life had taken hold—Jack would leave me notes on the blank pages at the back of books. Short cryptic notes I'd find when I stopped to reread my favorite book, which I did more often than not. Sure enough on the last page, dated the day before he died, he'd scrawled, *Fin, Sorry for the bad times. It wasn't your fault. Kiss the kids for me. Be strong like you always are. I love you. J.*

My eyes filled with tears, and I swallowed the lump in my throat.

"It arrived a few days after he died. He was a good analyst. It looks like two years ago, he followed a hunch that led him here. Of course, had Homeland or the Bureau known what he would have turned up, we would have provided more backup."

Donovan, the dark haired one, came up next to Rivera. "Yeah. It's hard to believe that one person could be tied to three deaths. You're quite the magnet for bad luck."

Rivera's concerned face morphed to horrified. "Dude, I can't believe you just said that to her. I'm not good with people, and even I know that sounds horrible."

Donovan shrugged. "What? She is a magnet for bad luck."

Rivera apologized for Donovan, and I tightened my fingers around the book. CJ came back with the blanket. His face still had smears of camouflage across it. I thought of the way he'd charged across that yard for me, gun drawn. He'd told me no one would go through him, and he'd kept his word.

My heart sank. All these people risked their lives for me. They could've been killed. CJ could've been killed. And Troy. What about Troy? Maybe Donovan was right. Maybe I was a magnet for bad luck. Maybe I'd always be—bad.

Chapter 62

CJ

I threw the blanket over Finley's shoulders and handed her a mug of steaming coffee—and whiskey. She took a sip and mouthed a thank you. I perched on the edge of her chair and rubbed a hand down her back. She leaned back into my hand, and a shot of warmth filled me.

Rivera squared his shoulders. "Here's what we've pieced together, or at least what Jack did. Before your parents died, Ian arrested Michael on a drug charge. They made a deal with him. He had to inform on your parents to stay out of jail and lure you into buying the drugs for him. Which he did."

Her back went rigid, sliding away from my touch. My stomach fell away. Owen had already told me this, but hearing it out loud from Rivera made it all the worse, like hearing a body count even after I'd seen casualties. She walked over to the bookcase and shifted some of the fallen books, with her hand sweeping up loose bits of pages into a pile.

"At the same time, Ahmeti, a crooked Albanian businessman, convinced your dad to go into business with him. The Albanians were just branching out from small stuff to more substantial crime. They were trying to get a foothold in the U.S., especially New York.

We're not sure if Ahmeti blackmailed your dad into going into business with him, using the info he had on your use of drugs from Ogilvy and Ian, or if your dad chose to do it because of his financial problems."

"No, that's not right. He didn't have financial problems."

"Well, our sources say he had been struggling, and it was pretty bad. We believe your dad unknowingly imported the heroin. When he realized it, he tried severing all ties to Ahmeti. Ahmeti's response was to order a hit on your dad, which Ian happily complied with because he needed money for his brother. Ogilvy and Ian covered it up by throwing the blame on Michael."

Rivera passed her a grainy black-and-white photo of her going into some rundown house. She blanched. "Michael said he needed it badly and couldn't go. I was petrified, but I went. I thought I was helping him. And well, I wanted some too. Just not as badly." She swallowed, met my gaze, and then dropped her eyes back to the picture.

"Yes," Rivera said, "well Ahmeti, with the help of the cops, did this to several people and businesses, blackmailing them. But with your dad, they hit pay dirt because his business was importing. Ahmeti wanted your dad's business, as is obvious because afterward he bought it from you."

She handed the picture back to Rivera and leaned back against the bookcase, her eyes averted.

"I think Captain Ogilvy and Ian assumed that they would get more than just money from Ahmeti for their role in the cover-up. But your dad cleared out his accounts and all that was left was a few thousand. It stuck in Ian's craw ever since. When Captain Ogilvy confessed to Jack before he died, Ian went haywire— thought he was going to take the fall for everything. He killed Jack to cover his tracks. But it was too late, we'd already had some correspondence with Jack, and we knew what he'd discovered."

"So, you investigated Jack's case all along?" I asked and looked over at Finley. I wanted her to come back over and sit down, but she remained alone against the bookcase. I was losing her. I could see it in her body stance, in her eyes that danced around the room never stopping on any one point for long, not returning my gaze. I motioned for her to come and sit down. She hesitated and then complied, sitting on the edge of her chair.

"Oh yeah, we knew something wasn't right." He turned back to Finley. "Before the investigation into your parents' deaths, Jack had been working on several ops involving the drug trade out of Afghanistan and through Tajikistan, a lot of it involving Albanians. Jack's blood analysis came back loaded with date-rape drug. We suspected Ian, but we couldn't rule out some angry member of the Albanian mob. We only closed the investigation of his death in order to draw one of them out, and the same with getting Michael released early. We figured Ian would get sloppy and nervous or maybe just greedy. Sure enough, greed and fear of the tightening noose won out."

Finley stood up, fists clenched at her sides. "And you weren't worried about me and my kids? About putting us in the line of fire?"

"Well, we had a car on you in D.C. But when you moved down here, and then I got the call from Owen and we knew Sin was nearby—" He shrugged. "—we didn't worry as much."

Finley sagged back down, the energy she'd mustered clearly gone. Her hand trembled as she took another sip of coffee. "What about Michael?"

"We've got him. Holed up in a safe house."

"You lied about him disappearing."

"We wanted to be careful and make sure no one knew. He almost blew everything by that stupid call he made to you."

Finley dropped her head and rubbed her brow. I moved a hand up to her neck to knead it for a second. Her muscles were as tight as a lug nut on a tire. She didn't move away this time, but neither did she relax.

"Anything else?" I asked. "It's been a long night." Maybe if I could get them gone, she'd be better.

Rivera shook his head. "We'll be in touch, but nothing that has to happen tonight."

Finley stood up. "I want to see my kids."

I followed suit. "I'll take you to Hank's. We need to fix both doors before you come back here."

She threw me a half-smile. "You and those doors. Let me go get some dry clothes."

I grabbed her hand as she walked past, but she gently tugged it free. I let her fingers slide out of mine. Something was going on with her. I could see it in her eyes—the distance, the space she was trying to put between us—but now was not the moment to address it. She was probably even more worn out than me, and I was pretty damn tired.

Exhausted or not, she bounded up Hank's stairs and into her kids' arms. I stood outside the room, witness to the reunion, thankful that I could help her and thankful that she'd caught Ginger and saved me that day all those weeks ago.

Owen stopped by on his way out.

"You leaving?" I asked.

"Trying to, before we get snowed in. Donovan and the guys are crashing at your place. I gave them your keys."

I nodded, my mind still focused on Finley. "I need a favor."

"Another one?"

"I've got an Animal Control agent drunk on power. He wants to take my horse Ginger. The one that gave Ian the final blow."

"I'll see what I can do." He followed my gaze to where it rested on Finley and the kids. "Donovan called her bad luck tonight."

I levered my exhausted body off the door jamb and rounded on him. "What?"

"You know him, he's awful with people. I think he thought he was making a joke."

"Some joke. What'd she say?"

"Not much, but I think she took it to heart." He patted my back and walked toward the door. "I'll call you tomorrow."

I nodded and went back to watching Finley snuggled up with the kids. A surge of anger at Donovan flashed through me. That was the reason why she'd left me in the living room, disentangling her hand from mine, and had been so quiet in the truck on the drive over here.

For two years, I'd tried to find that person I left on the floor of that bombed-out building. It'd been a futile mission. Only bits and pieces of me had survived that hell, but she'd shown me that who I was now was more important than what I'd lost. There was no going back; there was only forward. But that was okay because forward included her. I loved her and had no plans of being shoved aside.

Chapter 63

Finley

CJ showed up the next day with a pizza, an Xbox game for Cody, and a new phone for me. "With GPS, a camera, and a better antenna," he said. Jazz took one look at it and ripped the box open. She, Cody, and half the pizza disappeared upstairs with promises to get it set up for me.

He poured me a glass of wine and sat back, studying me from across the table, legs stretched out. "Troy's going to be okay. His vest stopped the bullets from penetrating, but the force of the shots did some internal damage. Good news is the docs said he'll heal."

I breathed a sigh of relief and took a long drink of my wine, keeping my gaze from his. It was easier to keep myself removed from him—keep myself from giving in to my urge to crawl into his lap—if I didn't meet his eyes.

He drummed his fingers on the table "Talk." It came out as an order. "I want to know what's going on. I think I deserve that much."

"Nothing's going on. I was at the barn today to see Ginger."

Out of the corner of my eyes, I could see his eyes narrow. "Talk to me."

I wasn't sure I knew what I'd say until the words

spilled from me. "Bad things happen to me. Bad things happen to the people I love. I'm bad luck. I put you in danger. I put my kids in danger. I can't do that again."

"Donovan, right? He's the one that said it to you."

I pulled my hair back and twisted it into a knot. "It doesn't matter who said it. He's right. Look at Troy."

"Troy was taken in by Ian and believed the wrong story. And he knows it. I'm not scared by some bad luck. The danger is over now."

"I almost got you killed. Who knows what lies around the corner? The kids don't have a choice, and that tears me up enough. You do."

"I thrive on bad odds. Besides, your life isn't dull. I like that."

I snorted.

"And I'm flattered to be stuck in the category of people you love."

My stomach lurched. Shit. Did I say that? "I'm not sure why. You almost got killed."

"I almost got killed in Tajikistan. At your house, you were the one doing all the heavy lifting. All I had to do was hit my mark. That's about it."

"Still—"

"Listen, I don't care if you're a magnet for danger or death, or whatever you think. We only have a limited time on this Earth. And I choose—if I get to choose—to spend that time with you. The last few weeks have been the best of my life. And I don't think you or anyone should walk away from something like that. But—" He leaned forward, hands on his knees, as if he wanted to make sure I heard and understood him.

I cocked my head. Despite myself, I was eager to hear what he said next. "But what?"

"The thing is, I've never actually asked you what you want. I guess I always figured you wanted what I did, and I just kind of bowled over anything in my path. So, now I'm asking. What is it you want?" His eyes were intense and piercing.

That was unexpected. He had this uncanny way of hijacking the direction or plan I had, stealing my focus and redirecting me on another path. Not that I minded that much.

I stood up and wandered over to the counter buying time. I knew what I wanted: I wanted him—but all that came with so many other things. Scary things, like commitment to staying and conversations with the kids over it and questions. I picked up a spatula and leaned against the counter, playing with it in my hands. "I'm not sure. My life is so—"

I stopped talking, unsure of where I was going.

"Can I say something more?"

I shrugged. "Sure."

He stood and approached me, stopping short of invading my space. "For a long time after I got hurt, I didn't understand it. How could I lose something I was so good at? Because I was. I was good at killing. And I loved the risk—I'll admit it. I found a purpose in serving my country. After I almost died and it was all taken away, I struggled for a long time to make sense of everything and to move forward. I've never thought about life in terms of good or bad luck, or even fate. But I have to wonder. If I'd never been hurt, would we have met? I'll never know. What I do know is the day Ginger barreled into your yard, the day you found me— that day was the best day of my life."

I didn't know what to say to that. He smiled and,

leaning in, cupped my chin and brushed his mouth against mine. I didn't move, just let him kiss me. When he stepped back, I licked my lips and tasted cherries.

"I love you," he whispered.

Before I could respond, he stepped back and left the kitchen. I heard the front door open and close. His truck engine revved up and was followed by the crunch of the tires in the gravel. I followed his path to the porch and stood there for a long time, staring at the space his truck had vacated.

I'd spent twenty years guarding my heart and my life, making sure I'd never feel anything too strongly, convinced that my passion and single-minded love for horses, and for Michael, had affected my judgment and killed my parents. And maybe it had played a role. But love had saved me too, just as it saved my kids. CJ had come as he promised that night, had run through the dark, through the storm, injured body be damned. Just as I'd sent the kids out through the hidden tunnel, knowing I could face Ian and save them by doing so.

I couldn't change the past, but maybe CJ was right: the past had made me too. All the little choices that had to happen to bring us both here to this present moment. The past made us. Would we have met without it?

I pulled my cardigan sweater tight around me and hugged myself, staring into the pine trees that dotted our property lines. I tried to imagine my life as if he'd never been in it, as if he were never in it again. But I couldn't do it. And more importantly, I didn't want to.

Chapter 64

CJ

The next morning, with two cups of coffee in, I was done. I chucked the invoices on my desk and strode out of the office.

"Where ya going?" Griff asked. He didn't even bother to roll out from under the car he was servicing.

"Back over there."

"To say what?"

"Anything." I'd relived yesterday enough times. I'd wanted her to come after me, but she hadn't, and I refused to sit here waiting and not knowing.

The crunch of car tires turning on the gravel drive filled the air.

"Another customer. Better get the clipboard." Griff said, head still stuck under the chassis.

"Fine." I stomped back into the office, swiped it off my desk, turned around, and ran smack into Finley in the doorway.

"Going somewhere?" she asked, pushing her sunglasses up on her head.

I shook my head, speechless. My chest so tight I could barely breathe.

"I wonder if you have a spare moment to check my new car?" She smiled and smoothed out the edges of her hair. It tempered her outward fiery self, made her seem just a bit nervous, and gave me a great picture of her slanted cheekbones. She slightly wet her lips, drawing my eyes to her mouth.

When I could finally clear my throat, I nodded. "I might be able to, but it'll cost you."

I dropped the clipboard onto the bench and walked toward her.

She met me halfway. "Really? A lot?"

"Oh yeah. A lot."

"Can we work it out in a game of ping-pong?" She licked her lips again and smiled.

Damn. "Maybe. Feeling lucky?" I couldn't keep a straight face with that lame-ass line.

She didn't take notice of my foolish grin. "I feel something." She moved even closer.

That was enough invitation for me. I wrapped my arms around her and pressed her against me.

"But you can't rush me,"

"I promise I won't." Hopefully she meant marriage and not sex. I'd dreamed of her every night since the day she'd jumped out of my truck. And I always woke hot, sweaty, and unable to walk straight.

I ran my hands up her arms, relishing the softness of her skin under my fingertips.

"You still owe me a bottle of Jack." She placed both hands on my chest and pushed until I stepped back. Then she turned and strode out to the barn.

I followed, enjoying the view from behind. "What do I owe you a bottle of Jack for? And, you know, you fit fine in my arms. Why'd you have to walk away?"

"You always push your luck. I gotta get Ginger and bring her back to my place. Now that the roads are clear, I'm not taking a chance with that Animal Control guy.

She grabbed Ginger's halter and lead that hung outside Ginger's stall.

Then she turned, her lips inches from mine. Her telltale scent of cinnamon and vanilla lingered in the air, and it took all my willpower not to kiss her, which she probably knew. "Sorry. The bottle of Jack?" I asked.

"It took Griff two tries to break the door. Not one."

I slid my hands up and under her hair and cupped her face. "Worth every damn penny." Then I captured her mouth with my own and time stopped moving.

Epilogue

Finley

On Christmas Eve, a letter showed up from California. With my heart fluttering in my chest, I slid a finger under the seal and pulled it out: a simple white card with a design of holly all over it. Inside was a photo. It was of me and my junior jumper, Paddy, at the Lake Placid horse show. I was in show clothes, and Paddy peered over my shoulder, his white stripe so distinctive against the dark color of his face. Attached to it was a small piece of paper.

Dear Whit,

I wanted to say sorry for everything that happened. I've spent years thinking of how badly it all turned out, how without me, your life would have gone on like normal and most likely you'd have become that professional horsewoman you dreamed of. I want you to know I did love you, in my own screwed-up way, and I never forgot the good times we had.

I've had this picture for twenty years. We met at this show, and I thought you were beautiful and kind. You were the only one who believed in me ever becoming more than a high California surfer boy. I wasn't wrong about you. Unfortunately, you were wrong about me, and you paid the price. I'm clean now and reconciled with my family, but that doesn't really do much for you. If I could go back in time and fix it, I would. I'm sorry. I never meant for any of it to happen. I hope things are better for you now.

Michael

CJ came from the garage, hammer in hand and lines across his forehead. I held out the picture and letter for him. He read it quickly and looked at me, lips rolled inward as he regarded me with those sharp green eyes.

"You okay?"

I nodded, suddenly aware that I really was. We'd been cruelly used, Michael and I, and we both had paid the price for our drug use, stupidity, and selfishness. But there was nothing to be done now but to let it go.

"Yes. For the first time in a really long time, I think I am."

He grinned at me, roped an arm around my shoulders, and dragged me back into the hard planes of his body, planting a kiss on the side of my neck. "I'm glad."

So was I. I slid the letter back into the envelope, but not the picture. It was a good one of Paddy and me. I'd find a space for it in the house.

CJ promised he wouldn't spend the night, trying to keep up a semblance of propriety, but decided it was pointless when the kids badgered him to stay. He left early to feed the horses and returned, smelling of hay and with the four dogs in tow, each with a new Christmas bone to chew. I pressed a fresh cup of coffee in his hands, and we retreated to the living room couch, cuddling close to the fire to wait for the kids.

They came down in a rush of excitement. CJ smiled at me over the crackling of paper and screams of delight. At thirteen and fifteen, we were teetering on the edge of losing the whole Christmas wonder and joy thing, but for another year we were safe. I smiled back, knowing how precious this time was. It wouldn't be long before they went off to college, demanding gift cards and money in lieu of tangible presents.

Afterward, we all descended on the kitchen for eggs, bacon, and biscuits. We sat down together and demolished the breakfast in short order. Cody and Jazz returned to their presents, still chewing.

"Good?" CJ asked, sipping coffee.

I slathered jam on the last bite of my biscuit and nodded. My heart too full to speak.

He slid a small box across the island at me.

"What's this?" I asked, eyeing it suspiciously. "I thought we were keeping things simple."

"I wanted to get you a new saddle, but there were so many choices. It overwhelmed me. Besides, a saddle is really something you need to sit in and choose for yourself. And the cost—crazy. You'd think they were made of diamonds. So, I figured I might as well just get you diamonds."

I picked up the box warily, undid the ribbon, and opened the lid. Nestled on the white velvet was a platinum band with three diamonds—one center one, bracketed with a smaller diamond on each side.

He motioned to each jewel. "You, Cody, and Jazz." He brushed his thumb over my knuckle. "Listen, I can't promise that we won't have bad times or run into problems or that I don't carry baggage from my service days, but what I can promise you is that I'll try my best, that I will be here for you and Jazz and Cody. And that I love you."

Grinning, tears in my eyes, I held my hand out, and he slipped the ring on my finger. Spreading my hands out on the counter, I regarded them both. My wedding band from Jack encircled my right ring finger. I had moved it there a month ago. CJ's ring sparkled from my left hand. Each felt right to me.

"I know you said you want to take things slow. So, it's whatever you want this ring to mean, whenever you want it. I just don't want to lose you. Ever. Besides, I plan to give you more diamonds than a Texas beauty pageant queen."

A memory of my dad crossed my mind. "That's too funny. My dad said something like that before my last show. I still remember his face glowing with pride as he handed me my saddle. 'For my daughter. The equestrian worthy of a seat of diamonds—' "

The last word died on my lips, and a vision flashed before me of my dad handing it over, and the way his voice shook on the word *diamonds*. My twenty-year-old saddle with the lopsided seat.

CJ forged right ahead. "Speaking of dads. Mine called this morning to tell me Merry Christmas and that he'll lend me the money for the land if I want it, which is convenient since Wade's deal fell through. Although I'm not sure I want his money, it would be helpful. The town board rejected Wade's proposed development, so the land is back on the market."

My mind, half-frozen on my memory, registered CJ's words but couldn't yet come into the present. "That's great."

CJ leaned in, eyes piercing, and gently tapped my forehead. "Earth to Fin, what's going on?"

I pushed my hair back, almost embarrassed by my

theory. "I know this is a long shot, but what if my dad changed his assets to gems and hid them in my saddle?"

CJ stared at me, wide-eyed. "That's either genius or off-the-hook insane."

I swallowed the incredibly large lump in my throat, pushed back from the island, and ran for the barn, CJ on my heels.

My saddle hung on a new saddle holder CJ had recently installed. I laid it pommel-down on the top of my trunk. "It always got reflocked before indoors. But I wasn't around the last time. My dad was there with the saddle fitter."

I pictured my dad's smile as he'd handed me that saddle. It was the first time he'd smiled in a long time—and the last I'd ever see.

I slipped my fingers into the narrow opening beneath the seat and the panel of the saddles, searching through the guts of wool flocking. My heart galloped along. When my fingers brushed velvet, I looked up at CJ and grinned.

I pulled gently, and a small navy bag popped out. With shaking fingers, I opened the drawstring and poured into CJ's outstretched hand twenty uncut diamonds.

"Oh my." I stared at the twinkling stones and tried to remember to breathe.

"That was a hell of a chance to take," CJ said, rolling the stones gently in his fingers. "What if you never figured it out?"

"What if I had sold the saddle?"

"My guess is, he was protecting his assets but didn't think he'd die for them or that you'd ever stop riding."

"Probably not." I touched one of the diamonds gingerly, trying to wrap my head around their actual physical existence. Until this moment, I'd never truly believed there'd been a fortune.

"What are you thinking?" CJ asked.

I heard a noise outside and glanced up sharply, but it was only Ellie, appearing at the door to check us out.

My eyes filled with tears, overcome with all that these rocks meant. "I don't know. What do you think?"

He shrugged his eyebrows. "I think my three pale in comparison."

I shook my head, laughing, brushing my cheeks. "Yours I'll have for the rest of my life. These, we could sell—the problem is, don't they sort of belong to the government?"

"Well, we can ask Owen and Rivera, but my guess is you're fine. No one can tell for sure if that money was tied to the drugs or the regular stuff he imported. He cleared out accounts to protect you guys. They tried to steal it from him, but it was his. Now, it's yours. Don't feel bad about it."

"What do we do with them?"

"That I don't know, but I'm sure we can find someone to help." He poured the diamonds back into the pouch and handed it to me. "I do know you can get that lock fixed now."

He threaded his fingers through mine, and we headed back to the house.

"Don't worry about it," he said. "You'll figure it out."

I slanted a look his way. "I have already."

"You have?"

"Yup. We're going to buy the forty acres, put in a

brand-new house with a pool for you and an industrial-size kitchen for me so I can bake, and we can rescue horses and do equine therapy and feed the clients good desserts."

"You never stop surprising me." He stopped, pulled me into him, and traced his hands down my back. "I love that about you."

Sliding my arms up and around his neck, I angled my head back to meet his eyes. "What else do you love?"

"You don't have enough time to hear it all."

"For the right incentive, I might make the time—"

Not waiting for me to finish, he leaned down, pressed his lips to mine, and stole the last word.

A Word About the Author

Dianne May discovered writing at the age of eight and romance novels in her twenties. A voracious reader, she reads and writes across all genres, but romance remains her true love. *The Perfect Distance* combines her passion for romance and her passion for horses. She lives with her husband and three kids, three horses, two cats, and a dog on a six-acre farm in North Carolina. A graduate of Connecticut College and Albany Law School, she practiced law before starting her family and discovering that late at night, when the house was finally quiet, she could pour out to her computer the stories that percolated in her mind all day. Her first novel, *Wynter's Horizon*, a paranormal new adult romance, was published in 2013 and will be re-released under a new title. *The Perfect Distance* is her second novel.

May is an advocate of horses, and she hopes her readers will join her cause. Approximately 100,000 horses are sent to slaughter a year. There are organizations that help, including equine therapy organizations that devote resources to helping veterans. Please consider donating to the following organizations:

Norwegian Fjord Horse Rescue (www.nfhmo.org)
Saratoga War Horse (www.saratogawarhorse.org)
Aiken Horse Rescue (aikenequinerescue.org)
Colby's Crew (colbyscrewrescue.org)
Mustang Heritage Foundation
(mustangheritagefoundation.org)

Thank you for purchasing
this publication of The Wild Rose Press, Inc.

For questions or more information
contact us at
info@thewildrosepress.com.

The Wild Rose Press, Inc.
www.thewildrosepress.com

CPSIA information can be obtained
at www.ICGtesting.com
Printed in the USA
BVHW041947220222
629804BV00013B/447